A Wicked Dance of Obsidian and Light

A Wicked Dance of Obsidian and Light

Echoes of Darkness Book 1

Published by Skye Publishing

Editor: Ayden Rails

Proofreader: Lindsey W.

Art: Everything is painted digitally by the author.

Paperback ISBN: *978-1-0687616-4-5*

E-book ISBN: *978-1-0687616-3-8*

A WICKED DANCE OF OBSIDIAN AND LIGHT

LUCIA SKYE

Content Warning

This book contains graphic violence and sexual content. It is not intended for anyone under the age of legal adulthood. All characters depicted herein are over 18 years of age.

Some contents within this book may be triggering or disturbing to some readers.

Reader discretion is strongly advised.

<u>Trigger warnings</u> include but are not limited to:

Alcohol consumption

Attempted rape (not by the MMCs)

Anal Play

Blood

Death

Depression

Dubious Consent

Car accident

Gore

Grief

Hospitalization

Kidnapping

Physical abuse

Raw sex

Restraint

Sexual assault

Sexually explicit scenes

Strong language/ profanity

Swallowing bodily fluids

Spanking/ Impact play

Torture

Voyeurism

Playlist

1. CHINCHILLA - Little Girl Gone
2. Chris Grey - MAKE THE ANGELS CRY
3. P!nk - Who Knew
4. BAD OMENS - Like A Villain
5. SAYGRACE - You Don't Own Me ft. G-Eazy
6. Sleep Token – Alkaline
7. Elley Duhé - MIDDLE OF THE NIGHT
8. Doja Cat x The Weeknd x Lana Del Rey - Streets
/ One Of The Girls / White Mustang [LIBERTO Remix]
9. Ex Habit - Who Do You Want
10. Camylio - over me
11. Two Feet - I Feel Like I'm Drowning
12. Kehlani - Gangsta
13. Camylio - Angel
14. Sam Smith - Fire On Fire
15. Mellina Tey - Obsession
16. Lusaint - Wicked Game
17. Arctic Monkeys - Do I Wanna Know?
18. Camylio – Trouble
19. Sleep Token - Granite
20. Stileto – Cravin
21. Jacob Lee – Demons
22. Hozier – Take me to church
23. Bad Omens- Limits

Author's Note

This book ends on a cliffhanger and

centers around a love triangle.

If that's not for you, I completely understand.

To you,

May you find the courage to dance on the edge of

darkness from time to time.

And for those of you who dream about being pinned to the wall by a 6'4" tattooed demon, Kaiden Black is waiting to fulfill your fantasy and make you his good girl.

1

"A woman was found dead in an alley in Ashville's Raven District. It happened early this morning. A sanitation worker discovered the unidentified woman's body behind a dumpster in the back alley of Ice Club. Now, a homicide investigation is underway. Theresa, our reporter, is outside the medical examiner's office with new information. She also spoke to the early commuters who unfortunately saw the woman's dead body before and after police arrived.

"That's right, Nate and Andrea. The unidentified white woman, who is believed to be in her early twenties, was drugged and sexually assaulted before the attacker strangled her to death. But, the gruesome detail that shocked the witnesses was the message 'demon whore' carved onto the woman's naked chest—"

"Ugh. What the fuck is wrong with people?" Samantha, my best friend, asks while shutting off the TV, indignation lacing her words. She's propped against the mountain of decorative pillows on my bed, her legs crossed in front of her, sipping on a glass of white wine.

"That's a weird thing to carve onto someone's body," I mumble pensively and pause with my hand on my closet door, then turn around to face Sam. "Isn't this like the third woman found this year in a back alley with the same message carved onto their body? Could a human have found out about the presence of demons and gone crazy? Or maybe it was one of those overzealous religious fre—"

"Nope, I'm not doing this right now," Sam interrupts me with a harrumph and points her eyes to the ceiling as if asking for divine intervention. "I already had the day from Hell with the flower deliveries being delayed, and I can't talk about depressing shit." She lets out an aggravated exhale and flits her gaze to me, her demeanor doing a one-eighty. "Soooo...do you think your secret admirer will send you a bouquet of flowers this year, too?" She waggles her eyebrows as she takes a sip of wine. "I bet he's hot."

"We don't know if it's a man, Sam. You bring me flowers all the time," I shoot back while rummaging for the hellseeker gear in my closet. I take it out, pull the pants on, zip them up, and reach for the reinforced corset. Like leather, the gear makes the wearer feel nothing short of a badass, but luckily, it's made out of *sanctifiber* and sturdy enough to withstand a demon fight. It also doesn't creak with every step you take and doesn't give you swamp ass when you run after a demon because, unlike leather, it's actually breathable.

She rolls her mossy green eyes, tucking a fiery copper strand of hair behind her ear. "That's because I own a flower boutique, you dumbass. Of course I bring you flowers all the time. C'mon, Iris...it has to be a man."

"Man or no man, I honestly don't care. I can't wait to taste that chocolate again." I sigh giddily, remembering the explosion of flavor on my tongue. Every single year on my birthday, without fault, ever since I woke up from the accident, someone has been sending me a big bouquet of irises and a box of black cherries soaked in liquor and dipped in the most decadent chocolate. They are the most delicious things I have ever tasted, and to say I'm obsessed with them would be an understatement. I could almost orgasm just by having a taste. I don't even let Sam have more than one.

Opening the door to the bathroom, I step in front of the sink and look in the round vintage mirror while I start taking my makeup off. There's only half an hour left before I have to go out on my shift, and wearing a full face of makeup while hunting demons doesn't go hand in hand, especially if some of the disgusting tar-like blood gets on my face. I hate it when that happens.

A hellseeker shift usually involves going out at around ten p.m. and scouring for demons in the area of the city I am assigned that week until around four a.m., unless Grayson calls a meeting at the compound and sends me on a mission.

Sam follows me and props her hip in the door frame. "Speaking of your birthday. I have tomorrow all planned." She takes a hearty sip from her almost empty glass.

I throw her a sidelong glance. "Can we just do something quiet at home?"

She folds her arms in front of her chest and pouts. "Yeah, not happening. It's your twenty-third birthday, not your sixtieth. You desperately need to have some fun and let loose a little. There's this new club that opened a month ago in the Raven district. It's called Sin. It's super exclusivist. The waiting list is like six months or something like that. I told you about Alex, right? He's a bodyguard there and will get us in. I already told him we're going."

"It's my birthday; don't I have a say in it?" I grumble while splashing some water onto my face.

Sam stomps her foot, pointing an angry finger in my direction. "I swear to Hecate, Iris. If we don't go out tomorrow night, I'm going to hex you to grow corpse flowers in your vagina, and cooties to go with them. When's the last time you went out with me? I fucking miss you. I want us to have some fun together like we used to. You take your damn job way too seriously."

My chest constricts and I saw my lip between my teeth, guilt washing over me at her words. Sam is right; I have been neglecting her lately. I scrunch my eyebrows, trying to think of the last time we went clubbing together or even went out, but I come out with nothing but demons.

"Yeah, that's what I thought, biatch. We're going to go out tomorrow night whether you like it or not," she declares, her full lips setting into a thin line, a glimmer in her eyes that promises to make good on her hex. I'm not afraid she's going to actually hex me. She only means it when she wants to strongarm me into doing her a favor or when I royally piss her off. There was this one time a few years back when, after a nasty fight, I had moss growing on my armpits for an entire week until I apologized.

"Fine, we'll go," I concede. "But you do understand I have to take my job seriously, right? Being a hellseeker is not something I can take lightly, Sam—"

"We're going to have so much fun!" she screams enthusiastically, jumping up and down on the balls of her feet until she reaches me. Then, she throws her arms around my neck, enveloping me in the heady smell of wisteria and jasmine that always clings to her skin.

A smile tugs at the corners of my lips as I hug her back. "Will you braid my hair? You do a far better job than I do."

She disentangles herself from me. "Sure."

We walk out of the bathroom into the small hallway, its walls full of framed pictures that remind me of every moment since I woke up from my accident, and we make our way to the living room.

The cyan couch is the first thing you see as you enter the eclectic one-bedroom apartment. There's a small, wooden coffee table in front of it. An open-spaced kitchen is to the right, with cream-colored French-style counters and copper accents, the fridge the same color as the couch.

A table that sits a maximum of four people is placed in the middle of the kitchen, and potted plants are scattered all throughout the apartment, courtesy of Samantha. But most of them sit on the floor, near the white arched windows. I love those arched windows to death, and aside from the cheap price, a steal really, those windows were one of the main reasons I decided to buy the apartment. To the left of the entrance is the hallway, the bathroom door in the middle of the left wall, and at the end of the hallway is my bedroom.

Samantha was horrified when I first told her that I bought it and was going to move in. The peeling on the depressing yellow wallpaper-covered walls, and the dirty floors that had holes in them didn't deter me. I've wanted to own a place that was my own for so long, and two years ago, I finally moved out of my aunt's house. It was a lot of hard work, and Sam helped me renovate it. I bought new furniture, and we painted the walls. It was the only time I had used some of the money I inherited from my mother's death.

Sam places the empty glass of wine in the sink and saunters toward the couch, sitting down with feline grace. As I pass the small wooden coffee table, my phone vibrates with an incoming text. I take it and plop down on the floor between Sam's legs, resting my back on the couch so she can start French braiding my hair. I unlock the screen and tap on the text.

> **Grayson: Covetorax demons in the city. Track and kill them.**

"Who is it?" Sam asks and peeks down at the screen.

"Grayson. He's sending me on a mission," I respond.

"Isn't he like a hundred years old or something? Does he even know how to text?"

I chuckle at her question, but she's kind of right. "Honestly, he's never texted me before and especially not for a mission," I muse. As I said, when sending us on a mission, the head of the Ashville Order usually summons a meeting at the compound or calls to personally notify us about it, and that's pretty rare, too. He usually assigns me missions with a higher level of difficulty, also, like hunting down draconic ravengers, souldrakes, or ghouls. These are the most dangerous demons that manage to slip through the cracks in the veil separating our worlds.

Covetorax demons are more suited for hellseekers who just finished their training at eighteen, since they're pretty easy to kill. I don't look too much into it, though; at the end of the day, a mission is still a mission, and it's my duty to fulfill any job the Order gives me.

"Ouch!" I exclaim when Sam pulls too hard on a hair strand.

"Shush! You wanted me to do your hair, remember? Stop complaining," she scolds me. "Anyway…maybe tomorrow night you'll finally lose your virginity. Find a hot guy at the club, bring him home, fuck his brains out."

Pursing my lips, I throw her an annoyed look over my shoulder. "I don't even know what to say to that, Sam."

"You don't have to bring him home. Just fuck him in the bathroom, get it over with."

I deadpan, "If I had a penny for every time you told me I should lose my virginity since we've met, I would be filthy rich by now."

"Iris, you're almost twenty-three years old, and you haven't ever had sex. You're wasting that body and those stripper tits of yours. You can't keep waiting for Noah to come back. It's been five years." She exhales loudly as though the solitary state of my vagina aggravates her. "Do you have a hair tie?"

My jaw locks with anger, and the crippling sadness that hung to me like a black fog for an entire year after he left threatens to swallow me whole at the mere mention of Noah's name. As much as I put up a strong front, him ghosting me still hurts like a bitch. "I'm not waiting for him to come back, Sam," I say through clenched teeth and slide the hair tie I always wear off my wrist, handing it to her.

"Then prove it. Move on. He ghosted you five years ago, and you're still living in the past..." She finishes my braid and secures it.

"No, I'm not. Are you done?" I bite back, harsher than I intended and totally proving her point. Noah is a very sensitive subject, even after all these years.

Sam sighs and hugs me from behind. "I'm sorry, okay? You know I love you. I just want to see you happy." She plants a kiss on the side of my head and lets me go.

Pushing myself up from my sitting position on the floor, I stride to the entryway table where all my weapons are scattered. "I'm happy, Sam, truly. I have you, my aunt, and my job. I don't need anything more," I say as I place the whip in its holster at my belt and then position the rest of the weapons on my body. Luckily, hellseeker weapons are invisible to the human eye, otherwise I would surely give someone a heart attack or get arrested as soon as I stepped foot on the street.

Sam stands from the couch, takes her designer bag from the kitchen table, and joins me at the door. We both slide our shoes on at the same time, Sam her stilettoes and me my beloved, over-the-knee Dr. Martens combat boots. We get out of the apartment and descend the stairs, Sam's heels making clicking sounds that echo loudly in the stairwell.

"Call me when you wake up?" Sam asks as she closes the front door of the building at her back.

"Yup," I respond, popping the *p*.

"'Kay. I'll come over and doll you up." She hugs me quickly. "See you tomorrow. Love you," she says over her shoulder, blows me a kiss, and starts walking toward her car.

"Love you too," I shoot back and take a deep, cleansing breath, clearing my mind of the Noah fog and everything else. I have some covetorax demons to hunt down.

2

I spot the two possessed humans with the help of my *ethereal sight*, their tainted black-greenish auras pulsing around their bodies, a clear indication of the possession. They've managed to break into an ATM and steal all the cash. I have to bide my time, though, and follow them until there aren't any witnesses around. Everything we do has to remain under the veil of secrecy. Humans aren't supposed to learn about the reality — or better said, horrors — of our world.

Covetorax demons are some really ugly motherfuckers, but out of all of the demons that escape through the veil into the human realm, these are the easiest to kill. They aren't very strong or smart and don't consume the light of a human soul as fast as other, more powerful demons. They personify greed, like shiny objects, and have a thing for robbing banks, jewelry stores, and anything of value.

The sickly smell of perfume, sweat, alcohol and bad decisions all mingle together to overpower my senses as the demons lead me smack dab into the center of Ashville, on the main street of the Raven District —

the busiest neighborhood in the city with summer right around the corner. At nighttime, swarms of partygoers take over the district, transforming it into a bustling beehive. I just prefer it much more during the day. Being sober and trying to weave your way through the throngs of people and the drunks that got shit-faced at the happy hour after work isn't an easy feat.

Most of them are still wearing suits and work-appropriate clothes, all haphazard after a few hours of drinking. Men with shirts no longer tucked in their pants, groups of women in high heels walking slow on unsteady feet, speech slurred and loud in an attempt to cover the blasting music spilling all over the street in a cacophony of beats as people are hopping in and out of bars.

Raven District is like a beacon for all the people trying to have a good time and indulge in the sinful promises whispered to them by their innermost-darkest desires. Under the moonlight and the influence of alcohol and drugs, everything is possible. The regret will only come the next morning when the stain of shame can't be washed by the water of their morning showers.

Humans aren't the only ones attracted by the nightlife and chaos in the Raven District. Demon activity is the strongest where lust, gluttony, and greed are delivered on a silver platter to feast off. Broken, damaged souls are the easiest to corrupt as the demonic influence slithers through their thoughts, taking control of their minds and actions. Fortunately, the lightborn, the members of the Order, can't be possessed. Our blood lineage is blessed by the archangels, making our bodies sanctified vessels that can't be breached by any type of demonic influence.

I remain in the shadows while passing Sin, following the possessed humans. It seems like half the city is waiting in line to get into the neighborhood's newest hot spot. In a stark difference from the after-work crowd, groups of gorgeous women wearing short, slinky dresses paired with sky-high heels and men looking sharp in their best clothes form the longest line I have ever seen in front of the sleek, three-story building. Huh, so Sam wasn't lying when she said this is the hottest place in town.

Still tailing the two demons toward the end of the street, keeping an unsuspecting distance while not letting them escape my sight, I barely dodge a guy stumbling out of the Irish Pub looking like the Devil is snapping at his heels. Probably a lawyer, judging by his expensive black suit that most likely cost more than my entire wardrobe.

I jump back right at the last second before his body jerks forward with a spasm, then suddenly bends over at the waist as he projectile vomits right in front of me.

Eww. Asshole.

He almost threw up on my boots. Luckily, only a few drops splattered my beloved Dr. Martens. Thank God for hellseeker reflexes. I step to the side, annoyed, and gag a little when I feel the stench of regurgitated alcohol and his last meal, which I suppose was a burger, burning my nose. *Ugh.* I hate hunting demons at the start of the Raven District weekend. I always want to kick someone's drunken ass by the end of the night. I throw the disgusting drunk an annoyed look over my shoulder and continue my pursuit.

Turning left at the end of the street, I stop when the covetorax demons do, getting ready to break into a jewelry store that's closed at this hour. The shop is small and quaint, with big windows adorned in a display of intricate pieces of jewelry that sparkle in the light cast by the lamppost.

The humans they possess are of average height, one bulkier than the other, and if I had to guess, they're both in their early twenties. The bulkier, shaved-head man on my left is dressed head to toe in black, a leather vest over his heavy metal band T-shirt. Tattoos cover every inch of exposed skin, and he has about ten piercings that I can see. He looks like he just got out of an MC Club meeting.

Whereas the one on my right is all limby and awkward mannerisms. With his pressed khakis, shiny shoes, and tucked shirt, he looks like the perfect churchgoing choir boy. He even wears thick-rimmed, round glasses while he wields a crowbar, trying to force the front door of the jewelry store open.

The image is so strange I almost burst into laughter, but I try to control myself as I put my back to the wall two buildings behind them, blending in with the shadows under the alcove of the entrance to Ciprianni's. The Italian restaurant is closed at this hour, and all I can think about is how hungry I am.

I haven't had time to eat dinner tonight, and I'm tiptoeing the line of becoming hangry. All I have to do is wait for them to break into the store, steal the jewelry, and run. I'll make my move on the retreat.

My "move" usually consists of tracking them to a back alley, killing the demons without witnesses, and handing the stolen goods to the police after ensuring that no harm was done to the human hosts (of course).

Humans surmise at all the hidden horrors of the world, hence all the scary movies out there, but they're supposed to live in blissful ignorance. Of course, people in high places and the intelligence agencies know about the presence of demons, but they usually leave the Order of Sariel to deal with anything demon-related, since it was, after all, formed at the command of the archangels.

My mouth waters and my stomach grumbles as I imagine a steaming bowl of shrimp truffle pasta in front of me…the same thing I ordered when Noah took me out on our first date at this very restaurant. *Fuck.* As much as I've tried to avoid thinking about him since my discussion with Sam, my mind keeps replaying all of our moments together on a loop like a sick movie. A special brand of torture that claws at my heart with steel-tipped talons, pooling blood from old wounds I thought long healed.

My blood simmers as our last kiss flashes before my eyes, and his empty promises ring in my ears. My nails dig deep into my palms, leaving crescent indentations behind.

The hurt is quickly replaced by the taste of betrayal. It burns through me like acid because I fell in love with him like a fool, and I believed him when he said before he left that he would never forget about me. It's been five years, and Noah hasn't sent a single text. Zero. Zilch. Nada. Well, fuck him. He clearly moved on, and so have I.

As I'm berating myself for letting the ghost of what Noah and I could have been tear me to pieces again, the two possessed humans suddenly turn around, their malice-filled gazes fixate on me and run before stealing anything as if they somehow knew I was onto them. That's never happened before. Covetorax demons are not smart at all, and the compulsion they feel to steal makes them oblivious to their surroundings.

Dumfounded by the fact that they ran before breaking into the jewelry store, I just stand there gaping like a newb. Usually, I like to think of myself as a badass bitch and all that since I'm one of the best hellseekers in the Order, and I kill demons on the regular. *Shit.* The covetorax are getting away while I'm frozen in place, gawking at their disappearing backs like the village idiot.

I quickly compose myself and start chasing after them, boots pounding fast on the pavement, soles burning my feet. I get some weird glances from people I pass on the streets since I'm not wearing running gear, and also, who the fuck would go for a jog at this hour in the middle of the night? As I get further away from the Raven District, though, there are fewer and fewer people, most of them sleeping peacefully in their beds, unaware of the dangers lurking in their dark alleys.

Thankfully, I'm able to track the covetorax demons to the edge of the forest, where the national park of Ashville starts. Grayson would've had my ass in a sling if I lost them. There aren't any people in the forest at night, so I can tap into that unearthly speed that all members of the Order possess and sprint after them.

The late-night spring air is crisper and a bit colder here in the forest compared to the air in the center of the city. It fills my lungs and burns the tip of my nose as leaves and fallen branches crunch under my combat boots. Balmy currents of pine-scented air mixing with chilly winds bite the skin on my cheeks with tiny pricks as I run faster and faster.

The stars twinkle and sparkle brightly in the sky, unhindered by the artificial city lights. The full moon, a bright orb of gray light, casts an eerie glow on the forest foliage, making the leaves appear translucent. I hope like hell there aren't any wolf shifters in the park tonight.

They usually stay in their community, not this close to the border of town, but last year, there were a lot of deaths caused by what humans believed to be animal attacks. I have a sneaky suspicion a rogue wolf shifter was involved. Wolf shifters, dark witches, vampires, and any other dark creatures are all under the jurisdiction of the Obsidian Conclave, though.

Without breaking any sweat, I run until I reach a clearing in the forest, right on the shore of Shadow Lake, where the humans possessed by the covetorax demons simply stand there, blank-faced and waiting for me.

This night could win an award for its weirdness so far.

"Well then, I guess you decided to make this really easy on me. Let's get this party started, boys! Ice cream and a new season of *The Vampire Diaries* are waiting for me at home," I say while approaching them and uncoiling my whip out of its holster. It's my weapon of choice when demon fighting.

Our weapons are sanctified by the archangels, and these are the only things able to kill demons; holy water is just laughable, honestly. The one downside, though, is the only weapons the archangels sanctified are old-fashioned ones. We can't use guns or any modern weapons; the bullets would go straight through them.

One of them snorts in response, since covetorax can't talk even when possessing a human. I blame it on their pea-sized brains, if they even have any. Then they both snarl at me at the same time, taking fighting positions.

Huh. This is pretty weird, too; I have never encountered a covetorax that would willingly get into a fight.

I tap the oval piece of onyx I'm wearing in the choker around my neck. Aside from the necklace with the amethyst pendant, the choker is the only piece of jewelry I wear. I never take either of them off, even when I shower.

The onyx stone glows red, and at the same time, the mouths of the two possessed humans open forcefully. Two smoke clouds leave their bodies that drop lifelessly with a thud to the ground, the thick-rimmed, round glasses shattering at the impact.

All of the Order members wear jewelry that encapsulates onyx. When we tap it, it has the power to extract demons from possessed humans, so we can kill them without harming their bodies. It works best on weaker demons, though, and never on Elite ones like Princes or Dukes of Hell, who don't need to possess humans because they come topside looking like them already.

Once the demons are extracted from their bodies, the humans usually wake up after a few hours and think they have the worst hangover of their lives and will go on like nothing happened. Unless their souls are tainted too far by the possession and we have to step in.

The smell of sulfur and soured meat fills my nostrils as the smoke starts taking the true form of the demons. Instead of the small and frail bodies of the covetorax, long muscular limbs with deadly claws, a cross between a hellhound and a panther with leathery reptilian skin, and two horned heads made only of razor-sharp teeth appear in front of me. I lay my eyes on the two draconic ravengers.

What in the actual fuck?

The shock pins me in place a second too long as one of the ravenger demons lets out a battle cry and flies at me on all fours with supernatural speed. It catches me off guard and slices my left forearm with its poisonous claws.

Motherfucker! That really hurt!

I manage to jump back right at the last second before those claws tear through my chest. When the other ravenger approaches and tries biting my head off, I crouch and roll on my right side. Making sure I'm far enough from its razor-sharp teeth, I propel myself up, then spin my whip in a circle above my head and throw it around the first ravenger's neck to immobilize it. It moves like a fish out of the water, its limbs and claws frantically swinging at me.

The previous ravenger comes at me again, but this time, I'm prepared, so I jump onto its back and use it as a springboard, launching myself into the air. Using the momentum, I unsheathe the sword strapped to my back and chop the head off the ravenger I have contained in my whip as I land into a nimble crouch.

The black rancid goop that sprays from its severed head gets into my eyes and mouth. I gag when I feel the taste of rot and sulfur on my tongue.

Eww.

For fucks sake, Iris, pull yourself together. Not turning your head to avoid the ichor is so amateur.

Its body disintegrates in seconds, leaving only black smoke and the acrid scent of rot behind.

The second one takes the opportunity to attack me while I'm furiously wiping at my eyes to get the disgusting goop off my face.

I dodge its attempt to hit me with its hind legs, but it unexpectedly swings its front claws at me, slicing through my pants and into the skin and muscle on the front of my thighs.

Sanctifiber might be sturdy enough, but it surely isn't foolproof. Red-hot pain shoots through me as blood starts seeping from the deep gashes. My rage threatens to boil over.

"These pants were new, dammit, and they make my ass look really good. Now I have to throw them out, you sorry excuse of a demon," I yell as I strike the demon with my whip and slice its legs off. It releases a high-pitched, deafening scream as it falls to the ground with a loud thump, so I bend down and decapitate it with my sword, carefully avoiding the nasty spray of goop this time. Cutting off the head is the only way to kill most demons.

Blowing out a breath of relief, already thinking about the pasta and ice cream I'm going to devour when I get home now that the job is done, I search for the vial of antidote in my corset. I need it for the poisoned wounds I got on my left forearm and my thigh. If the poison gets into the bloodstream and to the heart, it will kill a normal human instantly. Luckily, my hellseeker blood gives me an extra twenty-four hours.

I bring the antidote to my lips, when my skin breaks out in goosebumps all over my body. An ominous feeling unfurls in the center of my chest.

Something isn't right.

The temperature suddenly drops as currents of awareness zip down the ladder of my spine from the roots of my hair all the way down to my toes, and a heaviness settles in the depths of my stomach. That's when I turn my head and look toward the lake. Jaw slack, I do a double take because I can't believe what I'm seeing.

No…it…it can't be.

Right above the center of the lake, a black line appears out of nowhere, as if someone took a blade and sliced into thin air like it isn't immaterial. The tear starts transforming with the speed of light into a gaping hole that seems to suck all the light around it, like a vortex of hopelessness and despair.

No fucking way.

Did someone just open a portal to Hell?

Surely, the ravenger's poison is stronger than I think, and it's giving me some sort of a waking fever dream. As I try coming up with a different explanation for what I'm seeing, the onyx stone in the choker around my neck starts pulsating. It burns my skin like a piece of hot coal.

The air feels heavy, almost unbreathable, as if what I assume to be a portal sucks all the oxygen around it along with the light. The stars aren't visible anymore, and everything goes deadly silent. The rustling of the wind in the leaves, the lonely howl of a wolf in the distance, and the playful song of nightingales and cicadas, gone. The indecision of my next actions pins me in place with my mouth agape, staring at the jagged circle of doom.

Suddenly, the air crackles with lighting, and a strong wind starts out of nowhere as multiple shadowed flying figures enter through the tear, headed straight at me with unnatural speed, even for demons.

I have never encountered this type of demon before, but based on their speed and the way they look alone, it's pretty clear these shadow demons would be extremely hard to kill. And facing more than five on my own. Big no. I have to haul ass and fast.

The vial of antidote slips from my hand and drops to the ground as I start running, the broken shards of glass crunching under my boots. I have more at home; I just have to get there first. I take the phone out of the back pocket of my pants and try calling Grayson to send some reinforcements my way. He always answers his phone when a mission is given.

It goes straight to voicemail.

Shitshitshitshitshitshitshitshit!

3

Thump.

Thump.

Thump.

My heart thunders violently in my ears. The pressure in my chest and temples crushes all of my thoughts together in a tangled mess. I can't think about anything else aside from the fact that I have to escape whatever is chasing me. I have never run this fast in my entire life. My lungs are burning with every hurried breath I take, like I can't fit any more air in them, making my head swim with dizziness and coating my tongue in the coppery tang of blood.

I glance over my left shoulder to memorize what type of demon I'm running from. Maybe I can identify it later; I also need to describe it to Grayson so he can alert everyone from the Order. However, when I try to take a better look, I end up tripping over a rock.

Dammit.

Attempting to break the fall, I roll on my right side. Since I was using the hellseeker speed, I end up skidding on the ground and falling awkwardly with a loud thump. My right arm sits underneath me at an unnatural angle, and I'm desperately trying to get up as fast as possible, but fear grips me with poison-tipped claws.

Closer and closer.

A sharp pain stabs through my ankle. I probably sprained it. My shoulder also screams in protest when I attempt to get up again. Bile surges in the back of my throat as nausea constricts my stomach. It's dislocated, for sure. It isn't the first time, and it surely won't be the last time this happens, but I don't have time to put it back into its socket.

C'mon, Iris, get moving already!

Clenching my jaw hard, I ignore the throbbing pain as I jump up and come face to face with one of the demons. My breath freezes in my lungs, and it feels like the forest is also holding its breath as I use hellseeker speed to unsheathe the sword strapped to my back with my left hand. With a battle cry, I swing it in a wide arc, and it goes through the demon's shadowy neck. I honestly expect the sword to glide right through the immaterial flesh, but it does end up encountering resistance. How weird…I don't have time to dwell on it, though, because the demon's shriek makes my eardrums almost bleed as a blinding light erupts from the contact. The shadows disintegrate before my eyes.

However, the feeling of victory is short-lived because the moment I swing my sword again to counter the second demon's attack that comes flying at me, its tenebrous fingers seize the blade. The sword turns to useless ashes in my hand.

What. The. Fuck.

Acting purely on reflex, I uncoil my whip and snap it into the air. Before I get the chance to snare it around the demon's neck, it grabs me by the throat.

I freeze.

I look into the eyes of the dark-cloaked creature, and it's like staring into the fiery pits of Hell. Up close, it looks like a decaying corpse with mostly bones showing through its rotting flesh. It also has shadowy bat wings. My next breath is suffocating.

The demon singes my skin where it holds me by the throat, and I can't move. The onyx stone turns to a hot poker against my neck before it shatters. Tiny black shards stick to my chest, impaling me with the force of the explosion.

I forget all about the throbbing caused by my dislocated shoulder and the deep gashes in my thigh because the pain is so much more excruciating now. It's agony. To the point where I think I might faint. It feels as though my organs are incinerating from the inside out.

What in the holy hell? Why can't I move?

Demons are not supposed to be able to immobilize a hellseeker, dammit. My eyes and nose are the only parts of my body not paralyzed, obvious by the rancid, foul smell as the other Hellish creatures close in around me. In a frenzy, I try to think of something that can help me escape.

The one restraining me unexpectedly slaps its other rotting hand on the side of my head. It leaves fiery imprints on my scalp as it creeps closer to my face. White-hot pain detonates in my nerve endings, nearly blinding me as I feel something inside my brain—almost like a wall— crumble. The avalanche of agony that follows makes me convulse.

My heart slams into the back of my stomach with the speed of an anchor hitting the ocean floor.

This is how I die.

All of a sudden, there's a loud bang. A glaring orb of light explodes that takes over my eyesight. My vision swarms with little red and white dots, and the world moves around me like I'm on a spinning roller coaster. I vaguely notice the demon dropping me to the ground.

A blurry, flying figure with black hair and an exquisite body breaks through the vortex of what has become my reality. It picks me up against its chest with incredible gentleness. The intoxicating smell of black cherries and spiced rum envelops me in a warm cocoon. I'm either dead or hallucinating because this creature can't be real.

Or is it an avenging angel?

Can angels even have black wings?

"Are you the Angel of Death?" I manage to ask the blurry figure in a broken whisper. The pain intensifies to the point of madness, causing me to dry heave until I throw up in my mouth. I end up blacking out.

4

Darkness consumes me. I keep telling myself to open my eyes, but despite my best efforts, I'm not able to make my muscles listen to me. I still feel like my organs are incinerating themselves from the inside out while the smell of sulfur is stuck to my skin and burns the back of my throat. The loud ringing in my ears progressively dims as two voices I don't recognize argue in the background.

"Get the fuck out, Maeve! I'm not kidding. I will snap your neck in two if you as much as breathe too close to her," the deep, manly voice demands with anger.

"Are you out of your fucking mind, Kaiden? She's a hellseeker! Why the fuck did you save her? You've never even fucked me in your apartment, but you brought her here?! You put her on your bed? HER? This bitch deserves to die!" a very pissed-off and high-pitched woman's voice replies.

"Dominic, get her the hell out of here, or I swear I'm going to kill her. And call Malik, tell him to hurry. If he doesn't get here in the next five minutes,

I'm going to fucking kill him too," the angry man belts out with urgency.

Oddly, even if the manly voice is dripping with ire, I can't help but feel soothed by it, like a tiny part of my soul recognizes it, and I don't feel in danger at all. The sounds abruptly fade into nothingness as bone-deep tiredness washes over me. I let it pull me in like a tidal wave taking me under an infinite sea of oblivion.

My eyes snap open, and I blink a few times to clear my vision. A military parade has taken residence in my skull and is stomping all over my brain as the room spins with me. At least, that's how I feel—like I've spent hours banging my head against the wall. I also must have swallowed a bag full of cotton because it takes a few tries until I finally manage to unstick my tongue from the roof of my mouth.

Ugh.

The room finally stops spinning after a few minutes, and I look around, trying to make out my surroundings. I'm lying on a four-poster bed in the center of a room decorated in various shades of gray, white, and black. The room is sleek, modern, classy, and screams money.

Soft, warm light filters through the thick fabric of the drapes, covering what I assume are floor-to-ceiling windows. I wonder what time it is. The sheets are black, made out of the softest Egyptian cotton and their smell clings to my skin, spicy and warm. I suppress the urge to burrow my nose in them and inhale deeply. I feel weirdly naked under them. Grabbing the edge of the thin sheet that covers me, I lift it.

Dafuq?

I really am naked. I only have a pair of lacy panties and my amethyst necklace on. I mean, this is how I usually sleep; I often wake up in the middle of the night from night terrors that I never remember, drenched in sweat, tears in my eyes, and screaming until my throat is raw.

My best guess is the dreams are from my life before, from the accident when I lost my mother and all of my memories. I ruined so many pjs that I just stopped wearing anything. Being naked in my own bed is entirely different, though, from being naked in a stranger's bed in a room I don't recognize and wearing underwear that definitely isn't mine. I hope the panties are new, at least. Because if not...eww.

Blinking a few times, I realize I'm completely healed; my ankle doesn't hurt anymore, and my shoulder is back in its socket. I roll it a few times in a circle to see if I have full range of motion, and I do. Panic seizes my chest as I remember the white-hot pain caused by the touch of the mysterious shadowy demon.

There's a glass of water on the nightstand and a bottle of Tylenol. I pop two pills into my mouth and take small sips from the glass, trying not to upset my stomach.

The sound of water being turned off in the shower reaches my ears, and I realize there must be an en suite bathroom through the door at my right, and someone is in there.

Shit.

I look at the door and quickly grab the thin sheet, wrapping it around me as best as I can. I freeze, and my heart skips a beat as the door opens and the most beautiful man I have ever laid eyes upon steps out of the bathroom and stops at the threshold.

Fuck me.

Beautiful not in the traditional way, where beauty means everything that is good and light. But in the promises of a fallen angel whispered in the middle of the night, where all of your darkest fantasies come alive and bathe you in sin and moonlight. He's tall, sculpted, and hard, every ridge and sinewy muscle defined, wearing only a towel hanging deliciously low from his hips.

Droplets of water are sticking to his sun-kissed skin, covered in artful tattoos all over his chest, arms, and thighs. Even his knuckles and throat are tattooed. The only spot untouched by the needle is that right above his heart. I have never felt an attraction to guys with tattoos before. I mean, sure, I always appreciated the artistry behind the craft. But his are so intricate and unique, they stir something inside me.

I'm clearly having a stroke because I'm not able to look away from this walking wet dream of a man.

Ha, who am I kidding? I'm not just looking; I'm blatantly gawking like a weirdo. I'm afraid if I touch the corner of my lips, I will surely find some drool there, too.

Obsidian eyes streaked with gold and crimson ensnare mine. They burn a fire trail straight to my soul. "Like what you see, angel?" He winks and smirks while crossing his arms over his chest, his deep, rough voice rolling over me like molasses. Something about his posture is predatory—like a lion waiting to strike at any minute and sink its sharp teeth into its prey.

My face feels hot, and I know without having to look in a mirror that it must be as red as an overripe tomato in this moment. I want to kick myself for being so blatantly obvious.

"I wouldn't flatter myself too much if I were you. My neurons have probably been fried by that wannabe Dementor in the woods. And who told you, you could call me angel?" I fire back while squinting my eyes in annoyance, mostly at myself but also at how stupidly hot he is.

Ugh.

He sucks on his teeth before his gaze locks with mine. "And if I were

you, I wouldn't joke about the umbra demons." The tips of his raven black hair are touching his shoulders, still wet from the shower, a few droplets of water falling from them and cascading through the rivulets of muscles. Keeping eye contact is proving to be quite difficult. I swear my eyeballs have a mind of their own. Just like Sisyphus, they roll back down the muscle — ahem, hill.

Shit. Focus, you dumbass.

"And how do you know that?" I have never seen or heard about this type of demon before, and I've been with the Order for eight years now. "Who are you, and why did you bring me here?" I demand with urgency.

He cocks an eyebrow at me while resting his right hip on the door frame, crossing his legs at the ankles in a faux-relaxed way. I can feel his rapacious gaze, though, and there is nothing relaxed or comforting about it.

"Before you start with the third degree, you should probably thank me. You know, for saving your life," he drawls, annoyance dripping from his tone. He then strides toward another door at my left and disappears through it.

I quickly get up after I pull the sheet around me like a makeshift black dress. Stumbling a bit through the dizziness caused by my sudden movement, I try to keep my legs steady and follow him through the door. "Don't you dare walk away from me! I want answers, and I want them now!" I yell after him while entering what seems to be a dressing room and…

WHOA!

He's naked with his back facing me, pulling on a pair of distressed jeans over black boxers, his muscles dancing deliciously with the movement, the towel resting on the floor at his feet. I stare at his naked backside, feeling like my skin is pulled too tight over my bones, and tiny electric shocks take over my body.

His back is spectacular, adorned by a massive tattoo of black wings.

As I take a few steps in his direction, I see that it's actually a fallen angel bowing on one leg, its head resting on its forearm, as if in regret. The image is beautiful and soul-wrenching.

Damn, I feel like such a pervert. I need to get laid. I mean, for the first time ever since I haven't lost my virginity yet. It wasn't from the lack of trying, trust me. But every guy I went out with either bored me to death or made me want to drive a fork through their eyeballs. I would rather get myself off than let clean-cut Clive fuck me missionary style for about two minutes before he comes, thank you very much. Also, I always thought it would be Noah I would have my first time with, and maybe we could become more later as time passed. But he left the Order in Ashville to join the Order in another city with his parents when I turned eighteen. I haven't seen or heard from him since.

My mysterious savior spins on his heel and looks into my eyes, a devious smile tugging at his mouth. He can obviously tell I was ogling him again.

"Aren't you going to put a shirt on? And where are my clothes? My weapons?" I ask as I unsuccessfully try not to stare at his perfectly chiseled chest.

"So demanding and feisty," he says, approaching me with a predatory gait. "Do I need to remind you you're in my home? I had to throw out your clothes; they were torn and covered in demon blood. And for your weapons, I don't know. I think the umbra disintegrated them when it touched you." He pauses, lifts an eyebrow, and says, "My name's Kaiden Black."

What. The. Fuck.

"That thing disintegrated the rest of my weapons, too?" I ask in disbelief, mostly to myself. "Is that even possible? The weapons sanctified by the archangels? You have got to be kidding me. How powerful are these demons?" I rack my brain, trying to remember where I heard his name. It sounds so familiar, and I know for sure I've heard it before…I just don't know where.

The realization slams into me with the feeling of being thrown into a pool of ice-cold water.

I can't believe I'm stupid enough to not notice until now the Sigil of Baphomet inked on his right shoulder, the head of a goat in the center of a reversed pentagram, marking him as a member of the Obsidian Conclave. In my defense, though, he has so many tattoos that it got lost, blending perfectly with his full sleeve. And who am I kidding? I was too busy ogling him to notice.

"You're Kaiden Black, as in Kaiden Black, the head of the Obsidian Conclave?"

An Elite demon saved me—a very powerful Elite demon.

Fuck my life.

I have to get out of here!

NOW!

5

My heart leaps in my throat, hammering my blood through my veins as I throw out my right leg to spin kick him in the face. Kaiden's head snaps to the side as my foot connects with his jaw. His eyebrows draw together in a scowl as he brings his thumb to the corner of his lips to wipe the blood trickling down on his chin. Huh, his blood is not tar-like as I was expecting, but a very deep shade of crimson. His burning gaze slams into mine as he turns, disbelief evident on his stupidly gorgeous face before he starts...chuckling.

What the?

I freeze, taken aback by his reaction, the beautiful lilt of his laughter, and the way his whole face lit up, making my heart do crazy acrobatics inside my chest. Kaiden shakes his head as if he's sharing an inside joke with himself, and our gazes lock—mine confused as hell, and his flashing something akin to respect.

I bristle, aggravated by my body's reaction to hearing him laugh. "What the fuck is so funny?" I don't waste a second, cocking my arm and sending my fist flying in a powerful uppercut.

Lightning quick, Kaiden dodges my attack and uses my momentum to turn me around and pin me to the wall with his body, one arm around my waist, right under my breasts, keeping me in place. I dropped the sheet when he spun me around, and it's now pooling at my feet, so I'm standing only in my panties, his chest pressed to my back.

Damn it!

He's strong and fast. Faster than me.

Kaiden bends his head slightly, bringing his lips to my right ear while his still-wet, silky strands brush my cheek, making me shiver. "You're spectacular, you know that?" Our bodies are flush, the naked skin on his chest in direct contact with the naked skin on my back. I don't know where I end and he begins. His warm, sensual smell washes over me, spicy and musky with a hint of rum and black cherries. It reminds me of the decadent black cherries dipped in liquor and covered in chocolate. The ones I receive every year for my birthday. It makes my insides warm, like staying in front of a cozy fire on a cold winter day.

"I don't take compliments from demons," I bite back and buck my hips, trying to escape, but I'm met with his hard-on, pressing deliciously in my ass. I can feel how big he is, even with the rough fabric of his jeans covering it. Heat instantly pools between my legs, and my clit throbs when I feel he is as affected as I am by the contact of our bodies.

"So, this is how you thank me for saving you? I should spank you for this behavior. Tell me, Iris, would you like that?" he says gruffly, his voice thick and rough from his arousal. It wraps around me like liquid silk.

My heart skips a beat at my name on his lips.

How the fuck does he know my name?

His warm breath tingles the sensitive skin behind my ear, sending ripples of desire that make my core muscles clench as my juices wet my panties. My nipples pebble hard against the wall. The contact sets my skin on fire.

Kaiden's breath hitches before he inhales sharply, and a shudder goes through his body. "You *would* like that," he rasps, surprise and something else evident in his tone. I know this seems crazy, but he almost sounds...Nah, that can't be right. I'm reading too much into things. That's not...hope I'm hearing, is it?

Earth to Iris. A demon is holding you!

"Dream on, demon! I *would* never let you touch me. You make me sick!" I spew as I make another attempt to escape, stomping on his foot with my heel as hard as I can. The bastard doesn't even flinch.

He laughs, the sound hollow, almost as if my words deeply hurt him, and with ease, he separates my legs using his knee, immobilizing me further against the wall. "Don't give me this holier-than-thou attitude. I can smell your desire from here. I bet if I moved your panties and touched your pussy, I would find it drenched. My cock would slide right in," he snaps, his tone as cold as the Arctic.

Shit.

It's infuriating how right he is. My legs start shaking uncontrollably. I'm a heartbeat away from begging him to fuck me against the wall. To hell with all the consequences.

"I need you to promise me you won't try anything stupid again before I release you. As much as I would love dry fucking you against the wall, we have more important things to discuss," he says calmly and continues, "So here is how this is going to go, Iris. I'm going to release you; you're going to go to the bathroom, have a few minutes to yourself, calm down, and then we're going to talk over breakfast in my kitchen. After we talk, you can go on your way, unharmed. Okay? I need you to answer me now," he demands. His deep voice rolls over me like silk.

Ha, he must have hit his overly inflated head on something if he thinks I'm going to give up just like that.

"Okay," I snap.

"Promise you won't try anything stupid again."

"I won't try anything stupid again. I promise. Now release me," I clip out through clenched teeth while rolling my eyes in annoyance.

He relaxes his hold and releases me slowly to make sure I'm not going to attempt hitting him again. Yeah, sure, like that's even a possibility. One thing I'm proud of is that I never back down from a fight, even if the chances are stacked against me.

As Kaiden steps away from me, my stupid body almost weeps from the loss of delicious warmth. In the next breath, I turn around to face him and swing my right arm in an arc, aiming a fist at his annoyingly beautiful face.

My knuckles barely graze his jaw as he grabs my wrist with inhuman speed and tugs me with so much force toward his body that my front clashes with his chest, my breasts pressing against his pectorals while his hard-on digs exactly in my center. My back hits the wall. Hard. All the air leaves my lungs in a huff.

Holy shit.

He then grabs my other wrist and pins both of my hands above my head on the wall, keeping them fused together in one hand. Tattooed fingers collar my throat. His thumb presses on the fluttering artery on the side of my neck, the silver rings adorning his fingers cold against my heated skin.

My feet are dangling above the floor, and he's acting as if I weigh nothing more than a feather while bracing my whole weight with his body. I haven't even noticed until this very moment how Kaiden's six-four frame towers over me. It makes me feel small and dainty.

Ugh.

This up close and personal, I can truly appreciate his full, sinful lips. He also has a small bump in the middle of his otherwise straight nose, probably from having it broken and put back together more than once.

This imperfection doesn't take away from his beauty; it only makes it more striking.

His chiseled jawline is covered in a day's worth of stubble, and I suddenly have the urge to lift my hand and rub my fingers against it. Our bodies are aligned perfectly in all the ways that matter, and a heaviness settles in my breasts when my diamond-hard nipples rub onto his chest. My skin feels as if it's caught on fire, and my blood turns to molten lava into my veins.

Fuck. Fuck. Fuck me now.

I didn't think this through.

The air between us thickens and sparks. I whimper when he rolls his hips, creating friction with the rough fabric of his jeans on my overly sensitive clit, covered just by my very thin, drenched panties.

Our gazes collide, and the corner of his lips lifts in an infuriatingly sexy smirk. "I love how feisty you are, angel, but I would appreciate it if you would stop trying to hit me." His smile drops, and a muscle ticks around his jaw. "So. Don't." He pauses. Then his Adam's apple rolls with an audible swallow. "Do. That. Again." He's breathing hard, labored breaths, and his eyes are two obsidian pools of desire, the golden flecks swirling with red streaks as he looks up and down my body like he wants to devour every inch of me.

I'm frozen in place by the fire in his eyes, my limbs and brain turned to mush. Kaiden's scent is an inferno blazing through me, making my clit throb almost in pain. I need the release like I need my next breath. I'm so out of my mind with need I start to gyrate my hips slowly to create more of that mind-numbing friction.

Kaiden sucks in a jagged breath, and his nostrils flare as his gaze flicks between my eyes and lips, a deep frown pulling at his eyebrows. Obsidian fire traps me like a binding spell as his eyes snap back to mine...searching, and alight with so much emotion and longing that my heart jackhammers against my ribcage, and all my blood rushes in my ears. Desire sears me from the inside out. His tongue darts out to moisten his lips. The movement is so sexy I bite into my lower lip to suppress a moan. He swears loudly under his breath before his thumb comes up, freeing my trapped lip and running a fiery path across it with the pad of his finger.

He rests his forehead against mine. My heart sputters in my chest as we share the same breath.

One heartbeat passes.

Two.

Three.

I close my eyes and wait for that moment of devastating destruction when Kaiden's lips are going to meet mine, but it never comes. Instead, my world tilts on its axis as I'm thrown over his shoulder like a sack of potatoes.

All of this happens so fast, it takes a humiliating amount of time for my sex-induced brain to catch up. My ass sticks up in the air, and my breasts are pressed against his back, my eyeballs in direct contact with his ass, his grip on the underside of my knees strong and firm, keeping me in place, not giving me even an inch of wiggle room so I can try to escape.

I can't believe I feel disappointed that a demon didn't kiss me. Clearly, the umbra's touch fried all my working neurons. I even hallucinated that a demon had black angel-like wings.

"What in the actual fuck?! Are you insane? Put me down right now!" I screech, my anger fueled not only by the fact that he's manhandling me, but mostly because I'm still so turned on I can't see straight, my body strung high like a string over a bow, ready to snap at any moment.

He takes long strides to exit the dressing room and walks toward the bathroom attached to the bedroom I woke up in.

"Are you deaf? Put me down!" I scream again while banging my fists on his ass. Instead of answering, he slaps my left ass cheek hard three times in rapid-fire succession, and then he shocks the hell out of me by caressing the stinging skin.

My body is a live wire as I feel the vibration of those slaps right in the center of my pussy, my panties getting soaked again, if that is even possible. Liquid fire races through my veins as the image of Kaiden taking me over the knee and making me come just by using his hand flashes through my mind. I'm so angry I want to gouge his eyes out.

He enters the bathroom and doesn't even make a sound as he unceremoniously slides me down the front of his body. The contact fires my senses, making my skin tingle all over. I suck in a sharp breath. My feet slap the floor tiles hard when he drops me in the walk-in shower.

"You—" I don't get to finish what I was going to say because he moves his hand, and all of a sudden, ice-cold water starts pouring on my head.

He didn't just do that!

The cold water is so jarring I just stand there with my mouth agape, giving him a death stare while seething with anger. I wouldn't be surprised if fire starts coming out of my nose, dragon style.

"I'll let you cool off. I'll wait for you in the kitchen. We need to talk. You'll find some clothes on the side of the bed when you come out of the bathroom. Unless you want to finish what we started," he says while arching an eyebrow at me, his tongue rolling over his lower lip. Desire dances in his eyes like hot embers.

I feel his gaze on me like a physical caress. It only manages to make my blood boil in my veins even more. "Fuck! You! Get the fuck out!" I bellow. My fingers clench and unclench, my nails digging deep into my palms, leaving crescent indentations behind. I turn around, and the door shuts behind Kaiden as he leaves the bathroom.

6

Taking a few deep breaths in through my nose and expelling them through my mouth, I try to calm down. Obviously, fighting my way out didn't do me any good, so I have to take this shower, listen to what he has to say, and leave.

Switching the water from cold to hot, I take off my soaked panties, throwing them in the corner of the walk-in shower. Is he going to let me leave just like that? He did save my life, and aside from the fact that he stopped all of my attempts to hit him, he only restrained me without retaliating. Not even a hair on my head is harmed. I took a pretty bad blow to my ego, though, because it was so freakin' easy for him to immobilize me. He acted like I was an annoying insect, not a badass hellseeker.

I'll have to call Grayson and tell him what happened.

Shit.

How in the world am I going to explain this to him? Maybe I should tell him in person. Closing my eyes under the spray of hot water and massaging my hair with the heavenly-scented shampoo I found on the shelf, I imagine how the conversation would go.

"Um…so Grayson, you know…the mission you gave me on Friday night to kill those covetorax demons? Yeah, I did kill them in the end, after I found out they tricked me and turned out to be draconic ravengers. Anyway, after I killed them, all of a sudden, the sky tore open, and very powerful shadow-like demons attacked me in the woods, and I almost died. Hold on, though, because the story gets even better. An Elite demon saved me. I know, funny, right? His name is Kaiden Black…yeah, the Kaiden Black. I also tried to dry fuck him against the wall like a cat in heat. Apparently, tattoos and rugged man looks are totally my kryptonite because I can't seem to think straight when he is near or touching me."

Just thinking again about how his body felt against mine makes me weak in the knees. I start banging my forehead on the glass of the walk-in shower. I'm a shameless hussy and didn't even know it until this fucked up day. How I could act like that with someone I just met is beyond me — a demon on top of everything?

And you wanted him to kiss you, Iris. You almost begged him.

Oh, shut up!

I'm a twenty-three-year-old virgin, and I haven't been interested in a guy long enough to lose my virginity until now. I thought the pink vibrator sitting in my nightstand drawer at home was enough to satisfy me, but all that went out the window five minutes into meeting a sexy Elite demon.

A demon Iris, a fucking demon.

I just wanted to go home after killing those draconic ravengers, stuff my face with a bowl of delicious carbonara, eat my weight in ice cream, and veg out on the couch. Was that too much to ask? Can't a girl celebrate her birthday in peace?

Stepping out of the shower, I dry my body with a cloudlike, fluffy white towel that was hanging on a hook. *Ugh*, even his towels are perfect. I didn't get to appreciate the bathroom until this moment since Kaiden brought me in like a sack of potatoes, and I was too angry to take in my surroundings. I was also hanging upside down, so there's that.

The room is spacious, almost bigger than my apartment. You can fit around ten people in the walk-in shower, and they still wouldn't touch each other. To my right, a golden chandelier hangs above a Victorian claw foot bathtub with beautiful golden accents, and I want to move in it and never leave. I have always wanted a claw foot bathtub like this one, but the bathroom in my small apartment looks like a matchbox next to Kaiden's.

I could afford a more luxurious apartment with the money I inherited after my mother's death. It feels wrong, though, to use that money as if I'm happy she's dead. I won't touch it unless it's an emergency. The salary I get from the Order is enough to live a comfortable life.

The bathroom counters to my left and the wall behind are black, made out of marble, two oval-shaped sinks on top with golden faucets, and a huge, gilded mirror hanging from the wall above the counters. Judging by how luxurious everything looks, I don't think that's paint. The toilet is in another room, separated by a door. *Jeez, talk about money.* Of course he's filthy rich, being the head of the Obsidian Conclave.

Turning to the sink closest to me, I rest my hands on its sides while looking at my reflection in the mirror. My skin is paler than usual, my eyes bloodshot, the red splotchy veins making the weird colors of my irises pop even more. I was born with a rare case of heterochromia, and ever since I could remember, people have always assumed I'm wearing contact lenses. They never believe me when I tell them the cerulean pale irises outlined by two violet rings are real.

Dark circles surround them, and I look like I haven't slept in weeks…I guess brushing hands with death will do that to you. I rake my hand through the freshly washed ebony hair that sticks limply to my scalp, a stark contrast against my milk-colored skin.

I'm glad I don't usually wear any makeup when I go out hunting. I bet I would have looked like a hot mess right now, with mascara running down my face and patches of foundation everywhere. Just the thought of sleeping with a full face of makeup makes my skin crawl.

Lowering my fingers to the center of my chest, I roll the pendant that's resting there between the tips of my fingers. I wonder how the necklace survived the umbra attack since the onyx stone I had in the choker around my neck exploded. The golden pendant hangs from a delicate chain, and it's shaped like angel wings with a round amethyst gemstone in the middle. The stone is the same color as the rings of violet surrounding the blue of my irises. It's intricate and unique, and it's the only tangible thing I have left from my life when my mother was still alive.

The hollowness I feel inside my chest like a gaping wound threatens to swallow me whole and take me under. It's an empty space I filled with sadness and frustration at myself and at my weak mind over the passing years for not being able to remember her...or to even recognize myself. Thoughts about my lost past will come and go at different times of day, sometimes making me sick with how much I miss it, like a phantom limb, carrying its weight at all times. I snap my eyes shut, my very first memory after the accident assaulting my brain.

Beep.

Beep.

Beep.

The blinding lights burn through my retinas, intensifying the pounding in the back of my head tenfold. My throat is raw, like I swallowed a million razor blades as the harsh antiseptic smell crawls up my nose. Pain. So much pain. Everywhere. Radiating from my leg all over my body. A moan breaks loose through my lips as I unsuccessfully try to move my fingers. It feels like I'm entirely encased in cement. So heavy. So hard to break through. If only I could rub my eyes a little. Make the image clearer.

The hazy fog of blurriness finally lifts from my eyes after what feels like an eternity, but I only see white. A white ceiling. A dozen little beeps and dripping sounds. Where am I? I'm lying on my back and have something attached to my right hand. I move my eyes to see what it is with the speed of a snail. A big needle protrudes from my wrist, and it's attached to an IV drip. Am I in a hospital?

"Iris, can you hear me?" a voice I don't recognize breaks through my lethargic thoughts.

Huh? Who is Iris?

I sluggishly turn my head to the left and realize that I'm not alone in the room. A slim, tall, brunette woman with kind hazel eyes in a white coat is talking to me.

"Iris, can you hear me?" she repeats. "Blink if you can hear me, please."

I blink and look at her, confusion taking over my foggy mind. Iris? Is that my name? A sinking feeling of desperation unfurls in the pit of my stomach. I don't know who I am. How did I get here? There's something I need to remember. It's important. My body shakes with the mental effort. I have to remember. I have to.

"You were in a car accident. You are now in the ICU at the Heartland General Hospital. You've been in a coma for two weeks – "

What?

No. No. No.

That's impossible.

The doctor keeps talking, but her voice drowns in the jumbling thoughts inside my head. How can I not remember that I was in a car accident? I can't even remember my name.

"…you are the only survivor of the accident. I'm sorry to say this, but your mother passed away. The injuries she endured were too severe."

My heart rattles hard against my ribs as panic seizes my chest, folding my lungs in two. I'm surprised my ribs are not cracking under the pressure with how rapidly my heart is beating. Loud beeping sounds invade the room, their echoes bouncing off the walls.

"No! No! No!" I repeat in a broken whisper.

"Tachycardia! She's having a panic attack. I need a sedative stat!"

As the gaping wound in my chest expands to a bottomless pit, tiredness seeps into my bones, pulling me under. Blankness takes over my eyes, and I wish I would stay in the void and never wake up.

Unfortunately, I did wake up after a few hours. Despair took over every little cell of my being when the doctors told me again what happened…that my mother was dead, and I told them I didn't remember anything, that I couldn't even remember my name or how I looked.

They held up a mirror to my face, and the stranger staring back at me with lifeless, strange-colored eyes, reflecting the empty soul that lay beneath, told me silently that it would have been easier if I were dead, too. I didn't know who I was. I didn't remember significant details about my life, the void consuming me, my thoughts, my being. I was there when she died. I probably watched her take her last breath.

Strangely, I remembered current events like who the president was or the Pythagorean theorem, but nothing personal. The doctors said my mind was too shattered by what happened, and it protected itself from the trauma by not letting me remember the physical and emotional pain.

Eight years ago, we drove our car into a canyon. It left me with multiple internal injuries, scrapes, and cuts all over my body, a tibia-fibula fracture on my right leg, the bones sticking out of the skin on the side of my knee. My mother was found dead at the scene. Of course, the official cover-up version was that she died on the spot because of her injuries. The Order and I knew the truth, though. At the bottom of the canyon, a demon was waiting for us. The demon killed her, and it almost killed me too.

43

I found out the truth from my Aunt Josephine—the only family I have left—when she came for me at the hospital. Of course, there's also my father, a human. My mother fell in love with a man, left the Order for him, and ran away, leaving everything behind and cutting ties with everyone, even her sister. No one knows who he is; my birth certificate holds only my mother's name. If not for my aunt and the Order, I don't think I would be a sane person right now. I had to stay in a mental facility owned by the Order for almost a year until the doctors cleared me to leave.

A year of therapy and group sessions did nothing for my memory loss. It only slightly helped me crawl out of the pit of despair my deep depression threw me into. The doctors told me that my memory might come back one day or possibly never would.

Eventually, I had to make peace with it. At least, that's what I told everyone. I never did, though. The doubt and bitterness scraped with sharp claws at my heart's walls until there was nothing left behind but rage and a taste for revenge that is never sated, no matter how many demons I kill.

How could I forget my rage, the very reason I am able to face the world every day? After all, that's why I worked so hard on becoming a hellseeker, to avenge my mother's death. To find the demon that killed her and to prevent others from having the same fate as her.

"You have to remember who you are, Iris! What the demons did to you and your mother. Everything they took from you," I tell my reflection while clenching the sides of the sink, my fingers white from the pressure, and steeling my resolve further that I have to get out of here and forget all about Kaiden Black and his sinful body.

7

Wearing the towel as a dress, I make a beeline for the room I woke up in. On top of the bed, clothes are neatly folded and waiting for me as promised, with a pair of strappy sandals on top. Kaiden isn't anywhere in sight, so I presume he's in the kitchen, as he previously stated.

I was expecting a T-shirt and sweatpants from Kaiden's wardrobe, but am surprised to find women's clothing instead. My first thought is that he's giving me his girlfriend's clothes to wear, the notion making me want to rip these clothes to pieces. The unsuspected irrational pang of jealousy burns through my chest like venom.

Why the fuck do I even care?

But the clothes still have the tags attached to them, so I calm down, the Italian brand name sounding foreign on my tongue and too hard for me to pronounce correctly. I haven't even heard of it before, and I blanch at the price tag on each item.

Jeez. Does he eat money for breakfast?

Unfolding the clothes, I look at them. High-rise straight jeans and a pastel pink linen cropped top with billowy puffy sleeves. There's also a set of the sexiest lingerie I have ever seen or touched, the soft pink lace silky and partially see-through. Something that I would have never chosen to wear by myself. Well, mostly because I could never afford something like this. The clothes look weirdly sexy and sophisticated at the same time, though. I usually don't wear pastel colors or any colors; I mostly stick with black since it hides blood stains the best.

Discarding the wet towel at my feet, I start dressing myself, and I'm surprised at how well everything fits, as though Kaiden knows exactly my size. Sometimes, it's hard for me to find tops that fit nicely around my breasts since I have full D cups, and at times, some of them make me look like a stripper, showing too much cleavage. I always have to buy a bigger top than the bottom, but the clothes hug my body and feel like second skin, which makes me even more annoyed at how perfectly everything fits, even the bra and shoes.

Getting out of the bedroom, I pass a few closed doors on a spacious hallway and a small sitting area. At the end of it, I reach a staircase. The top of the stairs offers a view of the entire first floor of what seems to be a ginormous penthouse decorated in a minimalistic combination of white and black, with floor-to-ceiling windows overlooking the city and snow-capped mountains in the distance. The view is breathtaking. I can only imagine how beautiful it would look at night with all the tiny glimmering city lights. This is so not what I thought a demon's home would look like. It's bright and airy but classy and edgy at the same time with light woods and black marble accents. It's also so clean it almost looks staged.

It's early in the morning, judging by the placement of the sun in the sky, and it's sunny, with no traces of clouds. The sudden burst of light makes me blink a few times in order to adjust to the brightness. I'm not

46

used to waking up at this time of day since I work at night, and on the weekends, I like to sleep in.

I descend the stairs and walk slowly toward the kitchen. I stop near the bar, not mentally prepared for the sight of Kaiden flipping pancakes at the stove, barefoot, the movements making his back muscles dance in a way that gets my pulse spiking through the roof.

He thankfully has a black tee on that, at a closer look, somehow seems more erotic than him being naked. It fits him like a glove, hugging his muscles and accentuating the bronze hue of his skin. It all looks so domestic; I want to laugh at the irony. A demon cooking pancakes for a demon hunter. If this isn't a line from a joke, then I don't know what the hell is.

Am I trapped in one of Dante's circles of Hell and have no idea?

Two empty plates are on top of the bar, alongside a spread of scrambled egg whites, bacon, fresh strawberries, and freshly squeezed orange juice.

"Sit. We're going to eat, and then we can talk," Kaiden says while turning off the induction stovetop and placing the tower of chocolate-chip pancakes on the bar.

"I'm not hungry; I just want to go home. Say your piece, demon, and I'll get out of your hair," I bite back with indignation. As soon as I finish saying it, my stomach grumbles loudly at the smell of the delicious spread, and I want to die inside because I can feel my face getting redder by the minute.

Kaiden looks at me, the ghost of a smile turning up his lips in amusement at my embarrassment. "C'mon, take a seat and eat. You've been down for almost fifty-five hours. No wonder your stomach is making loud noises."

WHOA.

My mouth drops open involuntarily, my eyebrows shooting up all the way to my hairline. "WHAT? Fifty-five hours? I've been sleeping that long? What day is it?" I ask in a high-pitched tone. I slept through my twenty-third birthday and my plans with Sam.

"It's Monday. You didn't just sleep; you had to heal. You're lucky you're alive and that I found you when I did. If it weren't for my warlock friend, Malik, you would have been dead now."

"It's Monday?" I echo in disbelief. I also had dinner plans for Sunday evening with Aunt Josephine to celebrate my birthday. She must be worried sick since I didn't answer my phone. She probably called me a thousand times.

On top of that, I also have to go to the compound and let Grayson know about the attack. *Fuck.* He's going to be so mad when I tell him it happened on Friday, and two days have passed since then. Luckily, I wasn't on demon-hunting duty this past weekend. I normally have weekends off.

Pulling out a bar stool, I plop down on it. "Where's my phone?" I ask while staring into space, trying to make the best decision of what to do next. Banging my head on the bar seems like a good option.

"You didn't have a phone when I found you," Kaiden says as he pulls the bar stool next to mine. The moment he sits down, his left thigh grazes my right one, which pulls me out of my reverie and leaves a wake of shivers behind.

"Did you throw out my Dr. Martens too?"

"They were all torn up," he tells me as he starts stacking pancakes on my empty plate, his proximity engulfing me in his decadent, musky, spicy scent, making me hyper-aware of his presence. He's so close I can feel the body heat radiating off him.

Gah, why does he have to smell so good?

He inches slightly backward while putting some scrambled egg whites on his own empty plate. He doesn't give me much space, though, our bodies only a breath away, every movement eliciting tingles, starting a slow simmer that I can feel deep into my bones.

Feigning ignorance, I don't put any space between us. I don't want to show him how affected I am by our proximity. *Ah, what the hell.* I'm hungry anyway, and he did make me chocolate chip pancakes, which, by the way, are my favorite thing to eat in the morning.

Has he been stalking me or something?

After slicing a few strawberries on top of the pancakes, I take my first bite while Kaiden starts eating his boring egg whites. Do demons need to eat? I have never seen one eat before.

I suppress a loud moan when the melting chocolate flavor explodes on my tongue, making me almost dance with happiness. Judge me, I'm hungry as hell, and the pancakes are so freakin' fluffy and perfect.

We finish the rest of our meals in silence. I'm still trying to figure out how I'm going to tell Grayson about everything that happened. The Order is my entire life, it would destroy me if I got kicked out. As much as it pains me, I have to lie. There's no other option. But how much I'm going to lie and what I can tell still has to be decided.

I vaguely hear "...coffee?" and ask, "Huh?" when I realize Kaiden is now standing near the very expensive-looking coffee machine. I was so immersed in my thoughts again that I didn't notice him standing up.

"I said, do you want coffee?" he asks again, his back facing me while pressing a few buttons on the machine. It beeps loudly, and hot liquid starts pouring into the mug. Apparently, you need a degree just to make a cup of coffee. I'm sure if I touch it, I will break it or possibly set it on fire.

"Yeah...thanks. I'm trying to figure out what to report to the Order. I can't exactly tell them you saved me, you know. They would show me the door without a second thought," I sigh, the predicament I find myself in souring my mood.

He slides the steaming cup of java on the bar in front of me. "It's best if you don't tell them what happened. I have reasons to believe someone sent you directly into a trap on Friday night."

I blow on the surface of the hot liquid and chance a small sip, hoping I will still have taste buds left, and the coffee is perfect, exactly how I usually drink it. Two creams, two sugars, and it tastes as expensive as the machine it came out of looks.

"What do you mean? What reasons?" I flit my gaze to Kaiden.

He's now facing me on the other side of the bar while his inked forearms rest on top, protruding veins evident over thick ropes of muscles.

Jesus. Are forearms supposed to look this sexy?

"Did the night go as it usually does when you go out hunting, or did something weird happen?" he inquires while raising an eyebrow at me. He straightens and crosses his arms in front of his chest as if he wants to challenge me with his words. His tattooed biceps stand out even more with the move.

"Well, now that you mention it, a series of weird things happened." Can I really trust him with this? I trust just a few people from the Order with my life. But they took me in when my life was in shambles, and I was just a shadow of a person. Grayson would never do anything to hurt me, would he? I tear a hole in my cheek, trying to decide what to tell him and what I should keep to myself.

"Go on," Kaiden urges me to continue while tilting his head.

I tell him everything that happened since I started following the covetorax demons until the moment he found me in the woods, leaving out the part where Grayson sent me the text with the mission. I wasn't even sure he knew how to text until that very moment. He looks about fifty years old, but I know for a fact that he's closer to a hundred since we age slower than normal humans, and technology isn't something he bothers with very often. And then he wouldn't answer his phone. He is always a phone call away when he gives us missions in case something goes awry and we need backup. Did he send me to my death knowingly?

No…that's impossible.

Is it?

"The draconic ravengers were clearly just a decoy. Someone wanted you to be in the woods near Shadow Lake when the umbra came through the portal," Kaiden states calmly as he rests his back on the counter, facing me.

Slumping in the stool, I consider his theory. It's pretty clear someone sent me into a trap. The draconic ravengers posing as covetorax is a clear indication of that. A demon pretending to be another is unheard of; they even imitated the greenish-black aura unique to the covetorax when they possess a human.

"Fine, I'll entertain the idea that you're right for a second. Why me, though? I don't get it. I mean, yeah, sure, I am a hellseeker, and demons have beef with the Order. But in the grand scheme of things, I'm just a soldier and definitely not special enough for someone to open a portal to Hell for little old me and then send such powerful demons to kill me. It doesn't make sense," I scoff.

Kaiden isn't bothered by my mocking tone and continues as calmly as before, "I don't know why they chose you as a target. What I do know is that something big is coming. Mutinies have always happened in Hell, but the uprisings against Lucifer have become increasingly frequent in the last fifty years."

He takes a sip from the mug, looks down, and then his burning gaze locks back with mine. "In the last months, things have gotten so out of control that Lucifer went into hiding. Many demons don't agree with the Celestial Treaty. They believe all demons should be able to come topside whenever they want, not just a select few that work within the Obsidian Conclave and have Lucifer's permission."

If what he's saying is true, we are utterly fucked. "Lucifer went into hiding? Why doesn't the Order know about this by now? Shouldn't the archangels, the all-mighty beings of God, already be aware of the situation and warn the Order about it?" I muse, trying to keep up with all the questions popping up in my head.

He arches an eyebrow at me and takes another sip of coffee before he starts answering my string of questions. "Do you not remember why Lucifer was cast out of Heaven? It was because of his pride. He would never admit that things have gotten so out of control that he cannot rule Hell the way he used to. Admitting to mutinies, especially to the archangels and their chosen ones, the Order members, is simply out of the question for him. Even speaking about these things in his presence would make him go mad and tear every single piece of flesh from your bones while burning you alive."

"And how have I never heard about the umbra demons before? Also, isn't opening a portal to Hell a direct violation of the Celestial Treaty? I'm honestly surprised the archangels haven't paid us a visit yet," I exasperate as I start sipping my coffee now that it's not that hot anymore. It almost feels like blasphemy to waste it. It's practically liquid gold.

"The umbra are ancient demons that haven't been seen on Earth in hundreds of years, that's why. Lucifer hid or destroyed almost everything about them in his obsession to gain the upper hand against the Order. It's not the first time he's hidden information. No one from the Obsidian Conclave knows what the umbra are and why the portal was created in the first place. We barely managed to kill the ten in the forest."

He locks his gaze with mine and continues. "I'm just as surprised as you that the archangels didn't smite us all for the breach of the Celestial Treaty. That's why you can't tell anyone in the Order about the portal. It's going to start a war," Kaiden finally finishes his lengthy explanation, still sitting with his back at the counter. His forearms are no longer relaxed, though; his fingers grip hard the edges of the counter.

If all he's saying is true, then we are neck-deep in shit. But why trust a simple hellseeker from the Order with this information?

I lean back in my chair and rotate the cup of coffee in my hands. Then my gaze snaps back to his. "Okay, so if no one knows about the umbra, then how do you? Also, what happened to the portal?"

Kaiden answers with a cruel smile painting his face, "I just had to torture the right demon to get that information."

A chill goes down my spine at how casually he mentioned torture. I'm no stranger to the notion of it; of course, I have tortured demons before in a failed attempt to find the one who murdered my mother. It's also a tactic used by the Order in extreme situations. We even have a ruthless enforcer, Cain, who's brought in whenever the Order needs to get information. I know it's necessary at times, but still, the way he smiled, like he enjoyed every minute of said torture, makes me shudder. I can't forget who I'm talking to.

His eyes search mine, surely to gauge my reaction before he continues, "Portals to Hell are highly unstable. I don't know how much you know about them since the Celestial Treaty forbids the use of portals unless you are the leader of the Obsidian Conclave and have business in Hell. Depending on the demon's strength, it can only stay open for a few minutes. It was already closed when we arrived in the forest."

"Why should I trust you are telling me the truth?" I wouldn't put it past a demon to be deceitful in order to get what he wants. What is his plan, his ulterior motive? "I'm just a hellseeker, a good one, but I'm not a member of the Aureal Council, so I don't have any power to make decisions within the Order like Grayson does. And why did you save me? What, did you happen to casually take a stroll in the woods at three in the morning? Is that a demon thing?" I scoff with anger in my tone, my gaze hardening, trying to remember that I'm talking to an Elite demon after all.

A sexy as sin, delicious smelling demon, but nonetheless, still a demon. I can never put my trust in what he says or does, not after one of his kind murdered my mother and took everything from me.

One minute, I'm staring hard at Kaiden; the next, he disappears without a trace from the spot he was occupying at the counter. He suddenly appears at my back, turning me around in the barstool with inhuman speed to face him. He cages me against the bar with his arms.

What the fuck?

It took him less than a second to do all that. My legs open involuntarily, framing his sculpted hard as steel body, the contact of our legs touching firing my senses.

Shit.

Chest heaving and face hot, I stare back at Kaiden, anticipating his next move, my heart beating a mile a minute. His warm breath is coming in waves, touching my face as his gaze is boring into mine. The intensity of his eyes ensnares me, the red swirls dancing again with the golden streaks in the tumultuous obsidian sea. He's so handsome it almost hurts to look at him. When he starts speaking, a shiver works its way down my spine.

"I've been monitoring demon activity in Ashville for a long time. Especially around bodies of water where the veil that separates our worlds can be easily ripped into. I knew the day would come that the demon behind the mutinies in Hell would make a move. Don't forget who I am, Iris. I'm the head of the Obsidian Conclave, and I rule Ashville. I know everything that happens at all times. As to why I saved you… well, it's because you were targeted for a reason. You're special, and I need to find out why you're so important to them," he challenges, the deep tone of his voice rolling over my body.

"All of this is crazy. I'm not special. Get that out of your head. I've heard enough; I want to leave now." I shake my head in disbelief. The headache I woke up with earlier today threatens to take over again with a vengeance.

I need to think about everything that happened since starting my shift on Friday night, and I can't do that with Kaiden in the same room as I am, even more so when he's standing this close to me. We are practically sharing the same breath. The close proximity of our bodies is making me frazzled.

The weight of his eyes is like a physical caress, nailing me to the spot I'm in, unable to move because deep down, all I want is for him to close the space between us and kiss me. That makes my insides boil with anger at myself and at his stupidly handsome face.

Eyes on me, Kaiden licks his lips. "You should lay low for a while, take a break from your hellseeker responsibilities. The demon that targeted you will be back to finish what he started."

I snort a surprised laugh that dies quickly when I realize Kaiden is being dead serious. I abruptly stand up from the bar stool, pushing at his chest and putting distance between us. "Oh, I'm sorry. I didn't quite get the memo when a demon became my boss and could tell me what to do," I deadpan. "Clearly, you're fucking crazy if you think even for a second that me taking a break from my hellseeker responsibilities will ever happen in this reality."

I spin on my heel, giving Kaiden a withering glare. He's leaning on the bar, arms crossed over his chest, posture relaxed and head tilted, amusement dancing in his eyes, like I'm cute for getting mad. That gets my hackles rising even more. I want to wipe the stupid smirk off his face.

"You know what? Fuck this! I've been civil enough. I've heard everything you had to say, and now I'm leaving. Don't even fucking think about trying to stop me, or I will gut you and send you back to Hell, where you belong!" I yell while stomping my feet quickly toward the elevator. I swiftly enter it and jab the button for the first floor.

As I wait for the glass doors of the elevator to close, I sweep my eyes over the open-spaced floor of the penthouse, looking for Kaiden.

What the fuck? Where did he go?

He probably disappeared somewhere, Houdini-style, just like earlier when he caged me in at the bar.

Good fucking riddance.

The doors finally slide closed, and the elevator starts descending.

8

Kaiden materializes in the elevator, scaring the living shit out of me, making me scream murder while cramping the space with his big, muscly frame. He chuckles at my reaction. The sound and the carefree look on his stupidly gorgeous face melts the anger I was feeling before like an ice cube left in the scorching heat of the sun.

He's wearing a leather jacket over the black T-shirt, and he isn't barefoot anymore; black, worn motorcycle boots cover his feet. He looks hot as sin, and I want to get drunk on the Kool-Aid he's selling. I narrow my eyes at him, trying not to smile, forcing the corners of my lips to stay in place.

"What are you doing?" I ask with fake annoyance in my tone.

He pushes the parking button on the elevator, still smiling. "I'm taking you home."

"I can get home by myself, thank you very much. I'm twenty-three years old, not a freakin' child," I grumble while side-eyeing him.

"Trust me, angel, I know you're not a child anymore." His eyes feel hot on my skin, two pieces of burning coals sweeping my body up and down while he licks at his lower lip, his earlier demeanor forgotten. He looks like a dark-maned lion, waiting patiently for the opportunity to pounce on its prey. The small space in the elevator seems to shrink even further, making the pressure in my chest clamp down on my lungs as I expel a trembling breath.

Kaiden's warm, spicy scent of rum and black cherries envelops me with static energy that tingles my skin. Angry swarms of butterflies take over my stomach, fighting for the small space, making me queasy with anticipation.

"You don't have a phone or any money on you. How do you think you're getting home?" Kaiden challenges, his voice gruff. He's looking at the elevator door like it's holding the secrets of the universe, my presence forgotten. But, at a closer look, the way his fingers flex as if he's barely restraining himself betrays the fact that he's as affected as I am by the enclosed space we're in.

"I can manage somehow," I mumble under my breath while staring straight ahead, pretending the electricity zapping through the air between us as my right hand almost touches his left doesn't exist. I can't resist, though, stealing a glance at the raven-soft hair touching his shoulders. I'm tempted to ask if he uses a hair mask and if I can borrow it. He looks like he just stepped out of a hair commercial. Why do men have such good hair with so little effort? It isn't fair at all.

Blinking slowly, I imagine how it would feel if I ran my fingers through his soft strands or if I grabbed his locks greedily while he pushed me against the elevator wall to ravage me with a soul-consuming kiss. Molten lava starts coursing through my veins as the images assault my brain, making my heart skip a beat.

He's a demon. He's a demon. He's a demon.

The elevator stops to a halt as the sliding doors finally open with a loud ding, pulling me out of my dirty thoughts. Kaiden gets out of the elevator quickly — as if I'm on fire and he's doused in gasoline — leaving me no choice but to follow after him.

As I round the corner and enter the parking garage, around twenty luxurious cars come into view. There's also a big black motorcycle at the end of the row of parked cars. I spot a red Ferrari, an Escalade, a Lamborghini, and a Rolls Royce, and that's where my knowledge of cars ends.

Jesus, are all the residents in this building filthy rich?

I follow Kaiden until he stops next to a shiny motorcycle. "Put this on; you're going to need it," he says while taking off his leather jacket, holding it up for me.

"If you think I'm going to get on that piece of death metal, you're crazier than I thought, buddy." I cross my arms over my chest, arching an eyebrow in defiance at him.

He's still holding up the jacket for me, a challenging glint shining in his eyes. "It's a Ducati, not a death trap. I've been riding motorcycles my whole life; you're safe with me. Now, c'mon, get your ass on here. I don't have all day."

I snicker at his boldness. "Um, yeah...that's going to be a hard no for me. I'd rather walk home barefoot and naked like the day I was born than get on that," I grumble while turning around, walking briskly toward the elevator.

"Dammit, Iris, stop being so fucking stubborn," Kaiden spews angrily. He reaches me before I can even take three steps in and grabs my right arm. His touch sears my skin as he spins me around. "Either you put this jacket on and get onto that motorcycle, or I'll do it for you. And trust me; you're not going to like that," he says while looking down at me over the bridge of his nose, his eyes two tiny slits, crimson streaks starting to take over the onyx color of his irises.

"I've never ridden a motorcycle before," I mumble and turn my head to the side. My eyes burn a hole in the gray wall of the parking garage as I try to escape the strange connection I feel to Kaiden while his heated gaze sweeps over my face like he can stare right into the depths of my soul. I'm also mad at the fact that I have to admit I'm afraid of something. I don't like feeling weak and out of control.

I swallow hard, and for the life of me, I don't know why the next words leave my mouth. "I, um, I…I was in a car accident when I was fifteen, and I lost my mother and all my memories. I've always been afraid of getting in a car or on a motorcycle since then. Given the loss of my memory, you would think that since I don't remember the accident, I shouldn't be afraid…but I am," I say softly, almost whispering while keeping my eyes tightly shut. I don't want him to see the tears gathering in my eyes and blurring my vision.

I didn't even get my driver's license when I turned sixteen, like everybody else. I refused to learn how to drive despite my aunt's insistence. She offered to teach me many times, but I couldn't get behind the wheel. I had a panic attack every time I tried. I was so crippled by what had happened in my past that before the age of twenty, I couldn't even get in a car without the dread making me breathe like I had just run a marathon. I don't even know why I told him about all of this. The only people who know about it are my aunt, Sam, and Noah. It got better with time; I don't have a panic attack anymore when I'm not the one behind the wheel. It's not a pleasant experience, though.

"Fuck," is the only thing Kaiden says as he softens the hold he has on my arm. He then takes my hand in his and tugs me into his arms, embracing me and squeezing me tightly. I am so shocked that I open my eyes and just stand there with my arms hanging limply. The swarms of butterflies escape my stomach, taking over the entirety of my chest.

Electricity starts zapping all my nerve endings. It fries my neurons and leaves me in a puddle of goo on the floor. I can't get out of my head how well we fit together, like two pieces of puzzle. Inhaling deeply his warm, spicy scent that is now mixed with that of leather, I pick up some notes I didn't before — fresh cloves…maybe tobacco.

My heart lodges in my throat when he pulls back and frames my face with his big, rough hands, his warmth radiating through me. His thumbs caressing my cheeks make all the tiny hairs on my body stand up at attention. Kaiden's eyes search mine like he's trying to tell me so many things through them. Only a breath separates us, and I can't move. I'm frozen in place, pinned by his piercing gaze.

I suddenly get the feeling deep into my gut that I know him.

No, that's impossible.

Jesus, what's wrong with me? We just met. Why am I feeling this crazy connection to him?

"I'm so sorry…if you want, I can get the keys to one of my cars and drive you home. I thought it's a waste not to ride the motorcycle in this weather. The feeling you get from riding a bike is like nothing you have experienced before. I'm not going to ride too fast. I would never let anything happen to you, trust me," he says solemnly, regret and something else shining in his eyes, something I can't quite put my finger on.

My breath hitches in my throat, and my heart does a backflip at the cadence in his voice. A strange feeling creeps into the center of my chest, squeezing my heart. Words evade me as I stare into Kaiden's eyes, like a raft lost in the sea of emotions I can't read, pulled under by the unrelenting currents.

Sawing my bottom lip between my teeth, I honestly can't believe the next words that leave my mouth. "Fine! I'll ride with you on the motorcycle. But, if I die in a terrible accident, I'm going to come back as a ghost and hunt you for all eternity," I huff while narrowing my eyes at him.

Kaiden winks and offers me a roguish grin so beautiful it steals the air in my lungs, and I forget how to breathe for a second. "Trust me, I would enjoy that more than you think." Then he steps back. Immediately, I miss the warmth of his hands on my face as he turns around, walking the few steps to where the motorcycle is parked. He takes the leather jacket resting on the bike and holds it up again, waiting patiently. I follow him and spin around, my back facing Kaiden as I put my arms through its holes.

Oh my God!

As soon as the leather jacket touches my skin, Kaiden's sexy, decadent smell surrounds me like a blanket and makes my head spin. I fight against the instinct to take the lapels of the jacket to my nose and sniff it like a creep. He then takes a helmet out of the saddle bag, puts it over my head, and snaps it in place. I shiver when he touches the skin under my chin unconsciously.

"Aren't you going to wear a helmet?" I ask while Kaiden mounts the bike and looks at me.

"I only have one; I've never needed an extra until now. I don't need it anyway. Hop on," he says, excitement evident in his tone.

My heart does a somersault and starts crawling its way up my throat.

Shit. Shit. Shit.

I can't do this.

"I, um…I don't know if I can do this." I lower my eyes, looking at my feet while gulping hard. It pains me to show weakness again, but my stomach sinks all the way to the bottom of my feet as jitters take over my body.

"Iris, look at me. You *can* do this. If at any moment it becomes too much to bear, I'll stop," Kaiden's words are soft, soothing the anxiety that's creeping in the back of my throat.

My eyes snap back at him as I nod in response before swallowing a lungful of air. "Okay. All right. I'm a badass bitch, and I'm not afraid of anything," my voice wavers as I mount the motorcycle with trembling legs. Keeping as much distance as I can from the hard, hot body sitting in front of me on the small seat, I look for something to grab onto, but I can't find a place for my hands.

Kaiden laughs at my mantra of self-encouragement and grabs my hands with his, pulling me tight around his back while circling my arms around his middle and interlocking my fingers. The whole front of my body is pressing hard into his back. My nipples harden at the contact, a simmering heat unfurling in the bottom of my stomach.

"This is where you're supposed to keep your hands. Hold on tight," his voice deepens, proving I'm not the only one affected by the way our bodies are pressed together. He then starts the engine, and I can feel the vibrations right at my center, stimulating my clit, making it throb with need.

Shit, this thing is like a giant vibrator.

If I don't end up with a huge wet spot in the center of my crotch, it's going to be a Christmas miracle.

Concentrating on the vibrations and the way Kaiden's body feels against mine, I don't even notice when he takes off. I squeal when the realization kicks in, and I tighten my arms around his body in a vise-like grip while shutting my eyes hard. I'm sure wrinkles form at the corners with the pressure. I only open them when we exit the building, feeling the sun warm up the leather jacket on my back while taking in the sounds and smells of the city.

We start riding on the streets as Kaiden glides the motorcycle smoothly and effortlessly in between cars. I should be scared shitless, but oddly I feel safe with him, like something deep within me knows that I can trust him with my life. Well, he did save me, so that's where this feeling must come from.

From the tall modern skyscrapers we're passing, it's pretty obvious he lives in the southern part of Ashville. A few years ago, a huge dump site on the edge of the city was bought by a developer who transformed it into a luxurious neighborhood with tall buildings, high-end stores, restaurants, and cafes. My apartment is on the opposite side, where historical four-story buildings are the norm.

Kaiden swerves right and takes the scenic route, exiting the city toward the beltway. There's a mountain road that circles Ashville completely on its outskirts. Once we reach the beltway, he speeds up, the pine trees becoming a blur, the coldness of the mountain air mixing with warmer currents, burning the tip of my nose and filling my chest with pine-scented air. The snow-capped mountains are visible in the distance, and I realize he took this route to make me appreciate the ride and the feeling of the bike between my legs even more.

I don't want to admit it, but Kaiden was right; I've never experienced this feeling before. I feel like someone just opened up a cage and let me spread my wings and fly for the first time in my life. It feels different than being in a car. I don't feel trapped like the carrosserie is going to close in on me. I start smiling a huge, goofy grin as I feel the anxiety ebbing away bit by bit. I probably look stupid as fuck, but I don't care.

Kaiden slows down as he enters the city again and rides through the narrow cobblestone streets in the oldest part of town, where my apartment is. As we almost reach my apartment building, the thought that I haven't told him where I live pops into my head. In between being terrified and embarrassed by the deep scars left by my past and getting excited about the ride, the feeling of freedom coursing through my veins, I completely forgot about that.

How in the hell does he know so many things about me?

Kaiden stops the engine and I get off the motorcycle, losing my balance, my legs feeling too heavy all of a sudden as the soles of my feet touch the pavement. He grabs my arm softly, balancing me, only letting me go when he's sure I won't fall.

His gaze flits to me while he's still on his bike. "It's always harder to keep your balance after the first ride; your legs are going to be sore tomorrow."

I nod and clear my throat loudly. "Thank you, um, you know, for the ride home…" I suddenly feel awkward, not knowing what to do with my hands or what to say next.

What the hell is wrong with me?

I was ready to beg him to fuck me against the wall in his dressing room earlier today, and now I feel like a schoolgirl with a crush. Remembering I still have the helmet and his jacket on, I slide the leather jacket off my shoulders and unclasp the helmet. I pull it slowly over my head in a failed attempt to not put too much frizz into my hair. Welp, at least I tried. I can only hope I don't look like I lost a fight with an electrical fence.

"So, did you enjoy the ride?" he asks with a lopsided grin as he takes back his jacket and helmet from my outstretched hand. Our fingers brush slightly, and my heart leaps at the contact.

"I did. I felt like I was flying," I say softly, looking down at my feet, still feeling awkward.

"I'm glad I was the one to give you that experience for the first time." His words pull my gaze back to him. He already has his leather jacket back on, looking like the rock star or the bad boy of every woman's wet dream.

No, scratch that.

He isn't a boy; he's all man, with his shoulder-length raven hair and the five o'clock shadow on his marble-cut jaw, all topped off with the distressed jeans, leather jacket, and worn boots to go with the powerful motorcycle between his legs. Wet dream personified indeed. He puts the helmet back in the saddle bag and starts the engine.

"Kaiden?" I'm not sure he can hear me over the loud rumble the engine is making, but he turns his head slightly. The look in his eyes makes me weak in the knees. "Thank you…for saving my life," I say sincerely. "I'll consider what you asked—to not tell anyone from the

Order about the portal."

He nods instead of offering me a reply and takes off, revving the engine, the vibrations reverberating in the sidewalk where I stand, looking after him until he's a tiny blob in the distance.

So, I guess it's back to reality now.

9

Four-story Victorian and Georgian-style red-brick buildings stick to one another on the street I live on. Some even have fake wrought iron balconies in front of the windows, complete with climbing ivy on the walls that turn red in winter, now a vivid green. I moved here not only because of the charm but also because it was affordable. The street is beautiful and picturesque; however, most apartment buildings need serious improvements.

Reaching the front door of my building, I say a prayer and hope the lock is still broken because I don't have my keys. I grab the door handle and turn it down.

Dammit.

Out of all the days to fix the stupid lock, our lazy administrator chose today. I roll my eyes in annoyance and mentally prepare myself for my only solution. Pressing the intercom button right underneath my name, I wait patiently as it rings.

"Who is it?" Ms. Robbins asks, annoyance dripping from her tone.

"If you're trying to sell something, get lost!"

"No, Ms. Robbins, it's me, Iris Harper. Your neighbor, from 4B. I lost my key. Can you please open the front door for me?" I cringe as I wait for her reply, not sure if she's going to open it.

Ms. Robbins is a single woman in her sixties, living alone in 4A, the apartment next to mine. There are only two apartments on each floor. And unfortunately, she's the only person living in this building that I know for sure is at home at all times. I also don't think she has any family left because no one visits her, ever. So, I take it upon myself to do her grocery shopping each week because of her health condition. I also accompany her to the doctor every time she needs it.

Despite these things, she sometimes annoys the hell out of me; she's all up in my business. I like to think of it as a love-hate situation. She complains tirelessly every time I watch TV that I'm throwing a party in my apartment and maybe even some orgies. As if. I wish I were that level of cool to host an orgy in my apartment. I guess the walls are a little too thin, or her hearing is a little too sharp for her age and for her own good, so she can sometimes hear me masturbating. Oh well. A girl has to live a little. I'm a virgin, not a nun in a convent.

"Fine!" she huffs loudly, slamming the intercom's phone. I can already tell she has reached the limit of being annoyed for the day.

The door buzzes, and I finally enter the building and start climbing the stairs to the fourth floor. None of these historical buildings have an elevator, but I don't usually mind. It's like an extra workout in addition to running, martial arts, boxing, and combat training at the compound. Now, I feel like my legs have doubled in weight from the motorcycle ride, and I struggle a little to get to the fourth floor.

Reaching my door, I look for the extra key I keep under the mat in a fake pocket I sewed in myself. I have previously lost my keys in a lot of demon fights, so I had to make sure I can still get into my apartment at the end of my shift. Ms. Robbins's door opens slightly, the chain lock keeping it in place. I can only see one of her eyes and a portion of the silver hair on her head, which she usually keeps in a bun, through the small gap.

Here it goes.

"You weren't home this weekend. Where were you? And you should take better care of your belongings, young lady. What if a burglar finds the key you lost?" she mumbles angrily.

"Ms. Robbins, with all due respect, that's none of your business. The key didn't have the address on it, all right, so calm down. No one is going to break into this building," I say, trying not to snap at her.

She annoys the hell out of me, but strangely, I'm fond of her cranky ass. She slams the door shut, and I can hear her mumbling profanities at me through the closed door. I roll my eyes while finally opening my door.

"WHERE THE FUCK HAVE YOU BEEN?" the loud scream slices through the air, echoing off the walls and scaring me shitless. I clutch my chest above my heart, trying to still its rapid beating, and whip my head toward my cyan couch where Samantha, my best friend, is standing, an angry look painting her face. Near her, on the small wooden coffee table, sits a beautifully wrapped present, a gorgeous bouquet of black irises, and a box of the decadent cherries wrapped in chocolate.

"Jesus, Sam. You scared me to death." I heave out a loud sigh, relieved that it's her, not a banshee, and close the door. She has a spare key and always comes by whenever she feels like it. She also has taken it upon herself to keep the numerous plants she gifted me alive since I always forget to water them.

Sam's eyebrows shoot all the way to her hairline. "I scared you?" she asks incredulously. She lifts an angry finger toward me with murder in her eyes. "Don't *you* dare scare me like that ever again! I tried calling you a thousand times, and you haven't answered. I think I've left you at least two hundred voice messages and texts. What the hell, Iris? I thought you were dead. I was ready to go to the Order later today."

Sam takes the present from the coffee table and stalks to the front door. Without wasting a second, she throws her arms around my neck, hugging me with all her strength. "Happy birthday, ho-bag! You better have a good explanation for ruining everything I had planned for you."

"I can't breathe," I joke as I hug her back. We both know her physical strength is no match to mine, being a hellseeker and all. You wouldn't want to get a tongue-lashing from her, though. She pulls back, one arm thrown over my shoulders, still holding the present in the other, and looks at me while analyzing my outfit.

"Why do you smell like a hot guy? And what the fuck are you wearing? Don't get me wrong, you look hot as hell, but you usually wear black, and you could never afford these clothes on the salary you get from the Order."

She narrows her eyes at me. Then they widen almost comically. "Oh, my Goddess! Did you finally lose your virginity and have mind-blowing sex all weekend long? Because if that's the case, I fucking forgive you, and I need all the details like right this minute. Wait, let me open a bottle of wine first. You better start spilling, or I'm going to revoke your BFF in the whole wide world status!" She saunters to the kitchen, throws open the fridge, and starts looking for a bottle of wine.

I can't help but smile at my spitfire of a best friend, Samantha Ambrose. Her hair, a gorgeous copper—as fiery as her personality—cascades to the middle of her back along with doll-like green eyes that sparkle like emeralds and red painted lips.

She's only five-two in height but tough as nails and will set the world on fire for her friends. She's also a light witch and draws all her power from earth-bound elements only; like all witches, she worships the goddess Hecate. Her knowledge of plants and the ability to quickly grow any flower, or anything green for that matter, makes her the most sought-after florist in Ashville. She owns the most successful flower boutique in our city and is already thinking about expanding.

I met her on my first day of high school, being newly enrolled in junior year. I was huddled in a corner of the girl's bathroom, crying. Not even two hours in at that school, I had already become the target of the mean group of girls that also happened to be members of the Order. It was mandatory that we attended a normal high school on top of the classes and the battle training we went through at the compound.

The only difference between me and them was that I wasn't pure-blooded. Every member is supposed to marry within the Order. If you leave and get married to a human, you will never be accepted back in, as the powers bestowed by the archangels are kept alive by pure bloodlines. A half-human who had their powers intact or could use the sanctified weapons was never heard of — until me.

As soon as my aunt saw how fast I healed after the car accident, she immediately told Grayson, and they tested me. I passed all their tests with flying colors. My acceptance in the Order was submitted to a Council vote, though. It took some convincing, but Grayson was fond of my mom before she left the Order, and he managed to persuade the Aureal Council members to accept me in the end. But even after they took me in, I was under a lot of scrutiny. I always had to work harder than anyone else to prove my worth.

On top of that, the lightborn were all naturally blonde, and I was the only one with black hair. I guess the genes I inherited from my human father were stronger on that front since my mother was blonde with pale, cerulean eyes. At least I had inherited half of her eye color, but the purple rings of my irises make me even more of a freak show in their eyes.

Needless to say, I became a target for Veronica and her pack of hyenas as soon as I arrived at the compound after being released from the hospital at the age of sixteen. There, with all the adults present almost all the time, I could avoid them. But at school, it was their turf.

That day, Veronica, Tessa, and Britney cornered me in the bathroom after biology class and started telling me I was brought into the Order just because Grayson pitied me and he would throw my ass out the door the minute he realized my tainted blood was worth nothing.

Hurt by their words, my insecurities started settling deep into my bones, so I just remained there in a corner of the bathroom, crying my eyes out. I felt my whole world crashing down, my deep emotional scars bleeding all over the bathroom floor. I had no one else aside from my aunt, and the fact that I couldn't remember anything about my life before the accident filled me with crippling anxiety at every step.

That's how Sam found me. She entered the bathroom like a tornado, lifted me from the floor, and hugged me. I had never seen her before in my life. She told me she was sure a poor soul had been hurt, since those grade-A bitches left the bathroom with stupid, smug-looking faces.

Sam immediately adopted me as her best friend; from that moment forward, we've been attached at the hip. She's like a beacon of light, filling all the dark corners of my life with warmth and laughter. She also hexed Veronica and her pack of hyenas every time they tried bullying me. I love her fiercely, just like a sister. She's family.

Still at the door, I open the beautifully wrapped present Sam passed me. In the sage-colored box is a dagger with a white hilt, an intricate serpent carved around it and the sheath. "Wow, Sam. Is this real ivory? I have no words; this is stunning. Thank you! You shouldn't have spent so much money on me." Tears threaten to spill from my eyes because my best friend knows me so well.

"Don't get emotional on me, and don't tell me what to do with my money. It's vintage; I found it in that small store you like to shop at near the Raven district. The man that runs the store made me a really good deal. Now, where's the wine? You don't have any in the fridge."

I wipe at my eyes, place the dagger on the entryway table, and take off my shoes, joining Sam in the kitchen. "What time is it? Is it even noon? Are we going to start drinking this early?"

She looks at me like I'm crazy. "Since when do we judge day drinking? I mean, is there really such a thing as a wrong hour to start drinking wine? Besides, we haven't even celebrated your birthday."

She does have a point, and this isn't a discussion I can have without alcohol in my system, anyway. I open the cabinet door under the sink and take out a bottle of Chardonnay from my stash, passing it to her. "Put it in the freezer; it'll get cold faster. Can you also order a pizza while I go pee really fast?" I ask, already making my way to the bathroom in the small hallway.

The walls I pass are full of black-and-white and colorful photos of me, Sam, my aunt, and the few old ones I could find with my mother in my aunt's house. There's even one with me and Noah from before he left. Even if it's hard to admit, I miss him fiercely, and I'm still mad that he hasn't contacted me since he left five years ago.

We are both smiling in the photo as if we didn't have a care in the world. He has his arm wrapped around my shoulder, hugging me to his side, and we are sitting next to his piece-of-shit truck that always broke down when he needed it most. Sam took that photo. I don't have any memories from my life before, so I like to surround myself with the memories I made since I was allowed to leave the hospital. I don't want to forget ever again.

"Maybe you can eat pizza with that goddess body of yours, but with my height and how big my butt already is, I'll order a salad for me. I swear to Hecate, I hate you for being able to eat whatever the fuck you want without gaining an ounce of weight, you bitch!" Sam yells at me, still in the kitchen since I can hear her rummaging through my drawers, probably looking for the pizza flyers.

"What are you talking about, crazy? Your butt looks amazing! I wish I had a butt like yours; mine is as flat as a pancake. Trust me, you're going to need pizza with that wine for what I'm about to tell you," I bellow through the half-closed door of the bathroom while I take care of my business.

My small bathroom doesn't have a claw-foot bathtub, but it's enough for me. It has a walk-in shower that can barely fit two people—not that I have ever tried to shower with anybody else—and a sage counter. A round vintage mirror I found at the small antique store near the Raven District hangs above it. It's very French country chic, and I love it. I quickly wash my hands and amble back to the living room.

"I ordered a large pepperoni pizza. Now spill. I want to know everything. But make it fast; I left Trish in charge of the boutique. We both know she's amazing at caring for the flowers and can whip a mean bouquet out of anything, but she has very low people skills. I don't want her scaring the customers," Sam says as she pats the empty seat on the couch next to her.

By the time I finish telling her about everything that happened since I last saw her on Friday night, we have already eaten the whole pizza, the box discarded on the coffee table, and have drank almost all the wine in the bottle. I'm tiptoeing the tipsy line, but I'm careful to not get drunk. I still have to go to the headquarters and report to Grayson.

"I don't know what the fuck to say, honestly," Sam mumbles incredulously as she stares at me, a half-empty wine glass in her hand, her right leg resting underneath her floral sundress on the couch.

I tuck my hair behind my ear and roll the slender stem of the empty glass between my fingers before placing it on the table. "Yeah, that pretty much sums up what I kept telling myself after waking up in Kaiden's penthouse." Taking the box of black cherries dipped in chocolate from the coffee table, I open it and extend it toward Sam. We each take one. I moan at the explosion of flavor on my taste buds.

"These are so fucking good," Sam says, reaching for the box to take another one.

I swat her hand, scowling. "You know the rules. By the way, were you here when the bouquet got delivered?"

She throws me a dirty look, and then her eyebrows furrow. "Um, no…the bouquet and the box of chocolates were already on the table when I came to check up on you."

"That's weird," I muse. "Maybe Ms. Robbins let the delivery guy in and used my spare key."

"So how big was his dick really? I need some new material for my nightly one-on-one sessions, if you know what I mean." She waggles her eyebrows, a shit-eating grin taking over her face.

I cross my legs and roll my eyes at her. "I haven't seen his dick, Sam. He had his jeans on. Now, can you please concentrate? My whole life can change today after the report I'm going to give Grayson."

"C'mon, don't be a prude. I want to know," she whines, slapping my thigh with her left hand.

"Oh my GOD! Fine! Based on the massive hard-on he was sporting under his jeans, I would say his dick is epically big. Are you satisfied? Can we start talking about important stuff now?" I pinch the bridge of my nose. "I'm fucked. If I don't lie, they're going to kick my ass out of the Order. And how else will I be able to explain the situation?"

"If I were you, I would tell Grayson about the umbra thing that attacked you. I wouldn't tell him everything, though. Of course, you should keep out the fact that you almost lost your virginity to a hot Elite demon, and that you even met him. Maybe also keep out the portal-to-Hell part until you know more. I don't want to be caught in an angels-versus-demons war. I'm too young to die! And you can't die a virgin!" she exclaims dramatically.

"I don't know, Sam...I still don't know what to do." I start chewing my bottom lip nervously.

She rolls her eyes while sipping from her glass. "Listen, whatever you decide, I'm going to be here for you, okay? And if they want to kick you out, then so be it. It's going to be their loss. You know that aside from Noah, I never liked any of those elitist Order stuck-up bitches, right? They all think they're above every other being out there. You bent over backwards to prove yourself, but they never fully accepted you anyway. Just because your hair is not blonde and your blood is not pure. What the fuck does pure even mean anyway?"

Her phone pings with a text message, breaking the silence that settles between us as we both think of a way out of this crazy situation. She checks the screen, and her gaze flicks back at me. "Did Kaiden say anything more about you being the target?"

"He said I was important somehow, that I'm a piece of the puzzle or something like that."

"That's pretty vague," she muses.

Biting my bottom lip, I saw it between my teeth. "There's a big library at the compound where I can search for information about ancient demons. I'll see if I can find something about the umbra demons in there. Maybe Aunt Josephine will help me with that."

Sam stands up from the couch and walks to the front door. I follow her there. "All right then, it's settled. You do that and let me know how it goes. I need to get back to the flower boutique. Hopefully, Trish didn't scare all the customers away." She hugs me quickly. "And don't think that just because you almost died, I forgive you for ditching me on Saturday night. You're going out to Sin with me next weekend. We need to celebrate your birthday," she lets me know matter-of-factly.

"Fine. Jeez, you have a one-track mind," I mumble under my breath while holding the door for her.

"If it ain't broke, don't fix it." She winks at me as she exits. "Text me after you talk to Grayson," she half-yells, descending the stairs. "Oh, and your birthday cake is in the fridge. I stress ate half of it."

"I will. After I get a new phone," I shoot back before closing the apartment door.

Assuming Grayson doesn't kick my ass to the curb straight into a boring human life.

10

The house the Order uses as its headquarters sits on a massive piece of land in the residential area of Ashville, on the west side of the city. It's a three-story, Georgian-style gargantuan mansion made out of faded brick. It has a grand entrance adorned with four columns as tall as the house and a triangular roof. The numerous windows are all vitrails depicting angels battling demons, the fall of Lucifer into Hell, and the story of how the Order was created and continued the battle against demons. It's surrounded by a tall brick fence that keeps out inquiring eyes, and it's heavily warded against demons or any dark creature.

The Order of Sariel was created around the eleventh century with the initiation of the Knight Templars. They were believed to be the first bankers of Europe. But the true mission of the Knight Templars was hunting and killing all demons that escaped into the human realm. Because of their wealth and secrecy, the Knight Templars were viewed with suspicion and resentment. They were accused of being heretics, and in the thirteenth century, King Philip dissolved the organization to calm the masses, but only in the public eye.

The organization continued its work in secrecy and became the Order of Sariel. All Order members are descendants of the original knights. There are twelve Order compounds worldwide, and each house has a leader. All twelve leaders are members of the Aureal Council, which votes on the most important decisions.

Five hundred years ago, the fight against demons became too bloody, and the Order was pushed to the brink of extinction alongside all humanity. There were too many demons escaping through the Hell gates, ravaging souls and wreaking havoc on Earth. Remember the bubonic plague, the Black Death? Well, it wasn't caused by the rodents festering with infected fleas. We call it the demonic plague for a reason.

In the second wave of the demonic plague, the archangels intervened, closed all of the twelve Hell gates around the world, and imposed the Celestial Treaty, which Lucifer signed reluctantly under the threat of Hell being wiped out completely.

The Celestial Treaty is a set of documents initiated to restore the balance between evil and good on Earth. If the balance is broken again, the seraphim, alongside the archangels, will intervene by closing Heaven and wiping out Earth and Hell without a second thought.

According to these documents, there has to be an Order house in every city where there is a Hell gate. Only a few demons are granted permission to be on Earth, and all are members of the Obsidian Conclave. Still, the veil that separates Hell from Earth is highly unstable where the Hell gates are located, making it easier to breach. Sometimes, demons slip through the cracks unnoticed. The Order acts like the demon police, killing all the demons illegally on Earth.

Because there must be a balance, good cannot exist without evil. The Obsidian Conclave was created to check the power of the Order and as a solution to appease Lucifer and any displeased demons. It is stated that the Order will not hunt or kill any demons that have permission to be in the human realm or any dark creatures such as vampires, wolf shifters, dark witches, and warlocks as long as they don't kill humans. These creatures are in the jurisdiction of the Obsidian Conclave, marked by the Sigil of Baphomet, and have to abide by their rules.

It's forbidden for anyone in the Order to fraternize or even be seen in the presence of a Conclave member or a dark creature and vice versa.

That's why I'm standing in the gravel driveway, staring like a weirdo at the three-story mansion, nerves strung high while gnawing on my bottom lip. The years I've spent in this house learning everything there was to know about the reality of our world and training to be a hellseeker, just like my mother, flash through my eyes. Even though they never accepted me completely, aside from Noah and my aunt, the Order took me in and gave me a purpose. A life in which I can avenge my mother's death. It's all I have.

As I climb the stairs to the massive wooden front door, a resolve settles deep into my bones. I'm not going to tell Grayson about Kaiden. I'll be kicked out, and all my years of hard work and dedication will amount to nothing.

I finally open the front door and take in the entryway of the mansion that always manages to impress me with its grandeur, even if I've been here thousands of times. The tall ceilings are a staple throughout the house, but the one above the entrance is my favorite. An octagonal grand cupola with an exact replica of the Sistine Chapel fresco painted by Michelangelo, The Last Judgement in the middle, and the nine scenes from the Book of Genesis surrounding it in a circle. An enormous marble statue of Archangel Michael with his sword and a shield, ready for battle, sits in the center of the shiny white travertine floor. On each side of it, two curved stairways with dark wooden railings lead the way to the upper floors.

The mansion seems empty, an eerie silence thickening the air, making my stomach churn in anticipation. At this hour, everyone under eighteen is either at school or in one of the classrooms on the first floor, learning everything there is about our history and demons.

The library and Grayson's study are on the second floor alongside other smaller offices because, believe it or not, we even have an accountant and a tech guy who has to be on top of all the security issues. The dorms occupy half of the second story—rooms for the orphaned children, whose parents fell victim to our perpetual battle against the evil forces. And from time to time, hellseeker delegates visit from other compounds around the world. The training rooms, the gym, and the hospital are all on the third floor.

I make my way to the right staircase. As I put my foot on the first step, I see Grayson's grandson Erik descending, his icy, gunmetal gaze chilling me to the bone. I square my shoulders and keep my head high. I can feel his leering gaze as I look straight ahead, refusing to acknowledge his presence.

Five, four, three, two, one…

"Half-blood cunt," he spews as he intentionally pushes his shoulder into mine hard and continues his descent.

I bite the inside of my cheek, drawing blood, my hands trembling with the need to throat punch him, but I don't give him the satisfaction of reacting to his hateful words. I don't even look at him. I learned long ago that this is my best weapon against the unrelenting bullying I used to get.

As much as I respect Grayson, Erik gives me the creeps. His leering gaze lingers too much, not only on me but also on other women at the compound. I avoid him at all costs, and the incident a few years back when we were still high school students is the reason why.

He always teamed up with Veronica, Tessa, and Britney to make my life hell at school. After my first few months of training, I learned to fight back and not be a doormat anymore, so they mostly left me alone.

But one day, he took it too far. I was coming out of the bathroom in a hurry, trying to get to my next class because I was already ten minutes late, the hallway empty, when a hard body appeared out of nowhere and caged me in a corner against the wall.

Erik told me I should be taught a lesson for acting so high and mighty when I wasn't worthy enough to become a hellseeker, my tainted blood making me an abomination. He brought one of his hands to my throat, crushing my windpipe, and then pressed his lips to mine forcefully. I was about to knee him in the balls when hurried steps echoed in the distance.

He let go of me and disappeared as quickly as he appeared, leaving me shaking like a leaf against the wall. From that day forward, I've avoided him like the plague, always keeping my guard up. Who knows what would have happened if he hadn't been interrupted? I was so ashamed of what he did to me, but mostly that I acted so weak, I haven't even told Sam about the incident. But we aren't in high school anymore, and I'm not going to let myself be intimidated by him.

Brushing the unpleasant interaction off my shoulders, I resume climbing to the second floor, passing a few closed doors to Grayson's office. I knock and wait patiently for his response. My stomach fists into a ball of restless energy as a thousand scenarios play through my head.

"Come in," the gravely, powerful voice comes through the door.

I have to do a double take because I can't believe what I'm seeing. Then, my heart sinks all the way to the bottom of my feet, and I suddenly feel the need to sit down. Grayson is standing on the side of his desk, bent over a map and whispering something to…Noah.

Fuck me.

When did he get back?

The realization that I wasn't the first person he saw or told he was coming back cuts me deep like a dagger being impaled straight into my heart. Though, I honestly don't know why I was expecting that of him. It's not like we've spoken in the five years he has been gone doing God knows what.

I guess I am that easy to forget. A joke. Expendable.

He's even more beautiful than I remember. The five years I haven't seen Noah transformed him into a man, all hard-cut marble and sharp edges, the black jeans and gray tee molded to him like second skin. His honey-blond hair is cut short on the sides and longer on top. It looks like he just rolled out of bed but in a studied, perfected way.

His expression is serious as he says something to Grayson. My ears can't pick up what they're talking about, and I know it has to be a secret.

Shaking my head, I manage to piece myself together and close the door. Grayson and Noah straighten as they finally realize they aren't alone in the room. Noah's gray-blue gaze immediately captures mine as he looks me up and down, a shining glint transforming his eyes into burnished steel.

"Iris!" a huge smile takes over his face as he starts walking toward the door, where my feet are two blocks of cement. He tries hugging me, but I immediately come to my senses and step to the side.

"I need to talk to you. Alone," I tell Grayson, trying not to look at Noah, who keeps staring at me with a confused look on his face, the big smile long forgotten.

"C'mon, Iris, are you really going to pretend I'm not here?" Noah demands with annoyance.

So now he's the one annoyed.

Fuck that.

I keep my gaze straight on Grayson. He raises an eyebrow at my request.

"Everything you have to say to me can be said in the presence of Noah. He has clearance."

"Since when?" I huff loudly.

"Since I said so, Iris." Grayson has a deep, gravelly voice and hawk-like, stern eyes from a severe face hardened by his position as head of the Ashville Order, scolding me like a petulant child.

"Fine. Whatever." I cross my arms in front of my chest. "I have completed the mission you gave me on Friday night, but something else happened that I believe you should know about."

"What are you talking about? What mission?" His harshness is replaced with confusion as his eyebrows scrunch together.

"You texted me on Friday. Right before I went out on my shift, you gave me a mission to track and kill some covetorax demons, remember?" I shoot back, a bit unsure.

"I would never send a hunter of the Order on a mission by sending a text. And I hardly consider covetorax demons worthy of hellseeker missions. You already know that. I also misplaced my phone on Friday evening; I only managed to find it Saturday morning before my Council meeting."

"Well, I received a text message from you. It was your number," I exasperate.

Grayson takes out his phone and scrolls for a few minutes of blistering silence that makes my skin crawl. He finally looks at me. "There are no messages or calls from or to you, Iris. Give me your phone; I want to see the text. And sit, both of you. You're giving me a headache. You're acting like children, and I don't have time for this," Grayson says sternly while he sits down at his desk and extends his hand, waiting for me to pass him my phone.

"I don't have it," I mumble under my breath. Noah pulls the chair on the right so I can sit, but I roll my eyes as I sit down on the other one, trying to completely ignore the heady aroma of his cologne. He smells exactly as I remember: sandalwood and cedar, like taking a fresh breath of air on a crisp spring morning.

"What do you mean you don't have your phone? What happened to it?"

"I'm not sure. I think I lost it," I say, barely above a whisper. Grayson's inquiring gaze makes me feel like I'm five years old again. My face is probably as red as a beet at this point.

Great.

Grayson narrows his eyes at me, deep wrinkles forming at the corners. "And this is what was so important that you had to tell me alone? That you killed some covetorax demons on a mission I didn't give you?"

Something must have put him on edge before I came into his office for his patience to run so thin so soon. He is always serious, but not like this.

I clear my throat and regain my voice. "No. I chased the covetorax demons all the way to a clearing in the forest of the national park, right on the shore of Shadow Lake. The thing is, when I tapped the onyx stone, instead of covetorax demons leaving the possessed bodies, two draconic ravengers appeared. We fought, and I killed them. After that, I thought everything was fine until something pulled my attention toward the lake, and that's when I saw around ten winged demons, flying straight at me. I started running and called you, but you didn't pick up."

"What demons?" Grayson and Noah ask at the same time with urgency.

"I don't know...I have never seen this type of demon before or even heard of it. They looked like shadowy corpses with giant bat wings."

"The ley lines—these demons might have caused the massive disturbance," Noah chimes in from my right.

"And how are you reporting this to me now? It's Monday, Iris! Or have you not looked at the fucking calendar?" Grayson shouts at me and slaps his desk hard with both palms. I flinch at the booming, unexpected noise. He stands up abruptly, making the legs of his chair scrape abrasively against the wooden floor, and starts pacing his office.

Fuck. This is going worse than I imagined.

"It wasn't like I had a choice. I did manage to kill one of them, but then another managed to grab my sword. Its touch pulverized the sword…turned it to ashes in my hand. I have never seen a demon do that before. Then it grabbed me by the throat with its rotting, shadowy hands. It paralyzed me, and I felt like it was incinerating every organ in my body from the inside out while melting my brain at the same time. My onyx choker exploded at the contact, and the rest of my weapons disintegrated as well. I barely managed to escape by some miracle. But I was severely weakened and had deep gashes on my thigh from the draconic ravengers I killed. I realized at that point that I didn't have my phone anymore."

Taking a deep breath, I try to swallow the lump that suddenly forms in my throat and continue. "I ran as fast as I could until I got home and passed out from the pain. Luckily, Samantha, my friend, came over unannounced since we were supposed to go out. She got worried when I didn't answer her calls. She nursed me back to health, and if she hadn't found me, I would be dead right now. I was out for the count for the entire weekend. I just woke up today."

The lie came easily, but it feels heavy and wrong on my tongue, like I ate something spoiled. It makes my stomach clench. I fight against the instinct to rub my sweat-slicked palms on my thighs.

Grayson sits back in his chair while scrutinizing every inch of my body with his sharp eyes. "You don't look like someone who battled death for two days straight."

I gulp, hoping this interrogation will be over soon. I can't stand the pressure much longer. "Samantha is a light witch. She is really good with plants. The Order buys our antidotes from her, remember? She brewed some concoctions and made me drink them."

"Why didn't you run at the compound? It's closer to the national park. We have a hospital here and doctors that could have saved you," Grayson shoots back. The iciness dripping from his tone could freeze over an entire city.

Fuck.

I didn't think about that.

"I honestly don't know. I was in a lot of pain, barely conscious when I ran. I probably thought I could make it to the antidotes I have at home and wouldn't need healing," I lie again, fighting the sudden urge to look down and fidget as I lock my gaze with Grayson's, hoping he will believe me. If I let my gaze waver, he will definitely know something is off.

Noah is still looking at me from his chair. He's not saying a word, but his eyes are burning a hole through the side of my face. I refuse to acknowledge his presence more than I already have though.

The silence that falls in the room is thick with tension, and I hope like hell I don't have two big sweat stains under my armpits. At least I'm wearing my usual black T-shirt, so it won't be that obvious. Still, nothing can escape Grayson's hawk-like eyes. After a few moments of deliberation that feel like hours under his scrutinizing gaze, making my stomach quiver with the need to throw up, Grayson finally speaks again.

"You're dismissed. Go to Timothy and ask him for a new phone. Then go to the third floor and tell one of the doctors to check you out. I want a full exam."

I stand up on shaky legs and make a beeline for the door. Grayson and Noah resume their talk over the map, too low for me to hear, even with hellseeker-enhanced hearing. I turn the knob and exit the office.

Shit.

My legs are trembling, and my heart refuses to slow down. I lean my back on the closed door and try breathing in and out slowly for a few seconds. It doesn't work. But I can't just stay here, leaning on the door and breathing like a crazy person about to have a meltdown. Someone might come this way, or even worse, Noah or Grayson might open the door.

And I'm sure I have guilt painted all over my face. I've never lied to

Grayson before, and it was all made worse by Noah's presence throwing me off. Now that I am done with the meeting, all of my bottled-up anger blazes through my veins like acid, making me want to hit someone, Noah more precisely, or put a hole through the wall.

I don't do that though. I put the stopper on that bottle once more, fist my fingers, and clench my jaw as I walk the small distance to Timothy's office.

11

Timothy's office is a few doors down from Grayson's. The door is slightly ajar, and he's sitting on his leather swivel chair with his headphones on, his back facing me. He's staring at the big wall made out of monitors while checking out the surveillance footage.

"Tim?" I ask loudly after I knock on his door. He doesn't turn around or even notice that I'm in the room. "I swear to God, if we are ever under attack at the compound, he's going to be the one to die first," I mutter to myself and stalk forward, placing my hand on his right shoulder when I reach him.

He belts out a high-pitched shriek, almost falling off the chair. I would have found that really funny if I wasn't so pissed off over the encounter with Noah in Grayson's office.

"Shit, Iris! You scared me," he says as he removes his big headphones, the movement making his thick-rimmed glasses askew. Loud rock music is playing from his headphones, which explains why he didn't hear me.

Timothy is the same age as me; we graduated in the same year, but when I was set on becoming a hellseeker, Tim never had it in him. His shy demeanor, lanky body, and aversion to any type of violence also made him an easy target for bullying. But he's a genius and loves anything that has to do with tech and computers. His shoulder-length, dirty-blond hair is tied in a ponytail, and he's wearing a black Metallica T-shirt over dark blue denim. He's cute in a geeky, non-threatening way.

"What do you need?" he asks as he straightens the frame of his glasses.

"Grayson sent me to get a new phone."

He bends and rummages through the drawer in his desk. "You hellseekers sure lose and destroy your phones a lot."

His observation rubs me the wrong way. "Yeah, well, you kind of don't give a shit about your phone anymore when a demon is about to eat your face, and then use your bones as toothpicks. Not like you would ever know," I grumble the last part under my breath while I roll my eyes at him.

Tim flinches, and his whole face turns beet red at my words. *Fuck.* I'm being a bitch on purpose, and I have to calm down. I would never act or talk like this normally, especially to Tim, who never did or said anything bad to me.

I sigh. "Sorry, Tim, it's been a couple of rough days."

"No worries," he says as his face starts to regain its normal color.

"How's Roman? Did you guys go to that rock concert you were so excited about? What was the band's name?"

His gaze flits to mine with a pleased gleam as he pauses his search for a moment, and his cheeks flush again at the mention of his boyfriend. "Deadly Sins. Yeah, they were amazing. Roman had this whole romantic dinner planned before we left on the rooftop of his apartment building. He even hung fairy lights on the pergola in between the trailing vines. It was beautiful."

A soft smile turns the corners of my lips at Tim's dreamy expression.

Roman is one of the doctors who work at the compound. He visited from another compound in Europe two years ago and never left. It took Tim a whole year to garner the courage to ask him on a date, but since then, they've been in a steady relationship, and I couldn't be happier for them. "Wow. Do you have any pictures?"

"No…we um, well, you know," he stammers, visibly uncomfortable. "We were busy with other things," he blurts out and clears his throat loudly before extending his phone holding hand to me. "Here. You know the drill, it's already programmed with all the numbers you need."

"Would you do me a favor, please? I know I acted like a major bitch just now, but can you also program my number in it and see if you can back up all my calls and text messages?" I ask as sweetly as I can.

"I'm not sure. If it was in the cloud, it's possible; if not, I can't promise anything. Come back in ten minutes."

"You're a lifesaver. Thank you so much! I'll swing by in ten," I say while making my way to the door, then stop in my tracks and turn around. "Um, I also wanted to ask you if you, by any chance, saw something weird on the surveillance footage Friday night, let's say between nine and ten p.m.?"

He tilts his head to the side. "Like what?"

"I don't know…someone acting sketchy, going in Grayson's office without permission, that sort of thing."

He shakes his head. "No, nothing out of the ordinary happened," he says pensively, then his eyebrows drop in a frown. "Actually…"

My heart thunders in my ears as I wait for his next words with bated breath.

"…there was a glitch in the system, and I had to reboot it around nine thirty, so I didn't have any footage for a few minutes, but this happens at least once a month. It's nothing new."

Fuck. I deflate like a balloon as I exhale heavily. "'Kay, thanks, Tim."

"Wait. Why are you asking this?"

"It's nothing, don't worry about it. I'll see you in a bit," I tell him as I get out of his office and make my way to the library, where my aunt works.

Could the glitch be just a coincidence, or did someone cause it? I mean…it did happen at around nine thirty when I received the text. But who could be so tech-savvy to cause a glitch in an otherwise impenetrable system? I know we have top-notch security, and no expenses are spared to ensure the compound will never be breached. Maybe someone from the outside broke in, even if it seems impossible with the strong magical wards making this place a fortress.

I have to get my hands on the security footage and comb through it. I could ask for Tim's help, but I don't want to get him into trouble, and at the end of the day, anyone could have done it. What if Tim is behind it all? He's the only person I know with the brains to cause a glitch and hack into Grayson's phone.

I snort a quiet laugh at that thought as I step through the library's threshold. Tim wouldn't hurt a fly. The empty library hall is drenched in colorful filtered light as the afternoon sun radiates through the vitrail glass of the floor-to-ceiling windows. The walls and shelves are white, with golden plaster ornaments in the corners, and the ceiling is jaw-dropping. Six cupolas with elaborate lime-wood carvings are painted in the same lapis lazuli color Michelangelo used for the Last Judgement fresco. The paintings depict a grand imperial court made of pure gold surrounded by walls and streets garnished with the most precious stones, streams, and rivers that run through golden sands and blossoming trees. Cherubim, seraphim, and archangels fly or complete mundane tasks in the elaborate Elysium, the City of Angels.

Aunt Josephine is sitting at her desk at the library entrance, scribbling something in a notebook. She's wearing her usual gray pantsuit with a white shirt underneath, her hair pulled tight in a severe bun. She's fifty-two, five years older than my mother, but she doesn't look a day over thirty-five. The blood that runs in the veins of the lightborn is blessed, and it makes us age much slower than normal humans. I don't know how much of that applies to me, though, since I'm a half-blood, as Veronica and her pack of hyenas always like to remind me since my first day at the compound.

She used to be a hunter in the Order, but after her fiancé, Owen, suffered a horrible death at the hands of a draconic ravenger in a gruesome battle, she couldn't bear fighting anymore and chose to be the new librarian, occupying the position that was left empty when the one before died of old age.

Even though she doesn't look a day over thirty-five, her conservative clothes and the way she styles her dark-blonde hair age her a bit. She also doesn't look much like my mother. If someone told me they were sisters without me being aware of that fact, I would have said that was impossible. My mother's hair was much lighter, almost whiteish, and the cerulean hue of her almond-shaped eyes made her look otherworldly. In comparison, my aunt's eyes are warm brown and rounder in shape, but always kind and motherly.

The soles of my sneakers make loud, squeaky noises on the marble floor of the library, the dead silence heightening the sounds as I amble toward her desk. She hears me approach and lifts her head. When her eyes find mine, a dark shadow passes over them. Her whole face turns ashen.

It stops me in my tracks.

In the next second, stark relief floods her features, and I visibly relax. *Jeez, Iris, first Tim and then your aunt, who is next on the suspect list, Sam?* I shake my head, berating myself for letting paranoia get the best of me. I quickly come to my senses and continue walking until I'm standing right in front of her desk.

"I've been so worried about you! Where have you been?" she

demands loudly, anguish evident in her tone. "You didn't answer any of my calls." Her voice echoes off the tall walls of the enormous library.

"I was injured in a strange demon encounter and lost my phone. I'm sorry I missed our Sunday dinner," I tell her hesitantly. I don't want to add to her concern, but I need her help finding information about the umbra.

"Oh, I'm so sorry, dear. I lost my head." She shakes said head as she stands up, sidestepping her desk and hugging me. Her fragrant perfume envelops me; she always smells like roses.

My aunt smiles at me and sits back down behind her desk. "I'm glad you're okay. We can reschedule our dinner any time. Happy birthday, by the way!"

"Thank you! Let's talk on the phone and see how the week goes. Maybe we can go out to Ciprianni's for a change. My treat," I say while I bend slightly to rest my forearms on her desk.

She flaps her hand in the air like it's a non-issue. "Don't be silly. You know I love to cook for you."

"Can you maybe help me with something?" I ask.

"Of course. What is it?" Her questioning eyebrows make her doe-like eyes even bigger.

"I need a book on ancient demons that haven't been seen on Earth in hundreds of years, maybe more. Do we have anything like that in here?"

"Hmm, maybe in the archives in the basement. We have some books there that were written even before the initiation of the Knight Templars. Is there a specific demon you're looking for? I need to narrow down my search."

I tear a hole in my cheek as I deliberate what I can tell my aunt. But she took me in after the accident and gave me a life in the Order. I can trust her with my life; I'm sure of it.

"Yeah, there is. I believe umbra demons attacked me on Friday night, and I just wanted more information on them. Please keep this to yourself. I don't want anyone to know, not even Grayson. Until I have more details about it, of course," I say in a whisper. I don't want a random person who might pass near the library to overhear our conversation.

"Sure, you know I'd do anything for you, dear. How do you spell that? I have never heard about this type of demon before. Is it *u-m-b-r-a*?" she asks while writing down the name in the notebook.

"Yeah, I think so, but I'm not one hundred percent sure."

"All right, I'll look into it and let you know if I find something. It's going to take at least a couple of days, though, maybe even weeks. The books we have in the basement are very old and need to be tended with care. There are also over two thousand books that haven't been organized in a very long time," she tells me softly, catching on that I don't want anyone to overhear.

"Perfect. Thank you, Auntie! I don't know what I'd do without you." I bend over her desk and give her a peck on the cheek. "I have to go. I need to pick up my new phone and then I need to get some training in before I start my shift tonight."

"All right, dear. We'll talk soon." She waves at me before getting back to scribbling in her notebook.

I stride back to Tim's office and knock again on his door. This time, he hears me.

"Ah, there you are. I finished setting up your phone, but I could only recover your calls, photos, and everything else besides the text messages. And I don't know if you had everything stored in the cloud, so some might be missing. Sorry," he says as he rotates his chair to face me.

Damn it.

I really need my texts back. I wanted to prove to Grayson that I wasn't lying—well, at least about that.

"Is there any way I can get my texts back?" I exasperate.

He shrugs. "Unfortunately, no. I tried everything already."

"'Kay, thanks, Tim." I sigh in defeat and take my new phone from him.

As I exit Timothy's office again, Noah gets out of Grayson's study. *Shit.* The feeling that I need to punch something comes back with a vengeance. With all the blows I keep taking since Friday night, I feel like I can't catch a break.

I turn my head, pretending I haven't seen him, and quicken my pace toward the stairs. I have to get to the third floor, and I can feel him getting closer to me by the second.

"Fuck! Iris! Just wait a minute. I need to talk to you," he growls angrily as he grabs my right arm. The heat of his hand brands my skin and sends shivers all over my body. His sandalwood cologne invades my senses. Without intending to, I take in a deeper breath. I missed him and his stupid smell so much. I shake my arm free of his hold and narrow my eyes while turning around to face him.

"You're five years too late, Noah. And what about what I need, huh? Right now, what I need is to get away from you as soon as possible or else I'll flip the fuck out," I whisper-yell at him, not wanting to cause a scene. I turn around and resume my brisk walk, reaching the stairs.

"Oh my God! NOAH! I heard a rumor about you getting back, but I needed to make sure it was true with my own eyes," Veronica squeals ostentatiously in a stupidly fake sweet voice that makes my teeth want to fall out as she half-runs, half-walks, descending the stairs from the third floor.

Fuck my life.

I look up and huff loudly, praying for patience because I can't deal with this shit anymore. I would rather gouge my eyes out with rusty spoons than have to sit through this.

Veronica's platinum-blonde hair is held up in a perky ponytail that bounces with each step. She's wearing a short pink skirt paired with a low-cut T-shirt in the same color. She looks like a real version of a Barbie. At least she has her outside beauty going for her because I experienced first-hand how rotten she is on the inside.

"I was training when Britney told me she saw you arrive earlier today. I started looking for you immediately. I always knew you would come back for me," she says as she reaches us at the bottom of the stairs and hugs Noah, pushing her heavily padded boobs in his face while completely ignoring me.

I hate to admit it, but jealousy ignites my blood. "Yeah, in those clothes, you were training for sure," I mumble under my breath, and I know I'm being a petty bitch, but I don't care.

She side-eyes me and pretends she didn't hear a word I said because Noah is here, and she's desperate to get back with him. They were in a relationship a few years back but split up around the same time I joined the Order. She always talked about how perfect they were together and what beautiful babies they would make. She's still set on marrying him and makes sure everybody knows it. I can always pick up his name in her mindless conversations with her minions, Tessa and Britney.

I'm surprised I still have teeth with how strongly I'm grinding them. I start climbing the stairs, trying hard not to look behind and see what everybody else does: the golden couple. When I left Tim's office, I intended to do the medical exam first and then go train. But if I don't punch something soon, I will burn this place to the ground.

"Iris, wait! We haven't finished our talk," Noah shouts after me.

"We haven't even started it, Noah. Besides, you've been too busy for five years straight; what's another day?"

"So, tell me, what have you been up to since we last spoke?" Veronica's sickly-sweet voice reaches me at the top of the stairs, and I bite the inside of my cheek hard, drawing blood.

Noah says something back, but I can't hear his exact words.

12

Grateful I can't hear their voices anymore, I enter the first training room we use for boxing and sparring. Mattresses are scattered all around the floor, and the smell of fresh sweat tingles my nose. A few students are practicing their fighting skills with wooden swords on my right. They don't pay me any attention as I make my way to the punching bags in the back of the room.

I'm already wearing my black training clothes and sneakers, so I don't need to change. I choose the punching bag in the left corner and take a deep breath, cleansing my lungs while I start wrapping my hands with gauze. I slide off the hairband I always keep on my wrist and secure my braid. I hate it when hair gets in my face while I'm training.

Skipping the warm-up because I'm feeling too fired up to start slow, I think about the hope that filled every cell of my being when Noah left. He promised he would never forget me, and he did. I start throwing bitter punches in speedy jabs that hit the punching bag with loud thuds. Sweat gathers at my hairline and starts dripping on my face, a few droplets getting stuck in my eyelashes.

Every memory of him brings in more fury, and with it, my punches become more and more punishing. I wish he were here in front of me instead of the punching bag.

"You're holding the dagger wrong."

When I was released from the hospital and became a member of the Order, I kept mostly to myself. Everyone avoided me like I had a bad case of leprosy, and the only people who spoke to me were the professors, the fighting instructor, my aunt, and Grayson. I could hear all the other Order members whispering when I passed them in the hallways of the compound that I would never be good enough to become a hellseeker and learn everything I had to until the age of eighteen. How could I? My blood was tainted, after all. I was set on proving everyone wrong and avenging my mother's death, so I trained every night at the compound, everybody else already having left hours before, until I exhausted myself and couldn't stand anymore.

It was one of those nights I met Noah.

Particles of dust dance in the silver streaks of moonlight that shine through the open windows of the training room, illuminating the rubber floor and casting me in shadows. I'm practicing throwing knives at the dummies in the back of the room, already exhausted from a full day of school and demonology classes. On top of that, my body is covered in bruises, and my muscles are sore from all the times our fighting instructor, Ezekiel, threw me like a rag doll to the training mat. He kept telling me my posture was wrong, and if I didn't fix it, I had no chance against a demon in the real world. Still, I didn't give up and kept challenging him.

Everyone has already left, but despite how heavy and battered my body feels, I need to practice more. So here I am, at ten p.m., alone in the training room with all the lights turned off because I'm trying to simulate a real demon fight in the real world, as Ezekiel put it, throwing daggers at the dummy.

I have to prove to everyone, but most of all to myself, that they are all wrong, and I can do this. The only problem is that my aim is off, and for the life of me, I can't manage to make any of the daggers stick where I want them to. I throw another, aiming it at the dummy's head. It flies right by its left ear, getting stuck to the white wall behind it. Spiderweb cracks form at the impact.

"Fuck!" I let out a scream of frustration, throwing the rest of the daggers I'm holding to the floor.

"You're holding the dagger wrong," a deep voice booms loudly behind me.

I clutch my chest hard, right above my heart, and a squeaky, high-pitched sound leaves my mouth as I turn toward the disrupting voice.

"I didn't mean to scare you." The young man grins at me from the doorway.

Holy shit!

Noah Pierce is talking to me. To me!

Noah, with the tall, drool-worthy body and panty-dropping smile.

And I'm making a fool of myself.

God, if you take requests, please smite me now!

"I didn't know you were there," I shoot back, my cheeks flaming a deep crimson.

He approaches me with long strides and drops to his haunches, picking up the daggers I threw to the floor in a rage. Oh God, I didn't think it was possible, but he's even more beautiful this close. Shaggy, honey-colored hair falls over gray-blue eyes that twinkle as he stands from the crouch, now holding all the daggers in his right hand. He's standing so close to me that his sandalwood cologne makes me dizzy.

"May I?" he asks, a soft smile tugging at his lips.

"Um, sure…"

He keeps one dagger and goes over to the table at my left, where all the weapons are spread, placing the rest of the daggers on it. I move a few steps to my right, expecting him to get in my spot and show me how he does it. Instead, Noah takes me by surprise by coming behind me and placing his left hand on my hip. He then puts his right foot between mine and spreads them by a few inches.

"You need to widen your stance a bit and put more weight into your heels." His hot breath rolls over the side of my face. It leaves a wake of shivers behind that travel from the back of my neck all the way down to my toes. After that, he places the dagger in my right hand. Our fingers touch briefly, and my heart seems to have stopped as fireworks take over my belly.

"Hold it how you normally would."

I do.

The front of his body touches my back as he lifts my arm into the throwing position. I'm going to combust with every second that passes, with the feeling of him on my skin. He then curls his fingers around my hand and fumbles with my grip on the handle to correct my hold.

"This is what you need to change. Wrap your fingers around it a bit lower and loosen your grip. Relax. Take a deep breath, in and out, and close your eyes. Picture in your mind the exact spot where you want the dagger to hit."

His deep voice surrounds me as I close my eyes and picture the space between the dummy's eyebrows.

"Now open your eyes and throw. Don't overthink it. Just do it," he says confidently as he steps back.

The loss of his body heat at my back makes me sway with disappointment, but I quickly regain my balance and open my eyes, laser-focused on my target. I take another deep, cleansing breath and flick my wrist, sending the dagger flying at the dummy. It impales the rubber right in the spot I envisioned in my mind.

"Oh my God! I can't believe that worked!" I squeal, and in the spur of the moment, before I can think my actions through, I turn and throw my arms around Noah's neck.

"Thank you," I whisper, my body a live wire of desire as realization kicks in. I'm hugging Noah! Me! HUGGING Noah! And he's hugging me back. My head is nestled perfectly on his chest, and I can hear his heart beating loudly. Our bodies are melded together. I swear he shudders — almost like he's as affected as I am by him — while I step back awkwardly, not knowing what else to say.

His cheeks have a tint of red to them. "You're welcome! I knew you had it in you," his voice wavers slightly as he runs a hand through his hair.

After that night, he offered to train me, and every single day before his shift, he made it his personal mission to make me one of the best hunters in the Order. He was eighteen, two years older than me, and he had already started his hunting duty. I never complained while he put me through numerous tests, grueling exercises, and new fighting routines.

We became very good friends, and we spent a lot of time together. I even introduced him to Sam. My crush on him grew with every passing minute we spent together, but I was too shy to make the first move, and I couldn't even remember if I had kissed a guy before or dated anyone. Every time he touched me, my heart would pound like crazy, and heat would take over my body as if I jumped in a furnace. I especially loved it when we trained together in body combat; the close contact always leaving me wanting more.

I could tell he liked those sessions, too. Whenever our bodies touched, his eyes changed color, transforming to burnished steel, but he never made a move or asked me out. I eventually let go of the idea when, out of nowhere, two weeks before I turned eighteen and finished my training, he surprised me by asking me out on a date.

I start kicking the punching bag with my legs, alternating roundhouse kicks with wide hooks and speedy jabs, as I remember the day we went out on our date — my first date. I'm drenched in sweat while bringing myself to the point of exhaustion, but I don't care. I start tapping into the speed and force of a hellseeker as the memories keep assaulting my brain.

"Stop fretting! You will end up with raccoon eyes if you keep moving like that," Sam scolds me as she applies eyeshadow to my closed eyelids. I'm sitting cross-legged on my bed while Sam is getting me ready for the date with Noah, all the contents of her makeup bag covering every inch of the polka-dot comforter.

I chew on a hangnail. "Sorry," I say for the umpteenth time. "What if he tries to kiss me, Sam? I've never kissed anyone before – that I know of, at least. Oh God, what if we knock teeth awkwardly, or what if I get food stuck in my teeth and make a fool of myself?" I exasperate as every worst-case scenario plays in my head.

Sam pinches me hard on my left thigh.

"Ouch! What was that for?" I open my eyes and scowl at her.

She rolls her eyes dramatically. "For being so painfully oblivious! Have you not seen the way he looks at you? You could have a bloody tampon stuck in your teeth, and Noah would still French kiss the hell out of you! Now stop being annoying, and let me finish your makeup." She angrily points the eyeshadow brush at me.

"Ewwww. Thanks for putting that image in my head."

She pinches me again on my other thigh. "Shush! Or I'll leave, and you'll have to do your makeup all by yourself."

"Fine," I mumble and close my eyes, making an effort to stay as still as possible.

After what feels like an eternity but is more like an hour, I'm finally ready. The soft makeup look Sam did accentuates my eyes and makes them look cat-like. I wish I were as good as her at doing my own makeup. She also curled my hair in big fluffy waves that reach the middle of my back. After she leaves, I get dressed amidst whole-body jitters.

I bought a new periwinkle dress for the occasion. It has a sweetheart neckline, a flowy skirt that reaches just above the knees, puffy sleeves, and it cinches around my waist with a delicate belt. I feel beautiful and feminine in it. I even bought some short black heels that I have no idea how to walk in.

At seven p.m., not a minute later, a knock comes from the front door of my aunt's house. I quickly come down the stairs, the skirt of my dress swishing around my thighs, and I almost faceplant from the heels. I quickly regain my balance and open the door with trembling fingers.

"Hey. Wow! You look beautiful!" Noah beams as his gaze roves over my body.

I flush at his appraisal. "Thank you!"

He looks ravishing in gray slacks and a white button-down shirt, sleeves rolled up. He holds a big bouquet of white roses in his right hand, which he extends toward me. "These are for you," Noah says, shifting nervously from one foot to another.

"Oh, they're so beautiful!" I accept the bouquet, my cheeks flushing a deeper shade of crimson as I thank him. I go back into the house and put the flowers in a vase in my room, and then we leave for the restaurant.

We ride in Betsy, his red Toyota truck that has seen better days. I try my best not to freak out in the car, but I'm on the verge of an anxiety attack. Every second that passes constricts my lungs in a vice-like grip. Noah throws me a concerned look, his warm hand wrapping around mine, and the panic crawling in the back of my throat subsides. He only drops my hand when he has to shift gears; then he resumes holding it. He's also driving really slowly, not seemingly fazed by the honks of angry drivers; he just ignores them and keeps smiling at me until we reach the restaurant.

Noah got us a table at the best Italian restaurant in Ashville: Ciprianni's, in the Raven district. I have the shrimp and black truffle pasta, and he has the lasagna. At the end, we share a tiramisu, and he pays the bill, refusing my offer of splitting it. He also doesn't pay any attention to the waitress, who blatantly flirts with him the entirety of our meal, even if she could tell we were on a date.

As I'm about to get out of his car at the end of the night, my hand on the door handle, Noah calls out my name softly. "Iris…"

The moment I turn around, he gently places his hand on my cheek, cradling it, closing in the distance between us. I must be having a heart attack. I can't explain otherwise how my heart is beating so fast. It feels as though a hummingbird is trying to escape my chest. My palms start sweating.

"Can I kiss you?" he whispers against my lips, his hot breath rolling over my face.

I nod, gulping hard. I'm frozen in place by the look in his eyes, like I'm the most precious thing he has ever laid his gaze upon.

When his lips touch mine, I forget how to breathe altogether. His full, plump lips taste like tiramisu. He starts licking softly at my lips, and I opened them slightly for him.

It's weird at first, feeling his tongue in my mouth, but I start moving mine in tandem with his, and I whimper at the way the contact is sending pulses of need to my center. He groans, deepening the kiss, and we stay in the car, making out for what seems like forever. Disappointment floods me when he pulls back after a while. We are both breathing hard as he rests his forehead against mine, eyes closed.

"God, you taste so good, and I want more, so much more. But we need to stop. I promised I would get you home by ten thirty, and we wouldn't want your aunt to worry," his voice is gruff, thickened by desire, his hot breath rolling over my parted lips.

After that night, something intervened with his family, and we couldn't see each other for a few days, but we spoke on the phone every day. I was so in love with him that I couldn't believe my fantasies had become true. For the first time in my life, the gaping hole in my chest was filled with happiness, and the loss of my memory didn't hurt as much.

When we finally met again, he told me he had to move all the way to the Vatican; his parents were being sent on a special mission there indefinitely. He wanted to stay, but his parents wouldn't take no for an answer. My world seemed to have collapsed at that moment, but he reassured me that we would still talk every day. Noah even booked a flight back to Ashville in a few months to come see me. At least, that's what he claimed. Who knows if it was even true.

The day he left, I couldn't stop crying. A week passed, and I never heard from him. Then, a week turned into four, and a month turned into six. I asked Grayson every chance I got if there was any news from Noah or his parents. He told me what they were doing was classified, and he couldn't share that information with me. For a whole year, I cried myself to sleep, wishing he would send me a text, just one, telling me that he was still alive and that he missed me.

One day, I was at the compound, on my way to the library, when I passed Veronica, Tessa, and Britney going down the stairs. As always, I didn't look at them, but I heard Veronica clearly telling them Noah had called her again the night before, and they talked for an hour. *Again. For an hour.* My heart shattered right down the middle, and my knees buckled while my right foot missed a step.

I had to use all my body strength in order to balance myself as my eyes filled with unshed tears. I refused to show weakness and cry in front of other people. I immediately went home, sobbed uncontrollably for a few hours, and from that day moving forward, I pretended Noah never existed in my life, and I even started dating sparingly.

When I moved to my new apartment, I found the picture of us in one of the boxes I used for my stuff. My aunt probably put it there without my knowledge. I immediately threw it in the trash, but after a few minutes of deliberation, I took it out and hung it on the wall alongside the other photos.

Snapping my eyes shut, I let out a frustrated cry because I can't pause the assault of images that play like a broken record in my head, chipping more and more at my heart. I'm surprised there is anything left of the punching bag, honestly, with how much force I'm putting in every kick and punch I'm throwing. My braid is stuck to my drenched back, and rivulets of sweat trickle between my shoulder blades and on my face, but I can't stop.

"Ouch. I would hate to be that punching bag," the voice that is still the same but deepened by the passing years says from behind me with amusement.

I start a fire round of body shots on the bag, ignoring Noah.

"C'mon, Iris, please, stop ignoring me! Can you give me five minutes?

That's all I ask." Regret and something else thickens the timbre of his voice, almost as if he truly is sorry.

Yeah, sure.

He's a much better actor than I remember.

I snort a bitter laugh. "Not asking for much, are you? I imagine I am owed five years of ignoring you," I grumble while I stop my series of body shots, the punching bag not doing it for me anymore. I stalk to the shelf on my right, stacked with clean towels, and pull one out to wipe away some of the sweat running down my face.

Turning around, I amble toward the other room where the training dummies are, with Noah hot on my heels. The room is empty, and I make a beeline for the weapons laid on a long table on the far-left side of it. Again, I act as if Noah isn't even present as I grab a few daggers and start throwing them in rapid-fire motions. I flip one in the air, catch it by the tip, and throw it to the center of the forehead; I throw another to the heart and three more in the groin area, to make a point. I take out the daggers from the dummy and return to my spot, getting ready for another round.

Suddenly, a strong arm circles my waist from behind while Noah's right hand covers my dagger-throwing one. I freeze. I can feel every inch of him as our bodies align perfectly together. *Shit.* I close my eyes, trying to still my rapid heart.

"Your throwing knife skills are perfect. You must have had a good teacher." His lips almost touch my right ear as he speaks, his breath tickling the side of my neck, igniting a slow-burning fire in my belly.

Fuck.

I hate how affected I still am by his presence.

As I take a few deep breaths in, his scent envelops me completely, and I shake my head, trying to regain my composure. I can't help but remember the other body pressed into my back just earlier today. I didn't get any action for five years aside from some drunk, sloppy kisses from random guys I wasn't even interested in, and that were either trying too hard or not at all. And now, not even twenty-four hours apart, I've had two erections digging in my ass.

Kaiden's face flashes through my mind. It's like someone threw a bucket of ice-cold water at my face.

What the fuck am I doing?

I turn around quickly, throwing the daggers to the floor and pushing hard at his chest with both hands. "Leave me alone, Noah! Can't you tell I don't want to speak or even see you in front of my eyes? You had your chance already. You had five fucking years to talk to me. But you completely ghosted me. So, tell me, why would I spare even five minutes of my time on you?" I cross my arms in front of my chest, ready to strike at any second.

"I know I don't deserve your time. Trust me, no one knows that better than I do. I wanted nothing more than to talk to you all these years but couldn't. At first, something happened, and then I wasn't allowed to," his tone is soft, coaxing as he comes closer again.

I take a step back but hold my ground. "Bullshit! I don't care. I'm not the same naïve girl who can be fooled by sweet fake talk anymore. I know I was just some girl you fooled around with. Were you still fucking Veronica when you asked me out on a date? Did you go out with me on a dare? See if you can make the half-blood freak fall in love with you? Were the two years we spent together as friends a joke to you? What the fuck was it, Noah?" I scream loudly, not caring if I make a scene anymore.

"Don't you dare say those things about our date! That night was the best night of my life! And what the fuck are you talking about? I never spoke with anyone from Ashville in these five years, not even with Grayson. If you don't believe me, go ask him yourself." His anger matches my own, his eyes becoming smokey like when dark-gray clouds pull in, preparing for the incoming storm.

His temper is shorter now, that's for sure. He never snapped or yelled at me before he left, even if I drove him crazy. A darkness seems to cling to his features now. As if what he went through in these five years changed the very essence of his soul. I can still see the remnants of the boy with a golden heart shining through the cracks, though.

"FUCK!" He runs his fingers through his hair, pulling hard at the strands as he looks up toward the ceiling, ruining the faux just-rolled-out-of-bed look. He then takes a deep breath in and sighs through his nose. His gaze locks with mine. "I'm sorry. I don't want to fight with you. Please. Can you meet me at our spot in the garden? I want to explain everything, but I don't want to do it here," he says more calmly, and the desperation in his voice dulls my anger.

"I can't, I don't have time. I have to shower, do the medical exam, grab some weapons from the armory, and get ready for my shift. I work tonight," I reply, my voice scratchy from all the screaming.

"Please, Iris. Give me five minutes of your time. I've missed you so much," he pleads again.

"I don't know, Noah. You discarded me like I was yesterday's trash. You let me fall in love with you, then you left and never looked back." My voice trembles, and tears blur my vision with the admission of my heartbreak.

Stupid fucking feelings.

Noah closes the small distance between us and tries to hug me, but I don't let him. I push at his arms and step back again, looking down as I swallow through the lump in my throat, trying to clear the tears in my eyes. When I lift my head, his gaze is filled with regret. Sadness slumps his shoulders as if he's on the verge of giving up. Giving up on me.

"I'll wait for you in the garden until ten tonight. If you don't show up, I promise I'll never bother you again. You'll only hear from me for official reasons regarding your position in the Order, nothing more." He clears his throat and turns around, leaving the room, not sparing me one more glance.

13

Sitting on the exam table in one of the rooms reserved for the hospital on the third floor of the compound, I scroll on my phone as I wait for Dr. Corey to do the full-body checkup Grayson ordered of me. I have at least two hundred missed calls and some very colorful voice messages from Sam over the weekend, but nothing else backed up to the cloud, not even a single missed call from Aunt Josephine.

The clock on my brand-new phone screen shows it's six p.m., so I don't have much time until I have to start my shift. I already showered and changed with some spare clothes I always keep at the compound for after my training sessions. I hope the doctor will finish the exam quickly because I'm starting to get hungry, and I don't want to start my shift on an empty stomach again. That would really suck.

This day feels like the longest day on Earth, and tiredness is seeping into my bones. All I want to do is hop off the roller coaster of emotions I've been trapped into from the moment I woke up this morning.

Taking a deep breath in and expelling it through my mouth, I stare at the white wall of the doctor's office, indecisiveness plaguing my mind. I don't know what to do. I miss Noah so much, but I don't want to get sucked into my feelings for him again. I barely managed to get over him, and it required a lot of tequila, gallons of ice cream, and some really questionable choices. I fire a text to Sam, needing her advice.

> **Me: Noah is back. He wants to talk. What should I do???**

My phone immediately pings with her reply.

> **Sam: WHAT?!?!?**
>
> **NO FUCKING WAY!!!**
>
> **Are you sure it was him and not a ghost?**

I smile and roll my eyes at her words.

> **Me: 100% sure 😂😂😂 It was him I saw all right. I did do a double take when I saw him in Grayson's office. I thought I was having a stroke.**

> **Sam: Shit.**
>
> **Are you ok?**
>
> **Do you want me to come kick his lying ass?**

The string of messages come one after another. Sam is one of those people who isn't patient enough to send a full text; she just isn't wired like that.

> **Me: Yeah, I think so. Actually...I don't know if I'm ok.**

> I don't know what to do. Should I go talk to him or not? He's waiting for me at our spot in the garden... if I don't show up, he promised he won't bother me again. He told me he was sorry and that he wants to explain everything...

Sam: Maybe you should go and see what he has to say.

You never did get any closure. Dick punch him for me when you finish your talk, though.

Wait. Is he still hot?

The door opens, and I look up from the phone, putting it on silent. Dr. Corey walks in and stops in front of me. "What can I do for you today, Iris?" he asks with a warm smile. He's a very handsome man with deep, ebony skin that creates an unusual contrast with his natural, almost whiteish blond buzz cut and hazel eyes.

"Grayson told me to do a full exam. I was attacked by a demon this weekend, and he sent me here. He wants to see if I'm okay...at least, I guess that's what he wants," I mumble the last part mostly to myself while I look back at my phone. A few unread messages are flooding my screen.

Sam: ????? C'mon Iris. I want to know.

What are best friends for?

OMG.

I totally forgot!

What did you tell Grayson?

How did the meeting go?

I quickly type a reply. I don't want to be rude toward Doctor Corey, but I know Sam is like a dog with a bone and will send me a thousand texts if I don't answer her right this second.

Me: Jesus! YES, he is still hot. Actually, he is even hotter than when he left. He's all man now. Now stop being a psycho and stop sending me 100 texts. I'm at the doctor's office getting a full exam— Grayson's orders. Talk to you later. Xx

THE SUN IS setting on the horizon, painting the sky in vibrant orange and magenta hues as I descend the stairs at the back patio of the mansion, making my way toward the garden. As Sam said, I need closure. Even if I don't owe it to Noah to listen to what he has to say, I owe it to younger Iris, the one with the broken heart. Maybe I can finally close that chapter in my life forever and allow myself to fall in love again. Even though I repeat like a mantra in my head over and over again that I don't feel anything for him anymore, I know deep down that he is the reason I refuse to go further with anyone else.

The fragrant lilac air fills my lungs as I start walking on the pebbled mosaic garden path, passing the luxuriant lilac shrubs and a few hawthorn trees in full bloom on my way to our spot, as Noah called it. It was my spot at first, where I used to hide from the scrutinizing eyes of the other Order members and enjoy the beautiful garden as I sat on the grass, resting my back on the tree trunk or sprawled on a blanket under the ancient oak tree and did my homework or prepared for an exam. After that night in the training room, Noah met me there almost every day and it quickly became our spot. I did my homework as he read a book or helped me study.

The massive oak tree looms over the wrought iron bench Noah is seated on. The bench wasn't here before; I wasn't aware of the change until this moment. I haven't been back in this spot since he left. It hurt too much.

He's slightly bent over, looking at the ground, lost in thought, his elbows resting on his knees. His messy honey-blond hair is slumped over his forehead, covering his eyes. When Noah hears me approach, he lifts his head. Gray eyes flit to mine with a glint of relief.

"You came," he says as he straightens, pushing the hair out of his eyes.

"That doesn't mean I forgive you, Noah. You don't know what it's been like for me…" I swallow through the lump in my throat and continue, "So, talk. I don't have much time." My tone drips with iciness as I sit down stiffly on the other side of the bench, leaving as much space as possible between us.

God, it feels so weird to sit with him again under the oak tree, as if we are frozen in time, and he never left.

"I guess I deserve that," he sighs, looking down. "I wish things were different. I wish that day my parents told me they had a special mission and we had to leave the country never came because I would still have you. We would already be married by now, I'm sure of it."

He scrunches his eyebrows and shakes his head, continuing, "If there is one thing I deeply regret is that I waited so long to ask you out on a date. I was so fucking stupid, waiting for almost two years. Jesus, Iris, I fell in love with you the moment I saw you for the first time. I still am in love with you…I never stopped."

He meets my gaze, and the pain in his glistening, smokey eyes lands like a blow to my solar plexus. A tear crests over my eyelashes and rolls down my cheek. I break the eye contact and wipe at it quickly with trembling fingers.

Ugh, stupid fucking feelings.

My jaw ticks. "If you were so in love with me, why did you let five years pass without even a message? How can I believe you cared so deeply for me when you treated me like yesterday's trash, huh?" I demand angrily, still looking away from him, my heart raw, the old wounds I thought I had stitched carefully with tequila and sleepless nights threatening to open again and bleed me dry.

"When we arrived in Italy, my phone stopped working unexpectedly. I managed to find a repair shop and left it there, hoping they would fix it quickly. We were staying at a hotel, so I went back to my room, planning to call you, and that's when I realized I didn't have your phone number or any other number memorized. My parents already left on a secret mission they could tell me nothing about because it was classified. I waited for them to return so I could call Grayson from one of their phones and ask him for your number."

He takes a deep breath and exhales shakily. "My parents…they never did come back. They were killed in that mission." His words are laced with undisguised pain.

My head snaps back at him when I hear the last part. "What? Your parents are dead?" I pause and shake my head in disbelief. I take a deep breath and swallow before continuing, "Noah, I had no idea; I—I don't know what to say." I place my left hand over his, which rests on the bench in the empty space between us.

He turns it with his palm facing upward and interlocks our fingers, making my heart flutter at the contact. I withdraw it, though, after a few seconds. I'm sorry for what happened to him, but I can't bear his touch anymore. The lines are already starting to get blurry, and I can't let my feelings for him mess with my head again.

I tuck my freshly washed hair behind my ear. "But that was five years ago. Why didn't you call to tell me what happened? I would have jumped on the first plane to get to you. You know that."

"My parents were members of a special division in the Order called the Kabal. Everything they did was classified. A member of the Kabal contacted me in person at the hotel and told me an Elite demon killed them. He also told me I was supposed to be recruited into the special division, and that's why my parents insisted so much that I moved there with them, but they never got to tell me. Everyone in my family had been a member—it was my birthright."

Noah looks wistfully in the distance and continues, "I was so devastated by the news of what happened to my parents; I didn't want anything to do with the Order anymore. I locked myself in my hotel room for a week, and even if I picked up my phone, I couldn't reach out to anyone. My grief paralyzed me. If I didn't call and tell you about their deaths, then it couldn't have been real. If no one else knew…then maybe I could live in my bubble forever."

He heaves out a deep sigh and his sad eyes lock with mine. The purple, darkening sky reflects into his irises, making them almost the same color as the rings outlining mine. He doesn't say anything for at least a few seconds, just keeps me captive with the sadness in his kaleidoscope gaze. Then he starts talking again.

"The denial I was feeling soon turned into anger, and when the Kabal contacted me again, I told them I would join their special division if they let me kill the Elite demon. I wanted revenge, and that was the only way I could get it. They accepted my request, but I had to enroll in their special training program first, which lasted for three years. In the program, we weren't allowed to contact anyone from our previous lives. Attachments to the past are not accepted in the Kabal. In order to become the killing machines they wanted us to be, we had to let everyone from our pasts go."

Jesus, what the fuck?

Would he make up such an elaborate story just for me to forgive him?

No, that can't be. Noah never lied to me before. And I know his parents traveled all the time, probably for those special secret missions. But I don't know this new Noah sitting next to me on the bench. It all sounds way too freakin' crazy not to be true, though. He wouldn't lie about his parent's death.

Maybe I should have gotten day drunk with Sam because all of this would have been much easier to digest if I was at least slightly buzzed.

"And what about when you finished your special training? Why didn't you try to contact me then?" I inquire. "Why did you let two more years pass?"

"I didn't think you would still want to hear from me after so much time. I was sure you had already moved on. Look at you, Iris, you're gorgeous! You're so beautiful, not only on the outside. Any man would be lucky to be with you," he responds while his eyes rake over my body, a glint of desire shining in them.

"Maybe you shouldn't have taken that decision from me. It was mine to make," I scoff. "For what it's worth, I'm sorry about your family. I know how much you loved your parents and how close you were to them. But what are you doing here, Noah? I don't believe you appeared out of nowhere after five years just to have this conversation with me."

"The Kabal sent me. They monitor every ley line in the world, especially in the cities where the Hell gates are located. Something caused a massive disturbance in the ley lines on Saturday around three a.m. I believe it has something to do with the demons that attacked you in the forest. The Kabal sent me to investigate the disturbance."

My eyebrows draw together. "What are you talking about?"

"There are mutinies in Hell. The Kabal managed to trap a lesser demon in the Seal of Solomon about a year ago. After a few months of continuous torture, the demon started singing like a bird. It told us the leaders of the mutinies in Hell are getting more and more powerful. A lot of demons want to overthrow Lucifer, especially after he signed the Celestial Treaty," he replies.

"The Seal of Solomon? Aren't witches the only ones who can trap demons into that seal?" I ask, bewildered.

"The Kabal is working with a few dark witches. We get our missions directly from an archangel, so the organization is on another level than the Order and doesn't play by the same rules. Anyway, the situation is dire. Lucifer went into hiding, and Hell is in disarray. I'm afraid something big is coming."

So Kaiden was telling the truth after all. I pretend this is the first time I heard of such a thing and feign shock. "And Grayson knows about this? About everything you're telling me? Am I even allowed to know all of these things?" I ask with urgency.

"Grayson knows that I'm a member of the Kabal. He was told I was going to arrive today with a special mission to find what caused the disturbance in the ley lines and that he is supposed to help me in any way he can. He doesn't know about the mutinies or Lucifer. I trust you will not say anything to anyone about it. And no, you're not supposed to know any of the things I told you; everything is classified."

He scoots closer to me on the bench and takes my hands in his, pinning me in place with his burning gaze. "Something big is coming and you've already gotten hurt by those demons in the woods. I couldn't bear it if anything happened to you again. I can't lose you too," Noah's voice trails off on a broken whisper.

Looking away, I swallow, trying to escape the emotion shining in his eyes, but I don't withdraw my hands this time. I look at the sky, needing a moment to take in everything he told me, from the death of his parents to the secret organization and his declaration of love.

Dusk settles around us, and I take a deep breath, filling my lungs with the perfumed evening primrose air. I don't have much time until I have to start my shift.

"I have no words, honestly. Everything you've told me is so," I search for the right word, "convoluted." With a deep sigh, I get up from the bench. "I need to go; I still have to take some new weapons from the armory before my shift. I also need a new onyx stone."

Noah stands up at the same time as I do and stops me by placing his fingers softly on my left elbow. "Would you consider giving me another chance? I missed you so much. I want to be in your life again. There's nothing I want more in this world."

"I don't know. I need time to process all of this. I can't give you an answer right now."

A soft breeze tingles the back of my neck, lifting a few strands of my hair, blowing them into my face. Noah steps closer. The tips of his shoes touch mine as he grazes his knuckles over my cheek slowly before tucking the strands of hair under my left ear. A shiver works its way down my spine at the gentle touch. He's so close I can feel the ghost of his breath on my lips. The silver light cast by the moon dances in his eyes, making them glow.

"At least let me be your friend again," he almost whispers.

I inch back to break our connection. I'm surprised there isn't a hole in the ground between my feet with how hard I'm staring at it. "As I said, I need time."

"Take all the time you need. I'm ready to wait however long you think is necessary. But I will also need your help with the investigation. Can you please take me to the place in the national park where the demons attacked you?"

"Yeah, I can do that. Let's meet up tomorrow. Call me around twelve; that's when I usually wake up after my shift." I take another step. "Bye, Noah," I say as I put more distance between us, taking the pebbled path back to the mansion.

"Wait, what's your number?" Noah shouts after me.

"It's the same one. I never changed it," I shoot back over my shoulder.

I always hoped you'd call.

14

Sighing, I close the front door of my apartment and discard all of my weapons and the takeout food I brought with me on top of the entryway table so I can take off my old black leather combat boots. I just finished my shift scouring the city for any demons to kill. The thing is, I couldn't find any. All I did was circle the streets over and over again, but still nothing…not even one.

Which is strange. Even on the slow days, I can still find at least one or two lesser demons to kill. Tonight, though, the streets were one hundred percent dead. It was eerie quiet, like a storm brewing under the surface, on the precipice of unleashing its wrath on everything and everyone.

Weirdly, I feel more tired now than after fighting a hoard of demons. Call me a psycho, but I love my job. The chaos of being in a fight, the adrenaline buzzing through my veins, the way my sword slices through rotten meat and bones. The fact that I couldn't get into at least one fight with a demon tonight left me reeling. At least there weren't any drunks this early on a Tuesday morning to piss me off.

While I was roaming the streets aimlessly, my mind decided it needed a job, and I couldn't stop the loop of images playing on repeat, forcing me to remember everything that had happened since Friday night, from almost being murdered in the woods to waking up in Kaiden's penthouse and to Noah being back after all these years.

I desperately needed a release, and it was all made worse by the fact that I was so damn hungry. Barely having ten minutes to come back to my apartment before my shift, I got my spare hunting boots from the closet in my bedroom and called Sam to tell her about the meeting with Grayson. I didn't have time to eat after all, and I was still upset that Kaiden had to throw away my favorite boots.

Taking the bag filled with takeout boxes of Chinese food—fried rice, spring rolls, dumplings, and kung pao chicken, all my favorites—I make my way to my living room and place them on the small coffee table in front of my couch.

After turning on the TV, I stride to my fridge and take out the bottle of Pinot Gris I had chilling in it. I pour myself a glass before I return to the living room. Plopping down on the couch, I place the glass of wine on the table and the bottle next to it on the floor.

I start eating straight out of the cartons with the wooden chopsticks while pressing play on the remote. *The Vampire Diaries* opening credits fill the air as I relax into the cushion. Five minutes into the episode, my phone buzzes on the table. Pausing the show, I take my phone and tap on the screen. It's a text from an unknown number.

UN: My sheets still smell like you.

My heart does a flip-flop as I stare at the screen. I read the message several times before replying.

Me: Who are you?

It has to be Kaiden, right? I mean, it's pretty clear that I haven't been

123

in another man's bed. Ever. The response comes instantly, which means he was waiting for my reply. The thought makes my insides pitch.

> **UN: Do you make it a habit of lying in strange men's beds often, angel?**

Usually, I hate pet names, but Kaiden calling me angel does strange things to my heart. The vivid memory of him saying that to me for the first time, only wearing a towel, looking like a walking wet dream, is forever seared into my brain. I press my thighs together at the way that image makes my breath quicken. Jesus, what is wrong with me? He isn't even in the room. I have to have an orgasm soon, or else I'll combust.

> **Me: Kaiden? How did you get my number?**

No, seriously, how did he?

> **Kaiden: How did your meeting with Grayson go?**

I roll my eyes at him ignoring my question, and even though I know I shouldn't be talking to him at all, more so about matters of the Order, I feel the need to tell him anyway. He did save my life, after all.

> **Me: I told him nothing about the portal, just that some very powerful demons I had never seen before attacked me. I also lied about you rescuing me. He didn't quite buy it...Now answer me. How did you get my number?**

> **Kaiden: I always get what I want. Have dinner with me.**

I huff at his cockiness.

> **Me: Apparently not, because there's no chance in hell I'm going out with a demon. It's against the rules, or have you forgotten I'm a hellseeker?**

> **Kaiden: We could have dinner at my place where no one can see us.**

> **Me: Yeah...not happening.**

> **Kaiden: We'll see about that.**

> **Me: Someone needs a reality check.**

> **Kaiden: Goodnight, angel. Dream about me.**

I delete and rewrite my reply several times, but decide not to send the text in the end. I have to get my head straight. I can't be talking to a demon, even though he ignites something in me that I have never felt before. It makes me feel unhinged, unbalanced, and a little bit crazy, like having my foot over the edge of a cliff, ready to jump headfirst into the abyss.

The irrational attraction to Kaiden has me staring blankly at the wall for more than half an hour. Out of all the people in the world, I have to be lusting over a demon? Letting out a deep sigh, I try to bring myself back to reality, but I fail...miserably. Even though I just resumed the series, my mind keeps taking me back to the moment Kaiden pinned me to the wall.

Fuck.

I fill the fourth glass to the brim and discard the empty bottle on the floor next to the couch. I usually don't drink more than a single glass of wine after my shifts or that much in the middle of the week, to be honest, but I don't care. I'm too wound up and need alcohol in my bloodstream to make me forget about all the shit I've been through. I feel like my world is spinning off its axis. At least I can be a little tipsy and enjoy the fucked-up ride.

My focus is fully on the series now, so I mouth along with Damon, then with Elena about how much control they have over each other. No matter how many times I rewatch this season, Elena and Damon's break-up scene always leaves me depressed. I know what I need to make me feel better: some wine. Yeah, some more wine. Oh, and some ice cream. And music, definitely some music.

Standing up from the couch, I sway slightly and trip over an empty wine bottle. Who the fuck put that there? *Oh, I did.* I start laughing at my stupidity and go back to the fridge to look for another bottle. Shit, I can't find any.

With the hope that I still have some more wine in there, I open the cupboard under the sink. I don't. I only had two bottles left, and I forgot about the one I had drunk with Sam the day before. But I do have a half-full bottle of vodka that's in the back of the cupboard since New Year's Eve when I did shots with Sam. I ended up so shit-faced that I spent the whole first day of the year hugging the toilet.

Mixing wine and vodka.

Should I?

Fuck it! You only live once.

I plop down on the floor, with my back resting on the fridge, and dig into the ice cream container while drinking vodka straight from the bottle. The ice cream-vodka combo is delicious.

I'm a fucking genius.

When I remember I wanted to listen to music, I connect my phone to the small Bluetooth speaker I use when I work out at home. Bad Omens "Like a Villain" blasts through the apartment, making me tap my right foot to the beat.

Standing abruptly on unsteady feet, I start dancing and screaming at the top of my lungs at the same time as the lead singer while taking swigs directly from the bottle. I keep singing, jumping around, and dancing, the bottle of vodka my dance partner. The world becomes fuzzier and fuzzier with every drop of alcohol drenching my stomach and sloshing into my veins.

I don't know how much time has passed since I started dancing, but my clothes are plastered to my body; that's how sweaty I am. Suddenly, bone-deep tiredness washes over me in waves. All I want is to go to sleep. But the ground keeps moving under my feet as though I'm a passenger on a boat navigating treacherous waters. To top it off, the room is also spinning.

My slow blinks do nothing to clear the foggy wall that has fallen over my eyes. When the image finally sharpens a little, I stumble to the hallway leading to my bedroom.

What the fuck?

I don't remember the hallway being this long.

Keeping my body upright is nothing short of a Herculean task. Not even propping my hands on each wall helps. I'm stuck on a roller coaster ride that goes on and on and on. And the worst part? Each fumbling step I take is accompanied by painful stomach clenches and the acrid taste of bile as it carves its way up my throat.

Not today, Satan!

If I can only manage to get to my bedroom first, I'll fall asleep and won't be sick anymore.

Okay, Iris. You can do this!

After what feels like an eternity, I finally manage to get to my bedroom and fall face-first on the bed. The coolness of the sheets against my cheek feels like heaven. It only takes a few seconds for sweet blankness to take over my vision and my thoughts.

I WAKE WITH a start, blinking slowly, trying to adjust to the bright light burning my retinas. I realize I forgot to pull the drapes over my bedroom window and want to kick myself for this mistake. In an attempt to quiet the loud banging in my head, I take the extra pillow next to me and put it over my face and ears. *Ah fuck.* Someone took residence inside my skull and keeps hitting my brain with a hammer. At least, that's exactly how I feel.

Where the hell are my clothes?

I'm naked on the bed. The last thing I remember is getting tired from all the dancing and trying to get to my bedroom. I definitely don't remember undressing myself.

My throat feels like the Sahara Desert, and I desperately need to drink some water. I try lifting my head but feel the room spin with the move. So, I slowly slide to my bedside table, still on my back, and bring the glass of water on top of it to my lips without moving my head. I spill most of the water on the bed, but manage to get a sip in. *Fuck.* The second the water hits my stomach, the violent urge to throw up overtakes my entire body.

Jumping from the bed as fast as I can, I barely get to the bathroom in time before I start retching all the contents of my stomach into the toilet.

Fuck my life! I'm never drinking again!

Luckily, I also have an entrance to the bathroom from my bedroom; otherwise, I would have made a mess on the floor.

As I lift my head from the toilet, I realize the banging is not only in my mind; it's coming from my front door. Sam must have forgotten her key again. She can open the door with magic, she's a witch, after all, but she likes to fuck with me sometimes, just to piss me off. She's the definition of an annoying sibling. She's lucky I love her so much.

I quickly throw some ice-cold water onto my face and brush my teeth to get rid of the disgusting taste in my mouth. My reflection in the mirror is something else entirely. My hair resembles a bird's nest, sticking in every direction, and I look exactly how I feel. Like shit. I swiftly put it in a messy bun, using the hair tie on my wrist, and amble back into my bedroom.

The pounding keeps getting louder and louder, and I shout as I rummage for something to put on, "I'm coming, you psycho! Stop banging like a madwoman!" I immediately wince at the way my head pulses in pain at the loud sound.

I can't find my robe anywhere, so I open my closet and throw on the first thing I can find: a very old white T-shirt. It's basically see-through, but I don't care since it's just Sam. I pause as I slide open my underwear drawer, my eyebrows drawing in a deep frown. What the fuck? Did I drunkenly rearrange all my underwear? Also, the pale pink lingerie set Kaiden got me is missing. I distinctly remember putting it in the back of the drawer to only use it on special occasions because I could never afford to buy such luxurious lingerie. Did someone break in just to fuck with me, or am I just that weird when I'm drunk? Another loud bang pulls me out of my thoughts, and I hastily slide on the first pair of panties I can grab and stride toward the front door.

My hallway is a disaster. I don't know how, but a lot of the pictures that were hanging on the walls are on the floor. None of the glass is shattered, though. Thank God for that; otherwise, I would have stepped directly on broken glass. The empty takeout boxes are still on the small coffee table, the ice cream a melted puddle next to the fridge, the container tilted on its side, and the bottle of vodka empty in the middle of the living room. *Shit.* Did I drink all of it? No wonder I feel like a car ran me over.

The pounding on the door is incessant as I put my right hand on the knob. "Sam, I swear to God," I mutter angrily, yanking the door open.

I freeze as I stare at the person in front of my eyes.

Strong arms suddenly pull me in a bear-like hug, and I don't know how to react. My brain is a foggy mess.

"Um, Noah? What are you doing here?"

15

"You didn't answer your phone, and I got so worried. I've been calling for two hours non-stop. I thought something happened to you again. I got your address from Grayson and came to check up on you." Noah's still hugging me tightly, his fresh, crisp smell taking over my senses.

"Oh," I say in a breathy whisper as I suddenly become aware of the fact that I'm almost naked in his arms. I totally forgot that I had promised to show him the spot where the umbra attacked me in the forest.

My front is completely stuck to his, and I feel every single muscle and ridge of his body pressing against mine. He pulls me in slightly, allowing me to feel his erection poking at my belly. I inhale a shaky breath and swallow. Neither of us moves, and I know I have to be the first one to step back because I'm still deeply hurt by his actions. But I just can't. My brain is short-circuited by the memories of us, of what we could have been together.

Noah pulls back a little to look down at me, and I almost melt at the way his eyes rove over my body. How many times have I daydreamed and wished he would come back and look at me just like that? He then lifts his hand and brushes his thumb against my right nipple over the see-through fabric of my shirt. I can't stop the breathy moan that tumbles free at the contact.

His eyes are two mirrors of quicksilver as he closes the small space between us and brings his lips to mine in a searing kiss. The groan he lets out the moment our tongues meet is sexy as fuck. This kiss is nothing like the ones he gave me five years ago, which seem almost innocent in comparison.

Something happens, though, as the kiss deepens; Kaiden's face unexpectedly flashes through my mind. The heat I imagined coursing inside my veins a thousand times over as Noah kisses me is barely a flicker of a dying ember.

What the fuck is wrong with me? He's a demon.

Noah suddenly glides both of his palms on the back of my thighs and lifts me. The movement snaps me out of my thoughts. So, I circle my legs around his body in response and weave my fingers into his hair, pulling the strands hard and licking at his lips furiously. I refuse to recognize what this really is — a feeble attempt at erasing Kaiden's face, which seems to be etched on my brain. With a frustrated groan, I try hard to concentrate on the way Noah's hard-as-steel erection is pressing right at my center, dampening the lacy fabric of my thong.

Still not nearly as wet as when Kaiden had you pinned against the wall, the nagging voice in my brain screams at me.

I push it away as Noah closes the door by kicking it with his left heel and starts walking with me in his arms on the hallway that leads to my bedroom while devouring my mouth like a starved man.

He steps on one of the pictures, shattering the glass. We both land on the bed with him on top of me, right in between my legs. Lifting my T-shirt over my head and discarding it on the floor, he looks at me with awe in his eyes as he takes both of my breasts in his hands, making slow circles with his thumbs on my nipples.

"God, Iris," he breathes against my right nipple before he sucks it into his mouth greedily.

Pleasure zips through me. "Touch me. Please!" I beg with desperation. Maybe if he touches me, I will forget about Kaiden. I have to. *I have to!*

He palms my pussy and starts making soft circles with his fingers on my clit, over the damp fabric of my panties, as he keeps sucking and teasing my nipples with his tongue. I close my eyes, trying to stay in the moment, but in the darkness, I get another flashback of the way Kaiden collared my throat with his tattooed fingers.

This is wrong.

So wrong.

I can't do this to him. To me.

We have to stop.

As I'm about to push him away, Sam's loud voice travels through the apartment unexpectedly. "Iris! Are you still sleeping? I almost died laughing at the voice messages you sent me this morning."

"Fuck," Noah groans under his breath and lifts his head. His eyes lock with mine, brimming with disappointment.

Shit. Shit. Shit.

The reality of what I was about to do hits me all at once like a ton of bricks as the haze of desire completely disappears from my brain with the sound of the front door of the apartment slamming shut. I push Noah off me with inhuman speed and jump off the bed to close the door.

"What the fuck happened in here? Why are all the pictures on the floor? Oh my Goddess! Did you drink all the leftover vodka alone? Are you crazy?" Sam asks in disbelief, shock dripping from her tone. Her heels click loudly against the hardwood floor as she approaches my bedroom. She knocks. "Iris? I can hear you in there. Are you okay?"

"Yeah, I'm fine, just a little hungover. I'll be out in a minute. Let me put some clothes on," I reply breathlessly from the other side of the door.

"All right, weirdo. It's not like I haven't seen you naked before, but whatever."

The deep breath I take into my lungs does nothing to still my rapid pulse. I turn back to Noah, but I can't look into his eyes, so I take in his appearance instead. He's sitting on the bed, his erection bulging the material of his jeans, his golden hair messed up by my wandering hands. I suddenly don't know what to do.

I clear my throat loudly in an attempt to clear the blistering silence that has fallen between us as I stride to my closet. With my back to Noah, I sift through my clothes for something to wear. Taking out some dark blue sweats and a rock band tee, I hastily put them on.

"Iris, I—" Noah says softly.

I cut whatever he was trying to say while facing him again. "Can you please stay here? I'll get rid of her fast. It's just…I don't know how Sam's going to react if she sees you. She was the one to pick up the pieces when you left, and I can't deal with the drama right now," I whisper.

Knowing Sam, she will probably hex him with a small dick or impotence. She can be creative like that and also vindictive, especially if someone wronged me. Noah nods instead of offering a reply, and I leave him there, sitting on the edge of the bed, his elbows resting on his knees. I swiftly get out of the bedroom and close the door behind me.

The pictures are back on the hallway walls as if nothing ever happened, and the rest of the mess is picked up, the ice cream puddle nonexistent. Sam is sitting at the kitchen table, typing something on her phone. As always, she's dressed to impress in a black pencil skirt paired with a stunning burgundy ruffled blouse that accentuates her fiery hair, which is pulled in a sleek bun.

"Hey, thanks for cleaning up," I say as I approach her.

She lifts her gaze from the screen. "It's nothing. I just snapped my fingers, and everything was back in its place. Witch, remember?" She points her right thumb at herself and arches a perfect auburn eyebrow at me while analyzing me up and down. "Why are you so red in the face? And why are your lips swollen like you just had a sexy make-out session?"

"I was throwing up right before you came through the door, maybe because of that. I feel like shit. I came back after my shift last night and drank a bottle of wine and the rest of the vodka left from New Year's Eve by myself. I got so wasted; I don't even remember what the fuck I did half of the time before going to sleep," I answer, plopping down on the couch unceremoniously, hoping she's going to drop it.

"Iris Harper, I know you better than anyone! There's something you're not telling me. Spill, bitch!" she demands while narrowing her eyes at me.

I huff. "God, Sam, there's nothing. I'm so fucking hungover. I want to rot in bed and wallow in pain until I have to go out on my shift tonight."

"That's why I'm here, silly. I made something to help with the hangover." She opens her designer tote bag and fishes something from inside. The small glass bottle she takes out is filled to the brim with a questionable-looking liquid like someone puked something green in it.

"I listened to your voice messages when I woke up, and I almost peed myself. I immediately knew you got smashed, so I prepared my perfected hair of the dog for you, aka Sam's Hangover Miracle Juice," she says as she strides to the couch, sitting down with the grace of a ballerina before passing me the glass bottle.

Nausea comes back with a vengeance at the thought that I have to drink the repulsive looking glob. I press the heels of my palms into my eyes, but it does nothing to calm my rioting stomach. "I'm almost afraid to ask, but what voice messages?"

"You mostly mumbled something about Elena and Damon breaking up. Who the fuck are these people? I know I'm your only friend. Anyway, this one's my favorite," she says before she unlocks her phone. My drunken voice suddenly blasts through the apartment at full volume.

"Kaiden's so hot! I—I just dream about his abs you know? Like dude, duuuuude! I have never seen abs like that! I want to pour some chocolate sauce on him," there is a pause as I belch loudly like a real lady and then continue, "Oh, oh, and some whipped cream and then lick him like the delicious fucking bad-boy dessert he is. No! A MAN, NOT A BOY."

Shit.

I don't remember recording this voice message or any message, for that matter. I cringe hard and hope like hell Noah didn't hear any of this. But with the enhanced hellseeker hearing…

"Sam!" I protest loudly as I try wrestling the phone out of her hand, but she's surprisingly strong for her petite frame and pushes back at my hands. I blame my stupid hangover for my weakness; otherwise, she wouldn't have been able to overpower me.

"Stop it!" she scolds me. "Wait, the best is coming now." She laughs loudly, tears gathering at the corners of her eyes.

My voice booms again, making me shrink in embarrassment. "And then after he spanks me, I WANT TO RIDE HIS DICK LIKE A DISCO STICK!"

Sam's wheezing, not making any more sounds as she doubles over, laughing so hard her whole body is shaking and I—I want the floor to swallow me whole because there's absolutely no way Noah didn't hear me shout that.

"I didn't know you were so kinky," Sam snickers as she wipes at the corner of her eyes delicately, probably trying not to ruin her perfect makeup. "I'm so proud of you!" She pats my thigh like a proud parent.

"Now bottoms up! You'll feel better, I promise."

"The last time you made me drink one of these, I almost shit myself for three days straight." I scrunch my nose while all the times Sam used me as her personal lab rat for every new crazy potion she came up with flashes through my mind.

"I perfected it, okay? Trust me, it's good. I changed the recipe; it just needed some frog legs. I tested it on me first this time. Cross my heart."

"Frog legs? Are you for real?" A repulsed shudder ripples through me. She takes the bottle from my hand and uncaps it while bringing it to my lips like I'm a two-year-old. I gag hard when the stench of dirty feet hits my nose. It's like she tried her best to make this as disgusting as possible.

"If I shit myself again or if anything else happens to me, I'm revoking you as my best friend." Narrowing my eyes at her and pinching my nose, I drink the liquid in three gulps. Surprisingly, it doesn't taste as bad as it smells, and it immediately calms the queasiness in my stomach.

"See? In an hour, you're going to feel like yourself again. I have to go. I'm meeting a client for her wedding flower arrangements, and I'm already running late." She stands up from the couch and bends slightly, giving me a quick hug. "I'll see myself out. And by the way, I know you weren't alone when I came in. You're welcome," she whispers the last part and winks at me with a cat that ate the canary smile.

I gape after her, not able to speak as she puts on her stilettoes and closes the front door behind her. When I finally get my bearings, I walk back toward my bedroom with the intention of letting Noah know she left.

Before I can put my hand on the handle, he storms out of the room with a hard look in his eyes, clouds rolling in, making them a slate gray. The vein pulsing on the side of his forehead looks like it's about to pop any second now. He surprises me by locking me in between his arms with my back to the hallway wall.

I look up into his icy eyes. "What are you doing?"

He crowds me, his large body looming over me. We are so close, the tips of our noses almost touch. "Who the fuck is Kaiden?" he grits out through clenched teeth.

"Just some guy I met a few days ago," I lie and shake my head. Well, it's half a truth. I did meet Kaiden a few days ago, but he doesn't need to know the specifics of how. I want to throttle Sam because this is exactly the result she wanted by playing my drunken voice messages loudly — to make Noah jealous. I don't know how she figured out I wasn't alone and that it was Noah with me in my bedroom, though.

"Did you let him fuck you?" Noah demands, ire dripping from his tone.

He did not just ask that. The audacity of this man!

His question burns through me like the blistering heat of a thousand suns. My nostrils flare, and a muscle thrums in my jaw. "What the fuck is it to you? How did you get in your head the fact that you have the right to know, huh? It's been five fucking years, Noah!" I push hard at his chest, needing space to breathe, and continue with the same fire in my voice, "What? Was I supposed to wait for you like a good little virgin all my fucking life until you suddenly remembered I existed and came back for me?" I ask on a derisive laugh. "You never called! You. Ghosted. Me."

I clench and unclench my fingers, indignation coating every word. "As far as I knew, I was dead to you, so stop acting like a jealous boyfriend! You lost that right five years ago when you left and never looked back." I start pacing at this point, not being able to douse the rage bubbling in my veins. "And don't tell me all these years you haven't been with anyone. How many women have you fucked since you left, huh?"

He doesn't answer. Instead, he evades my gaze, his eyes drilling a hole in the wall, jaw ticking. He doesn't have to say a word because I have my answer right here.

"Yeah, that's what I thought. Talk about double standards," I scoff and shake my head with equal parts anger and disappointment. I know it shouldn't hurt so much that he moved on, but a tiny part of me still hoped he didn't. I couldn't be a bigger fool even if I tried.

His shoulders slump, and his lips draw in a thin line. "Fuck...I'm sorry. It's just that you let me kiss you again, and then we did more, and I thought—"

I cut off whatever he's trying to say. "You thought what? That you own me? Yeah, news flash, you don't! And now, if you'll excuse me, I'm going to take a shower, and if you are still here when I get out of the bathroom, we can go to the national park. If not, you can go by yourself. I don't give a fuck." I sidestep his big frame, careful not to touch him as I enter the bathroom, slamming the door behind me.

I pull my clothes off with more force than necessary and turn on the water in the shower, stepping into the cold spray. The cold water feels like heaven on my overly heated skin. How my life became so fucking complicated, I have no idea. And why did I kiss him, dammit?! I shouldn't have. I blame my stupid hangover brain for that and the fact that I've been horny as hell since leaving Kaiden's apartment.

I also feel the strong need to hit something again because, despite what I said, I *did* wait for Noah to come back like a good little virgin. *Stupid Iris. Stupid. Stupid.* He probably fucked a dozen women since he left, and all I did was have some really boring dates with random dudes that I didn't even like all that much.

Stepping out of the shower, I wrap a towel around my body and enter my bedroom to grab some clothes. I settle on a pair of leggings and a loose black T-shirt since we're going to walk around a forest. I quickly blow-dry my hair and put it into a ponytail. I also dab a bit of foundation and blush on my face in an attempt to mask the fact that I'm still hungover.

My stomach isn't queasy anymore, though, so that's an improvement. At least Sam's concoction seemed to work a little, despite the frog legs.

Ugh.

When I finally get out of my bedroom, I almost bump into Noah. He's holding one of the framed pictures that's normally hanging on the wall, looking at it with a strange intensity.

"You have a photo of us," he says in a whisper while turning his head to look at me. "I remember this day; it was right before I asked you out on our date."

"Yeah, Sam took it. I almost threw it out, but I guess I wanted a reminder of how simple and happy my life used to be back then." I shrug nonchalantly and try to pass by him, but he blocks my way, stepping in front of me. The hallway is pretty narrow, so I can't avoid him.

"I'm sorry about earlier…I can't seem to think straight whenever you're involved, and for what it's worth, I've only been with a few women since I left. They were all drunken mistakes, and I couldn't stop picturing your face. I swear." His words are laced with sorrow and regret.

"It's none of my business, Noah…as far as I'm concerned, we were broken up the moment you ignored my calls. You could have fucked a thousand women. I don't care." The lie makes my stomach clench. "Can we please go now? I want to have some time to myself before I start my shift tonight."

I take a small step forward, hoping he will take the hint and move, but he doesn't budge. Instead, he invades my space, framing my face with his hand. He tilts my head slightly and looks directly into my eyes. The contact makes my pulse scatter.

"I don't care how long it takes, but I'm going to prove to you how much I love you, and I will fight for you, Iris. It doesn't matter who this guy Kaiden is or whomever you've been with since I left. All that matters is that I'm here now, and I'm not leaving." He then bends slightly, kissing me chastely on the lips.

The kiss is so swift, it almost feels like I imagined it. After that, he turns around and places the framed picture back on the wall, leaving me speechless and frozen in the middle of the hallway. I bring my fingers to my lips and swallow hard.

Trying to snap out of it, I blink a few times and shake my head as I finally manage to move my feet toward the entrance, where Noah is waiting for me. I make quick work of sliding two daggers into my boots after I slip them on. With my whip in one hand, I open the front door. As I lock it, I spot Ms. Robbins coming up the stairs, struggling with four bags of groceries, barely keeping her balance. Her usually neat bun is messy, most of the wild strands stuck to her sweaty forehead.

She looks up from the bottom of the stairs and huffs loudly when she sees me. The sharp glare she gives me could level an entire city. Her bony knees are in bad shape, and she can barely climb the stairs as is, but having to carry the heavy grocery bags on top of that must be torture. I'm the one who normally does her grocery run at the beginning of the week, but with the events of the past few days, I totally forgot. Shame and guilt filter through me, even if she annoys me more than half the time.

Before I can, Noah moves fast, descending the stairs to where she is. He takes all four grocery bags in one hand like it's a piece of cake, offering Ms. Robbins the other to help her with the stairs.

"Oh, thank you, young man!" She beams at Noah, which surprises me because she rarely smiles. Then she pats his arm, saying as loudly as she can, "I wouldn't mingle with this one if I were you. She likes to throw orgies in her apartment. Everyone in the building knows."

No, she did not say that. The old bat.

My entire face flushes red at her words, and Noah's eyebrows shoot up. He bursts into laughter at my expense.

All of a sudden, I don't feel guilty anymore.

"I don't throw orgies, Ms. Robbins. Stop telling people that!" I shriek, my voice coming out loud and squeaky.

Reaching the top of the stairs, she throws me a dirty look, still holding Noah's arm. "You kept me up all morning with the screaming and that awfully loud music. You should be ashamed of yourself! You should also close the door when you are having sex; you almost gave me a heart attack earlier." She scowls at me. The grimace deepens the wrinkles on her face even more. "And don't tell me you don't throw orgies when I saw that redhead coming to join you two."

Oh God, she saw me kissing Noah only in my underwear and a see-through shirt. That's how Sam probably found out Noah was with me. Ms. Robbins must have told her. The whole building will probably know by tomorrow.

Ugh. I'm going to die of embarrassment.

"C'mon, Ms. Robbins, we both know you don't sleep past four a.m. in your old age," I say as I roll my eyes at her. "And we did close the door; we were just kissing, not having sex. Stop being dramatic," I grumble. The tips of my ears will probably catch fire if this encounter doesn't end soon.

"It sure looked like you were having sex to me. You were as good as naked," she says vehemently, pointing an accusatory finger at me while inserting the key in the lock of her door, mumbling, "Kids nowadays don't have manners anymore. Everyone has sex in plain sight."

Noah is waiting patiently for her to open the door. Judging by the big smile on his face, he doesn't want this impromptu meeting to end as soon as I do.

Ms. Robbins finally opens the door and winks at Noah cheekily. "I wouldn't have minded, though, if you were the naked one."

A surprised laugh bubbles out of me. I don't know if I should be shocked or cringe in awkwardness. That's a side of Ms. Robbins I haven't seen before.

"Do you want me to bring these in for you, ma'am?" Noah asks, his big smile not at all bothered by her remark.

"Oh, if you don't mind, sure. Right there in the kitchen." She moves aside to let Noah pass. "Maybe you could stay for some tea. She's not invited, though," she says before she throws me another dirty look from the doorway.

"Yeah, like I'm not the one taking you to all your doctor appointments or buying your groceries weekly. I forget one week, and suddenly I'm the Devil," I mutter under my breath, thinking Ms. Robbins didn't hear me, but she definitely did because she snaps her head back at me with a scowl.

"I can't right now, unfortunately; I have somewhere to be. Maybe another time," Noah tells her charmingly while exiting the apartment.

"Anytime you want," Ms. Robbins shoots back. Her smile is so big that you can see the entirety of her dentures. She then closes the door, not sparing me another glance.

"I like her," Noah says as he closes the distance between us on the small hallway.

"Yeah, I bet, since you bring out her inner cougar."

He chuckles at my response, and we start descending the stairs at the same time.

16

"I can't believe you still have Betsy. I also can't believe the engine didn't die on you when you started it," I say incredulously from the passenger seat of Noah's old, red Toyota pickup as I look through the window, watching the city pass by.

Oddly, I don't feel anxious at all about being in a moving car. Maybe the motorcycle ride with Kaiden cured me of my panic attacks. At least, I hope that's the case. Or I have just really missed Betsy and the musty smell that always seems to cling to the interior, mixing with Noah's cologne. It smells like memories—all the times he unsuccessfully tried to teach me how to drive, our date, especially the moments after he drove me back to my aunt's house when we made-out in the backseat. It feels like all that happened a lifetime ago.

"I put it in storage before I left. I couldn't bring myself to sell it. My mom tried to convince me to take it to the auto park numerous times and get a new car, but I'm glad I didn't listen to her. I have too many good memories attached to it," Noah shoots back while changing gears, snapping me out of my thoughts.

His right hand on the stick shift grazes my thigh slightly with the movement. A shiver goes down the ladder of my spine at the contact. I gulp as the car's interior shrinks all of a sudden. So much for being cured. Claustrophobia carves a path in the lining of my stomach. It's nothing new, but still, I mentally prepare myself in case it gets worse.

He turns his head to look at me, drawing my attention from the window. "How are you feeling? You seem to be doing better with being in a car…"

"Yeah, well, a lot of things have changed since you left. I still dread it, but it's nothing like it used to be. I'm fine today, no panic attack on the horizon," I reply softly.

Noah nods in response. I'm grateful he doesn't feel the need to fill the empty space with meaningless chit-chat. That's one of the things I missed the most about him. We ride in companionable silence until we reach the parking lot of the national park. There are no free spots, so we have to circle it a few times before we finally manage to find one.

It's a beautiful cloudless day, the sun high in the sky, and with summer right around the corner, it isn't a surprise the parking lot is so full, even if it is only Tuesday. The park is vastly different during the day. People are all around us as we walk on the path to Shadow Lake, jogging, taking a stroll, or sprawled on blankets where they could find a clearing, enjoying the sun while reading or eating their picnics, happy and oblivious to the true horrors of our world.

The idyllic scene is heightened by the sun rays flickering through the trees, dancing on the forest floor, and the happy trill of bird songs. The fragrant pine-scented air is warm and pleasant, without the bite mountain air usually still carries in the spring.

It takes us about thirty minutes of brisk walking to reach the lake. Since there are so many people around us, we can't use supernatural hellseeker speed to get there faster.

"I think this is the spot where I killed the draconic ravengers," I tell Noah as we reach the clearing where the demons were waiting for me on Friday night. The new onyx stone I'm wearing in a choker around my neck, resembling my older one, warms slightly at the remnants of demon activity that haven't completely disappeared, the soil still holding the darkness of their goopy tar-like blood. Here and there, holes stand out in the vibrant green grass, where the earth looks scorched and dead.

"And those other flying demons came at me from the direction of the lake." I point my finger toward the lake. "When I saw them flying at warp speed toward me, I realized I was neck deep in shit, and I started running really fast, the fastest I have ever ran in my entire life and went through those trees." I point again with my finger, this time to the pine trees on my right.

"Lead the way," Noah says from my back. He keeps up with me as I start retracing my failed escape route.

After fifteen minutes of walking in silence, we reach the spot where I was attacked by the umbra. Ice sloshes through my veins at the memory of how much pain I was in. Slamming my eyes shut, I breathe in and out a few times in an attempt to regain my composure.

As I turn in a circle and take in the scenery before my eyes, I can't believe I survived something that left so much destruction in its wake. When the umbra grabbed me, I couldn't register anything else. But now that I can see all of it…the whole perimeter surrounding us looks as if a violent forest fire ravaged the vegetation, the trees almost completely obliterated.

A flash catches my peripheral vision as I turn to my right again, and I have to blink a few times, because what I'm seeing is more than ridiculous. A transparent human-shaped form is sitting on a badly burnt branch that clearly can't support any weight. As I get closer, the humanoid form morphs into a solid, dark-skinned, bare-chested young man, wearing only a sequined pair of golden pants, with a shaved head and a bored expression. Did Sam drug me or something? I'm going to kill her if she spiked the potion she made me drink. Noah is silent beside me, taking in the destruction before our eyes.

"Um, Noah? Do you see that? On top of that branch, there?" I tilt my head to my right, where the strange willowy guy is swinging his legs in a childish manner.

"What? I don't see anything. What did you see?" Noah arches his eyebrow before he throws me a weird look.

"Nothing. I think I'm still a little hungover," I mumble. "Fucking Sam," I swear under my breath, for my ears only. When I turn my head to look at the strange guy again, he's gone.

Great, now I'm hallucinating on top of everything.

"Iris, I have to ask. How the hell did you survive this and manage to escape? I have never seen something like this before…not even in my years working for the Kabal." Noah's gravelly voice and piercing gray-blue eyes snap me out of the long list of profanities I'm addressing Sam in my head.

"I honestly don't know. I didn't even realize it was this bad until now," my voice trails off at the end. Of course I know. Kaiden was how I survived. Jesus, Noah is right; no Order member could have survived this, not even with the pure blood running through their veins, and I am a half-blood. How is this possible? I mean, even if Kaiden didn't intervene and if the umbra did so much damage only by grabbing my arm, how did I not die on the spot, right then and there? Could it be possible that the umbra didn't do this? But who could have so much power…Kaiden?

"I'm going to see how much the burnt area expands. I also need to take some videos and photos to send to the Kabal with my report. Are you coming?"

"No, go ahead. I'm just going to stay here until you finish. I, um, I need a few moments." I gulp and snap my eyes shut, remembering the searing pain as the bony, shadowy fingers circled my throat.

"Hey, are you okay?" Noah comes closer. His fingers wrap around my shoulders.

I open my eyes and stare at his perfect face. Why does he have to be so stunningly beautiful? With his sparkling eyes, bedroom hair, and perfectly contoured pouty lips, he looks like he just stepped off a runway. It isn't fair at all.

He's not Kaiden, though, the nagging voice in my brain pipes out.

Shut up!

"Iris?" he asks again, and I shake my head to clear my mind.

"Yeah, I'm fine…go, I'll wait for you here until you finish."

"Are you sure?" A glint of worry shines in his eyes.

"One hundred, I just, I can't believe I survived this," I mumble.

"Yeah, it's weird you managed to escape. If the forest looks this bad, I can't even imagine how you looked…and you don't even have a scratch on you." He narrows his eyes, looking me up and down as if he's trying to figure out whether I'm lying or not.

Great, me and my big mouth.

Why did I have to say that out loud? It's like painting a huge red sign on my forehead that says *liar* in capital letters. Coming here with Noah was definitely not a smart move, but what could I have done instead? Refusing to show him the spot would have looked even more suspicious.

"I told you, Sam is an amazing witch. She brought me back to life," I shoot back, my stomach a ball of restless energy.

Ugh. I hate lying.

"But she's only a light witch, right?" His eyes narrow even further with his question.

"Yeah, she draws her power from earth-bound elements only," I answer firmly, hoping my tone is sure enough to stop his string of questions.

"Hmm. Then she must be the most powerful light witch on Earth," Noah's voice hardens.

Maybe he believed me before, but seeing the destruction left behind, he's starting to doubt my story. Noah is too smart. I suddenly feel like I'm being put in the hot seat, and he's interrogating me.

My throat bobs as I swallow. "Sam comes from a very powerful coven; her ancestors are known worldwide for their healing potions. Are you going to go take those pictures? I don't want to stay here more than necessary." I can't stand the pressure of having to lie any longer. I don't like it. At all. At least I didn't lie about Sam's ancestors or coven, but he's right; even if light magic is the only one able to heal, there's no way it could have cured me. Not completely anyway.

Noah sighs, clearly unhappy with my answer, but he lets go of my shoulders, dropping the interrogation. "Okay, I'll be back in a few minutes. Wait right here," he says as he puts more and more distance between us.

"I'm not going anywhere," I shout at his back and expel a deep breath, relieved.

I don't know what I expected from coming here. I don't even want to think what Grayson will do when he sees the pictures and the videos. He's definitely suspicious about my report. Maybe Noah will only send those to the Kabal and not show them to Grayson.

"I wish my life wasn't so complicated," I groan loudly, looking at the sky.

"At least you're still alive, buttercup," a chirpy voice says from beside me all of a sudden. I screech because there are no people in this area. The voice comes from the strangely dressed guy who was sitting on the tree branch earlier. He popped out of thin air exactly like Kaiden, right next to me. I didn't even know demons could do that until Kaiden.

149

I only thought archangels and seraphim could appear and disappear at whim. But I had never met an Elite demon before, either. However, this guy can't be a demon because my onyx stone didn't alert me of his presence. Maybe the strong demon activity left over from the umbra is messing with it.

I immediately take a few steps back. "What the fuck are you? And why are you half-naked and wearing sequined pants in the middle of the day?" I ask menacingly as I take the whip out of its holster and uncoil it in a swift, experienced motion.

"If I told you, it wouldn't be fun anymore, now would it?" he answers calmly, with a bored expression painting his face as he looks at his fingernails and rubs them on his naked chest. Then he snaps his fingers in front of my face. "Now focus, buttercup, 'cause I've been waiting for a long time for someone to finally see me. I need your help. My friend is in danger."

"What friend? What are you talking about?"

His mouth slants, and deep concentration draws his eyebrows together as he presses his fingers into his temples. "Fuck. It's getting harder and harder to remember. I forgot her name. You need to help her. She's my friend. They're watching her, and she's —"

Suddenly, his form starts flickering like a bad lightbulb, cutting off his sentence. When it finally settles, his demeanor does a one eighty, his face serene as if I'm talking to a different person entirely. The change is so abrupt it gives me whiplash. "Now tell me, where is that gorgeous specimen of a man that saved you on Friday night?" he demands in a sing-song.

"Who? You were there when I was attacked?" I ask, bewildered.

He disappears again and reappears closer to me. "Oh, you know. The hunk with shoulder length midnight hair, tattoos all over, delicious man candy." He winks at me and pops off. I search for him in a circle, and he appears right in front of me again, his face a hair's breadth away from mine while floating a few inches above the ground.

Did Sam put acid in that hungover cure?

I throw out my leg in a powerful kick, but it goes straight through him, his body rippling like water where my leg was supposed to touch him.

"Ugh, so rude. You hellseekers have no manners," he puffs and rolls his eyes at me.

"Wait, are you…a ghost?" I can't believe I just asked that, but there's no other explanation for what I'm seeing. No, I'm hallucinating…it can't be. I can't see ghosts. *I mean, what the fuck?* I'm just a hellseeker. Only seers, angels, and the fallen angels of the City of Ghosts are able to see spirits. I'm definitely not part of any of those categories. "You were talking about your friend before, the one that needs help?"

He tilts his head before his eyebrows knit. "Huh? What friend? I don't know what you're talking about. And wipe that frown off your pretty little face, buttercup; it's going to leave some deep wrinkles," he scolds me as he passes right through me, leaving a trail of goosebumps behind.

Gah, that felt weird.

"And yes…I'm a ghost…unfortunately. Good thing I got rid of that awful wig and mustache I was wearing before I died. Imagine me with a fake mustache for the rest of eternity," he sighs dramatically.

I shudder and turn on my heel to face the mysterious half-naked ghost. Nothing could have prepared me for this. I mean, am I having some sort of a lucid dream? I pinch myself for good measure. *Ouch.* No, no such luck. There's only one explanation; Sam and her fucking hangover cure.

Narrowing my eyes at him, I say, "Nope, I refuse to believe you're real. I can't possibly see ghosts; I'm just a hellseeker. This is all happening in my head."

"This is real, all right." He snaps his fingers, a smug look on his face. All of a sudden, his body is covered in gruesome wounds that look like a lion mauled him, or better yet, a draconic ravenger. His neck is so threadbare that I can see the pine trees through it. It barely supports his head. And the chest is nothing more than a mangled cavernous hole where his heart should have been. Compared to everything else, the tattered sequined pants don't even faze me.

My eyes almost bulge out of my head. "What happened to you?" I ask as I bring my fingers to my O-shaped lips.

"Oh, you know, just your friendly neighborhood wolf shifter. I was having a very fun make-out session here in the forest with a gorgeous firefighter I had just picked up at a Halloween bonfire party near the lake. I always wanted to be Freddy Mercury; hence the fabulous pants." He shrugs and yawns dramatically.

"Who are you speaking to?" Noah's voice startles me. I was so absorbed by the ghost/freaky hallucination—I'm still not sure which one—that I didn't even see or feel him approach.

"No one," I reply quickly, trying to come up with an excuse for addressing the air. "I was singing this song I can't get out of my head," I mumble the first thing that comes to my mind while coiling and putting the whip back in its holster.

"How rude," the ghost, who is now back to having no wounds on his body, says while hovering in front of a completely oblivious Noah.

"Tony. Enchanté!" The specter extends his hand toward Noah, but his fingers go right through his right arm. "You are not the broody dark-haired stud I wanted to see today, but you're not too bad yourself, pretty boy. I'm more of a tortured soul and bad boy type of a man, but you could do just fine." The ghost/hallucination apparently named Tony is now stroking Noah's cheek, his fingers disappearing into the side of his face.

I scowl at Tony and clear my throat loudly. "Did you find where the burnt area ends?"

"Yeah...it extends pretty far from here. I also took photos and everything I needed for my report."

"So, can we go now?" I'm having trouble concentrating on my conversation with Noah because Tony is now trying to lick his face.

What the hell?!

It's official. I belong in the looney bin.

"Sure." He frowns. "Why are you looking at me like that? Do I have something on my face?" Noah asks, raising a questioning eyebrow at me and wiping at his face with his right hand as we start making our way back to the car.

"No, you're perfect," I answer while I try really hard not to stare at Tony again, who is twirling like a ballerina in front of us.

"Uh, damn straight you are, pretty boy!" Tony exclaims dramatically as he pops in front of Noah and bats his eyelashes at him.

Noah smiles widely at my remark. I realize my mistake and roll my eyes, trying to play it cool. "I mean, you don't have anything on your face. I'm just hungry. I haven't eaten at all since I woke up." My stomach grumbles loudly as if suddenly awakened by my words. Why does it always do this in the presence of hot guys? Heat scorches the shells of my ears.

"Smooth." Tony nods while laughing at my expense, now floating on my left side. Noah laughs too at my awkwardness as he takes my hand in his and starts tracing circles in my palm with his thumb. The heat of his skin radiates all the way up my arm.

"Do you want to grab something to eat?" Noah asks as he walks beside me on the path, not letting go of my hand. We look like a couple taking a stroll in the park, and I know I'm giving him mixed signals by letting him hold my hand, but I just don't have the heart to let it go. He seems so happy that I didn't pull away, and it also feels nice.

"Um, sure," I respond.

17

Jane's Diner is one of the oldest restaurants in Ashville. It's quaint and cozy, squeezed between two Victorian-style buildings in the oldest part of town, on a small street not too far from my apartment. It's the place I always go to when I feel like eating a burger. It's also one of the places we used to hang out before, Noah and I, and sometimes even Sam would join us. But that was before Noah and his family left the country five years ago.

"This place hasn't changed at all," Noah says as he opens the restaurant door for me to enter. He parked a few streets over, and we walked to the diner. In the car, he asked me a lot of questions about my life since he's been gone, and about Sam's flower shop and business. All that while still holding my hand and me pretending a ghost/freaky hallucination wasn't following every step we took. He even rode in the car with us, making non-stop comments from the backseat about how hot Noah is.

Jesus, the craziness in my life keeps stacking up like a bad game of Tetris.

"Thank you, sweety!" Tony chirps happily at Noah, throwing him a megawatt smile as he floats right through my body to enter the restaurant before I can. A shudder passes violently from the tips of my hair all the way to my toes.

"Can you stop doing that?" I hiss under my breath at Tony. He turns around and sticks his tongue out at me.

"What?" Noah asks dubiously from behind me.

Noted. I probably shouldn't talk to the ghost since I'm the only one able to see it, and I don't want to look certifiably insane. I clear my throat and turn my head toward Noah. "I said, yeah, it's the same. Nothing much has changed here in Ashville since you've been gone." I shrug, following Tony through the door and looking at the restaurant's interior.

The walls are covered in white-washed oak panel wood, the bar and tables made of a darker cherry wood, and the floor is in a navy and white tile checkboard pattern. A few tables are occupied, and a group of girls start giggling loudly and whispering while looking at Noah.

"Oh my God! He's so hot!" one of them says to the others as we pass their table. I roll my eyes at that and peek at Noah, who seems to ignore them completely. Maybe he's being polite; the girls are so loud, there's no chance in hell he didn't hear them.

We take a seat at one of the orange leather booths, Noah sitting across from me, with Tony squeezed between him and the window. He's looking at the menu over Noah's shoulder, pretending to be invested in picking something to eat. I pinch the bridge of my nose hard and try to understand how in the world I'm seeing a ghost that just doesn't want to go away.

Donna, the waitress who's been working here since the first time I stepped foot in the diner a few years back, approaches our table. "Hey, Iris! Will you be having the usual?" she asks me with a big smile. She is a middle-aged woman with beautiful oval-shaped hazel eyes, thick lashes, and chocolate brown hair pulled in a low ponytail, with a few strands of gray showing through.

"Hi, Donna. Yes, thank you!" I smile back at her.

"And what about you, handsome? What can I bring you?" she asks Noah with the same warm smile—the kind that forms deep wrinkles at the corners of her eyes.

"I'll have the Texas chilly burger and a beer. Thank you, Donna!" Noah says as he lifts his head from the menu.

"Christ on a cracker!" Donna exclaims loudly, her eyes bugging out of her head. "Noah, is that you? When did you come back? Look at you! I almost didn't recognize you. You're all grown-up!" She shakes her head and sighs while fanning herself with her pad. "If only I were fifteen years younger."

"Back off my man candy, lady!" Tony hisses at her. I roll my eyes because there is nothing else I can do.

"I just arrived yesterday," Noah shoots back with a lopsided grin.

"Well, I hope you're not going to be leaving again; otherwise, some other man is going to swoop right in and snatch Iris here and leave you in the dust." She winks at me. "She did bring some of her dates here, but none of the guys were as handsome as you," she whispers conspiratorially to Noah. "There were also no repeats, so I think you're lucky." She winks again, this time at Noah.

"Donna," I scold her and blush fiercely.

"I'm not planning on leaving, and trust me, I know I'm lucky," Noah says as he places his right hand over mine on the table. All humor is gone from his face, and his gray-blue eyes sparkle with resolve as he looks deeply into mine. A fresh wave of heat scorches my cheeks while I clear my throat in an attempt to break the intensity that seems to shimmer in the air between us.

"Oh, you two look like the perfect couple," Donna gushes over us.

"I'll be right back with your orders." She backs away from our table, making a beeline for the kitchen.

"I'll have a Noah, please! Two hot buns and Noah in the middle with a side of mayo," Tony yells after her. Then, he resumes what seems to be his favorite activity: batting his eyelashes dreamily at Noah with his head propped on his hand.

I clear my throat again and slide my hands from under Noah's. "I'm going to the restroom. I'll be right back," I say as I stand up from the booth.

"Okay," Noah replies, looking at me, a soft smile turning up the corners of his perfectly shaped lips.

"Oh! We are finally alone! What do you want to do?" Tony squeals ostentatiously at Noah as I shuffle to the bathroom.

I quickly text Sam while I wait for the person in the restroom to come out. It's a very small bathroom that can only accommodate one person.

> **Me: Can you talk?**

> **Sam: Shoot. I'm not busy.**

Entering the restroom, I lock the door while tapping my finger over Sam's contact. I wait for her to answer as I look at my reflection in the mirror.

"So, how's Prince Charming?" Sam's voice travels through the phone.

"What the fuck did you put in that thing you made me drink?" I ask, my tone dripping with ire. "I'm having hallucinations, Sam! Did you fucking drug me?" I whisper-yell.

"Whoa! I didn't put anything in it to make you hallucinate. I promise. I would never do that, weirdo. Not on purpose, anyway. What kind of hallucinations?"

"I'm seeing a ghost! A bare-chested, gay black ghost only wearing a pair of sequined gold pants. He followed Noah and me from the national park to Jane's diner. He is now sitting next to Noah in the booth, batting his eyelashes at him." I run my hand over my face at how stupid this sounds.

There is a big pause on the line. I'm pretty sure Sam is shocked by all the insane that just spilled from my mouth. "I honestly don't know what to say to that. Are you the only one that can see this presumed ghost?"

"Yes! His name is Tony. I couldn't make this shit up even if I tried. Am I going crazy?" I ask with desperation in my tone.

"Tony? Who names their kid Tony? It sounds like the perfect name for a forty-year-old Italian mobster."

As if summoned by our talk, Tony suddenly appears in the bathroom at my back, scaring the living shit out of me. I scream loudly into the phone as I clutch my chest with my free hand.

"Uh ruuude! Why are you gossiping about me?" he lifts his nose in the air, seemingly offended. "If you really want to know, my mother was obsessed with *The Sopranos* when she was pregnant with me." He rolls his eyes dramatically. "Trust me, I've been bullied enough over it." He sticks his tongue out at me before he disappears abruptly. *Oh, God.* Now I have upset the ghost. I'm feeling weirdly guilty about it.

"Miss, are you okay?" a man's voice travels through the door as someone knocks.

"I'm fine! I just saw a spider," I reply, trying to still my rapid pulse.

"What just happened?" Sam's urgent voice catches my attention.

"He appeared in the bathroom, Sam. He was upset we were gossiping about him. He said his mom was obsessed with *The Sopranos* while pregnant. I'm losing my marbles, aren't I?"

"Oh, that makes sense…about the name," Sam observes calmly. "What if it really is a ghost? I didn't put anything weird in that hangover cure. I swear. Maybe those demons did something to your brain when you were attacked in the woods."

"And how can I test that out?"

"Well, you can try throwing some salt at it. If it disappears, it truly is a ghost; if not…you're fucked."

"I think I'm fucked either way. I mean, how could I be seeing a ghost? I'm just a hellseeker," I exasperate as I massage two fingers into my temple, trying to keep the imminent headache at bay.

"Calm down. Try throwing some salt at it first, see what happens, and then if he doesn't disappear, we will cross that bridge when you come to it."

"Okay, I can do that." I blow out a breath, trying to regain some normalcy and crawl out of the crazy pit I found myself in. "There's also something that doesn't sit right with me. Immediately after Tony appeared in front of me, he asked for my help, saying that he waited a long time for someone to finally notice him. He said his friend is in danger but that he can't remember her name. He also said something about people watching her, and then all of a sudden, he started flickering. When he materialized again, he seemed to have had a personality transplant and started fawning over Noah like a love-sick puppy. I even asked him about it, but it was like I was talking to a different person. Do you think he suffers from a multiple personality disorder, or should I check myself in at a mental hospital already?" I ask as I pinch the bridge of my nose.

"Hmm, interesting," Sam mumbles, and I can almost hear the gears turning in her head. "Grammie had a friend who was a seer. She died last year, so I can't call her to ask about this. However, I remember her telling me a few years back that ghosts are supposed to pass over to the other side quickly after their death, but some remain anchored to the human world because of unfinished business. Unfortunately, because they're not supposed to be here anymore, the longer they remain on Earth and refuse to cross over, their minds will slip further away until there is nothing left but a shadow of their old selves. That's why most of the ghosts that spend too much time on Earth turn into poltergeists; they eventually go mad, forgetting why they stayed in the first place."

"Wow, that's really sad…and it fits with Tony's sudden memory loss."

"Did he mention something about his death? Ghosts with violent deaths are usually the ones who refuse to cross. They want justice."

"He was mauled to death by a wolf shifter right next to Shadow Lake at a Halloween party. He showed me how his body looked when he died. He didn't even have a heart anymore, Sam."

"Shit."

"I know. But still, Tony didn't seem to want justice for his death; he was quite blasé about it in contrast to his friend needing help. All I gathered from the conversation is that the friend is a woman."

"Maybe we can help him cross over," Sam muses. "I'll look online, see if I can find something about his death or any information about his family or friends. If he reappears, ask him again about her. Perhaps it will help spark some moments of lucidity. Remember, if he acts crazy, just throw some salt at him. Let me know how it goes. A customer just walked in. Talk to you later. Love you."

"Love you too." My fingers white-knuckle the sink as I drop my head between my shoulders. Then, I look up in the mirror. "You are a badass hellseeker. If a souldrake doesn't scare you, a ghost named Tony should be a piece of cake," I say to my reflection and get out of the bathroom.

One of the two girls waiting in line huffs loudly, "Finally!" when I come out. I roll my eyes at her and amble to the table. Noah is typing something on his phone, and Tony is nowhere to be seen.

"I was getting worried. I was two minutes away from coming to get you," Noah says as his gaze finds mine.

"Sorry, I started feeling sick again," I lie, yet again. Albeit it's a small one, but I want the lies to stop, small or big. Lying is far more exhausting than I expected it to be.

The sound of Noah's phone ringing cuts through the thick awkwardness that blankets the air between us. "Sorry, I have to take this, and then I'll be all yours." He smiles charmingly at me, melting my insides. "It will only take two minutes."

"Sure, no worries," I reply, and he takes long, purposeful strides toward the exit.

"Here's your food. Enjoy!" Donna smiles sweetly at me as she slides the plates with steaming hot burgers and French fries on the table.

"Where's my hot Noah burger?" Tony pops out of thin air next to me, scowling at Donna. "The service here is terrible!" He crosses his arms in front of his chest and pouts.

It takes a lot of effort not to flinch at his sudden appearance. "Thank you, Donna!" I say with a brittle smile as Donna backs away from the table to take the order from a couple that just walked in.

I slide my phone out of my pocket and put it to my ear, pretending I'm calling someone so I don't look batshit crazy to the other patrons as I lock eyes with Tony and say, "Tony, listen to me. I believe you're still here for a reason. You mentioned a friend of yours needing help. I think she's a woman."

A flicker of recognition passes over his features, and the first version of Tony, the one that appeared in the national park, surfaces again as his form ripples. "Yes, she's my friend. She needs help…they're coming for her," he whispers.

His sadness is so palpable it makes my eyes mist. "Who is coming for her?"

"I don't know. They are lurking in the shadows. I can't see their faces. But they're always watching…waiting."

"Can you try remembering her name? Or some details that I can use to track her down? How did you two meet?"

A few moments of silence pass as his fingers clench and unclench in his lap, and his jaw tenses with visible effort. He starts hitting his head repeatedly with his hands, saying, "I can't! I can't! I can't! I need to help her," anguish coating every word.

"Calm down, please," I say in a soothing tone.

He doesn't seem to hear me as horror fills his eyes as if he remembered something. A silent tear crests his eyelashes before it trickles down his cheek. "He hurt her; he almost killed her. I tried to warn her. I screamed and screamed and screamed, and no one heard me." The brief moment of clarity seems to dissipate like sand between his fingers as he howls at the top of his lungs, "NO ONE!" like a broken record while he starts flying through the room at breakneck speed, bouncing off the walls.

The overhead neon lights start flickering, and the sound of a plate being smashed to the floor in the kitchen slices through the air. The patrons seem oblivious, though, to the ghost having a meltdown in the tiny restaurant. Their murmured conversation is a humming buzz that fades into Tony's ear-splitting shrieks. They ring so loudly that I'm surprised blood doesn't trickle down from my eardrums.

As inconspicuously as I can, I pour some salt from the shaker on the table in the palm of my hand and wait. The moment he passes my table, I throw it in the air at his rapidly moving form.

He halts. "You witch!" Tony screeches, pointing an accusatory finger at me.

At first, nothing happens, and I deflate like a balloon, thinking I've got more than one screw loose, but in the next second, his form seems to thin, and static takes over like a bad-functioning old tube TV. He disappears with a bright light and a small pop. Just in time, because Noah walks back into the restaurant.

Huh, so he really is a ghost.

I sigh and thank God.

18

I'm in the passenger seat of a car spinning at a startling speed. The smell of burnt rubber is so potent, it burns a hole through my brain. My stomach dips, and a horrible feeling churns in my gut as the car lurches over the side of the road. We start rolling into the canyon on our right, the car making sickening crunching noises.

Pine trees abruptly stop our fall, and my teeth clamp together with the force of the jarring impact. A fresh burst of red-hot pain shoots through me as I hit the side of my head on the window. The airbag unexpectedly inflates and smacks into my face while I try gasping for air. Looking through my window, I take a deep breath and exhale in relief when I see we still have a long way to go until we reach the bottom of the canyon. The car is rolled on its right side, held in place by the trees.

Thank God for the trees!

I turn my head slowly to look at my mother. She's passed out, her head and nose heavily bleeding. She hit her head on the roof pretty badly when the car was rolling. Grabbing her right shoulder, I try waking her up. "Mom, are *you okay? Please wake up! We need to get out of the car," I say with urgency as tears start falling from my eyes. She doesn't respond to any of my attempts.*

Suddenly, there is a loud crack, and the car jostles violently.

No, no, no, no, no, no, no.

Please don't!

Panic punches a hole through my chest as the pine trees start snapping under the weight of the car one by one, losing the fight with gravity. With a sickening, loud snapping sound as the last tree splits, we start rolling again into the abyss. Metal crunches and gives way. Terror-filled shrieks rip from my lungs, but I can't hear anything over the ringing in my ears and the pounding in my chest.

I wake with a violent start, screaming and shaking, my body propelled forward in a sitting position with the force of the terrible nightmare. Sweat covers every inch of my skin.

Oh, God, Mom. I saw Mom.

I can't believe it.

We were in a car; she was hurt.

My stomach fists into a ball, and the urge to throw up overtakes my entire body as bile floods my mouth. I try to get up as fast as I can, wanting to reach the bathroom in time, but my legs feel weak, disjointed, so I end up vomiting the contents of my stomach all over the rug on my bedroom floor.

After I finish retching my last meal on the fluffy white carpet, I remain there, on my knees, in my underwear, not caring about the mess I made as tears stream down my cheeks mercilessly.

The first year after waking up in that hospital, I would get nightmares as violent as these almost every night. The nightmares dwindled as the years went by. I now get them only a few days a week, two or even one if I'm lucky. One thing is constant, though: I never ever remember what I dreamed about — until now. And it wasn't just a dream; it was a memory. I'm sure of it. I can feel it in the very fabric of my soul.

My first memory.

While it's a horrible thing to remember, the car crash that changed the course of my life forever, and even if it made me sick, I'm grateful for it, to be able to have something back from my old life. And the image of my mom, I'm the most grateful for that; even bloody and unconscious, she still looked like an angel.

I don't know how much time passes while I just sit here, trying to remember every single snippet of the horrible flashback, memorizing my mother's face. If only I could have more.

Just a little more.

A dull headache blooms in the back of my head, and I hope it won't get worse. Since the umbra attack, I have been getting headaches every single day. Some more time passes before I sigh and press my palms on the floor to stand up. My legs fell asleep since I spent so much time in the same position, and now they're full of pins and needles. I do a little dance, trying to shake the weird sensation off. Bending at the waist, I roll the rug, pick it up from the floor, and take it into the kitchen.

Going back to the bedroom, I slip on an oversized T-shirt then shuffle back to the kitchen. After twenty minutes of scrubbing the rug with a brush, I still can't get the stain off. It's ruined, the stain permanently marring the pristine white of the fibers, just like the stain left behind by the crash on my life.

With a deep sigh, I make my way to the bathroom and crank the hot water almost to the max before I step into the shower. I need it to scorch my skin. To cleanse not only the tears and sweat from my body but also the awful feeling of guilt that always clings to me whenever I remember I'm the one who survived and my mom suffered a horrible death.

Sadly, when I step out, I don't feel any better, so I decide to go for a run. The walls of the apartment suddenly feel too small, closing up on me and making me feel claustrophobic. I need some fresh air. Besides, I have to work out anyway. I go through the motions of getting ready, while the fact that Kaiden hasn't contacted me since sending me those texts gnaws at me.

What is wrong with you? He's a demon, Iris.

Dark clouds are rolling in on the portion of gray sky visible from my arched windows, so I grab a light jacket from my closet and quickly put it on. I decide to leave my phone at home since I don't feel like listening to music. I need peace to be able to sift through my feelings.

As I exit the apartment building and stretch my calves a little, the rain starts with a light drizzle. The fine droplets of water stick to my braided hair and eyelashes when I begin running, the soles of my sneakers pounding on the asphalt, making splashing noises as the rain intensifies. Today, the air is cooler. It fills my lungs and burns my nose as I inhale deeply, picking up speed.

Even if it's raining, people are out and about, huddled under umbrellas or wandering into restaurants or cafes. It's Saturday, a little past noon, so naturally, everyone wants to enjoy the first day of their weekend.

After lunch with Noah and Tony, Noah walked me home and kissed me sweetly on the forehead, not making any attempts for more, and I haven't seen him since. He's probably busy with classified missions from the Kabal. Thankfully, the rest of the week went on without a hitch or any more craziness. I think I had enough in those first few days to last me a lifetime.

Tony also hasn't shown his face again, but I plan to research his death and see if I can find something about his friend. Sam didn't get the chance to look into it since she was crazy busy with her flower boutique.

There is one thing that's still extremely strange, though: the streets are clear of demons. In all the years working for the Order, I have never had multiple nights of not finding even one demon to kill. It's like the umbra made them go into hiding; at least, that's one of the theories I came up with. Not like I can ask anyone about this aside from Kaiden; he's the only person I know who can give me more information about the ancient demons.

My aunt hasn't found anything about them in the library yet, either. I've been texting her multiple times a day about it, and I think she'll probably want to hurl her phone at my head the next time she sees me, but not finding even one clue about the umbra and who's behind the trap is making my skin itch.

Taking a turn at the end of the street, following my usual running route to the national park, where I can tap into the hellseeker speed and run faster, deep into the forest with no people around, I remember I promised Sam I would go out with her tonight to Sin. *Ugh.* I really don't feel like it; I just want to binge-watch the rest of *The Vampire Diaries* season, eat until my stomach feels too full, and stuff my face with ice cream.

As soon as I get home from my run, my clothes drenched from the pouring rain dripping on the floorboards of my small apartment, a few missed calls and messages flood the screen of my phone — all of them, of course, from my psycho best friend.

Sam: Iris, you better answer the phone!

Hecate, help me; if you're ignoring me on purpose,

I'm going to hex your flat ass.

You're going out with me tonight whether you like it

or not!

Iris Harper, you better not be dead in a ditch

somewhere.

> **If you don't answer the phone in the next two hours,**
>
> **I'll send a SWAT team to your apartment.**
>
> **Or better yet, Ms. Robbins.**
>
> **Iris, I'm getting worried. Seriously, though, let me**
>
> **know you're safe! Love you! Xx**

I guess me almost dying a week ago brought up the mother hen in Sam. She always felt protective of me, though, ever since finding me huddled in a corner of the school's bathroom eight years ago, crying pathetically because I let Bitchasaurus Rex and her friends bully me. Even if she pushes my buttons and makes me crazy sometimes, I love her to pieces.

She's my favorite person in the world, the sister I always wished I had. But you don't need to share blood with someone for them to become your family. I quickly type a reply, not wanting her to be more stressed out than she already is.

> **Me: I'm alive...just went for a run and left my phone**
>
> **at home. Don't worry about me. I'll see you later.**
>
> **Kick ass at the wedding! Love you too! Xx**

She works her ass off with the flower arrangements she does for events, and she is now two towns over, making sure everything is perfect at a wedding of a very influential couple. She must be stressed to the max. This is one of the biggest jobs she has ever gotten, and if it all goes well, she will finally be able to open a second flower shop here in Ashville — something she has been wanting to do for a long time now.

I spend the next few hours slumped under a blanket on my couch, laptop perched in my lap as I research every death caused by an animal attack that happened around Halloween. None of the articles I found online mentioned Tony's death, though. Which is weird since the news covered a few deaths similar to his before and after Halloween about a year and a half ago, all of the victims with their hearts missing. I even go through the obituary section from the past two years. But again, no mention of Tony.

The news anchor's voice announcing the gruesome death of a woman in the national park following an animal attack is bouncing off the walls of the apartment when Sam barrels through my front door. Her emerald gaze flits to my slumped body on the couch. "You look like shit. Did something happen?" In stark contrast to her words, Sam looks like a million bucks, dressed in a chic chartreuse pantsuit with a cream blouse underneath, her hair in a sleek bun. But I don't miss the strain evident in the lines around her eyes and the dark circles under them.

"Wow, you're not mincing words tonight," I mutter as I pause the old video and place the laptop on the coffee table, closing it. She's right, though. The last time I caught my reflection in the mirror, I looked like a hot mess. I haven't been able to shake the dream and the memory of my mother for the first time in eight years. Since coming home from my run, I got into couch potato mode. I've only gotten up to receive the pizza delivery and to go to the bathroom.

Sam sighs deeply while she toes off her slingbacks. She drops her designer tote bag on the kitchen table before stopping in front of me. "So, I guess we're not going out tonight after all?" she asks, pouting.

"I really, really don't feel like it, Sam. Seriously. Not even for a million dollars, and I still don't think I can drink alcohol just yet. My stomach is still pissed at me for mixing vodka and wine like a dumbass. I can't even be in the vicinity of alcohol."

"C'mon, scoot over and make some room for me," Sam says bossily as she pushes my legs out of the way. She plops down and steals half of my blanket while narrowing her mossy green eyes at me. "You better have a good reason for not wanting to go out." She takes off her suit jacket, draping it on the back of the couch. Then she slides her bra off while still keeping her blouse on. "Ugh. This bra was killing me."

I heave out a deep sigh. "I had a flashback today. My first memory after the accident."

Her eyes widen, and her eyebrows shoot up in surprise. "Oh my Goddess! What did you remember?"

My throat bobs when I swallow, and sweat slicks my palms as I grip the blanket. "The accident. I saw Mom." Sam's face gets blurry through the curtain of tears gathering in my eyes. "The car lurched over the side of the road, and we fell into a canyon. She was hurt; she had blood trickling down from her head and her nose. The trees stopped the car, and then they started snapping under the weight, and we started rolling again into the canyon. That's when I woke up. It was a nightmare, but I'm telling you, Sam. It felt real, so fucking real," my voice breaks, and tears run down my face freely.

"Holy shit! I'm so sorry, Iris," Sam says before throwing her arms around me.

Sniffling, I wipe at my cheeks. "I'm not. It hurt like hell, but I remembered something at least. And I saw Mom. God, Sam…she was so beautiful. The photos don't do her justice, I'm telling you." Taking a big breath in and expelling it through my nose, I say, "And…I think I look like her. It was never evident to me before because the photos my aunt gave me are so old, but our eyes tilt at the exact same angle, and our noses look like carbon copies. I know it sounds crazy because I only saw her for a few seconds, but I swear she had the exact same number of freckles I have smattered on the bridge of my nose. She even had the one above her lip that looks like a beauty mark."

She pulls back and squeezes my hand. "Of course you do, dummy. I've been telling you that since I first saw her photos. You're the spitting image of your mom, sans the hair." We remain like that for a few moments, Sam holding my clammy, trembling hand in hers as I cry silent, bittersweet tears. After I finally calm down, she grabs the remote and turns on the TV. "What do you want to watch?"

"*The Vampire Diaries.*" I chew on my bottom lip, making my best puppy eyes at her. "So…you're not mad at me? We can go out next weekend."

"I can't; I have to leave the country for the rituals I do with Grammie every year before the Summer Solstice, remember?" She gives me a side-eye and takes the remote, searching for the show in my list. "I'm really fucking tired anyway. This wedding kicked my ass."

"Thank God and baby Jesus," I sigh dramatically.

There's a pause before she asks, "What were you watching earlier? Was it something about those animal attacks that happened in the national park?"

"Yeah, I was researching Tony's death, but I couldn't find anything. I was sure at first that it had something to do with the attacks that happened a few months before and after Halloween about a year and a half ago given the fact that all of the victims had their hearts missing, exactly like Tony. But I'm now starting to think it might not be related since I couldn't find anything. He could have died ten years ago, for all we know."

She taps a finger on her chin pensively. "Hmm, I think he would already be a poltergeist if that were the case. It had to have been recent. Ask him his full name next time you see him. Maybe we can find something about him if we know his surname too."

"If he doesn't flip the fuck out on me again. The last time I tried to pry information out of him, he was bouncing off the walls at the speed of light," I grumble.

"Maybe you could coax it slowly out of him. Try asking for his full name first before you ask him about his friend again."

"'Kay, I'll do that…if I ever see him again."

"Maybe you're lucky, and it was a one-time thing. A glitch in your brain caused by that umbra attack. You said you keep getting migraines since, right?"

"Yeah, almost every day now."

"That's not good. Did the doctor say something after your exam?"

I shrug. "No, he said everything looks good."

"I'll brew you something to help alleviate the pain if you get another one. I think you should ask for another exam if things get worse, though," Sam says as she presses play on the remote. She restarts the series from the beginning, but I don't mind. "Man, these Salvatore brothers are so freakin' hot," she pipes up after a while, getting deeply invested in the show.

After I give Sam some sweats to change into, we spend the rest of the night binge-watching *The Vampire Diaries* and eating our weight in junk food and ice cream.

19

The bell chimes as I open the door of the Nostalgic Vault, and as soon as I step inside the vintage shop, a cloud of slightly dusty air, tinged with the scent of aged wood, leather, and old paper, transports me to a different era.

"Hi, Iris. Haven't seen you in a while," Barry, the owner, greets me from behind the counter.

"Hey, Barry, yeah…life's been kind of crazy these past few weeks," I shoot back, ambling toward him.

"Oh, did you like the dagger your friend got you for your birthday?" he asks as he wipes a crystal cup with a rag, his ruddy cheeks lifting in a genuine smile. He's a stocky man with an impressive six-foot-seven frame. That, coupled with the thick mustache and bald head, gives him an uncanny resemblance to a walrus. Not at all what one would imagine someone who owns an antique store.

I nod. "I loved it. It's gorgeous."

"I knew you would," he says, turning around and placing the

cup back on the shelf behind him, displaying various teacups, candle holders, and rare sets of China with intricate flower designs. He spins on his heel, his gaze locking with mine. "Is there something I can do for you today, or would you just like to take a look around?"

I lean forward to rest my elbows on the counter. "Actually, I need information that can possibly be found in an old book or document, and I remembered you saying in passing once that you know someone who sells extremely rare, old religious books." Another week has passed, and my aunt still hasn't found anything about the umbra demons in the library, so I decided to take matters into my own hands.

His smile drops, and his eyebrows knit together in a deep frown. "Oh, I did, didn't I? I must have had one too many glasses of Chianti during the day," he mumbles and continues, "Well, you see…it's more of an acquaintance. She's my grandmama's neighbor. She moved here a few years ago from New Orleans." He clears his throat. "The woman is kind of…How do I say this? Eccentric, to put it mildly. She's a bit cuckoo if you ask me." He accentuates his last statement by rotating a finger on the side of his head, then leans forward, whispering, probably not wanting the other customers browsing the store to hear. "She's always saying how demons and all these other evil creatures are all around us, hiding in plain sight."

I choke on my own saliva as it goes down with my next swallow. Smoothing it out with a cough, I match Barry's whispered tone, "Wow, she really sounds crazy."

Barry hikes a shoulder. "Right?" He flops a hand in the air, his voice regaining his deep baritone. "I think it's just an act to sell her image, though. She does palm readings at the carnival that's taking place now until the end of summer. The one at the edge of Ashville. You can't miss her trailer; it says 'Madame La Flamme Palm Readings' in big, flaming letters."

"'Kay, thanks, Barry," I tell him straightening.

"You're leaving already?" he asks with a hint of disappointment in his tone. "I just got this Turkish rug that would go amazing with your couch, and I wanted to show it to you."

"I'm in a bit of a rush, but I'll swing back next week."

"Don't take too long because I'll probably sell it."

"I won't. See you then," I throw over my shoulder before stepping out of the store and hailing a cab to take me to the carnival.

"HEY! ARE YOU crazy?" the taxi driver bellows as I throw the bills at him with a mumbled "thank you" and open the door of the still-moving vehicle with a jerky movement, my fingers so clenched they refuse to let go of the handle.

Fuck, fuck, fuck, fuck, fuck, fuck.

The tires screech loudly as he slams the brakes. I don't waste a second, throwing myself out of the car into the carnival's parking lot, shutting the door behind me with a loud bang. The driver opens his window and shouts some profanities my way before speeding off, but I don't pay him any attention as I stagger forward, my lungs battling for air, folding in two inside my chest.

I grab the fence in front of me before pressing my cheek to the cold metal. I hold onto it for dear life as I snap my eyes shut and try to cram as much air as I can into my useless lungs. Tears leak from the corners of my eyes and stream down my face with the effort.

The entire ride, dread spiked my blood until I felt like I was going to pass out in the backseat. On top of that, the driver was a blabbermouth, and I could barely answer his string of annoying questions through the panic attack seizing my chest. *Fuck.* It hasn't been this bad in years…not since I was a teenager. I thought I had it under control, but oh boy, was I wrong. The flashback I got from the car accident must have brought it all back with a vengeance.

Great.

Just great.

I really hope this is a once-in-blue-moon situation because if I'll get like this every time I ride in a car again…fuck my life.

Heaving out a weighted sigh, I finally manage to shake off the mind-numbing terror. However, it still lingers in the back of my throat with the remnants of bile.

Ugh.

When I jumped from the cab like from a burning building, the carnival seemed almost abandoned, save for one or two people riding the Ferris wheel. Now, the parking lot is almost full, and I have to wait in line for more than twenty minutes before I finally manage to purchase a ticket.

The late evening air is thick with the smell of buttery popcorn and the sickly-sweet tang of cotton candy and taffy apples as I weave my way through the maze of booths. Raucous laughter, children screaming, blasting music from the carnival rides, and the occasional roar of excitement coming from the roller coaster at my right are grating on my already spread-too-thin nerves. The sounds are what one would normally expect at a carnival, but they still make the pounding in the back of my head feel like an ice pick spearing my brain. I'm always sensitive to sounds after a panic attack. Now, though, it feels intensified by a hundredfold as my temples throb fiercely.

I finally spot the trailer right next to the House of Mirrors and take my place in line behind two teenage girls giggling about their crushes and wanting to find out if they will end up together. Gritting my teeth, I try shoving the pain deep down but fail miserably. Then I remember Sam brewed me something specifically for these migraines, insisting I keep at least one vial on me, and I want to kiss her at this moment as I fish the vial out of my jean shorts front pocket and down it in one go. I feel its calming effects immediately.

When it's my turn, I climb the stairs, and as I step through the threshold, I almost choke on the potent smell of incense burning my nostrils. The interior is strategically illuminated by candles, a hazy fog floating in the air, enhancing the mysterious atmosphere. It looks straight out of a movie with the rounded table in the middle, two purple velvet chairs, beaded curtain, and the cherry on top: the fake crystal ball, next to a set of Tarot cards.

Seriously? I honestly don't know what I was expecting. I roll my eyes in annoyance at the thought that I wasted my time and want to kick myself for being so stupid, thinking that I could get information about the umbra from a con artist.

"Take a seat, *s'il vous plaît*. I'll be right with you," a feminine voice with a strong French accent travels from behind the bead curtain.

"Yeah, no, thank you," I mutter for my ears only, and just as I'm about to spin on my heel, the curtain parts.

"Let's find out what *le future* ho—" The woman pauses when her shrewd citrine eyes fixate on my onyx choker. Her gaze flicks to my hair, back to my choker, and to my hair again before it snares mine, a deep frown etching into her already lined forehead, where the passing of years has left its mark. "*Putain!*" she lets out sharply under her breath.

Interesting.

"I do not deal with your kind, hellseeker," she snaps icily before fully stepping into the small space. Her deep ebony skin glows in the candlelight, which starts flickering as the temperature in the room drops a few degrees. The air thickens with the flow of dark magic as some of her power seeps into the room. Clearly, this is an attempt to intimidate me. I'm not fazed, though.

"I just need five minutes of your ti—"

The dark witch cuts me off, her eyes narrowing at me. "You have no right to be here. I haven't broken the law, and I'm under the protection of the Obsidian Conclave." She lifts the fabric of the deep plum, bell-shaped sleeve covering her arm. Then turns it to show me the Sigil of Baphomet tattooed on the inside of her wrist. "So leave."

"I'm not looking—"

She tilts her head, interrupting me. "Why is your hair black? I thought all hellseekers had light hair," she asks as curiosity gets the best of her.

"My father's a human, that's why," I retort and take advantage of the silence that stretches between us. "I'm not looking to cause you any trouble," I try again, pausing to gauge if she has the intention of cutting me off again, then continue when she simply folds her arms in front of her chest with a hard look in her eyes. "I'm a loyal customer of Barry's, the owner of the Nostalgic Vault. He mentioned you sell very old and rare religious books. I am looking for information about a specific demon, and I thought that maybe if I'm lucky, I can find that in one of your books. That's all."

She pinches her lips together, taking a moment to absorb my words. "You're lucky Barry's grandmother is one of my dearest friends. What is the name of *le démon* you seek information about?"

"It's an ancient demon called an umbra."

The witch frames her chin with one hand and taps a finger over her lips, deep in thought. "Hmm, I think I heard that name once when I was a child. Wait here, and don't touch anything," she says pointedly, then throws me a scathing glare before disappearing through the beaded curtain.

I puff out a breath and shuffle on my feet as half an hour passes with no sign of the witch. At first, I thought that maybe she left through another door than the one at my back, but she soon starts making a ruckus as she rummages through things.

An unintelligible sound of victory travels through the trailer before the woman finally reappears through the curtain, holding a timeworn leather-bound book with a pentagram inside a circle filled with weird symbols on the cover. Her limp is evident as she bypasses the table to shuffle forward. She stops right in front of me, opening the book with gentle movements.

She flips the first two pages. "This is an Enochian book from the fifteenth century passed down through generations in my family after it was stolen from the Vatican's secret vault along with other rare books. It's a glossary of demons. My grandmother translated the table of contents," she says while running her finger over the pencil scribblings that sit atop the Enochian symbols.

She passes a few demons I recognize until her finger stops on what clearly says umbra. My breath catches in my throat as excitement bubbles through my veins. The second I reach for the book to take a better look, the witch snatches it from my grasp, closes it, and tucks it between her arm and body. "Ah-ah. Not so fast, hellseeker. I will need my payment first before you can have the book," she tells me, limping to the other side of the table and pulling the velvet chair out before sitting down.

"How much?"

She snorts a derisive laugh. "Money is not the currency I seek."

I huff impatiently. "Fine, then what do you want?"

"Siren blood. It has been proven quite difficult in the past years to come across. Oh, and also one of your blessed daggers. I was also going to ask for an onyx stone, but given the fact that the book is in Enochian and you will have to find a translator, these will do."

"Why would you need a blessed dagger? It can only be wielded by hellseekers. And where am I supposed to find siren blood?" I bite back. Well, I do know a sexy Elite demon with the face of a fallen angel and a body made for sin that I'm certain knows how to procure said siren blood, but I'm not keen on asking him for help.

She shrugs nonchalantly before cutting me a faux smile. "You want the book, *non*?"

Fuck.

A muscle pops in my cheek as I take out my phone from my back pocket. "Just give me a minute," I tell the witch and turn around, stepping outside for some privacy. My heart flip-flops inside my chest as I press Kaiden's contact.

He answers on the first ring, surprising me. "Angel, to what do I owe this pleasure?" his velvety smooth voice wraps around me, making my pulse hiccup.

I swallow hard as a shiver skitters down my spine. Jesus. How can he have this effect on me and not even be present? Even if the next words pain me, I say them anyway. It's the only solution I have. "I need your help. I have found someone with a book mentioning the umbra, but they want siren blood as payment. Do you know how I can get some?"

"Sirens are very hard to come by, but I can get you a vile of blood."

I let out a relieved breath. "Great, then it's sett—"

"I'll need something in return, though," he says, cutting me off.

Of course he does. I bite the inside of my cheek as I wait for his next words.

"Have dinner with me, and you can have the blood."

A surprised guffaw slips out of me. My heart stalls. Then kicks off with such speed it feels like it's trying to crawl its way out of my chest.

Clearing my throat, I try to regain my composure. I fail. "I can't do that, Kaiden," I hiss and crook a finger in the collar of my T-shirt to pull on it. It feels as though the temperature has risen a few degrees in the span of a few seconds. Even while dark clouds gather on the sky, a clear sign of an impending storm. "As you very well know, it's against the ru—"

"You want the siren blood. Yes or no?"

"Was I mistaken in thinking that you want the information about the umbra as much as I do?" I snap, indignation lacing my tone.

"Oh, I do want the information, but I want to take you out on a date more. So, what's it going to be, Iris?"

I clench and unclench the fingers of my free hand, my other threatening to crush the phone to smithereens. "Fine. I'll go out on a date with you," I grit out through clenched teeth, then add hastily, "But it needs to be somewhere private with no one around."

"Don't worry. It's only going to be us. I'll send you the details tomorrow. And, angel?"

"What?"

"I told you I always get what I want." With that, he ends the call.

That smug demon bastard. Letting out a breath through flared nostrils, I pocket my phone, snap my eyes shut, and pinch the bridge of my nose. I'm going to be breaking the rules for the second time since I joined the Order eight years ago in just a matter of weeks because of an Elite demon. And this time it's going to be out of my own free will.

Dammit.

The worst part? My rage is a mere band-aid, a feeble attempt to mask the heady excitement and giddy anticipation that surges through my veins like lightning at the thought of seeing Kaiden Black again.

20

Someone's been in my apartment…at least, that's what I think. Or I could be finally going insane; you never know. Over the last few weeks, I've noticed small changes, like the chairs at my kitchen table being slightly shifted, things that I previously put in one place disappearing and appearing in another, and last of all, some of my underwear is missing.

The changes are so minute that a person without an acute sense of awareness would surely miss them. Still, I can't be certain my tired mind is not playing games on me. The nightmares have been increasing in frequency since the memory flashback, and I've been waking up groggy every day since, feeling like a herd of elephants danced the Macarena on my head.

For all I know, the washing machine could have played hocus pocus with my underwear. I can't even remember how many times I searched for socks over the years to only find one out of the pair. The incertitude is driving me up the wall, and I'm seriously considering installing a security system. I even took out the key that I used to keep in the fake pocket I had sewn under the mat at my front door.

Oh, and let's not forget about the fact that the lingerie set I got from Kaiden disappeared into thin air, too. Well, that could have also been me, or better said, the stupid drunken version of me that possibly found it offensive to wear lingerie from an Elite demon and threw it out.

Now, I regret not going through the trash that day to make sure I did throw it out, but I was too hungover when I woke up and then got caught up in other things—other people, more precisely. I want to kick myself in the shin because that was the softest, most luxurious fabric to ever grace my skin, and I probably won't get the chance to wear something like that again, dammit.

"What 'cha doing?" Tony's sudden appearance pulls me out of my thoughts forcefully and the mascara wand misses my lashes, poking me in the eyeball hard and smearing black streaks all over my left eyelid as I blink on instinct.

"Ow!" I mutter a sharp curse under my breath and give his reflection in the bathroom mirror the stink eye. "You could have better timing, you know. How the fuck am I going to fix this?" I blow out a frustrated breath as my eyes start watering.

"Sorry, buttercup. I didn't mean to scare you. If you wait for the mascara to dry, then flick it off with one of those spooly thingies you use for your eyebrows, it should come off just fine."

"Oh, I didn't know that. Thanks," I say, sniffling, and wipe the tears at the corners of my eyes gently with a tissue, then move on to applying blush to the apples of my cheeks. Now that Tony's here, I want to ask him about his past. He seems lucid, but I don't want to bombard him with questions right off the bat. Maybe If we engage in normal conversation for a while, I could coax information out of him slowly.

"Sure. Going somewhere fancy?" he asks, popping off and appearing in a seated position over the closed lid of my toilet. He waggles his eyebrows at me. The gesture reminds me of Sam. "Please do share. I'm bored to fucking death, pun intended."

"I'm going on a date." My heart somersaults as my nervous excitement comes back with a vengeance.

He sighs dreamily, steepling his fingers under his chin. "Uuuuh. Who's the lucky guy?"

I apply a thin layer of lip gloss before saying, "It's the guy who saved me that night you first saw me in the national park."

"The broody, gorgeous tattooed guy? I didn't quite see his face, but his body is to die for. Is he a demon? I couldn't get an exact read on him. I tried to get a better look, but this bright light blinded and scattered me. It was pretty annoying."

I gape at him. "You know what he is?"

"Of course. When you die, you suddenly become aware of the existence of demons and all of the other creatures of the world. It's like the rose-colored glasses are lifted. How do you think I was aware a wolf shifter killed me?" he asks with a pointed look my way.

"Well, I haven't thought about that. I was too busy freaking out that I can see a ghost," I mumble.

"All this information pours into you once your soul separates from your body, but lately, everything that I've learned seems to be slipping through my fingers like sand, along with all my memories." Tony heaves a deep sigh, and I can't help but feel the sadness in his words pressing over my chest like a heavy weight. "Sooo, what's his name?"

"Kaiden Black," I tell him and try flicking the smudged mascara off now that it's dry. Huh. It's working better than I expected.

"Isn't he the head of the Obsidian Conclave?"

"Yup."

"Wow. Can you even date a demon? Aren't you, like...supposed to hunt and kill them?"

"Well, we're not allowed to kill demons that have permission to be here and are under the Conclave's wing, only the ones that slip through the veil. But it's a hundred percent forbidden to fraternize with them. Let's not even talk about going out on a date. The thing is, Kaiden has something I need, and he strongarmed me into going on a date with him in exchange for it."

Tony snickers before he gives me a wry grin. "Um-hum...don't look so devastated about it." He changes the subject, thankfully. "The Obsidian Conclave is in charge of the dark creatures, right?"

"Yup," I say as I take the hair out of my bun and start brushing it. "I assume the one who killed you was a rogue, which is the majority of dark creatures, unfortunately. All dark creatures that don't bear the Sigil of Baphomet are considered lawless. But even if they do have the Sigil, any dark creature that breaks the fundamental law will be punished at the hands of the Conclave. Hellseekers are not allowed to meddle unless they witness a dark creature killing a human."

Taking out the hair straightener from the drawer under my sink, I plug it in, then start parting my hair into sections while the straightener heats.

"What about hellseekers? Are you like a special race? You're all in an Order if I remember correctly."

Taking a moment to gather my thoughts, I consider how best to explain the intricacies of our world to Tony. "So," I begin, pointing the hair straightener at him before running it through the first section of hair. "A hellseeker is essentially a warrior, one who hunts demons. Some members of our Order are not hellseekers; they have other roles, such as doctors, accountants, surveillance...you get the gist. My aunt, for instance, works at the library's compound. We're all referred to as lightborn, since we have blessed blood running through our veins. So, in a way, you could say we're a distinct race, but lightborn were once human."

185

"Can lightborn leave the Order? What happens to them?"

"Some left, wanting a normal life, so yeah, you can leave if you want. My mother did. Only if you do, or if you get kicked out, you can't come back. You have to live as a human and by their rules. And, of course, you're not allowed to tell anyone about the Order or the reality of our world."

"Mkay, enough about this. What are you planning on wearing for the date?" Tony inquires with excitement. He floats after me as I stride to the bedroom to finish getting ready.

"Will you help me choose?" I ask, opening my closet.

"Sure, buttercup. If there's something I know, it's clothes. I had the biggest closet at home, and I loved playing dress up as a kid. Well, not just as a kid. Halloween was my favorite holiday."

"Anything else you remember?" I say casually while taking out the three outfit options for tonight and draping them over my bed. My stomach is a restless ball of nervous energy as I sneak a look at the clock perched on the wall. I only have half an hour left until Kaiden's going to be here.

"Oh yeah, that's why I popped into your bathroom in the first place. I remembered that I used to work as a server at a bar in the Raven district and wanted to tell you. Don't remember why, though. So, what are we working with here? Did Kaiden tell you where he's taking you?"

"He said he's picking me up on his bike and that the rest is a surprise, but to dress casually. You don't remember anything else? The name of the bar…maybe your surname or how long ago you died?"

He pops off and appears near my bed, analyzing the clothes I laid out. "Unfortunately, no. That's the first thing I remembered in a long time." He pauses, then tilts his head. "Hmm, I think I like the second pair of jeans, but none of the tops. I love that red number I saw hanging in your closet, though. The one with the tag still on."

I worry my lower lip between my teeth. "I don't know about that. I mostly wear black."

His lips twist in amusement as he raises one eyebrow in my direction. "You don't say. I couldn't tell with the soulless void that is your closet," he deadpans. "Trust me, you're going to look amazing in it. You're a true cool winter."

"Huh, what's that?"

"Your color palette. Now, c'mon, get dressed. You can change if you don't like it, but I guarantee you won't want to once you see how good you look in red."

"Fine," I say, rolling my eyes dramatically while striding into the bathroom to change. The second I step back into the bedroom, Tony whistles, making me laugh, and I do a little pirouette for him. "Well, you were right. The top was a gift from my best friend, and I never even tried it on because I didn't think it would look good on me. Now I feel like a dumbass." Checking myself in the mirror again, I say, "I don't think I have ever worn red be—"

"My friend's favorite color is red," Tony interrupts me.

I whip my head around to look at him. "Can you remember anything else about her?"

Suddenly, his form starts flickering. He reappears at my back, head tilted. I don't get a response because he starts laughing with a high pitch that rattles the windows. Then, he vanishes into thin air. I wait patiently for him to show up again, but he never does.

My phone vibrates in my back pocket, startling me, and my stomach takes a nosedive. I almost drop it from my sweat-slicked palm as I fish it out and tap on the screen.

Kaiden: I'm outside.

Me: 'Kay. I'll be down in 5.

I'm ready, but I need the extra minutes for a pep talk. "You better not forget he's a demon, Iris. You are not risking your whole future for a sexy as sin, tattooed demon. Are we clear?" I say, jabbing a finger at my reflection in the mirror. With a deep inhale, I spin on my heel, grab my leather jacket from the upholstered chair in the corner, and make my way downstairs.

21

With my heart lodged in my throat, I close the front door of the apartment building and spot Kaiden across the street. He's leaning casually on a different motorcycle than the one we rode the last time, arms crossed over his chest. The sun casts the back of his spectacular body in a halo of golden light, making him look like a dark, avenging angel, and I forget how to breathe entirely as his gaze does a slow perusal of my body before slamming into mine.

He's clad in a similar outfit as the day I woke up at his penthouse, wearing his confidence like a dark cloak, his beauty as deadly as the sharpest obsidian blade. His eyes don't leave me as I stride to him. It's hard to admit, but my legs feel as though I'm wading through shifting sand.

Don't trip. Don't trip. Don't you dare trip, Iris!

Kaiden's lips turn up in a soft smile as I stop in front of him. "Hello, angel." His deep, gravelly voice rolls down the ladder of my spine like a caress.

That's when I expect my onyx choker to start warming at his

presence. But it never does. *What the?* I make a mental note to change it for a new one in case it's defective.

"Do you have the siren blood?" I inquire, forgoing the pleasantries and trying to push the strange attraction I feel toward him away.

Spoiler alert. It doesn't work.

He arches an eyebrow, smile widening. Of course his teeth are pearly-white and annoyingly perfect. *Ugh.* "Getting straight to business, I see. Wasn't expecting anything less from you." He fishes a vial of blood out of the front pocket of his black jeans, showing it to me before sliding it back in.

"We're going to your place?"

"No," he replies without offering more information.

Folding my arms in front of my chest, I insist, "Then where are we going?"

"It's a surprise," Kaiden answers as he takes the helmet that was resting on the handle and holds it out for me.

Squaring my shoulders, I ignore his outstretched hand. "I don't like surprises."

"You're going to like this one, I promise. I can only tell you that the place we're going is about an hour away."

"Funny, promises made by demons don't tend to hold much weight. Plus, you bargained for dinner. Going on a ride with you wasn't part of the pact."

He straddles the bike and turns to look at me, unfazed. "We're going to have dinner when we arrive. You wanted a private place where nobody could see us. The ride is just a means to get there."

"Fine," I grumble and slip into my leather jacket before taking the helmet from him and putting it on. I slide behind Kaiden as he keeps the motorcycle steady for me. "What's with the new bike?"

"It's a Harley CVO Limited. I just bought it. Do you like it?"

"Yeah, it's much more comfortable than the other one."

"That's why I got it; it's made for two passengers."

"Oh," I breathe. Did he get a new motorcycle just for our date? *Wow, Iris, quite the high opinion you have about yourself.*

"Hold on," Kaiden says before starting the engine. The sound snaps me out of my thoughts. His rough, calloused hands snake around my wrists, his touch singeing me as he pulls the front of my body flush to his muscular back and wraps my arms tightly around his middle. My heart trips over itself at the contact. To make matters worse, his sensual scent wraps around me in drugging waves.

Fuck. I forgot how sinfully good he smells.

Effortlessly, Kaiden guides the motorcycle into the evening traffic, revving the engine. Not before long, we exit the city and start riding on mountain roads off the beaten path. I hate to acknowledge it, but the feeling of freedom I felt the first time riding with Kaiden has intensified tenfold.

My cheeks are hurting; that's how big my smile is as the crisp pine-scented air whooshes around us and bites at my exposed skin. I can tell we're in the national park, though I haven't ventured to this part before. I think we're somewhere in wolf shifter territory.

The blob in the distance transforms into a charming wooden cabin as we get closer to it, and my eyebrows shoot up nearly to my hairline when Kaiden stops the engine right in front of it.

"I have to get something from inside. It will only take a minute," Kaiden tells me.

"'Kay," I shoot back, and we dismount.

As Kaiden pops off, I turn around and take in the scenery before me, jaw slack. The mountains look like ancient giants burnished in gold as the sun makes its descent on the crimson horizon.

Kaiden reappears with a large picnic basket in one hand and a blanket in the other.

"This is beautiful. Is the cabin yours?"

"No. It belongs to a good friend of mine, Logan."

"We're in the national park, right?"

"Yeah, but it's wolf shifter territory, so it can't be accessed by anyone but them, as you probably already know," Kaiden tells me, confirming my earlier assumptions. "C'mon, we're going on foot from here." He turns on his heel and starts walking in the direction of the pine trees on the right side of the cabin.

"Are we seriously going to have a picnic in the woods?" I huff as I hurry my pace to match Kaiden's. "The sun is going to set soon."

"That's the idea," he drawls.

We walk in silence on the narrow forest path, the only sounds being the pine needles crunching under our feet, the bird songs in the distance, and the branches dancing in the breeze. After about fifteen minutes, the pine trees start dwindling. It takes us five more to enter a clearing with a spectacular view of the mountain peaks. Kaiden stalks forward and bends at the waist to lay the blanket atop the lush grass. He places the basket next to it.

I stomp toward him, still not seeing the logic in having a picnic so late in the day. If a mountain lion jumps on my head, I'm blaming him. He takes off his leather jacket, puts it next to the basket, and sits on the blanket. Then, he pats the space next to him, giving me a roguish grin that knocks the wind from my lungs for a second. "Take a seat, Iris. I don't bite...unless you want me to." He winks devilishly, and I almost melt into a puddle at his feet.

What is wrong with me?

Rolling my eyes at his remark, I slide out of my leather jacket and throw it on top of his before plopping down unceremoniously. I leave as much space as I can between us. "So, do you bring a lot of women here? Is this like your thing, picnic in the woods when it's almost dark? It's kinda creepy if you ask me," I say, face stoic.

He doesn't react to my jab. "No, actually, you're the only one I have ever brought here." Kaiden opens the basket, takes out four food containers, a bottle of white wine that surely cost more than my entire rent for a month, two tulip-shaped glasses, and two bottles of water.

"I stumbled upon this place at Logan's wedding. He got married to his mate in a meadow full of wild violets not far from here. I needed a quiet place to think, away from the party, and kept walking until I found the clearing. Whenever I'm overwhelmed or need to organize my thoughts, this is where I come. The one-hour bike ride also helps me clear my head."

Kaiden's admission renders me speechless for a moment. I didn't expect him to be so candid and almost vulnerable, in a way. I quietly accept a glass of wine from him and take a sip, the crisp, citrusy flavor bursting on my tongue. Damn, this is good wine. "I guess being the head of the Obsidian Conclave is not as easy as one would think, huh?"

What the fuck, Iris? Since when did you start being considerate of...a demon's burdens?

Kaiden chuckles darkly, the sound bitter, almost sad. "Yeah. But it's also a chance to make things better...do some good."

I snort a laugh, not able to imagine what in the world Kaiden's *good* could be. "What do you mean?"

He takes a sip of wine, and I gulp at the way his throat rolls with the swallow.

Gah, why is everything he does so insanely attractive?

He isn't even fazed by my mocking tone. "Mammon, the Elite demon that was the head of Conclave before me, was a greedy fucker. He wanted as much money and power as he could get his dirty hands on. He made the Conclave the largest distributor of drugs and illegal weapons in the world. But most of his fortune came from the flesh trade, trafficking women and children, not only dark creatures but humans too." Kaiden pauses, surely to give me a chance to absorb this information. He opens the fancy food containers filled with gourmet cold cuts, all types of cheeses, mini burgers that look divine, French fries, and strawberries covered in chocolate. My mouth waters at the display of delicious-looking food. I pluck a fry that, surprisingly, is still hot, biting into it absentmindedly.

How did I not know about this? I mean, yeah, sure, even if the Order didn't teach us much about the Obsidian Conclave aside from the basics, I knew the Conclave had to be involved in illegal stuff. They had to be making money somehow. And without evil, good cannot exist. Still, I never imagined something at this scale.

Kaiden starts speaking again, interrupting my train of thought. "He was so focused on how to make more that he completely ignored the rising hostility between species. Soon, the animosity reached a pinnacle, and wars broke out between the wolf shifters and vampires. Then, the dark witches got involved. Thousands died every year, and the bloodshed continued until I managed to banish Mammon to Hell and convinced Lucifer to appoint me as the new leader."

He heaves out a deep breath. "Since then, we've been waging a relentless battle against the corruption that Mammon spread like poison. We successfully dismantled the flesh trade conducted by the Conclave, and we're now tackling other issues…such as legalizing businesses, investing in properties, and providing real jobs to the dark creatures and demons under our protection."

My eyebrows knit together in confusion. "We? I thought you were the head of the Obsidian Conclave."

Kaiden leans forward, hooking his elbows on top of his knees, and shakes his head. "I understand you may have preconceived notions about the Conclave…about me, but I'm not a dictator, Iris. Almost every dark creature species has a representative within the Conclave. We make collective decisions, vote on them, discuss strategies. I may have the final say in some situations, but disagreements are rare. Ultimately, it was the inclusion of the dark creatures' voices and granting their rights that brought peace between the species."

My cheeks and the tips of my ears start burning under the weight of my ignorance. "I, um…I don't know what to say. I had no idea about any of this."

Kaiden scoffs. "Why would you? The Order is only interested in making perfect little soldiers who blindly obey every command. You don't need to think in order to fight, do you?" He lets out a breath through his nose. "Let's eat."

My jaw ticks at Kaiden's rebuke, and the glass almost shatters in my hand with how strongly my fingers are gripping it. I swallow the barb I was about to throw at him, though. I don't think Kaiden was trying to insult me…he only seems to disapprove of how the Order does things.

And in a way, he's right. Even I can recognize that. The Order could have done a better job at providing more insight into what the Conclave does. With the scraps of information they shared with us, they painted the Conclave as evil through and through. But at the end of the day, that doesn't make much of a difference…Kaiden is still a demon, and I'm still a hellseeker. Nothing will change that.

"Not hungry?" Kaiden asks before biting into one of the mini burgers. As if awakened by his words, my stomach makes a growling sound.

Ugh.

Kill me now, please.

He only chuckles as my face gets as red as a pickled beet and extends the container with the mini burgers toward me. I thank him softly and grab one. How the hell is it still warm? I guess the fancy-looking containers are doing some kind of magic.

A comfortable silence settles between us as we enjoy the food, which is so good that I have to keep reminding myself not to moan at every new bite. Dusk descends as the sun slips beneath the horizon. Indigo takes over the lavender sky, making the forest seem almost ethereal while the first stars of the night twinkle into existence.

As I bite into a strawberry, the juice dribbles from the corner of my lips down my chin, and before I get the chance to lick it away, a warm hand wraps around my jaw. My chest rises and falls at the contact, and my gaze lifts to collide with Kaiden's.

He's right in front of me; he probably did his Houdini thing, and I haven't even noticed until now. My pulse hammers on the side of my neck like a hummingbird taking flight as his half-lidded eyes drop to my lips. His thumb wipes the juice slowly, then moves over the curve of my lower lip, almost with…longing.

He surprises me by lifting his thumb to his mouth and sucking the juice from it as though he's tasting my lips. The gesture is so erotic that it sends a rush of heat in between my thighs. "Have I told you how stunning you look?" he rasps.

Fuck. The deep cadence of his gravelly voice and his words send my heart into a frenzy. I don't know what to say, so I swallow hard and shake my head, which causes a strand of hair to fall over my eyes.

Kaiden's right hand comes up again, and he gently pushes it away, tracing the side of my face before tucking it behind my ear. "Then I am a fool because you are the most beautiful woman I have ever seen, Iris." He inches forward, and I get lost in his gaze. Obsidian fire enthralls me in a binding spell. I suck in a choppy breath as Kaiden bridges the gap between us.

"It's starting," he breathes against my lips, a soft smile tugging at his mouth.

"Huh?" I asked, confused as he pulls back, bursting the bubble we were wrapped into. Disappointment that he didn't kiss me knocks the air out of my lungs with such force my chest constricts painfully. But I don't get the chance to read too much into it because the tiny meadow looks as though the stars from the sky are dancing all around us to the tune of a collective low hum. Hundreds of tiny lights blink in and out of existence, and all I can do is stare.

"Oh my God, Kaiden. Are these fireflies?" I ask, voice thick with emotion. My gaze flicks to his.

"Yes," he answers simply. His Adam's apple bobs in his throat. "Can I hold you?"

The word "no" sits on the tip of my tongue. It's the right thing to say. I don't know why I can't move my lips and utter it, though. As if a strange entity has taken control over my brain, I nod instead, and Kaiden slides behind me, bracketing my body with his muscular thighs. Then, his arms band across my middle. My pulse is a war drum in my ears as he pulls me flush to him. He buries his nose in my hair and inhales deeply as though he can't help himself. The ghost of his breath electrifies my skin.

Time loses meaning in Kaiden's arms. Leaning back and resting my head on Kaiden's chest, I swear I can hear his heart thundering as hard as mine. The warmth in my own chest scares me; it feels like…home. Like I belong here. I tuck it deep inside, in a corner of my soul, so I can pull it out later and examine it in the confines of my space, where there's no one to judge me but my own conscience.

"Kaiden?" I say softly, breaking the silence blanketing the air.

"Hmm?"

"This is the most beautiful thing I have ever seen in my entire life." I pause to trap his intoxicating scent into my lungs. "Thank you…for sharing this place with me."

"You're welcome, angel."

Silence falls between us again, and I revel in it, in this perfect moment, wanting to sponge every single second. I have never felt more at peace. I can't believe the best date of my life is with...a demon. This has got to be some sick joke played by the universe. There's a strange urge, a current in my fingers compelling me to pick up a pencil and sketch, etch this moment into posterity so I can come back to it over and over again.

I brush it off my shoulders, and as I raise the second cup of wine to my lips and take a sip, an idea pops into my head. I can't believe I haven't thought about this before.

"If I need your help with something, will you strongarm me into another deal?"

"I don't know. Depends on what you need help with." I can hear the smile in Kaiden's voice as he says, "I'm already planning our second date in my head."

His words are playful. Still, the realization that I'm enjoying this date far more than I should makes me suck in an unsteady breath. Like someone sucker-punched me straight to reality. What am I doing?

"Forget about it," I snap, breaking out of his hold and pushing against the blanket to stand. "I think we should go. It's late."

I shouldn't have let him hold me. Fuck, I let a demon almost kiss me. This is wrong on so many levels I can't even compute the implications of what this could mean for me. It's one thing to be attracted to someone on a visceral level. That's just lust. But I'm afraid I'm starting to like him....and that's something out of the realm of possibility for me.

Kaiden disappears from his seated position and reappears in front of me. "I promise I'll try to help you. No strings attached."

I tear a hole in my cheek, debating if I should tell him about Tony or not. My and Sam's research amounted to nothing, and every time Tony has decided to show his face, pulling information out of him proved to be a Sisyphean task. "Okay. I don't even know how to say this because I might sound crazy…heck, I'm not even entirely sure I'm not," I mumble the last part to myself. "So, after the umbra attack, I visited the national park again and, um…" I pause, clearing my throat. C'mon, Iris, just say it. "…that's where I met a ghost," I blurt out on an awkward chuckle.

Kaiden's tanned complexion turns ashen, and his eyebrows drop in a deep frown. Something flashes in his eyes that looks a lot like…fear. "What?"

"Yeah, um, it was a shock to me too. I mean…I legit thought I was batshit crazy. But it turns out he really was a ghost. I even tested it with salt. Did you know that if you throw salt at a ghost, it disappears?" Dear God, why am I blabbing so much? "Anyway, he asked for my help. He said his friend is in danger, and he tried to warn her, but failed. I couldn't find anything about him online. I think he was killed by a rogue wolf shifter, and that's why I thought you might be able to help."

Kaiden listens with rapt attention to my every word as I continue telling him everything about my interactions with Tony so far. Of course, I leave out all the Noah parts and why we were in the national park to begin with.

When I finish, a weighted silence thickens the air. Kaiden's jaw is an iron bar of tension, the playfulness and vulnerability he showed earlier gone.

"So, do you know anything about his death?" I ask.

"Yeah, the rogue did kill him. The reason you weren't able to find anything about his death is that we had to do damage control. The rogue murdered a lot of people, and the ones you saw in the media were just those we couldn't get to in time and were discovered by humans who called the police. That many deaths would have been suspicious if we didn't bury the information."

"What about his friend? Will you help me find her?"

Kaiden nods. "Tony was an acquaintance. I used to frequent the bar he worked at in the Raven district, the Shabby Shotglass. It's closed now. Anyway…I'll look for his friend. I'm confident I'll be able to find her and see if she really is in danger."

"Thank you," I murmur as I rack my brain. I'm sure I heard the name of the bar before. "Oh, I've been there once, at the Shabby Shotglass." The memory of the extremely boring date almost two years ago flashes in my mind, making me shudder. I can't believe I let that guy kiss me. He was a slobber. The kiss disgusted me so much I raced to the bathroom to rinse my mouth with water. When I came back to the table, he was gone, and the bill was paid. I thanked my lucky stars and bolted out of there like a souldrake was nipping at my heels.

Kaiden grunts, then grimaces as though he swallowed something sour before crouching, gathering the containers, and stacking them back into the basket. He quickly folds the blanket, grabs our things, and pushes to his feet. "C'mon, let's go. I have to call a Conclave meeting."

"Okay," I say, a bit confused by the urgency in his tone, and follow him back to the cabin. At least he'll look for Tony's friend. Maybe that will help him get some closure and finally move on.

22

The meeting has been dragging on for almost two hours, and I can't concentrate on a word coming out of Grayson's mouth because I can't shake the last encounter with the dark witch out of my head.

I went back to her trailer yesterday to give her the items she requested as payment. As I grabbed the book out of her hand, our fingers touched briefly. Her eyes widened almost comically, and all the color drained from her face.

"There is a shadow over your soul," she whispered, voice trembling, abject fear marring her features.

"What do you mean?" I chuckled uncomfortably.

"There's *darkness* inside you, girl."

I didn't know what to say, so I just stared back, mouth agape, before she shouted, "Out!" and ushered me out of her trailer, slamming the door and locking it behind me with urgency.

A sharp pain in my ribs brings me into the present. "Ow," I mutter under my breath and scowl at Raquelle, the hellseeker sitting on my right, who nudged me with her elbow.

"Glad to know I'm not boring you, Iris," Grayson drawls while giving me a death stare. I wilt under his disapproving glare as everyone in the room turns to look at me. I feel like the kid who got caught with his hand in the cookie jar.

Shit.

"Sorry, I was reminding myself to go to the armory and sharpen my daggers," I blurt out the first thing that comes to my mind. Erik lets out a derisive snort from his seat at Grayson's right. His stare has been sending icy shivers down my spine the whole meeting. He's always been creepy as fuck, but now it somehow feels ten times worse. Someone is going to make a documentary about him one day, mark my words. And it definitely won't be the good kind.

Grayson arches an eyebrow at my response before announcing, "The meeting is over."

All the other hellseekers collectively stand up and start filing out of the room. Just as I'm about to push back my chair, Grayson's voice makes me freeze. "Iris, a word?"

I remain seated, clenching my sweat-slicked palms into fists under the long table, and meet his hawk-like eyes.

"Doctor Corey said you've been having migraines since the strange demon attack, but there was nothing out of the ordinary with your exam. How are you feeling?" Grayson steeples his fingers on the table in front of him, waiting for my answer.

He's wearing a dark navy suit with a button-down, and the way he holds himself demands attention and respect—his training as one of the best hellseekers in the Order never forgotten.

"I'm good; I haven't had a migraine in a few days."

He tilts his head. "Noah told me you took him to where you were attacked in the national park. I saw the footage. I'm surprised you don't have any burn marks."

I gulp as my stomach twists into painful knots. "Yeah…me too—"

"Any other strange demon encounters since then?"

"If that were the case, I would have come to report it. But as all other hellseekers and I already said earlier, the streets are strangely empty."

He nods, seemingly pondering my words. "Fine. You're dismissed."

My forehead crinkles with a frown.

That easy?

Well, I'm not going to look a gift horse in the mouth. Without a word, I stand on trembling legs and shuffle out of the room. As soon as I shut the door at my back, I let out a shaky breath.

"Iris, you okay?" Roman asks, startling me.

"Hey, yeah, sorry. I didn't see you there. How are you?" I offer a brittle smile.

"Good, I just took my lunch break. I wanted to eat in the garden and get some fresh air, take advantage of the good weather, you know. I called Tim like a thousand times to ask him to join me, but I think he's blasting music in those noise-canceling headphones again. I should have gotten him something else for his birthday. I swear he never answers his phone." He rolls his eyes and flaps a hand in the air. "Anyway, sorry for the rant."

"Do you want me to go tell him you're waiting for him in the garden? I'm going that way anyway to see my aunt." I'm not, but I'm not going to waste this opportunity to sneak a peak at the surveillance footage of the night the umbra came through the portal. Tim has been stuck like Velcro to those goddamn screens.

Roman's kind cinnamon eyes crinkle at the corners with his smile. "Oh, that's really thoughtful of you. Thanks."

"Sure," I tell him over my shoulder and make my way to the second floor.

The discussion with Grayson is at the forefront of my mind as I ascend the stairs. I'm grateful he let me off the hook so easily, but it left me with a sour taste and an unpleasant feeling crawling beneath my skin...so at odds with the Grayson I know. He's acting weird. Or maybe I'm projecting my own insecurities on our every interaction because I was never in the position to lie to him before, and it's eating at my insides like battery acid.

As expected, rock music is blasting from Tim's headphones, but this time, he sees me walk into his office. He pauses the music and removes the headphones, tilting his chin in my direction. "Hey, what's up? Do you need anything?"

Leaning my hips into the door frame and folding my arms in front of my chest, I say, "No, that's not why I came. I bumped into Roman a few minutes ago. He said he's waiting for you in the garden. He just took his lunch break. He was also kinda peeved you didn't answer your phone."

"Shit," he mutters under his breath before he lifts his phone from the desk to check the screen. He slaps his forehead. "Ah, fuck, he called me five times, and I'm already in the doghouse for being almost an hour late on our last date." He brushes a hand over his face and heaves out a breath. "I can't leave; someone's got to be here to watch the monitors, and Christopher is running late today," he tells me, referring to the other guy in charge of surveillance. Tim is the only one with the brains to be in charge of both tech and surveillance.

I hike a shoulder nonchalantly. "I can watch the screens while you take your lunch break."

A glimmer of hope shines in Tim's eyes. "You don't have training or anything?"

"I'm in no rush. I can spare twenty minutes."

"You sure?" He chews on his bottom lip nervously. "If Grayson finds out about this, he's not going to be hap—"

Rolling my eyes, I cut him off, "He's not going to find out if we don't tell him. Besides, it's just twenty minutes in the middle of the day. What could happen?"

"Okay," he relents, then quickly stands and shoves his phone into the back pocket of his jeans. "Just take a seat in my place and watch out for anything out of the ordinary," he says as he stops next to me.

I push off the door frame and amble toward the desk. "Just go already. I promise I won't set anything on fire."

He chuckles. "Thanks, Iris. I'll owe you one," he says before leaving the room.

Heart thumping loudly in my ears, I close the door before plopping down on the wheeled chair. My fingers drum on top of the desk as I wait a few minutes to make sure Tim didn't forget anything or change his mind. After I feel enough time has passed, I grab the mouse and start browsing through the folders on Tim's laptop. He left in such a hurry that he forgot to lock the screen.

It doesn't take long to find the folder with the surveillance footage since everything is organized by dates. I double-click on the videos from that day and open them in different windows on the screen. Chewing on a hangnail, I fast forward the footage and watch Grayson pocket his phone around six p.m. and exit his office. He then gets in his car and leaves the compound immediately after that. It's impossible to tell where he went, but he doesn't come back until the next morning.

Well, this is…underwhelming.

Since Tim mentioned the glitch, I was hoping that someone interfered with the surveillance, and I could catch a glimpse of them getting into Grayson's office and messing with his phone or something. That's the movie I made in my head, and I am severely disappointed that it was just a glitch, nothing more. So far, everything points at Grayson. I still don't know what happened from that time until nine thirty when I received his text, but what if he lied? What if he didn't misplace his phone?

Ugh.

I close all open windows and slump in the chair, waiting for Tim to come back.

Ezekiel's shrewd caramel-brown eyes analyze my every move as we circle each other, swords at the ready, our shadows caught in the same dance on the grass beneath our feet. We decided to take advantage of the cloudless sky today and train outside, near the garden.

He took off his T-shirt earlier, and the scars marring his tawny skin are fully on display alongside his bulky muscles and perfectly carved six-pack. His dirty-blond hair is cropped short in a military buzz cut, and the fine lines etched into the corner of his eyes and forehead deepen with concentration as he watches me. He is no longer my instructor since I graduated a few years ago, but we still enjoy training with each other and meet at least once a week at the compound.

A fine sheen of perspiration coats my entire body. The light breeze that rustles the leaves feels like heaven against my heated skin. As soon as I step into the sunlight, my sword gleams, blinding me momentarily. The bright light sends a stab of white-hot pain directly to my brain. I inhale a sharp breath and clench my teeth while willing the headache to go away.

Ezekiel takes advantage of the hesitation in my steps, lunging at me full force. Our swords clash with a loud metallic clang, and the impact reverberates through my entire body as I parry with precision.

"Ah, playing dirty, are we?" I cluck my tongue and curve my lips in a smile as I seamlessly transition into a riposte and launch my attack.

He blocks me swiftly and lets out a deep belly laugh at my jab while shifting effortlessly between low and high guards, forcing me to adapt to the changing dynamics. "Is this all you got, Iris?" His pearly white teeth catch the light.

"I didn't want to startle you and cause you to pull a muscle or worse, break a bone at your old age," I deadpan and twirl as I tap into the hellseeker speed, tracing a wide arc through the air before our swords meet again in a jarring impact. The high-pitched metallic sound rings loudly. The birds that just a second ago were chirping happily in the trees surrounding us scatter into the air with rapid flaps of wings.

"Brat." Ezekiel arches an eyebrow at me. "Who's playing dirty now?"

I shrug. "C'mon, old man. Stop coddling me." He's far from looking old, and we both know it; he's about my aunt's age, so he looks about thirty-five, but it's my preferred jab when we spar. I call him old, and he calls me a brat.

A series of swings and slashes follow, the blades cutting through the air as we engage in a mesmerizing dance of gleaming steel and rapid footwork while we both use the hellseeker speed. Sweat dots my forehead and gathers at the nape of my neck, dripping down my spine. My breathing turns ragged, my muscles beginning to strain.

A tall silhouette approaching us catches my attention. My heart does a backflip at Noah coming into view, and my movements falter. He's wearing low-slung gray sweats and a muscle shirt that stretches over his chest like second skin. Using the momentary distraction to his advantage, Ezekiel breaks off by raising the hilt of his sword. He traps my blade in between his upper arm and torso and disarms me with a blow to my wrist.

"I see you're still the undefeated champion," Noah chimes in from the sidelines as he reaches us, lifting his chin in greeting.

Ezekiel looks at me with a lopsided grin. "Iris disarms me without any problem most days, but I think she got a little distracted today."

"Well then, it's a good thing demons don't use swords if Iris gets so easily distracted," Noah jests with a smug smirk.

Heat crawls up my chest all the way to my cheeks. I roll my eyes at them and resist the urge to stick out my tongue like a toddler. "Hardy har har." Making my way to my gym bag, I bend to unzip it and wipe the sweat off my face with a towel. Noah approaches us, giving Ezekiel one of those bro-hugs with a pat on the back. "How are you, Zeke?"

"I'm good. Iris didn't mention you were back," Ezekiel says while bending to place the swords on the grass.

Noah folds his arms in front of his chest. His muscles bulge with the movement, and his gaze flits to mine briefly at Ezekiel's words. "Yeah, I'm planning to stay a while. How's Christina?" he asks, referring to Ezekiel's wife.

"She's at home with the kids. They're a handful," Ezekiel responds, his whole face lighting up as it always does when he talks about his family.

Noah's eyebrows rise, and he tilts his head. "You've got kids? Multiple?"

"Yeah. A boy and a girl." Ezekiel takes out his phone from his bag and slides his finger on the screen to show Noah pictures of little Rhett and Alice.

"They're beautiful. You're lucky they take after their mother," Noah chuckles out.

Ezekiel slugs him playfully in the shoulder. "What about you? Married? Kids? A special someone waiting for you?"

"Nah, too focused on the job for that. Besides, there is only one woman I wanted to do all that with, and I left her behind."

I choke on the water I'm drinking, and my stomach does a somersault. I start coughing like I'm about to hack out a lung.

Smooth, Iris.

Real smooth.

"You good there?" Ezekiel raises a knowing eyebrow in my direction, his lips twisting up in amusement.

"Peachy," I mumble and wipe my mouth with the back of my hand when the coughing finally subsides. I put the cap back on the bottle and throw it on top of my bag. "Are we doing hand-to-hand today, too?" I ask Ezekiel. "I'm having dinner tonight with my aunt, and I have to go in an hour."

"Do you mind if I step in?" Noah juts in before Ezekiel can answer.

"No, actually. I promised Christina I'd go to the store and pick up some things before going home, so I'll leave you guys to it," Ezekiel says before bending to lift his bag alongside the swords. He looks at me over his shoulder. "Same time next week?"

"Yup," I respond, popping the *p*.

Ezekiel nods and makes his way to the back of the mansion.

Noah's gaze roves over my body as he comes closer, a glimmer of desire shining in his eyes. His sun-streaked hair is artfully mussed with that perfected, just-got-out-of-bed look, and the way his clothes cling to his body sends my pulse spiking through the roof. He cracks his neck from side to side and widens his stance. "Let's see if you got any better, Harper. If I remember correctly, your footwork was always kind of sloppy," he taunts.

I get my fists ready at the same time as Noah. "Ah, aren't you cute, Pierce," I say and move back as he initiates a series of feints, testing my defense. We fall in sync with the controlled rhythm of each other's footwork, and soon it's like Noah never left.

Noah launches a swift punch, aiming for my midsection. I respond with a precise block while inhaling a deep breath and countering with a low kick that he blocks easily. We continue in a fluid choreography of jabs and kicks, our chests moving rapidly with every breath. A sweat bead gets stuck in my eyelashes as I launch a flurry of rapid kicks. One catches Noah in the chin, and I manage to throw him off balance for a second.

He laughs, wipes the blood trickling down from the corner of his lips with his thumb, and comes at me. I subtly shift my weight, and the moment he's within reach, my fingers find purchase in his T-shirt. Using his momentum, I pivot my hips and step inside his stance while disrupting his balance. Engaging my core muscles, I put his weight onto my hip as I rotate and throw him to the ground. He lands with a loud thud on his back.

"How's that for sloppy foot—" I don't get to finish my jab because Noah kicks my legs from under me, and I end up falling on top of him. All the air leaves my lungs in a huff as our bodies collide.

"I'll say you still have to work on it," Noah rasps, and with a swift move, he rolls us and comes on top, knee in between my legs. My heart drums a staccato rhythm in my ears as my blood rushes into my veins. His fingers come up and brush a sweaty strand of hair off my face.

Noah closes the space between us until we're nose to nose. His Adam's apple bobs in his throat as his quicksilver gaze zeros in on my lips. I suck in a jagged breath, and his crisp sandalwood cologne mixed with the musk of fresh sweat envelops me.

All the times we trained together like this flash through my mind, and the carefully placed stitches around my heart start to unravel one by one. They leave my heart an open wound as I remember the sleepless nights, the sadness that weighted my bones, and how I moved as if trapped in a foggy, murky mist for an entire year.

The worst part about the person you love ghosting you is that you're trapped in the uncertainty of not knowing why; it leaves you suspended in doubt and prevents you from fully moving on. It's a special kind of purgatory. It would have been better if he would have broken up with me before he left. That way, it would have been a clean cut, and even if it hurt like a bitch…at least I would have had the chance to heal. What Noah did to me was much worse.

Noah dips, but right at the last moment, I turn my head, and his lips make contact with my cheek instead of my lips. The air between us grows thick with awkwardness as I push him off me. We both stand.

Brows drawn, he runs his hand over the back of his neck. "Iris, I—"

I cut him off as I bend, take my bag, and sling it over my shoulder. "I meant what I said, Noah. I need time to figure out if I even want you as a friend. You suddenly barge into my life five years after ghosting me and want to pick up where we left off like nothing happened?" I huff and shake my head. "I can't do this with you right now." I turn on my heel and stalk to the mansion.

"Fuck! Iris! Wait!" Noah shouts after me and starts jogging, easily reaching me and matching my hurried steps. "I'm sorry, okay?"

A muscle thrums in my jaw, and I tighten my grip on the strap of my gym bag. I don't look at him, though; I keep my gaze forward, pretending he's not walking next to me.

"I'm sorry I ghosted you. I'm so unbelievably sorry for that. But I'm not going to apologize for trying to kiss you. When you're near, I can't control myself. All I want to do is kiss you, touch you. You make me crazy; you're all I think about. Please tell me how to make this right. I'll do anything."

I stop as I reach the steps to the back entrance of the mansion and heave out a deep sigh. My gaze flicks to Noah's stormy one and his disheveled appearance. His clothes are sweaty, glued to his muscles, and stained green from rolling in the grass. A golden lock falls over his forehead, and I resist the urge to brush it back, to feel his skin against mine. "Okay, paint this picture for me. Let's say I forgive you, and that's a big fucking if, and we get back together. You say you're going to stay here for a while. What happens when the Kabal calls, and you have to leave? What about me then?"

He rakes a hand through his hair. "I would never ghost you again. There's nothing I regret more than doing that to you. I will take you with me this time."

A bitter laugh bubbles out of me. My lips draw in a thin line, and I suck on my teeth. "Quite presumptuous of you, don't you think? To believe that I would leave everything to be with you. Believe it or not, I have a life here." I shake my head and scoff. "The thing that you failed to realize five years ago is that, then, I would have followed you to the ends of the Earth. Now, I actually know my worth," I say, my tone dripping with iciness as I climb the stairs and enter the mansion, not looking back.

"So, Noah's back, huh?" my aunt asks as she takes the lasagna out of the oven, the hot steam and the delicious smell wafting through the air.

"Yeah," I say dryly, then start pouring red wine into the two glasses on the wooden counter in front of me.

Her gaze flicks to me while she places the hot pan on a trivet and starts cutting the lasagna into squares. "And, how do you feel about him being back?"

I put the cork back on the bottle and shrug. "It's been a long time,

Auntie. I'm fine," I respond, taking two plates from the cupboard to my right and placing them next to the pan on the counter.

Aunt Josephine side-eyes me. "Uh-huh. And I was born yesterday." She sighs. "You know you can tell me anything, right, dear?" She scoops two large portions of lasagna onto the plates I laid out and turns her body toward me, facing me fully. Her hair is in a messy bun, and she's wearing jeans and the pink T-shirt I got her as a gift last Christmas. It says 'I have no shelf control' above a shelf of books. It already has a few holes from how often she wears it. I make a mental note to get her more bookish T-shirts.

"You didn't leave your room for months, Iris, and your eyes were always puffy and bloodshot from crying. You thought I didn't notice, but I did. I mean, I was living with a broken-hearted, moody teenager…it was kind of hard not to," Aunt Josephine says with a pointed look my way.

"Gee, I thought I was being a bit more inconspicuous," I grumble. Looking down, I inhale deeply. "I'm not fine," I admit as I pick up the plates and take them to the kitchen table, placing them next to the cutlery. "I don't know how I feel. I guess being confused is the best way to put it. Maybe angry, hurt…happy that he's alive, but in an I-want-to-gouge-his-eyes-out-and-kiss-him-at-the-same-time kind of way." I shrug and plop down on the chair. "I don't know…"

Aunt Josephine brings the glasses of wine and sits down next to me with a pensive look on her face. "Have you spoken to him?"

Taking a hearty sip of wine, I look at her. "Yeah, actually, I did. A few times. I didn't want to at first, but he was relentless."

"So, did he at least explain why he phantomed you?"

I almost spit out the wine as a surprised laugh belts out of me. "I think you meant to say ghosted. You sure don't look your age, but I swear to God, when you say things like this, you sound like an old lady," I chuckle out. "How did you even think that phantomed is a word? You

213

work in a library for God's sake."

She narrows her eyes at me and kicks my shin under the table with her foot. "Oh, come on, like ghosted is a better word choice. Stop being a brat." She takes a sip of wine, making an impatient gesture with her hand in the air. "Well? I'm not getting any younger here."

My lips curve up in amusement. "He did explain, and I guess it was a pretty good reason. I somewhat understand his point of view, but he still let five years pass and didn't contact me at all." I cut a piece of lasagna and stab it with the fork before bringing it to my mouth. It's still pretty hot and burns my tongue, but it's worth it just to feel the taste. I'm always hungry as hell after training.

"And, what was the reason?" she asks, blowing softly on the piece of lasagna before popping it into her mouth.

"It's not really my place to say. It's personal." I also don't know what parts of the story Noah told me are classified. She could mention something to someone from the Order by accident, so even if I trust her completely, I don't want to risk it. Especially since Sam already knows everything.

"Oh, c'mon. Can't you at least give me a hint or something?"

"Jeez, you're nosier than Sam." She gives me a dirty look, and I say, "Sorry, Auntie, but I really can't tell you."

"'Kay, well, you know I'm here for you if you want to talk or need my advice, right?"

"I know." I smile softly and give her a peck on the cheek before digging back into the lasagna.

We finish the rest of our meal in silence after I help myself to a second portion and then top our wine glasses. "Did you have a chance to go over the Enochian text I gave you?" I ask.

"I did. It took me almost all day yesterday to translate it, but I finally finished it last night. Lemme go grab it." She stands up and exits the kitchen.

Her steps echo through the house as she goes up and down the stairs.

Nervous excitement bubbles in my veins, and I wait with bated breath as my aunt brings the leather-bound book alongside her own notebook. She sits down, rifling through the pages of her notebook. "Where is it?" she mumbles and stops on a page. "Ah, here it is." She turns it toward me.

My eyebrows pinch in concentration as I read the translation.

"'Beware of the shadow that lurks in the dead of the night. It whispers of forgotten souls and eclipses the light of life.

"'Beware of the nocturnal wind that carries the mournful wails of those denied peaceful rest.

"'Beware the dying breath, for the umbra seeks to ensnare those who linger between worlds, compelling them to a never-ending, soul-stealing twilight.

"'No escape shall be granted, for the umbra's grip tightens, and the stolen souls become eternally entwined in the ominous dance of celestial thievery.

"'A cosmic cataclysm, foretold in the shadows and unleashed at the hands of the Harbinger of Death, the Daughter of Starlight and Shadows.'"

As I finish reading the words, a sense of dread skitters down my spine. I fold my lower lip in between my teeth, trying to decipher the meaning, but come up empty. It all sounds like some weird foreboding premonition to me.

My gaze flicks to my aunt. "What do you think it means?"

"I'm not sure, honestly. The book is very old, though..."

I fish the phone out of my pocket and snap a photo of the translation.

She rips the page from the notebook and gives it to me. "Here, take it."

"Thank you, Auntie," I say before pocketing the page. "And thank you for dinner. It was delicious. You go rest, I'll clean the kitchen, and then I'll head out; I work tonight."

"You're welcome, dear. Do you mind if I go take a bath?"

"No worries; I'll see myself out." I hug her, and we say our goodbyes before she leaves the kitchen.

Drumming my fingers on the table, I debate if I should tell Kaiden about the translation. After staring at my phone screen for a few minutes, I send him the photo I took of the page.

> **Me: My aunt translated the Enochian text from the book I got from the dark witch.**

The little verification mark appears, which means he read the text, but he still doesn't reply.

Really, Kaiden? You're going to leave me on read?

I huff out an annoyed breath and take the plates and wine glasses from the table, rinsing them in the sink before placing them in the dishwasher. After I clean the counters and the sink, I wipe my hands on a rag and look at my phone again.

> **Kaiden: Sorry, angel. I'm in a meeting.**

> **Me: Oh, we can talk later. I didn't mean to disturb you.**

> **Kaiden: You didn't. I always have time for you. You didn't mention the text was in Enochian. I could have translated it.**

> **Me: You know Enochian??? Well, it's better I gave it to my aunt. Who knows what you would have asked**

in return for the translation. Anyway...what do you think it means?

Kaiden: I'm not sure. I'll look into it.

23

A fine mist hangs in the air as I enter the dingy alley situated between two aging buildings. The brick walls are stained by time and weather, with patches of peeling paint and graffiti. The *drip, drip, drip* noise coming from a busted pipe gets swallowed momentarily by the hum of traffic in the distance. The windows I pass are cracked and boarded up, and the pavement underneath my new Dr. Martens combat boots is uneven and littered with trash. As I continue my trek on the narrow alley, I step on something sticky.

Eww.

Earlier, when I arrived home, a box with a brand-new pair of over-the-knee Dr. Martens combat boots was waiting for me on the coffee table. It was beautifully wrapped, and it had a handwritten note that said,

'Sorry I threw the old ones out.

K.'

I don't want to admit it, but my insides melted as I opened the box and got the boots out. Aside from Sam, no one has ever done anything as thoughtful as this for me before. I freakin' loved my Dr. Martens, and the fact that they got destroyed when the umbra chased me equally enraged and made me sad. I can't believe Kaiden went through the trouble of getting me a new pair. My heart skips a beat when I think about him, and I shake my head, concentrating on my task while repeating my mantra in my head.

He's a demon. He's a demon. You're not attracted to a demon, Iris!

The musty odor, a combination of dampness, garbage, and neglect, alongside the pungent smell of rotting meat, crawls up my nose and makes my stomach roil with disgust as I advance on the alley. My onyx choker warms slightly while I get closer and closer to my target; it only alerts me of the remnants of demon activity.

The flickering lamppost casts eerie shadows as I round the corner. I nearly lose my dinner on the pavement when my eyes land on a zombie chomping happily on what looks to be a human arm in the corner, his back to a chain link fence. Another zombie is digging through the dumpster pushed against the exposed brick wall on my left.

Random human body parts scattered throughout the neighborhood led me to this alley. Zombies are not exactly subtle when they feed, especially since they operate on zero brain cells. When a demon possesses a human, it starts feeding on its soul. After it consumes the soul entirely and jumps to another host, there's nothing left of the human but a decaying husk with a penchant for consuming human flesh.

The zombie surfing through the dumpster turns around when I take out the sword strapped to my back and approach it. From the long, brown hair clinging in clumps to its scalp and what I can make out of the meat body dangling precariously off its bones, I can tell it was once a woman. It makes a garbled sound from deep within its chest, probably identifying me as its next meal, and stalks toward me. As it tries to grab me, I sidestep its clumsy attempt, and the razor-sharp blade of my sword goes through its rotting neck as I sever its head from its body.

The sound of tearing flesh and a pained animalistic moan fills the alley as the smell of death and rot burns my nostrils. The now lifeless body falls to the pavement with a loud thud along with the head, making the other zombie alert of the threat I possess. It jumps up from its crouched position in the corner and comes at me with a finger still dangling from its decaying teeth, which are partially exposed through hanging, rotting lips. I swear I'll have nightmares with this exact image for a few years to come.

This zombie is surprisingly agile, probably because it just ate. It brushes against my side as it tries to grab me with its bony fingers before I get the chance to fully dodge its attack. I shudder in revulsion and twirl before bringing my sword down and severing its neck from its body. The head smacks down the pavement, and it starts rolling toward the chain link fence while the body crumbles to the ground with a loud thump. I try not to gag as I wipe my sword on what's left of its clothes and put it back into its sheath, strapped to my back.

I'm about to exit the alley when a blood-curdling scream pierces the air. Despite my apprehension, I tap into hellseeker speed and sprint toward the loud sound. In another narrow alley two streets over, a man looms over a woman, his mouth latched onto her neck as blood trickles down her clothes. She is crying and trying to push at the man, but he simply grips her in a chokehold against the brick wall and feasts on her blood. Clearly, his strength outmatches hers because he is a vampire.

Since she's not dead or dying, and assuming he's part of the Obsidian Conclave, I am technically not allowed to get involved. But I can't sit by idly while a vampire attacks a woman in front of me.

"Let her go!" I grit out through clenched teeth as I uncoil the whip before swinging it over my head and cracking it forward. The loud snap slashes through the air.

However, the vampire doesn't seem scared in the slightest. A lazy smile tugs at his lips as he turns toward me like he has all the time in the world. His tall, lanky body is clad in a cheap-looking black suit. "I'm not breaking any rules, hellseeker," the vampire snaps with an oily voice, his hand still gripping the woman's throat tightly.

"P-p-please," the woman stutters. Tears run down her face in rivulets, blue eyes wide and pleading.

My nostrils flare. "I'll be the one that decides that. Are you a Conclave member?"

He shoots me a bloody grin, which looks downright sinister paired with the translucency of his skin. Extended canines flash in the artificial light cast by the neon sign of the bar across the street. "Of course I'm a Conclave member."

"Then come closer and show me your tattoo," I demand, my grip white-knuckled on the whip's handle.

"I thought you'd never ask." His smile turns dangerous, all teeth and sharp edges, as he drops his hold on the woman. She falls to her knees, and her gaze flicks to mine. I tilt my head as a sign for her to take the opportunity and run. Before she can move a muscle, the vampire grabs hold of her and thrusts his hand into the woman's chest, pulling out her still-beating heart. Her face is trapped in a silent wail of horror and surprise as she falls to the pavement in a pool of blood.

Red hot anger bubbles beneath my skin with the force of a hurricane. With a flick of my wrist, the whip coils around the vampire's legs like a serpent, tightening with a satisfying snap. The vampire, momentarily surprised, narrows his eyes and snarls at me, exposing his fangs. As I'm about to yank him toward me, the shadows around us shift and move. With a dazzling speed, about ten more vampires surround me in a circle.

I have no choice but to let the vampire go and pull back my whip. I welcome the adrenaline that sharpens my vision as a smile curves my lips. I'm outnumbered, and I know my chances of getting out of here alive are slim. I'm not going down without a fight, though.

"What is this, the sparkle convention?" I ask as the grip on my whip tightens, and with my left hand, I feel the weight of the daggers sheathed at my sides. "Wait, don't answer that. I know what you're going to say." I clear my throat and thicken my voice with mock exaggeration. "This is the skin of a killer, hellseeker."

The redhead in front of me hisses. I guess she didn't like my joke. Oh well, not everyone can appreciate good humor. I anticipate her move before she lunges at me, teeth bared. Cracking my whip in a figure-eight pattern, I coil it around her ankles and yank to the side using the hellseeker force. She crashes into the other two vampires on my right.

Chaos erupts in the next second.

Everything is a blur, a live wire of electricity zipping through me as I swing the whip in the air, creating a makeshift barrier between me and the vampires while I send my daggers flying. Shouts of agony resound as the daggers find their marks. I'm especially proud when one of them impales an eyeball with a wet crack since I'm using my left hand, my right being occupied with the whip.

One of the vampires manages to catch the end of my whip. He yanks hard. Muscles screaming in agony, I let him pull me toward him as I unsheathe my sword. With a swift arc, I sever his head from his body. Blood shoots out from the cut, and as much as I try to avoid the spray, it still covers the front of my corset. Luckily, none of it got in my mouth. Another one sizes the opportunity and grabs me by the hair. My scalp catches fire as multiple strands snap from the root. In my disorientation, I drop the whip. As soon as I recover, though, I surprise him by launching myself backward, making him lose his footing. I twirl and make a clean cut through his wrist, severing the hand holding my braid from his body.

His agony-filled scream is cut short when I swing my sword again, and the sharp blade goes through his neck. His head bounces off the asphalt as more blood shoots out, some of it getting into my mouth this time. Dammit. As I spit it out, a brawny male vampire, tall as a mountain, who looks like he's on a diet of steroid blood and could flip a truck with the flick of his finger, comes at me.

I thrust my sword forward, and he catches the blade mid-air, yanking it from my grip easily as if he just took a toy from a toddler. He throws it to the ground and punches me so hard my head flies to the side with a sickening snapping sound.

The metallic taste of blood coats my tongue as I stagger on my feet and blink a few times to clear my vision. My right leg shoots out in a powerful kick that he blocks with ease.

The vampire that was feeding from the woman earlier shouts, "Don't kill her! We need her alive," before the beefy vampire picks me up by the throat and hurls me at the brick wall like I'm a rag doll.

Fuckfuckfuckfuckfuckfuck.

I collide with the bricks so hard my lungs rattle inside my chest. The world tilts on its axis as shockwaves of white-hot pain pass through my entire body until I feel my bones vibrating. It blinds me momentarily with its intensity. Blood trickles down from the back of my head, warm and sticky as I fall to the cold asphalt with a loud thud. I suck in a jagged breath only to let it out in a muffled cry as I try my best to get up and fail.

A strange feeling slithers through my veins, like a newfound energy fighting to the surface. I don't have the strength to stop it if I wanted to. But before I can make sense of what is happening to me, I feel the prick of a needle in the side of my neck, and everything goes black.

24

*S*prawled on a blanket in the garden near the fairy house, I'm drawing a portrait of my new friend Amanda. "Heeeey," I whine when her form flickers and turns transparent.

Her eyes widen. "Sorry, I didn't realize I was doing it again," she says, her body fully materializing in front of me.

"S'ok," I tell her. I stick out my tongue in concentration, and my eyebrows draw together as I erase the lines of her mouth and start again. The sun is warming up my skin, making pretty shadows dance on the leaves in the forest. A breeze ruffles my hair softly, and a smile spreads on my face.

I'm wearing my favorite blue dress with white flowers on it. I heard Daddy telling Mommy earlier today before leaving that he saved a boy, and we will meet him tonight. I'm so excited butterflies are fighting for space in my stomach. I can't wait to see him. I never meet other kids; my Mommy says it's not safe for me, but maybe this boy will live with us, and then he will be my friend. I have lots of friends, but it would be nice if, for once, I could actually play with someone who can hold something in their hand or throw a ball.

"I'm done." I smile at Amanda and turn my sketchbook over so she can see the finished drawing.

"Her nose is a little bigger in reality, don't you think?" Chester says as he pops out of thin air next to me. He's a cranky old man with a crooked nose and a shiny bald head. He looks like one of those desert vultures I saw in the animal documentary Mommy put on the TV for me to watch earlier today.

Amanda scowls at him. "You're one to talk."

Her eyes soften as her gaze flicks to mine. "It's lovely. Thank you! You're very talented for being only five years old."

I smile brightly. "I know; Mommy tells me I'm going to be an artist."

"Iris, where are you?" Mommy shouts while looking for me in a panic from the back door of the house. Our house looks exactly like the one in the book my Mommy reads to me every night before going to sleep, The Fairy Princess, but it's so much bigger.

Living here is the best thing ever because I can play in the forest all the time. Mommy and Daddy play with me, too. I love it when Daddy pushes me in the swing; I always tell him, "Higher, Daddy! I want to touch the clouds with my fingers!" and he always does as I ask while I squeal in delight.

"I'm here, Mommy! In the garden," I shout back.

"Honey, we need to leave. Something happened, and it's not safe here anymore."

"But, Mooom!" My chest heaves, and my lower lip wobbles as tears stream down my face. "I don't want to move to another house again, I love the fairy house and, a-and Daddy is b-bringing a boy! I want to play with him! And… and my hands are dirty," I say through gulps of air and hiccups.

I grip my sketchbook as she picks me up and hurries to the car while keeping my head on her chest. I start sobbing, and Mommy's blouse gets wet. We move a lot, and I don't want to leave this house.

"I know, baby. I'm so sorry, but we need to leave. The boy will come visit when we find a new home, okay? I promise," she says while putting me in the safety seat and snapping the seatbelt in place. She closes my door, jogs around *the car, and opens the driver's door, sliding in behind the wheel.*

"Hold on, okay? Mommy's going to drive faster than usual," she says while looking at me over her right shoulder as she starts reversing the car in the driveway. I'm still crying, so I just sniffle and nod. While she drives off in a hurry, I take a look through the back window as the fairy house gets smaller and smaller in the distance. Then ugly, giant monsters appear on the front lawn, and start running after the car.

I wake with a jolt, a pained moan leaving my mouth as I blink a few times, trying to clear the sleep cobwebs from my mind. The dream clings to me—I can still feel the warmth of the sun on my face and the soft breeze combing through my hair as the image of my mother flashes through my mind.

A sharp pain pierces my brain, bringing me into the present. Another broken moan breaks loose as I stir slightly. Trying to bring my hand to my temple, I realize I can't. Something cold and heavy presses into my wrists. A shiver passes through my body, locking my muscles painfully. It's so damn cold.

What the hell? Where am I?

My chest expands with my next breath, and it feels as though I'm inhaling fire as the dense, musty air clings to my lungs. I can tell I have at least one or two broken ribs. My vision finally clears somewhat, though it's pretty dark, the only light provided by a sconce on the wall to my right, holding two flickering candles. My legs are secured in shackles, my hands bound at my back, and the cold, rough floor digs into the skin on my right side. It chills me to the bone.

Using my core muscles and pushing against the slab of stone with my shoulder, I manage to lift my upper body to a sitting position. Scooting forward, dragging my ass on the cold floor, I crane my head over my shoulder and see my hands are also in a pair of heavy shackles attached by a short chain, just like my legs. Only this chain is secured with another in an iron ring embedded into the wall at my back.

Great. Just my luck.

I pull on my restraints with as much strength as I can muster at this moment. But I only manage to make the shackles dig painfully into my skin. The clanking sound of the metal bounces off the walls loudly with my next attempt.

"Motherfucker," I swear through clenched teeth.

"You're awake," a feminine voice whispers. At first, I think I'm hallucinating, but as my eyes get accustomed to the scarce lighting, the silhouette of a woman materializes. She's sitting on top of a mattress on the floor to my far left. "How are you feeling?" she asks in the same soft tone.

"As if a speeding car crashed into me, and then a giant decided to play football with my head," I grumble and blink slowly, trying to make out my surroundings.

My eyes adjust to the lack of light in small increments. The ancient-looking walls made of weathered stone appear first, the flickering candle casting shadows that dance across the uneven surface. They're covered in a thick layer of grime, and there might be a mural of an angel beneath the dirt, but I can't be sure.

Next is the low vaulted ceiling. Thick cobwebs hang from it like creepy garlands. As I blink a few more times, the woman sitting on the mattress takes shape completely, hugging her knees to her chest, the candlelight making her sepia skin glow. Her otherworldly beauty shines through, even if it's pretty clear she's been here a while. I can tell by the unkempt state of her clothes. Also, her long, curly chestnut hair falls limply over her shoulders.

Her legs are shackled just like mine, but instead of her hands being bound at her back and secured to the wall, she has a metal collar around her neck with a crystal in the center that's secured to the wall with a chain. Several empty foam mattresses are strewn across the stone floor, and there's also a bucket in the corner.

"What's your name?" I ask her.

"I'm Ophelia," she responds in a hushed tone. "But you can call me Lia."

"I'm Iris. I would say it's nice to meet you, but I would be lying, given the circumstances."

Lia snickers at my words. "Yeah…I know the feeling." Her gaze flicks rapidly to the stairs in the dark corner as her dark skin pales slightly. "Try keeping your voice low. They don't like it when we talk."

"Oh," I whisper and scoot backward to rest my back on the cold stone wall. "Were you here when they brought me in? How long have I been out?"

She nods, sawing her lower lip between her teeth. "I'm not sure. About twelve hours. It's hard to tell since we have no windows here."

"How long have you been here?"

Fuck.

My bladder feels as if it's about to burst. I suppose the bucket is some sort of a makeshift toilet. How the hell am I supposed to reach it or even use it with my hands and feet bound?

Lia pops a shoulder. "I don't know…two weeks and a half, maybe three."

"Do you know why they took you?"

She arches an eyebrow and tucks her hair beneath her ears. I gasp and do a double take at her pointy ears.

No, that's impossible.

But how do you explain the ears then, Iris?

I dart out my tongue to moisten my cracked lips and tilt my head. "Are you—?"

Lia cuts me off. "Fae? Yup."

"B-but how?" I stutter. "I don't understand. How is it possible? I thought the fae fled the human realm hundreds of years ago because of the vampires."

"That's true. The vampires hunted the fae almost to extinction, and my people were forced to leave through portals back into Faerie or risk being enslaved by vampires and used for our blood." Her eyebrows draw together as she sighs. "Unfortunately, a war between the Seelie and Unseelie courts started about fifty years ago. My family was forced to cross back to the human realm when I was just a baby and start a new life here. There are many of us hiding under the pretense of being mortals."

My eyebrows knit together as I shake my head in disbelief. "I don't understand. How the heck haven't I heard about faeries being back until now?"

"We use magic to hide in plain sight, but the vampires manage to find us anyway. They hunt us down using lycans. They use an *aetherium* crystal to strip us of our powers when they capture us. That's what you see embedded in the collar."

I'm speechless as she continues, "I thought that the vampires hunting us down was just a cautionary tale our parents used to tell us at bedtime when we were little. Until I woke up in the middle of the night with a lycan snarling on top of me on my bed."

"That's fucked up," I mumble.

She lets out a bitter laugh. "This whole thing is fucked up."

I clear my scratchy throat. "Why do they want your blood so much, though? I heard some stories about the fae blood allowing vampires to walk in the sunlight. Is it true?"

She rests her chin on top of her knees. "It is. It also heals them, makes them stronger, induces euphoria like no other. Imagine heroin times a thousand. There's nothing more coveted by vampires than faerie blood."

Taking a moment to absorb all of this, I test my restraints again. They bite into my skin viciously and seem to tighten as my efforts increase.

What the fuck?

"Stop doing that! The chains are spelled," Lia whispers harshly. "It's impossible to escape. Me and the others tried almost every day."

I wince in pain and inhale deeply. "There were others?"

Lia makes a gesture with her hand in the air. "What do you think the other mattresses are for?"

Trying to ease the pressure from the restraints, I flex my fingers and rotate my wrists and ankles slowly. "What happened to them?"

She sucks in a shaky breath. "I'm not sure. There were four other fae women when they brought me here. After a few days, the vampires took them, and I never saw them again. I've been alone in this cell until they brought you in." Her swallow is audible, and concern is evident in the creases around her eyes. "I think…I think they sell us. That's what the others said. That there's a black market for faeries. These vampires sell us in auction to the highest bidder."

My jaw drops. "Holy shit."

"Mmhm." She looks away and starts whispering again after a few beats of silence. "So, why are you here? You're a hellseeker, right? I've only heard stories about your kind."

The sound of a door being unlocked and the creak of rusty hinges echoes, traveling down the stairs. Before I can answer Lia, a male vampire zips through the air and pins her to the stone wall by her throat. "You should know the rules by now. No fucking talking!" he screams in her face, and she crumbles within herself, making her body as small as possible, her eyes brimming with tears.

"Why don't you pick on someone your size, dipshit?" I snap and jump to my feet. The short chain connecting the shackles on my ankles hinder my balance, but I manage it. My ribs scream in protest and my vision blurs slightly with the movement.

He uses the dizzying speed again, letting go of Lia and appearing in front of me. "Shut the fuck up, cunt!" he snarls and backhands me hard on my already bruised cheek.

Pain singes me as my head snaps to the side, and I bite my tongue, drawing blood. I regain my balance, turn my head, and send a glob of spit mixed with blood right in between his eyes.

His nostrils flare, and he puffs air out of them like a bull in a fighting arena. "You're going to wish you hadn't done that!" He wipes the spit away and lunges at me. I sidestep, and before he can grab ahold of me, I headbutt him as hard as I can. Blood shoots out of his nose like a geyser, and he sways on his feet.

A deep belly laugh bubbles out of me. "Who's the cunt now?" I feel as though a fiery knife is piercing my already throbbing brain, and nausea overtakes me with the intense pain, but it was totally worth it.

Until he sends a powerful kick to my chest. The sole of his boot lands with such force I'm sure it left a deep imprint on my sternum. My back collides with the wall with a loud thud and a crack. A breath saws out of my lungs as I slide on the cold stone floor, inhaling fire instead of air. I think he just broke another rib. I don't give him the satisfaction of knowing how much pain I'm in, though. I bite the inside of my cheek so hard the taste of copper invades my mouth, and my nails bite into my palms with how hard I'm clenching my fists, but I don't make a sound.

"You're not so tough anymore, huh?" he snorts a derisive laugh before walking away. The reverb of his steps feels like a jagged knife slicing through my brain. "Stand up. You're coming with me," he snaps, and the clang of metal against stone echoes off the walls as he grabs Lia's chain.

"No, p-please," Lia pleads in a coaxing tone, her voice shaky.

"Let her go," I manage to get out through clenched teeth, but my voice is barely above a broken whisper. The room starts swaying in front of my eyes like a ship navigating treacherous waters.

Lia's desperate pleas resonate loudly as the vampire pulls her toward the stairs. There's nothing I can do about it. Guilt tightens around me like a venomous serpent, twisting my stomach into knots.

25

I drift in and out of consciousness, completely losing the notion of time. At some point, my eyes fly open at the sound of someone coming down the stairs. It's the vampire that attacked the woman in the alley and pulled her heart out of her chest. The one with the lanky body and raven hair, wearing the cheap-looking suit. He stalks toward me with an exaggerated lazy gait.

It would be more impressive if it weren't so obvious that he rehearsed it in the mirror. I bet he saw it in a movie somewhere. Shadows obscure his face, and his shiny oxfords slap the stone floor loudly before he steps closer to me with a bottle of water and a piece of stale bread in his hand.

"You hellseekers like to act so high and mighty. Well, look at you now," he says with a smug smirk, towering over me.

A muscle thrums in my jaw, and I arch an unimpressed eyebrow at him. "Big words coming from the guy who needed about ten other vampires to immobilize me. Get these shackles off me; let's fight fair and square and see who comes out alive," I snap.

He snorts. "You really think that's going to work on me?" Crouching in front of my bent legs, he uncaps the water bottle and brings it to my mouth.

Even though I feel like I've been wandering beneath the blistering desert sun for days, I press my lips in a thin line, then jerk my head to the side. They already drugged me once in the alley, injecting me with God knows what. I can't risk drinking something that might be spiked.

"You're not thirsty?" he asks in a bored tone. When I don't move my head, he sucks on his teeth, puts the cap back on the bottle, and throws it on the floor next to me. He shrugs. "Okay then. Suit yourself. I guess you're not hungry either." He discards the piece of bread next to the bottle as he stands, brushes off the lines in his pants, and turns on his heel.

"Wait," I call out. "Why are you doing this?"

He turns to face me again. Then, he folds his arms in front of his chest. With a mocking tone, he says, "Aw, wouldn't you like to know."

"What do you want in exchange for the information?"

He laughs deep in his belly. "You really think you're in the position to bargain with me?"

"There must be something you want…"

Tilting his head, he flashes his canines and zips through the air until he's crouching with his nose pressed close to the side of my head, sniffing my blood-soaked hair. A repulsed shudder passes through my body. My fingers itch with the need to punch him, but I need to see how this plays out first. "Fuck. Your blood smells sweeter than any faerie I drank from. Might as well get a taste."

"I'll let you bite me if you tell me why you brought me here."

He snickers. "Do you think I need your approval? I can just take what I want."

"If you try to take my blood by force, I'm going to put up a hell of a fight. You saw me fighting in the alley. Wouldn't it be nicer to have a willing participant? I might throw in another favor if you tell me," I say as seductively as I can.

Ugh. I think I just threw up in my mouth.

A slimy smile spreads on his face. "Deal."

I bat my eyelashes at him. "Can you tell me first? What if I pass out after you drink from me? I've never done this before."

"Fine. But you'll suck my cock too."

Bile surges in my throat, and I bite hard on my tongue as I nod, pooling blood. I'd rather let someone skin me alive with a blunt knife and then pour boiling water on my exposed organs.

"There's a bounty on your head. Congratulations. You, Iris Harper, are on Hell's most wanted list," he whispers in my ear.

My mind spins as soon as I register his words.

Dafuq?

I know I'm a hellseeker, but I'm one of many. It doesn't make any sense. "Who put a bounty on me?"

He lifts a shoulder nonchalantly. "Don't know. Don't care. I'm just the middleman. I deliver you and get the money. Now pay up."

I need to escape before he manages to hand me over to whatever demon put the bounty on me. "I need to pee first," I blurt out.

Rolling his eyes, he stands, fishes a set of keys from his pants pocket, and comes closer. "Don't even think of trying anything," he fires back before using one of the keys to unlock the shackles around my wrists.

Bringing my hands in front of me, I let out a breath of relief as I start rubbing gently at the raw skin with my fingers.

"Stand up," he commands.

As I push up, the room spins with me. Taking a deep breath that quickly backfires because my ribs stab me repeatedly in the lungs, I start walking at a snail's pace.

"Hurry the fuck up, I don't have all day, and I'm hungry," he snaps and pushes me from behind.

Pretending to trip on my legs, I wait until he's close enough and twirl on the balls of my feet, sending my fist flying in a powerful uppercut. The vampire's head snaps back as he staggers on his feet.

He bares his fangs at me in a snarl. "You stupid bitch!" he bellows, then lunges at me at warp speed. I manage to get another punch in before he grabs me, spins me around, and puts me in a rear headlock. In the next second, he sinks his fangs in the juncture between my neck and shoulder. Blinding pain surges through me as his sharp teeth pierce my skin. He starts gobbling my blood like a leech. I lodge my fingers in the space between his forearm and my neck. Bending my knees at the same time, I move the center of gravity so I can throw him off me.

However, I never get the chance because all of a sudden, he lets me go. I stagger forward, almost face-planting, my movements restricted by the shackles around my ankles. At the last moment, I manage to find my balance and turn around. I'm ready to gouge his eyes out for biting me and drinking my blood. But my movements falter at the look on his face.

Both of his hands are around his throat as if he's choking on something, his whole face scrunched in horror, his eyes as big as saucers. His veins are turning black as if poisoned blood is circulating through them. "Y-you…y-your blood. What a-are you?" he stammers. Before I can blink, he starts desiccating and disintegrating in front of my eyes until only a pile of dust is left. His clothes fall to the floor with a shuffling sound.

I'm frozen in place, my mouth agape and my heart galloping in my chest. *Um, what the hell just happened?* I rub my eyes and then blink a few times for good measure. Yup, he's still toast. Well, I didn't see that coming.

It takes more than a few minutes for my brain to finally catch up to the fact that this is my opportunity to escape. Dropping to my haunches,

I dig into the trousers lying on the floor and get the keys he used earlier, then plant my ass on the cold slab of stone to unlock my shackles. After a few tries, I finally find the right key.

When they snap open, a breath of relief leaves my lungs, and I jump to my feet. The movement jostles my ribs, and my vision blurs at the edges slightly as I hiss in pain. I go to the bucket in the corner to take care of my business before ambling toward the stairs. I climb them carefully, listening to every sound. It's not that easy, though, with the pulsing war drum in my ears.

Reaching the top of the stairs, I'm faced with a wooden door. It looks ancient. I curl my fingers around the rusty handle before pressing on it carefully. It's locked. Luckily, I took the keys with me. I lodge one of the keys that looks big enough to fit into the lock and turn it slowly. The door opens with a soft creak, and I slide through the small opening, praying that no one is on the other side. I get out on a narrow hallway lit with sconces. The flickering candlelight casts creepy shadows on the walls. Relief washes over me when it's clear I'm completely alone, and I close the door at my back.

Tip-toeing, I make my way through the hallway and pause in my tracks at the voices coming through a slightly ajar door on my right. I don't even breathe as I approach it. The sound spilling from the room is filled with music and raucous laughter, echoing off the stone walls.

As I inch forward, I peek through the small gap. There's a huge marble tomb at the back of the room. Cobwebs hang from it, dirt and grime thick on its surface. An ancient-looking angel statue is at its back, its wings chipped and looking as dirty and old as the tomb. I have to do a double take because next to it is a man tied to a cross in an x shape, naked and passed out, his skin ashen. Two vampires are feeding from him; the male latched to his neck while the female sucks on his wrist.

Music blasts from a speaker. A group of vampires dances lasciviously to the beat. Around ten more sit around a rickety wooden table in the corner, playing a card game—poker, if I'm not mistaken. They throw insults at each other and sip on an amber liquid in highball glasses.

My hand shoots out on its own accord, wrapping around the door handle. But I drop it when the realization that I can't save the man twists my stomach into knots. I'm injured, and I have no weapons…I'll get us both killed. Fuck. The only way I can help him is to escape and come back with reinforcements. I make a silent promise to the man that I'll be back. Hopefully, it's not going to be too late.

Clenching my jaw and steeling my resolve, I swallow hard and don't even breathe as I bridge the gap from one side of the door to the other. A chair scrapes loudly on the stone floor. I freeze. The breath I've been holding turns into icicles inside my lungs. Time stretches painfully as a long second passes. Then another. Finally, someone says, "Move. It's my turn to eat."

My heart rate slows with a relieved huff as I continue tip-toeing in the dimly lit hallway. It ends in a spiraling set of stairs. Reaching the top, I encounter yet another closed door. This one is not locked, so I turn the handle. Light spills in the dark corridor through the small crack. It reveals the side of what seems to be an ornate altar. Judging by the decaying remnants of pews, the long-forgotten candles melted into grotesque wax sculptures, and the thick layers of dust that cover every surface, this is an abandoned church.

Stained-glass windows once adorned with vibrant depictions of saints and angels are boarded up. A few streaks of light filter through the gaps, casting eerie patterns on the dusty marble floor. Movement catches the corner of my eye. There's a female vampire doing rounds. It's the redhead from the alley. I wait for her to turn her back on me to open the door and slide through the crack as quickly as I can.

With my heart thundering in my ears, I duck around the corner and flatten myself to the wall. Moving on the balls of my feet, I crouch and hide behind a Virgin Mary statue. My eyes dart around in search of something I can use as a weapon. Through the small opening in the door, I could barely make out the space, but now I realize it's more of an abandoned cathedral than a church. A towering, vaulted ceiling soars high above, adorned with once-glorious frescoes, now crumbled and faded by the passing of time.

There's a jagged piece of wood that I could use as a stake, but it's right in the middle of the nave, on the marble floor, so to get it, I would be exposing myself. *Fuck.* A wooden stake impaled into a vampire's heart is not fatal, but it does put them in a temporary paralysis state until someone takes it out. I have to at least try and get it.

The vampire has now reached the massive wooden door of the entrance, still with her back to me. On my hands and knees, I shuffle to the pews on my right, then flatten myself to the wood. I lift my head over the bench. The vampire is now on my left, in the aisle opposite me, walking toward the altar but still close to the entrance. I duck and continue on my hands and knees on the aisle, using the pews as cover until I reach the center of the cathedral.

It's now or never.

Sliding in the space between pews, I reach the nave. I peek over the wooden bench for the redhead, but I can't see her anymore.

What the fuck? Where did she go?

A *tsk, tsk, tsk* sound from behind makes me whirl around so fast I get whiplash.

"Well, well, what do we have here? If it isn't the little hellseeker bitch trying to escape." She's standing on the other end of the pew, looking at me with a Cheshire cat grin. She puts her fingers in her mouth and whistles like a referee, probably to alert the others. The loud, high-pitched sound bounces off the walls in waves.

My heart rattles against my ribcage, pumping adrenaline through my veins as I stand and launch myself in the air at the same time the vampire lunges at me. Right as my fingers wrap around the jagged piece of wood, she lands on top of me. The impact steals the breath from my lungs. Like a claw, her hand grabs the back of my head. Then her nails bite savagely into my scalp before she smashes my forehead into the marble floor.

Red-hot pain explodes in my nerve endings, and blood shoots out of my nose. My vision dims and blackens at the edges. I lose consciousness for a second, then come to in the next. Biting the inside of my cheek hard, I push through it, and tapping into the hellseeker strength, I send my elbow into her side. She lets go of my head with a sharp curse under her breath. Not wasting any time, I flip onto my back and impale the jagged piece of wood right through her heart. An anger-filled, ear-splitting shriek echoes in the vast space as the color drains from her skin. Her body turns to an unmoving corpse before it falls on top of me. She's heavier than she looks, and the impact jolts my already battered ribs.

If the other vampires didn't hear her whistle before, they surely heard the scream. I have to get out of here, *now*.

With a grunt, I push the redhead off me and jump up, ignoring the pain shooting from my ribs. Pumping my arms, I start running as fast as I can toward the massive wooden door.

C'mon, Iris! You're so close.

Blurry figures zip through the air, and before I can reach the door, I'm completely surrounded by vampires with no idea where the hell they came from. There are at least thirty of them. I'm running so fast that when I halt, my momentum propels me forward, and I collide with a hard chest, bouncing off it slightly, bones rattling.

Shit. Shit. Shit.

My stomach takes a nosedive when I realize it's the vampire that looks like a jacked-up professional wrestler.

26

His meaty hand shoots out at the same time I take a step back and slam into something hard, again. But this time, an intoxicatingly warm, sensual scent fills my nostrils—black cherries, fresh cloves, leather, with just a hint of rum.

"Hello, angel," someone whispers in my ear, the gravelly voice rolling over me like honey.

My breath hitches in my chest. I know this voice. "Kaiden?" I murmur, and my heart starts doing acrobatics in my chest as his arm bands protectively across my midriff, fusing my back completely with his front while the other lunges and blocks the vampire's attempt to punch me. His tattooed fingers wrap around the fist, stopping it mid-air.

"No one fucking touches what's mine!" Kaiden growls possessively as he tightens his hold. The sickening sound of bones crunching fills the air.

Um, what did he just say?

I barely have time to register his words because all of a sudden, the vampire is engulfed in a red fire so deep it almost looks black. He howls in pain as he's being burnt to a crisp while the other vampires hiss and tighten their circle around us. The smell of charred meat burns the back of my throat, making my eyes water.

Kaiden pulls me back from the scorching flames. "Stay here. Don't move," he commands in my ear.

With a frown, I touch my onyx choker. It should have alerted me of Kaiden's presence. This is the second time this has happened. Maybe it's not defective after all…

Suddenly, one of the barricaded stained-glass windows explodes, sending tiny shards of glass and wood splinters everywhere. We all turn toward the commotion as a silvery-black panther lands nimbly in front of the altar, its fur glinting as if made of pure moonlight. I do a double take when it's followed by what I assume is a gigantic wolf shifter with ash brown fur and honey eyes. The glass crunches under its humongous paws as they make contact with the marble floor.

When I think I've seen it all, a man in a black designer suit zips through the air from the direction of the shattered window, landing in a crouch next to the panther, holding a machete. He straightens his muscular body, brushing his shoulder of the remaining pieces of glass. Arresting blue-green eyes snap to mine when he catches me staring, and he flashes a devious grin in my direction before baring his fangs and snarling at the vampires surrounding us.

"What is happening?" I mumble in disbelief.

The panther roars menacingly, the animalistic sound bouncing off the decaying marble walls as it pounces on the line of vampires, starting to decapitate them using only the snap of its jaws and claws. In the next second, madness ensues. Everyone collides in a flurry of movements almost too rapid for my eyes to track.

I'm speechless, jaw on the floor, staring at the magnificent nine-foot feline made out of pure muscles as it decimates the vampires alongside the equally powerful gigantic wolf and the strange vampire in the designer suit who wields the machete as if it's an extension of his body. They all work together synchronously, like a well-oiled machine, the vampires not standing a chance.

Kaiden joins the fray, popping in and out of thin air at will, disorienting them while ripping their limbs and heads off with his bare hands and setting them on fire. He's even more powerful than I thought. My eyes drink him in, the way he fights like he was born just for this purpose, his magnificent body decked in black jeans, a leather jacket over a black tee, and combat boots. He moves gracefully as if he is death itself. He doesn't even get blood on him; that's how fast he is.

Sensing my burning gaze, Kaiden turns to look at me and tilts his head. He winks and shoots me a panty-dropping grin while holding a bloody head. A shiver passes down my spine the moment our gazes collide—his irises engulfed completely in crimson, the same color as the flames shooting from his palms. His scleras are turned black.

I break the eye contact, and rapidly approaching a broken-down pew, I send my leg in a powerful kick, splintering what is left of the wood. I manage to dislodge a few jagged pieces and dive head-first into the fight as a female vampire sneaks at Kaiden's back while he's busy dismembering another. The bitch is holding my sword.

She lunges at Kaiden, and at the same time, I jump, propelling myself into the air while swinging my arm in a wide arc. I impale the sharp piece of wood into her back, right where her heart is. The wail she lets out gets lost in the booming sounds of the battle as her body freezes, turning immobile. Using my left hand, I wrap my fingers around the hilt of my sword to take it back. But just as I'm about to face plant into her back, an arm snakes along my middle, stopping my movement.

I don't even have to look to know who it is; the current surging through me is evidence enough. Swallowing hard, I whirl, and I'm face to face with Kaiden. The hand he has splayed on my lower back burns through my gear. He tightens his hold on me, pulling me closer. Something ignites in me and turns my blood into molten lava. My nipples draw to hard tips as they brush against the hard planes of his chest, and our heavy breaths mingle, chests heaving.

His jaw ticks. "I told you not to move," he snaps while looking down his nose at me. His narrowed eyes are nothing more than two crimson slits. A few tendrils of inky hair have escaped the leather tie, framing his stupidly gorgeous face that looks too perfect to be real.

Ugh.

My palm itches with the need to brush them back. I clench my fingers and resist the urge. "Seriously?" I arch an eyebrow, huffing. "I think you meant to say 'thank you, Iris,'" I snark with a saccharine smile.

His nostrils flare. "I didn't need your help."

I scoff. "You sure looked like you did to me."

"You could have gotten hurt," he fires back, acidly.

"I can hold my own, thank you very much."

"Can you?" He tilts his head. "You have at least two broken ribs with the way your breath wheezes out of your lungs. Your pupils are blown out, surely from a concussion, and you're so full of blood and bruises you look like you've been in a fucking car wreck."

"It's not all mine," I mutter.

Kaiden's gaze drops to the juncture between my neck and shoulder. A muscle thrums in his jaw, and the vein on the side of his forehead looks like it's about to burst as his hand comes up. The pads of his fingers brush over my skin gently, making me shiver. "Who. The. Fuck. Did. This. To. You?" he grits out through clenched teeth. Golden sparks swirl with the crimson in his eyes. The floor starts to shake violently beneath my feet, chandeliers, and ornate altar statues threatening to topple down.

What in the? Is…is Kaiden doing this?

"He's dead," I say quickly. Deep cracks start forming in the already dilapidated walls. *Fuck.* If he doesn't stop, the whole cathedral is going to crumble on top of us.

"Kaiden. What the hell, man? You're going to bury us here," the hot vampire with the machete bellows from somewhere behind Kaiden.

As soon as he finishes saying that, the Virgin Mary statue turns to rubble, and a piece of the wall smashes against the floor, leaving a dusty cloud and a gaping hole behind. Gold rapidly takes over the crimson in Kaiden's eyes as his sclera turns a blinding white.

"Kaiden, you need to calm down," I murmur, framing his jaw with my hand. At my touch, he seems to snap out of it, and the earthquake stops abruptly as he sucks in a sharp breath, body shaking. He blinks. Then his eyes turn back to normal.

I let out a breath of relief, and my tongue darts out to wet my cracked lips.

Kaiden's eyes snap to my lips. The air sparks between us. Everything around us fades into a blurry background. My heart skips a beat; then it thuds hard against my ribcage. Butterflies swarm angrily in my stomach as they fight to escape the enclosed space. I'm mesmerized by the hunger in his eyes. He dips his head, but before his lips make contact with mine, movement catches the corner of my eye.

"DUCK!" I scream, and Kaiden pops off. He reappears at the back of the vampire who tried sneaking up on us, grabbing him by the nape of his neck and stopping his momentum.

Swinging my sword, I decapitate the vampire with a clean sweep, missing Kaiden's fingers by half an inch. The head drops with a wet thud to the marble floor, and blood shoots out. It paints Kaiden's face, and some of it drips down his clothes. He discards the cadaver, throwing me a scathing glare and wiping at his face with the back of his hand.

With another saccharine smile, I deadpan, "You're welcome."

Apparently, this was the last vampire to kill. An eerie silence fills the air as my eyes take in the carnage before me. Headless corpses, scattered limbs, and bloody heads cover the marble floor like a gory blanket thrown over a pool of blood. The musty smell of decay mingles with that of charred flesh, blood, and death. It coats my lungs and makes my stomach churn unpleasantly.

"Malik, Iris is injured." Kaiden's powerful voice snaps me out of it as the panther prowls toward us, stepping over the headless bodies.

The air shimmers slightly around its form, and all of a sudden, a man is standing in front of us instead of the panther. My eyebrows shoot up in surprise. I know about the existence of shifters other than wolves, but I also know they're very rare. And isn't Malik supposed to be a warlock? I have never heard of a black magic wielder who can shift into an animal at the same time.

He's striking, with slanted, catlike, pale hazel eyes, the taupe hue of his skin enhanced by the long silver hair reaching his waist. I don't think I have ever seen hair like his, shimmering and lively as if spun by moonlight. Even his body resembles that of a feline in the way he moves, as if he's fluid, muscular, and lean at the same time. The black leather duster he's wearing would look ridiculous if he weren't so freakin' hot.

Malik steps next to Kaiden. "I need to pull some juice from you. I used everything I had in the fight," he says, his gaze locked with Kaiden's.

"Take as much as you need," Kaiden tells Malik.

"There's no need; I'm fine," I mumble. But as I inhale, I'm reminded of the state of my ribs, the pain shooting through my body making me dizzy. I sway slightly on my feet. Now that the fight is over, the adrenaline crash is starting to settle in.

"You're not fine." Kaiden's shrewd eyes flick to mine. He arches an eyebrow as he tilts his head.

Malik takes two steps, stopping right in front of me. The piercing in his septum glints slightly when it catches the light of a flickering candle. "May I?"

Placing the sword in its sheath at my back, I simply nod, and he brings his warm hand to the center of my chest at the same time as Kaiden comes to stand next to him. Malik places his other hand on Kaiden's chest. His eyes snap shut, wrinkles forming with the pressure at the corners as he starts chanting, his veins swirling with inky, dark magic. It flows in the air like a thick fog before it wraps around me until I'm surrounded only by darkness. A strange feeling overtakes me. With every inhale, I feel something inside of me mending as if skin and bone start to piece themselves back together.

The chanting stops after a few minutes, and the dark fog dissipates as Malik drops his arms at the sides of his body. His shoulders slump, and his face takes on a gaunt appearance, dark circles forming under his eyes as if the use of dark magic took its toll on his body.

"Thank you for healing me, and I also haven't had a chance to thank you for the last time, you know, when the umbra attacked me," I say.

Malik winks. "No worries, sweets. Kaiden would have murdered me if I let you die. I happen to like my head attached to my neck, thank you very much." His feline eyes bore into mine like he's searching for something.

Kaiden clears his throat, and he quickly steps back. "Where's Logan?" he asks, addressing the vampire that's now standing next to him.

"He went outside to shift and get dressed. His clothes were in his truck," he answers. "I did a full sweep of the grounds. We killed all of them." His gaze flicks to mine. "I believe these are yours," he says as he extends five daggers, my phone, and my whip toward me.

"Thanks." I take my weapons and slide my phone into the back pocket of my pants. "Wait, there was this guy tied to a wooden cross."

A muscle ticks in his jaw. He's incredibly handsome, with olive-tan skin, a short beard, and a proud Roman nose, his raven locks swept back with a clean shave on the sides, longer on top and wavy. "He's dead. They drained all of his blood."

"Oh," I sigh, biting my lip. Another lost life.

"I'm Dominic, by the way."

"Iris, nice to meet you," I say before coiling the whip tightly to place it in its holster. Grateful to feel the weight of my daggers again, I slide them back one by one in their place at my ribs.

Dominic rakes a hand through his hair as his lips curl in a dangerous smile. "Oh, I know who you are. We met the night the umbra attacked you, though you were unconscious, so I guess it doesn't count. Also, Kaiden can't shut up about you." He chuckles, making me blush.

A laugh belts out of Malik. "That he can't. I swear to God my ear is going to fall any day now."

"Shut the fuck up, dipshits," Kaiden bites back with a snarl, earning a shit-eating grin in response from Dominic.

"I would shake your hand, but you look like you've bathed in blood, and I haven't had the chance to feed today," Dominic says. There's a glint of animalistic hunger in his eyes. The way he scans my body up and down isn't sexual by any means, though.

"Hate to break it to you, buddy, but you would turn into a pile of dust if you tasted my blood," I tell him, arching an eyebrow, folding my arms in front of my chest.

Dominic, Kaiden, and Malik share *a look* before Kaiden asks, "What do you mean?"

"Well, I didn't have time to explain this since you blew a gasket and almost buried us in rubble earlier. Anyway, they kept me in a crypt below ground. This vampire bit me when I tried to escape, but he acted as if he ingested poison. He asked me what I am, and then he started to disintegrate right before my eyes until only dust was left. That's weird, right?"

Kaiden frowns, sucking on his teeth as if in thought. "Yeah," he says after a few seconds of silence.

"Is this supposed to happen when a vampire bites a lightborn? I mean, I've never heard something like this happening before. Could it be the blessed bloodline?" I press while my gaze flits to Dominic. He must have an answer since he's a vampire.

"It's not the bloodline. Vampires have fed off lightborn and been fine before," he responds but doesn't offer anything more.

My lips purse. I feel as though there's something they're purposefully leaving out. Before I can pester them with more questions, Malik says, "I'm beat. Can we go? The smell of death is burning a hole through my brain."

Without waiting for our response, he strides to the massive wooden door that is now open and steps through it. We follow him out of the church.

27

A gust of wind slams into my face, ruffling the strands of hair that escaped my braid. I push them back while I inhale deeply. The crisp air feels like heaven after being locked for so many hours in that crypt. Dawn breaks on the horizon, painting the moonless indigo sky in vibrant burnt orange and fuchsia streaks.

"Where are we?" I ask, looking left and right, but we're only surrounded by overgrown grass and some cars parked to the side that I assume were used by the vampires.

"Bumfuck nowhere," Malik says before taking a hair tie out of the pocket of his leather duster to tie his hair in a low ponytail at the base of his nape. He and Dominic are walking in front of me and Kaiden.

"We're three hours outside of Ashville. There's an abandoned town half an hour from here," Kaiden juts in. He's walking so close to me that I can feel the heat radiating from his body. His sensual black cherry scent wraps around me in waves, with a hint of fresh sweat. I resist the urge to rub against him like a cat.

The sounds of chirping crickets fill the air, and droplets of dew stick to my Dr. Martens as we make our way through the overgrown grass. "What day is it? I kind of lost track of time in that crypt. It was early Friday morning, and I was just about to finish my shift when the vampires jumped me in a dingy alley."

"It's Sunday," Dominic answers.

Ugh.

And there goes another one of my weekends.

"How did you guys find me?" I ask.

Malik looks over his shoulder at me. "Tracking spell."

"Well, um, thank you for getting me out of there. To all of you," I say. I never imagined dark creatures would come to my aid, ever, especially ones part of the Obsidian Conclave.

They all mumble a "You're welcome," in my direction.

"But why?" I ask softly.

Dominic turns slightly, eyebrows drawn. "Why what?"

"Why did you guys track me? I mean, how did you know I was in trouble?"

"I called you a few times, and you didn't answer, so I came by your place, and your neighbor said she hadn't seen you in some time, so I got worried," Kaiden offers.

Why does that make my insides pitch? "Oh," I breathe.

Malik chokes on a laugh. "Yeah...*worried*. I thought you were going to level Ashville to the ground, and I swear I saw my life flash before my eyes when the first tracking spell failed," he mutters, giving Kaiden a pointed look over his shoulder.

Kaiden doesn't deny any of the things Malik said, he just grunts, and my heart does a backflip as I sneak a look at him. He's so damn serious. I can't help but compare this Kaiden to the one when he's alone with me. He's so different. It's as though he's two different people.

"Pay up, fuckface," Malik says all of a sudden, breaking the silence.

"Oh, c'mon, you killed what, just one more than I did?" Dominic grumbles, fishing out a wallet from his breast pocket. He slaps a few hundred-dollar bills in Malik's awaiting palm.

Malik pockets the money. "For your information, I killed two more, thank you very much."

My eyebrows crinkle as I throw them a confused look.

Kaiden rolls his eyes. "They like to bet on shit. It's their thing."

A laugh bubbles out of me. "You bet on how many vampires you would kill tonight?"

Malik turns slightly, smiling roguishly. "Actually, we bet on which of us is the best fighter. Obviously, I won. These fuckers don't stand a chance."

Dominic punches him in the shoulder. "Dream on, dickbag."

They keep throwing insults at each other for a few more minutes until we encounter a dirt road with two cars parked on the side: a truck and an SUV. A massive guy is leaning with his back on the fancy-looking truck, his arms crossed in front of his chest and muscles bulging the fabric of his forest green Henley. The color makes his deep amber skin pop. A mop of artfully messed-up ash-brown curls sits atop his head, the sides buzzed short, and his full lips curl up in a smile the moment he sees us approaching. He must be the wolf shifter.

"C'mon, fuckers, hurry up. Ava's waiting for me at home," he says, and then his eyes flick to me. He lifts his chin in greeting, the sunrise-streaked sky reflecting in his honey-colored eyes. "Hey, I'm Logan."

I wave awkwardly because I don't know what else to do. "I'm Iris."

"I know." He gives me a roguish grin, displaying a row of perfectly straight, pearly white teeth while opening the truck's back door.

Lifting an eyebrow, I ask, "Let me guess, we met on the night the umbra attacked me, but I was unconscious?"

Logan nods. "Pretty much, yeah."

"Shotgun," Dominic calls out like he's not older than fifteen before climbing in the passenger seat. "I'll see you around, *bella*." He winks at me and closes the door.

"Asshole," Malik grumbles, sliding in the back. He presses the heels of his palms into his eyes with a weighted sigh. "I'm going to need a fucking week to recover from this."

Guilt twists my insides. I'm sure my injuries were no walk in the park to heal.

"We have to stop for ice cream on the way. My girl's craving some mint chocolate chip," Logan says before rounding the hood.

Malik visibly shudders at that. "Is she going to dip pickles in that too? I mean, it's bad enough that shit tastes like straight-up toothpaste."

Logan laughs. "Probably. Yesterday, she had peanut butter on toast with hot sauce and pickles." He slides behind the wheel and starts the engine.

Malik gags. "Pregnancy cravings are fucking crazy, man. Remind me not to stop by your house at lunchtime anymore. I think I'll be scarred for life if I see her eat tuna and ice cream again." He turns his head to look at Kaiden, his hand on the door handle. "Are we still doing the Conclave meeting tonight?"

"Not sure. I'll let you know," Kaiden responds.

"'K." Malik closes the door, and the truck peels off, leaving a dust cloud behind.

"C'mon. Let's go." Kaiden places his hand at the small of my back, guiding me to the blacked-out Escalade. He opens the passenger door for me.

I unbuckle my sword's holster, throwing it in the back seat before sitting down. With a deep sigh, I sink into the comfortable leather chair, then tilt my head back on the rest, eyes closed. They fly open when I feel Kaiden's body heat. He brushes against me as he bends to snap my seat belt in place. Fireworks go off at every point of contact between our bodies, and I swallow hard when he turns slightly, grazing his knuckles on the side of my face. My pulse scatters.

"I'll be right back," he murmurs before dropping a large bottle of water in my lap and closing the door. He pops off. His absence leaves me cold, and I shiver slightly. I take a deep breath, but it does nothing to still my erratic heartbeat as Kaiden's smell invades my senses. It clings to the interior of the car, warming up my insides.

Fuck me. He smells like sex and sin wrapped into one glorious tattooed package.

I down half of the water in the bottle in three gulps. As I put the cap back on, Kaiden pops out of thin air behind the wheel, throws the SUV into drive, and speeds away. "Alkaline" by Sleep Token plays softly in the speakers, and I murmur along with the lyrics. The cathedral is engulfed in giant crimson flames reflecting in the side mirror as I look through it, so tall they blend in with the sunrise-kissed sky. So that's what Kaiden disappeared to do.

My sweat-slicked fingers curl in my lap as the familiar dread creeps up in the back of my throat. *Shit.* Not again. I really hoped that taxi ride was just a fluke, but the car crash flashback fucked me up good. The scenery is a blur in my window as I lean my head on the cold glass. Panic tastes like ash on my tongue as numbness seeps into my limbs. Sucking in a jagged breath and clenching my jaw, I try to keep it contained.

"Iris?" A warm hand wrapped around my upper thigh snaps me out of it. "You need me to stop?" he asks, concern evident in the lines etched in the corners of his eyes and mouth. Tingles bloom from his touch all throughout my body.

"No," I mumble. "It's not necessary. The panic usually goes away after a while."

"Do you want me to open the window? Maybe some fresh air will help."

I simply nod. I would have done it, but my fingers are so clenched I don't think I can move them. The window rolls down halfway, and

I inhale deeply, trapping the crisp morning air into my lungs while closing my eyes. It cools off my skin as it ruffles my hair. Kaiden doesn't remove his hand, and I don't ask him to. His touch grounds me. Keeps me in the present. I don't know what this says about me, that I am so comforted by a demon's touch, but I can't seem to bring myself to care at this moment. He saved me again. He killed for me.

After a while, the dread subsides, and my muscles relax. I don't think that the way my heart's thudding against my ribcage has anything to do with my car anxiety anymore, but with the hot demon sitting next to me, his touch burning through my pants. I press the button to roll up the window.

Kaiden's gaze flits to my face. "Feeling better?"

"Yeah, thanks." I grab the amethyst pendant between my fingers to play with it, as I often do to distract myself when in a moving car. When the pads unconsciously brush against the onyx choker, I drop my hand in my lap with a deep frown. "Whenever I'm near you, my onyx choker doesn't signal that I'm in the proximity of a demon. At first, I thought it was broken, and I even changed it for a new one, but now I'm starting to believe it's because of you. Do you know why this is happening?"

His hands tighten on the wheel. "Might be because of my blood," he replies, and I wait for him to expand on the response, but he doesn't.

Then I remember that when I clipped him with my foot in the jaw, he didn't bleed like a normal demon would. Huh. "I don't understand. Are your parents a special race of demons or what?"

"Something like that," he says cryptically.

I resist the urge to roll my eyes at him and opt to change the subject to something else I found weird when Kaiden and his friends came in through the church window, guns blazing. "When you said your warlock friend saved me, I didn't picture him being a dark magic wielder. I thought only light witches had healing abilities."

"Malik is just…special."

Wow. Shocking. Another vague response to which I let out a huff in response. I also want to ask how the hell is Malik able to shift into a panther like that and not even damage his clothes in the process. But I bite my tongue instead. An awkward silence stretches between us. I can't stand it. It makes my skin itch. Besides, I need to distract myself from another impending panic attack, so I say, "There was a fae held captive in the crypt when they brought me in. Her name is Ophelia. They took her away before I had the chance to escape. Did you know about the fae being back?"

His eyes snap back to the road. "For some time now, yeah. They've managed to hide pretty well, though, since they've crossed back into the human realm." He drums a rhythm with his fingers on the steering wheel. "Rogue vampires are hunting them. When we eradicated the flesh trade from the Conclave, it created a void. The rogue vampires took advantage of that and created their own trafficking ring. They pay dark witches to put wards on their hideouts. It's a fucking nightmare tracking them down. We're working on infiltrating Dominic to dismantle the ring. It's been proven very difficult so far, though. This den—we've been looking for it for over a year. They've been taking other creatures too, selling them."

"Lia said there were four other fae women with her in that crypt before they took them, and she never saw them again." I swallow as I fumble with my fingers in my lap. "Jesus, this is crazy. How the fuck did the Order members not know about this? Maybe we could help somehow. It's sick…what they're doing. Selling them like meat."

"The Order and the Obsidian Conclave working together?" Kaiden huffs a derisive laugh. "Do you believe the Order does not know? They don't fucking care as long as it involves dark creatures. They don't give a shit about us. They call us lesser beings for a reason."

I open my mouth, then snap my jaw shut because what the hell can I say? He's right. That doesn't mean that this sits right with me. My job in the Order is my whole life, and everything they taught us is ingrained into the marrow of my bones. Still, the injustice for what is happening to the poor fae slithers through my veins like wildfire.

"You're moving in with me. I'll take you to my penthouse, and then I'll arrange for someone to bring all your stuff to my place as soon as possible. Let Grayson know you'll take a vacation or something, pretend to be sick, whatever you want. I'm the only one that can keep you safe," Kaiden says matter-of-factly after a few beats of silence.

A surprised laugh bubbles out of me. It dies quickly when I realize he's not joking. My mouth opens and closes a few times in shock at the words that came out of his mouth. Soon enough, anger replaces the shock, igniting my blood. "Are you on crack or something?" I mutter in disbelief. "Hell will freeze over before I move in with a demon."

Kaiden pulls back his hand from my thigh, white-knuckling the wheel, and the absence of his touch twists my stomach into knots. His jaw ticks. "You don't fucking get it, do you? You're in danger, Iris. Do you think this was a coincidence? I told you someone's after you. I can't protect you if you're not with me at all times."

"I can protect myself," I scoff. "Get it through your thick skull, pretty boy. Me moving in with you. Not happening."

He throws me a scathing glare, his voice dropping down an octave. "Oh yeah? Then how the fuck did you end up here?"

Why does he care so much?

I suck in a serrated breath as realization kicks in. "You knew," I say shakily. "The vampire that bit me, he told me there's a bounty on my head. That I'm on Hell's most wanted list and that he was going to hand me over to the demon that put me there. You knew about that, didn't you? That's why you told me to lay low and take a break from my hellseeker responsibilities."

Kaiden's jaw ticks, and his grip on the steering wheel tightens, but he doesn't say anything. I don't need a response; I can read it on his face.

My nostrils flare, and my fingers curl into fists in my lap. "Why the fuck didn't you tell me?" I screech.

"I didn't want to scare you, not until I knew more."

"You lied to me," I seethe.

The vein at his temple looks like it's about to burst any second now. "I didn't lie to you; I told you I don't know who is after you and that I want to find out. I just left that part out. I did tell you that you were in danger and that they were going to come after you again, didn't I? What the fuck do you think that meant?"

I snicker. "Are you for real? The part that you decided to leave out was pretty fucking important, don't you think? I mean, hello, there's a bounty on me." My teeth grind together. "You're taking me home. End. Of. Discussion." Turning my head, I look through the window, refusing to acknowledge Kaiden anymore. If I do, I'm not sure I won't throat-punch him.

Move in with him, my ass.

"Fine," he snaps.

My breath slows down, and not before long, tiredness seeps deep into my bones, the weight of the weekend pulling at my eyelids.

A SLIGHT JOLT brings me back to reality, but I don't want to open my eyes just yet. I feel safe and warm and downright perfect. Another jolt follows, and I grumble a protest, not ready to wake up. My eyelids crack open at the soft chuckle that makes my whole body vibrate. When the sleep cobwebs finally clear from my mind, I realize Kaiden's holding me in his arms like a bride, climbing the stairs to my apartment, and my face is pressed against his chest. The close proximity sends my heart into overdrive.

"What are you doing?" I ask groggily, voice thick with sleep.

"Taking you home like you asked."

I struggle in his hold, but he only pulls me closer to his body. "I can walk, you know; I'm not some damsel in distress. Why didn't you wake me up?"

He looks down at me, cocking an eyebrow. "Trust me, I tried. You were so deep in it you were snoring louder than a hellhound."

My mouth opens in shock as the heat crawling up the back of my neck scorches my ears. "I don't snore," I harrumph.

Kaiden laughs, and I refuse to acknowledge its effect on me and my heart. "Keep telling yourself that. I never thought something so small could produce that kind of sound."

"Shut up and put me down," I fire back, narrowing my eyes at him. How dare he say that I snore?

I don't, do I?

How would you know, Iris? Knowing would actually require sleeping with someone.

Ugh. I really hate him and his stupidly perfect face.

Kaiden ignores me as we reach my floor, and he cuts through the corridor, sliding me down his body slowly in front of my door.. I swallow. Hard. An ember of heat stirs to life in my belly, igniting my blood at the way his body fits against mine. His hand gliding up the curve of my hip leaves a fiery path behind. My knees almost buckle when he reaches the apex of my thighs, and his fingers brush over my center slowly. It's embarrassing how wet my panties get. I suck in a shaky breath as he licks his lips, his gaze roving over my body slowly like a physical caress.

He bends slightly, and I close my eyes as his breath ghosts my lips. My heart is hammering as if it wants to crawl out of my chest to get to him. Kaiden's finally going to kiss me, and damn it all to hell; there's nothing I want more at this moment. When his fingers start traveling upward, I almost catch fire. He sneaks one into the front pocket of my pants, fishing out my keys.

My eyes snap open when he steps back, takes my hand in his, and places the keys in my palm with a devious smirk and a raised eyebrow. He fucking played me, and I folded faster than a cheap lawn chair.

Rage burns through me as my fingers curl into fists. I'm so angry and embarrassed that my face is probably the same color as a pickled beet. "I would say it was a pleasure seeing you again, but I would be lying, so kindly fuck off," I grit out and turn my back to him, jamming the key into the lock so hard I'm surprised it didn't snap in two.

Suddenly, I'm whirled around as Kaiden cages me in with my back to the door. The sound of his hands slapping against the wood on either side of my head reverberates in my ears. He towers over me, all broad shoulders and taut muscles, his eyes two pools of desire as he dips, traps my earlobe between his teeth, and then licks the bite of pain away. Electricity zips down my spine until I feel the zap in between my legs. My clit throbs in need.

"Oh, angel. I'm going to enjoy so much spanking the sass out of you. I'm going to get your perfect ass so red and your pussy so wet you're going to beg for my cock," he growls in my ear. His voice is liquid silk dancing across my skin. He pops off into thin air, leaving me a trembling mess against my door and so turned on I can barely see straight.

I cuss him out as my head falls back and hits the back of the door with a loud thud. I hate the way my body responds to his words. How they leave dents in the thick walls I erected around myself and my heart. How, every time he is near, my body gravitates toward him, unconsciously seeking his warmth. How, out of all the people in the world, I'm dangerously and madly attracted to a demon.

It takes an embarrassing amount of time for me to gather my wits and make my body function properly again so I can open my door. When I finally get into my apartment, I discard my weapons on my entryway table, take my combat boots off, and fix myself a sandwich, inhaling it in record time, even for me. I send a quick text to Sam, letting her know that I'm alive, recounting in a few sentences what went down since the vampires jumped me in the alley without checking the string of messages she sent me.

I don't have the energy to deal with her dramatics right now. If she weren't outside the country performing the purifying rituals with her grandmother for the upcoming Summer Solstice, she would have probably already been here chewing my head off for disappearing again on her. Not like I had a choice.

With a deep sigh, I plug my charger into my phone since the battery is at a whopping two percent and stride directly into the bathroom, slowly unsticking the hellseeker gear from my body.

Lethargy pulls at my muscles, and I almost drift off in the shower with the hot water pounding down on me. After an eternity, I manage to wash all the dried blood from my hair, and I don't even bother blow-drying it as I make my way to the bedroom, draw the drapes over the window before face-planting into the bed, and fall asleep in less than a second.

28

My entire body is alight with need. Eyes still closed, I replay the wet dream in my head again and again like a broken record. The way Kaiden's hands roamed my naked body as his cock pounded in my dripping pussy. *Fuck*. A desperate whimper leaves my mouth as one of my hands travels in between the valley of my breasts. I cup one and rub my puckered nipple between my thumb and forefinger as my other hand drifts lower, pushing the soaked panties to the side. My hips buck as the pads of my fingers fan over my engorged clit. I begin stroking it up and down while envisioning Kaiden is the one touching me, licking my nipples, biting them.

I let my other hand drop in between my thighs, pushing two fingers inside, pumping them in and out while stroking my clit at the same time. My imagination runs wild at all the things I would let him do to me. I moan loudly when I feel his intoxicating scent wrapping around me in waves. It's as though I managed to conjure him in the room with me.

"Kaiden," I pant with desperation, imagining him fucking me

instead of my fingers.

"Mmm, such a dirty little angel," Kaiden purrs. "Add one more finger in that pretty pussy. Let me see how desperate you are for my cock."

I add another finger. Then freeze.

What the hell?

Since when is my brain able to create such real fantasies?

Wait a damn minute.

My eyes snap open, and my breath hitches in my throat as my gaze collides with Kaiden's burning one. It stalls the beat of my heart before it accelerates to the point of madness.

Holy shit!

"Don't you dare stop!" Kaiden commands and my body obeys before my mind can even catch on to what is happening. "That's my good girl," he rumbles darkly.

Kaiden's praise nearly makes me combust. He's seated on the upholstered chair in the corner of my room, covered in shadows, posture relaxed, legs spread wide, allowing me a clear view of the massive erection tenting the fabric of his pants. At a closer look, I can see the way his fingers curl, digging into the armrests as he watches me through hooded eyes.

His lust-filled gaze is like an electrical bolt. It surges through my body as desire sparks and hisses in the air between us. My lips part on a moan, and my breasts bounce along with my heaving chest. I'm so wet the air is filled with suction noises as my fingers slide in and out of my drenched pussy.

Fire licks at my skin, scorching, obliterating every coherent thought. The moans and whimpers coming from me are embarrassingly loud and would normally make me want to hide under the bed and never show my face in public again, but I'm over the point of caring. My body almost vibrates with the need for Kaiden to fuck me.

Kaiden sinks his teeth into his lower lip, eyes at half-mast with pupils blown, red streaks swirling with gold in the obsidian abyss. "Fuck. You're perfect, Iris. So goddamn beautiful. That's it. Come for me. I want to see my angel fall apart." Kaiden's gravelly voice is low, hypnotic.

His words push me over the edge as my back bows off the bed. The orgasm seizes my body with the force of a tornado. Stars explode in the back of my eyelids until I'm floating on a cloud of pure bliss, my body jellified, boneless.

My eyes open at the sound of shuffling. Kaiden stands and prowls toward me with the gait of a black-maned lion cornering its next meal. Stopping next to my bed, he locks me in against the mattress as he straddles my hips.

My throat bobs audibly with a hard swallow. "What are you doing?" I breathe, my voice thick with the remnants of my orgasm. The expectation of his touch is maddening, fraying every single one of my nerve endings as my heart ratches against its cage.

Kaiden doesn't answer; instead, with his eyes fixated on mine, he takes the three drenched fingers that were just seconds before inside my pussy and sucks them into his mouth like they're the best thing he has ever tasted. A low rumble of pleasure leaves his chest, and he lets them go with a wet pop.

"So damn sweet," Kaiden says, voice like satin. His tattooed hand collars my throat, his rings cold against my heated skin. He drops his forehead to mine, and his hot breath comes out in short pants that fan over my lips. The gleam of undisguised hunger in his eyes is enough to set me ablaze. He breathes me in and releases a deep, throaty groan as he suddenly disappears and appears at the foot of my bed. Chest heaving and hands trembling, he says gruffly, "Dinner is ready," before popping off.

What the hell just happened?

Did I just finger myself in front of Kaiden?

Holy motherfucking shit!

I am so screwed.

My hand pressing on top of my chest does nothing to slow down my heart, so I take a few deep breaths in and out. This doesn't work either. I feel as though I just had an out-of-body experience. Am I still dreaming? I pinch myself for good measure, but nope, what just happened is one hundred percent real. Did he say that dinner is ready? What is he doing here? Jesus Christ, my mind is scrambled by the most scorching, mind-numbing orgasm of my life. How am I supposed to face him again?

After a few minutes, I finally get out of bed and stride to the bathroom. Catching my reflection in the mirror, I stop. My hair is a tangled mess, my skin flushed, and my pupils still blown.

After brushing the bird nest on top of my head and taking care of my business in the bathroom, I change into a soft gray cotton tee and some jean shorts. As I get out of the bedroom, I do a double take at Kaiden sitting casually at my kitchen table, scrolling on his phone like it's the most natural thing in the world. He changed from his blood-splattered clothes, now wearing a pair of black slacks and a crisp white shirt with the sleeves rolled up. His tattooed forearms look like freakin' arm porn.

The smell of delicious food hits my nose, and my mouth waters instantly. He set the table as though we are on a romantic date at a fancy restaurant, a candle burning next to a vase full of violet peonies placed right in the middle. Him being here in my space is deeply disturbing to me. It sets me off-kilter. How the hell did he do all of this without me hearing anything? I mean, sure, I was out cold since I got home this morning, but still, I must have been more tired than I realized. I guess being held captive in a crypt by vampires will do that to you.

What it definitely wouldn't do is give you extremely vivid wet dreams of Elite demons. That must have been all me. My whole body is still vibrating with the remnants of the explosive orgasm.

Kaiden's head swivels toward me with a cocky grin like he has a direct link to my dirty thoughts. God, he's so insanely beautiful I want to punch him in the face. The bastard would probably look good even with a shiner and a broken nose. He might even look sexier if that's even possible, enhancing those bad-boy looks of his.

"Hungry?" he asks, pocketing his phone and resting his back in the chair.

As though awakened by his words, my stomach rumbles loudly because the little bitch takes every chance at embarrassing me, and I already feel my cheeks getting a deeper shade of crimson.

Ugh. Someone, please kill me now.

He doesn't even have to ask; of course, I'm hungry. I'm always freakin' hungry. I love to eat. Instead of answering him, I say with a scowl, "What are you doing here?"

Kaiden stands and pulls out the chair next to his, motioning with his hand toward it. "Let's eat. The food is getting cold."

Huffing, I cut through the hallway and plop down on the chair. Kaiden strides to the stove, brings a steaming pan with him to the table, and serves me a healthy portion of shrimp and truffle pasta before filling his own plate as well. He then opens a bottle of Pinot Gris that looks expensive as shit, definitely not one from my stash, and fills the tulip-shaped glasses.

"Well?" I press as he sits down, crossing my arms in front of my chest, even though I want to attack the plate with the finesse of someone who was forced to eat only salad and carrots for a whole month. I always order this when I go out at Ciprianni's, and it's one of my favorite dishes. The fact that he cooked me one of my favorite meals not once but twice now is suspicious as hell.

He finally graces me with an answer after taking a sip of wine. "If the Mountain won't go to Mohammed, then Mohammed must come to the Mountain."

I arch an eyebrow. "What's that supposed to mean?"

"You didn't want to move in with me, so…I'm going to stay here with you."

"Ha, that's a good one, buddy." With a saccharine smile, I say, "No, you're not."

Kaiden lets out a derisive laugh, then his expression turns serious. "You must think you have a say in this, Iris. You don't."

I take a hearty sip of wine, needing the liquid courage. "Are you deranged? I can't let a demon move into my apartment," I snap once I've swallowed.

With a smile that's all teeth and sharp edges, Kaiden deadpans, "Ah, but you can definitely let one watch you play with that pretty pussy and then scream his name as you come."

I choke on a second sip of wine and start coughing. My eyes water instantly. *Jesus.* Kaiden and his filthy mouth are going to be the death of me. It takes me a full minute to regain the proper function of my lungs. "You're not moving in with me, Kaiden."

A muscle jumps in his cheek. "Don't test me, Iris."

"Or what?" I seethe, shooting daggers at him with my eyes.

Kaiden rests his elbows on the table, pinning me with an icy glare. "Or I'll personally arrange a meeting with Grayson and tell him how his perfect little hellseeker has been spending her free time in the company of an Elite demon. Oh, and let's not forget about how you lied to him."

"You wouldn't," I croak. "You can't be caught spending time with a hellseeker just as much as I can't be caught in the presence of a demon or a dark creature. You'll be shooting yourself in the foot if you go to Grayson."

"Try me, Iris. Just fucking try me. Do you think I give a shit about a stupid archaic rule? I'm the head of the Obsidian Conclave. I make the fucking rules." He runs his tongue over his front teeth. "If that's what it takes for me to keep you safe, to get you kicked out of the Order, I'll do it, and then you can move in with me. Easy."

I go from zero to a hundred in less than a second as rage fills my veins almost to the point of boiling over. My nails bite into my palms viciously under the table. "Why do you care so much about what happens to me? I'm no one to you."

Kaiden shuts his eyes, wrinkles forming at the corners with the pressure, and he lets out a deep breath as he massages the bulging vein in his temple. He looks like he's gathering his patience and trying to hold back from throttling me at the same time. When he opens his eyes, he completely ignores my questions and says, "Whether you like it or not, I'll be your fucking shadow from now on. And don't think that I make idle threats because I'm more serious than a fucking heart attack. If you don't want to get kicked out of the Order, you'll do as I say." Lifting the glass to his lips, he takes another sip and looks at me over the rim. "End. Of. Discussion. Now eat."

The bastard used my words against me. "For how long?" I clip out. I'm grinding my teeth so hard I'm surprised they don't crumble to dust inside my mouth.

"For however long it's necessary. Until we find out why you have a bounty on your head and who is behind it, you're not safe," he answers.

I'm shaking in my chair, literally vibrating with anger because there's nothing I can do. I can't risk him going to Grayson. Being a hellseeker is all I have, the only way I can avenge my mother's death. Kaiden ignores my glare and starts eating, unbothered by the blistering silence that stretches between us and makes my skin itch.

After a few minutes of seething with anger, I stab the fork into the pasta, pretending it's Kaiden's eyeball, and shove a forkful in my mouth without care at all for decorum. Even cold, the pasta is delicious, buttery, and cooked to perfection with just the right amount of garlic. I press my lips together to suppress the moan of appreciation for how delicious the food Kaiden made is. I don't want him to know how much I like it.

Half an hour later, I'm loading the dishwasher while stealing furtive glances at Kaiden, who parked his ass on my couch. He's watching the news like he owns the place. I take out my phone from my back pocket and shoot Sam a text.

> Me: Help!!! I woke up with Kaiden in my apartment!
>
> He threatened to tell Grayson everything if I don't let him shadow me and move in with me until we find out who put a bounty on my head.
>
> What do I do?!?

> Sam: Holy Hecate!
>
> Is he there right now?

> Me: Yup. He's sitting on my couch watching the news, if you can believe this shit.

> Sam: Oh my Goddess! Take a photo. I want to see who my bestie is lusting after.

> Me: I'm not taking a photo of him, you weirdo. I need your help to get out of this situation.

> Sam: Sorry to break it to you, but I think he's right.

Me: What?!? You're my best friend! You can't side with him. It's the best friend number one rule, you're obligated to be on my side no matter what.

Sam: I actually think it's a good idea. I mean, hello, you got kidnapped by fucking vampires. You almost died twice in the span of a month. It's like you're trying to break some sort of morbid record.

So yeah, let him take care of you, boo.

Plus, having some eye candy to stare at is an added bonus.

Me: I don't need him to take care of me! I need him gone.

Sam: What you need is to jump his bones. 😏

C'mon, snap a photo.

Knowing Sam will pester me relentlessly until I send her a photo of Kaiden, I lean on the counter and snap a photo of him as inconspicuously as I can. The only problem is that I forgot to turn the volume down.

"Did you just take a photo of me?" Kaiden asks, his head swiveling in my direction, amusement dancing in his eyes.

"Of course not," I squeak. My voice is so high-pitched I couldn't be more obvious even if I tried.

"It's good you're not an actress. I don't think I have ever seen someone lie as poorly as you," he chuckles as he shakes his head. "You know, if you want to take some more photos, I can lose the shirt, maybe the pants too, and give you a full show. You can use them next time you want to finger that pretty pussy." He smiles roguishly at me while slinging an arm on the back of the couch, winking.

I crinkle my nose in mock disgust because apparently, my body didn't get the memo that we're not supposed to like a certain dangerous Elite demon, and I have to press my thighs in a failed attempt to stop the pulsing in my clit at his words. "Don't flatter yourself too much. Your head might implode," I deadpan and turn around, cleaning an already sparkling counter and using my free hand to send Sam the photo.

> **Me: I hope you're happy because he noticed me taking it.**

> **Sam: Holy Hotness! This man is so hot he makes all my celebrity crushes look like trash. I hope you know this photo is going straight to my spank bank.**

> **Me: Oh, God. Please don't masturbate to his photo. It's gross.**

> **Sam: Why? Are you planning to?**

> **Me: I kind of already did masturbate with him watching me.**

> **Sam: WHAT????**

Me: In my defense, I thought I was alone in the room; I didn't know he was Joe Golberging my ass and sitting in the corner, watching me sleep like a creep.

Sam: Did something else happen? Please tell me you had hot, sweaty sex for the first time.

Me: Jeez, Sam. You're not worried at all that he watched me sleep serial killer style? He's a demon!

Sam: Oh, c'mon...be for fucking real. Do you need a reminder of the voice message you sent me not too long ago about how you want him to spank you, and then you want to ride him like a disco stick?
Spill, bitch!
And don't skimp on the details.

Me: We didn't fuck. He just watched me, that's it.
Sam: Oh...well, you still have time now that you live together and all that.

Me: Urgh, thanks for reminding me.

Sam: That's what besties are for.

Me: Enough about me. How are you?

Sam: Good. Having a blast with Grammie. She took too much peyote last night and made a tree sprout from this warlock's ass; she said he was being an asshole.

Me: Wish I was there to see it.

Sam: It was pretty epic. Ttyl. Love you.

Me: Love you too. Xx.

29

Music is blasting in my wireless earbuds, and sweat rolls down my spine as I pour all of my frustration while kicking the shit out of the punching bag at the compound. It's the only place Kaiden can't follow me. Two weeks have passed since he announced he was moving in with me, and I think I'm going crazy. I can't escape him. Even here. Because he's in every single one of my thoughts.

True to his word, he's been shadowing me everywhere. At the store. To pick up Ms. Robbin's meds. When I go for a run and on my shifts. I don't understand how the heck he gets anything else done because he's spending every second with me. He also cooks for us every day. I'm an okay cook; I love to eat more than I love to cook and treat it more as a chore, but everything Kaiden makes is borderline orgasm-inducing, and if he weren't a demon, I would beg him to marry me and make me food for the rest of my life.

I'm also paranoid and jumpy whenever we step foot out of my apartment because I'm afraid someone from the Order is finally going to see us together. I avoid going outside unless I absolutely have to.

The worst part is that I'm in a constant state of arousal around him. The temperature in the room rises to dangerous levels as my mind replays he popped into my bedroom last week.

I'm still screaming as the force of my nightmare propels my body forward like a jackknife. My throat is raw, and my tee is plastered to my body with sweat while tears stream down my face like pouring rain.

Kaiden suddenly appears in front of me. "What happened?" he asks. His head swivels around in the dark room, trying to find the source of my distress, his voice laced with panic.

I clutch my chest. "F-fuck. Y-you scared me," I stammer through the sobs wracking my body. "I h-had a n-nightmare." As per usual, I don't know what it was about, but my body seems to remember, and I'm filled with a sorrow so deep it spreads like black ink into every crevice of my soul. I haven't had one this bad in years.

Kaiden bends, and his fingers find the hem of my tee. "I'm just going to take this off and bring you a dry one, okay?"

My teeth sink into my lower lip, and I nod, not being able to do anything more at this moment. My body is shaking so badly that I can barely concentrate on anything. Kaiden peels off the wet tee, discards it on the floor, and brings a clean one from my closet. He pulls it over my head like I'm a child.

He then lies next to me on the bed, and with a swift move, he drapes me over his chest, one hand wrapped around the small of my back and the other thumbing the tears away gently.

"Shh, angel," Kaiden breathes. "I got you." His incredible scent blankets me like a cocoon, and the warmth of his body sinks deep into my bones. He continues caressing the back of my head and whispering sweet nothings in my ear until the shaking finally stops, and I'm no longer crying.

"What was the nightmare about?" he asks, his deep voice and the way his knuckles graze the side of my face sending shivers down my spine and my pulse

rate into overdrive.

It doesn't escape me how well our bodies fit together, like two pieces of puzzle. And despite everything, desire coils deep in my belly. It spreads to the area between my thighs, soaking my panties.

"It's okay if you don't want to talk about it," he offers, and I realize I didn't answer him. I was too focused on my dirty thoughts and the way his body feels against mine.

I swallow hard through the knot in my throat. "I don't know. I can't remember," I answer, my voice coming out all coarse and scratchy. "I used to get them every day since I woke up from the accident but I never remembered what the nightmares were about. Until a few weeks ago." And then there's that weird dream I had before waking up in the crypt after the vampires jumped me in the alley. That one wasn't a nightmare, but it still felt like a memory from when I was a kid. I don't mention it though.

Kaiden's body stiffens as he inhales a sharp breath. His heart kicks up a notch against the side of my face. "You remembered the accident?"

"Just a part of the accident…I saw Mom. She was hurt and unconscious. I tried to wake her up, but then the trees snapped under the weight of the car. We fell into the abyss, and I woke up," I say, my voice trembling. I don't realize I'm crying again until Kaiden gently wipes the tears running down my cheeks with his thumb.

"Did you remember anything else from your past?" His fingers shake slightly as he runs them through my hair.

"No…I mean, maybe. Once. After the vampires jumped me in the alley. I'm not sure it was a memory, though. I wish I remembered everything," I murmur brokenly. "Tell me something real," I blurt out after a few beats of silence.

"What?" he asks, confusion evident in his tone.

"Something about you that you've never shared with anyone before," I say—no…demand. Kaiden witnessing one of my most vulnerable moments left me raw, like being dragged through gravel at breakneck speed. I feel naked…

exposed, while I know almost nothing about him. I desperately need him to balance the scale, even if only for a moment.

He takes a minute to absorb my words, and he seems to understand as he starts talking, his voice thick, steeped in pain. "I never met my mother. When I was just a kid, I used to imagine that one day, she would come to rescue me from my father's claws." He laughs bitterly. "What a fool I was." He pauses as he swallows. "As I grew up, I understood that she never will, and it broke me more than I would like to admit."

Inhaling deeply, he continues. "He kept me locked…somewhere dark, no windows. The only person to ever show me tenderness and a semblance of what a mother's love could be in that place was a woman working for my father. She would sneak me out for a few minutes whenever she could on her cigarette breaks. The first time I stepped through the door, I was almost blinded by the abundance of light. It felt as though my eyes would melt off, but it was worth it to experience the first ray of sunshine on my skin. That moment will forever be seared in my brain because I got a taste of freedom, even if fleeting. I will never forget how it tasted, how it smelled…like sunshine and cigarette smoke." He clears his throat. "Smoking brings me back to that moment."

Words fail me, and my heart breaks for him, for the child desperately wanting to be loved and getting only crumbs in return. I would have never thought so looking at Kaiden, but I realize now that maybe we're not so different…him and I.

We just wear the scars left by our past differently. Some people wear them like open wounds for the whole world to see, while others hide them beneath walls so thick, nothing can break through. It seems as though he barricaded his beneath a titanium facade while I've let mine bleed like an overflowing river before honing all that pain to steel, transforming it into rage. Still, I sometimes feel as though I'm teetering on the edge of that blade, afraid that one day I will fall and impale myself in its sharp tip.

"Thank you. For sharing that with me," I say softly, breaking the silence *that blankets the air. A million questions sit on the tip of my tongue. I want to know more about Kaiden, about his past. Hell…I want to know everything, but I don't want to push him too far. "What was her name?" I settle on asking.*

"Theresa," Kaiden responds.

"What happened with her? Did you get to se –"

"She's dead. My father found out about the cigarette breaks and killed her," he cuts me off with a gruff voice, muscles pulled taut with tension.

Fuck. My heartstrings turn into painful knots. "I'm so sorry, Kaiden. For everything you went through, for what happened to Theresa."

He softens at that. "It's okay, angel. It's all in the past." He punctuates the words with a gentle caress on the curve of my cheek. A few moments pass before Kaiden speaks again. "It's late. You should go back to sleep."

"'Kay," I say tiredly and yawn. Exhaustion pulls at my eyelids, so I close my eyes as the steady rhythm of Kaiden's breath lulls me to sleep. I'm in the space between dream and reality when I feel soft lips against my forehead.

"I wish you would remember too…" Kaiden whispers after a few beats of silence. I think I also hear him say, "remember me," but my grasp on reality slips, and it all seems like I imagined it, like my brain is playing with me, and it's all wishful thinking.

Since that day, Kaiden finds his way to my bed every night, but only after I already fall asleep. He holds me to his chest, and I pretend to still be asleep. With bated breath, I wait for him to touch me, to do something about the sizzling electricity that sparks between us every time we touch because I'm too chicken shit to initiate anything.

I'm afraid that once I do, I'll lose myself forever in his touch. I know that the second we cross that line, I will be ruined for anybody else. And it terrifies me—more than anything. I usually fall asleep again at some point, and he sneaks out before I wake up. It almost seems like I've dreamt him there with me, but I feel him in every cell of my being, in every beat of my heart. Of course, we don't acknowledge it, and we don't talk about it. It's driving me insane.

A hand wrapped around my elbow stops me mid-punch and brings me back to reality. As I turn around, my gaze slams into Noah's sparkling blue-gray eyes.

Fuck.

My heart jumps in my chest, not prepared to be face to face with him. If I'm completely honest with myself, ever since those vampires jumped me in the alley and Kaiden has become my shadow, I haven't thought about Noah once. Even when he was gone he was always there in the back of my mind, my thoughts always drifting to him unconsciously.

"Hey," he says after I pull out my earbuds. He looks good, actually more than good. He's as gorgeous as ever, decked in jeans and an aquamarine V-neck tee that makes the blue in his eyes pop, though, for some reason, I don't feel those butterflies swarming my stomach or that racing in my pulse like every other time he was near me before. There's still something there, though more subdued.

"Hey," I echo and amble to the rack of towels, pulling one out and patting my sweaty face with it. "What's up?"

Noah runs a hand through his sun-streaked hair as he smiles softly at me. "Do you have a minute?"

"Sure."

"Can we talk in private?"

I nod and follow him out of the training room, trying my best to ignore Erik, Grayson's grandson, who's sparring with another hellseeker on one of the mats. His gaze has been burning holes in the back of my head the whole time I've been here, staring at me with those serial killer eyes. It makes my skin crawl. I shake the unpleasant feeling off and match Noah's steps until we reach the empty corridor and stop near the stairs.

"Listen," Noah says, and his eyebrows drop in a frown, "before we talk about official business regarding the Order, I wanted to say that I know you're still pissed at me, and that's why I haven't reached out to you. I wanted to give you some time to cool off, but I'm not giving up on us, Iris. I'll never give up on us." He takes my hand in his, and with a finger under my chin, he tilts my head up until our gazes meet. "Can I take you out on a date?"

My skin breaks out in goosebumps, and my heart does a little flip-flop in my chest. As much as I hate it, his touch still affects me. "I don't know...I don't think it's a good idea," I scoff, stepping back and pulling my tingling hand away.

The hurt flashing in his eyes transforms them to a stormy grey. "Just think about it, okay? There's no rush. As I said, I'll wait for you, however long it's necessary."

Sighing deeply, I say, "Did you want something else? I need to take a shower and head out."

"I received word from the Kabal. They analyzed the video and the pictures I took for my report. There's something you're not telling me."

Fuck.

"I told you everything I could remember from that night," I say, my tone dripping with annoyance. The lie tastes foul on my tongue.

His jaw ticks. "Are you sure?"

"We've been through this already," I clip out, resisting the urge to rub my sweat-slicked palms on my leggings.

"Fine," he bites back. "Did you, by any chance, see an archangel appear the night you were attacked by those demons?"

A surprised laugh bubbles out of me; then I realize he's serious, and my smile drops. "Of course not. I would have told you if I did. Why?"

"The fire that obliterated the forest was caused by *illum*."

"What? Are you sure?" I ask as my eyes almost bulge out of my head. *Illum* is the power wielded by the strongest of angels; only archangels and seraphim are able to use it. It's the divine light. It burns hotter than any flame, even hellfire.

He tilts his head, folding his arms in front of his chest. "The scientists working for the Kabal were able to confirm it after I sent them a portion of the scorched earth."

I shake my head in disbelief. "There was no angel whatsoever. Just me and the demons. That's it." And Kaiden Black. Of course, I don't mention him. An image of Kaiden's eyes getting all bright and weird when he lost his shit that night in the abandoned cathedral the moment he saw the vampire marks on my skin flashes through my mind. But he's an Elite demon, so it doesn't explain the *illum* at all.

However, I did see with my own two eyes the way the portion of the forest looked as if a wildfire like no other obliterated everything in its path. If *illum* was involved, then it would also explain the fact that we have barely encountered any demons on the streets since the night the umbra attacked me. They would be scared shitless of the possibility of coming face to face with an archangel.

Noah sucks on his teeth. "I hope you're telling me the truth because if not, you're digging both of our graves here. Yours if you're lying and mine for trusting you." With stiff shoulders and a granite jaw, he turns on his heel and leaves.

Great. Just what I needed.

An hour later, after taking a shower and spending some time with my aunt in the library, I make my way to the alley, where I know Kaiden is waiting for me. He always drops me off there when I go to the compound and then picks me up again when I'm done.

Fiery red clouds cover the apricot sky as the sun dips into the horizon. The air is still fresh and crisp even if summer is finally here. Because of the mountains surrounding Ashville, the heat never gets to be suffocating, and I love that. A shiver rolls down my spine with the sensation of being watched. I turn around to scan the street for anything suspicious.

There's the usual evening traffic, the honking of horns in the distance, and some kids playing basketball across the street, but no one else. Man, this paranoia is getting the best of me. I'm constantly on high alert, and it shows. I shake my head, annoyed that I'm being so jumpy.

The ping of an incoming email forcefully pulls me out of my thoughts and into the present. I take my phone out of my crossbody bag, tapping on the screen to see who is it from.

Dammit.

My jaw ticks as my eyes register the words, my fingers clenching the phone in a white-knuckled grip. I've hired a tech guy, who cost me an arm and a leg, to look into Grayson's text with the hope that maybe someone hacked into his phone and sent the message. But he couldn't find any evidence of that. He also couldn't trace Grayson's location after he left the compound, as I asked. Apparently, there's a strong encryption blocking anyone who tries, so my best guess is that Tim must have worked his magic on that front. I mean, Grayson is the leader of the Order in Ashville, so I don't know why that surprises me.

What can I do next? I've tried everything that I could think of to help me get an answer regarding the text, and asking Grayson point-blank if he sent me into a trap is something I can't do for obvious reasons. The text message was really the catalyst for the whole incident, but after hitting two dead ends, I have no idea where to turn. I suppose focusing on learning more about the umbra and the bounty from Hell is my best bet, and hopefully, then I can unravel everything from the top down.

Heaving a deep sigh, I shove my phone back into the bag and continue my trek. As I round the corner and enter the narrow alley, my heart starts doing the rumba inside my chest when I spot Kaiden waiting for me next to his bike, a lit cigarette between his full lips. A Zippo is dangling from his fingers as he plays with it. He pockets it when our gazes collide.

The sharp angles of his jaw and cheeks stand out even more today since his hair is tied back. He looks like the prince of darkness dressed in his usual black attire, leather jacket, and worn boots. Letting out a plume of smoke, he stubs the lit cherry to the wall next to him, flicks it to the trash container, and takes out my helmet. One of my conditions for letting him give me a ride everywhere I went was that we both wore helmets so no one could recognize us.

"Training good?" Kaiden asks, handing me the helmet as I stop in front of him.

"Yeah," I respond, and a current passes through me as our fingers touch. All the hair on my body stands on end.

He mounts the bike, but before starting the engine, he says, "We have plans for tonight. We'll go home to change and then head out."

God, the way he said home like we're a couple that lives together does things to my insides I'm not ready to admit to yet. "What plans? You know I can't go anywhere. I work tonight," I scoff. I want to ask Kaiden about the *illum*, but it all sounds too crazy to be true, so I bite my tongue and decide to keep it for myself for a while longer.

"Well, I have to go, so you're going with me. I'm not letting you out of my sight. Besides, you want answers, don't you? That's what we're doing, getting some answers," he says vaguely.

"Fine," I fire back, put on my helmet, snap it closed, and then hop on behind Kaiden. I inhale deeply to trap his intoxicating scent in my lungs and glue my front to his back, interlacing my fingers in front of his taut abs.

He slides his helmet on before revving the engine. The pavement vibrates beneath us as Kaiden glides the motorcycle out of the alley and into the evening traffic.

KAIDEN'S BEEN CRYPTIC about where we're going tonight, only saying it's a party, so I lock myself in the bathroom, do my go-to makeup look, and straighten my hair since it got wavy from being in a braid. It doesn't look as good as when Sam dolls me up, but I did my best. Entering my bedroom, I make my way to my bed. There are two ivory boxes on top of it. One is bigger than the other, with the same brand name stamped on top that I don't recognize, but it sounds foreign, and the items inside probably cost more than a lung on the black market.

Opening the bigger one, I take out the piece of silk chiffon material and unfold what must be the most stunning dress I have ever seen and touched. It's black, with a strappy form-fitting corset on top adorned with delicate flowers on its side made out of golden filigree. At a closer look, I can tell the flowers are irises. The floor-length skirt has two slits running down the sides. I get out of my robe and put the dress on, looking in the oval-shaped mirror next to my closet.

Holy shit!

I have never worn something sexier in my entire life. I almost don't recognize myself. The dress fits me like a glove, as if Kaiden has my exact curves memorized to perfection. The slits are so high they come up almost to my navel, and it's the type of dress that can't be worn with underwear because it shows every little line. I hook my thumbs into my panties and slide them off, then open the other box and take out the pair of high-heeled strappy sandals inside. I slip them on and rotate in front of the mirror. I start chewing on a hangnail on my thumb. I'm so far out of my comfort zone wearing this dress.

"Iris, are you ready? We're going to be late if we don't leave now," Kaiden's voice travels through the door as he knocks.

"Yeah," I say, turning around. Before I can take a step, he barges in and stops in his tracks, his Adam's apple bobbing in his throat as he swallows.

Kaiden shakes his head while running a hand over his clean-shaven jaw. "Fuck, angel, you look…" His voice is a deep, gravely rasp as his heated gaze travels every inch of my body like a physical caress, from the tips of my toes to the crown of my head, leaving a fiery path behind.

Time stands still as we take each other in, and I struggle to breathe as if he sucked all the air in the room with his presence. Heat crawls its way from my chest all the way to my face.

He licks his lips, and his eyebrows slant together. "I keep trying to find a word that can do you justice, but there isn't one. Beautiful, gorgeous, arresting…they all fail to describe you."

"You look pretty good yourself," I breathe, not recognizing my voice because it comes out all throaty, and I offer him a soft smile.

Kaiden in his usual clothes is hot as sin, but Kaiden in a black suit is downright lethal.

He's not wearing a tie, and the two buttons at the top of his white dress shirt are left undone, the tattoos on his throat and chest peeking through the gap. He closes the space between us, and his hand shakes slightly as he brings it up, letting his knuckles run down the column of my throat. My skin blooms in goosebumps before he unclasps my onyx choker.

"You're not going to need this," he says and strides to the bedside table, placing it on top. "You also can't take any hellseeker weapons with you."

My forehead crinkles in confusion. "Why?" I ask. I never ever take my onyx choker off.

"Because we're going to a succubus party."

"You can't be serious. Why on earth would we go to a succubus party?" I snap.

"To kidnap Adramelech," he responds casually as he shoves his hands in his pockets.

I rack my brain, trying to remember where I've heard that name before, and then it hits me. A clear image of Mrs. Hawthorn explaining Hell's hierarchy to us in demonology class a few years back when I was still in training flashes through my mind. Adramelech is the name of Lucifer's chancellor, his right-hand man or, better said, right-hand demon. He wants us to kidnap Hell's chancellor?

What. The. Fuck.

30

"So, how exactly are we going to do this?" I ask from the passenger seat of Kaiden's Escalade, digging my fingers in the smooth leather as the usual vengeful anxiety slowly ebbs away. The panic still clings to me, though, leaving behind an unpleasant, ashy taste in the back of my throat.

Kaiden's gaze flits to mine briefly. With his right hand, he takes out a syringe from the inside pocket of his suit jacket, shows it to me, and then shoves it back in. "This type of party only happens twice a year, and Adramelech never misses it, so we're going to find him and drug him with something special prepared by Malik. Everything is arranged already. I have someone on the inside working for me."

"What do you know about succubae and incubi demons?" he asks after a few beats of silence.

"I know they embody beautiful women and men and that they exude powerful pheromones that make people go crazy with lust and hump each other's bones at the snap of their fingers. I also know that the pheromones enhance sexual experiences, and the more people in the room fucking, the better because that's how succubae and incubi feed: from the desire, lust, and sex."

Kaiden nods. "The party we're going to might seem…wild, and it's going to be filled with dark creatures that don't pertain to the Conclave along with some very high profile humans, so keep an open mind and don't drink anything there, okay?"

"'Kay,' I say. "Do you think he knows something?"

"He's Lucifer's right-hand man. If someone knows something, it's him."

"But don't you think Lucifer's going to be furious? Do you really want to risk angering him? I mean, c'mon…"

"Well, if Lucifer wanted to protect his chancellor, he should have taken him with him the moment he went into hiding. Besides, what he doesn't know can't hurt him."

Kaiden turns right on what seems to be a private road, pushes the brake, and stops the car on the side of the road. "Can you pass me the box from the backseat?"

Turning around, I grab the black velvet box and place it in Kaiden's awaiting palm.

"Put this on." He opens it and hands me a black masquerade mask with intricate gold embossing.

Kaiden takes out a more masculine version of the mask he gave me. We both put them on, and I pull down the sun visor to look in the mirror. The mask is stunning. It covers half of my face and leaves a portion of my nose out, along with my lips.

He eases his foot on the break and pulls back onto the road, driving until we approach an opulent two-story mansion that exudes wealth and sophistication in every meticulously crafted detail. As the car idles on the gravel driveway, I take in the patterned gold-hued stone and the massive windows, framed by delicate tracery that punctuates the façade at regular intervals. Through the glass, I can see glimpses of the twinkling chandeliers hanging from vaulted ceilings. In my mind, a dungeon would seem more fitting for a succubus party than this, a house that looks straight out of *The Great Gatsby*.

A valet opens the door on my side. At the same time, Kaiden gets out and rounds the hood before placing the keys, along with some bills, in his palm. He then bends to whisper something in the valet's ear. With a toothless smile, the valet nods and scurries away.

Pocketing the ticket he received from the valet, Kaiden offers me a hand to help me out of the car. When I step next to him, he places the hand at the small of my back, guiding me to the grand entrance of the mansion. The warmth of his touch singes my skin as shivers roll down my spine.

"Kaiden," a gorgeous woman with East Asian features says in greeting. The seductive tone in her voice pulls my attention from the foyer's sweeping staircase flanked by two ornate balustrades. A mask covers the right side of her face, and her coal-black hair is cut short in a flattering bob. If I thought my dress was provocative, hers is just a sheer crimson chiffon over lacy underwear that doesn't leave anything to the imagination. Good for her; she looks amazing. I wish I were as confident as her to wear something like this in public.

Kaiden lifts his chin. "Maeve."

Maeve gives him a come-hither smile that clearly says they've fucked at some point, her eyes drinking him in ravenously, and the unexpected pang of jealousy spreads through my veins like acid. When she turns to me, she gives me a withering glare.

"Oh, I see you brought a pet. I thought you were coming alone." Her nose crinkles in blatant disgust, a slight accusation in her tone. "You usually have better taste," she deadpans.

She did not just say that. The fucking bitch.

My fingers curl into fists at my sides, and I bite the inside of my cheek hard, almost drawing blood in order to stop myself from punching her.

"If I ever give a flying fuck about your opinion, Maeve, you'll know," Kaiden clips out, his tone dripping with ice. "Now, let's get this over with."

Maeve's nostrils flare as she approaches Kaiden. She starts to pat him down for weapons, and I realize she must be the person he has on the inside because we wouldn't be allowed to enter with the syringe in his breast pocket. Kaiden said we weren't even allowed with phones inside, so we left them in the car.

Maeve is making a show out of it, touching him with languid strokes and bending seductively while pushing her tits and ass out as her hands move upwards on the inside of Kaiden's legs. She stops a second too long when she reaches his crotch and palms him seductively while biting her lower lip.

I see red, vibrating with a blistering rage as I hold myself back from grabbing her wrist and snapping it in two. Blood pools in my palms where my nails are biting into my skin. I would rather let a hellhound skin me alive and watch it eat my organs than sit through another second of this.

I chance a glance at Kaiden, who couldn't look more bored even if he tried to. He doesn't even make eye contact with Maeve—his gaze fixated in front of him with a blank stare while waiting for her to finish making a fool out of herself. That manages to calm me down a bit, but only by a fraction. I still want to gouge her eyes out.

She finally moves to me and starts patting me down, her lips twisted in a mix of contempt and revulsion. When she finishes, I shoulder-check her and, not so accidentally, step on her toes with my heel as hard as I can. Oopsie. I know it's petty, but I don't care. I do surprise myself though; I've never acted like this before, not even when Veronica was blatantly throwing herself at Noah. She cusses me out under her breath, and I can feel her eyes drilling holes in the back of my head as I make my way to Kaiden, who's waiting for me near a woman serving champagne.

The busty blonde, wearing nothing more than a lace teddy, hands us each a flute from a tray, and we take them. Kaiden offers me his elbow, and I wrap my fingers around it as we round the corner, reaching a massive door.

"Welcome to the place where your dirtiest fantasies come alive," a brown-skinned attractive man clad only in a satin pair of boxers says before opening the door with a flourish.

As soon as we step through the threshold, the arousal hits me like a ton of bricks, making my clit pulse with need to the beat of the seductive song reverberating from the walls and high ceiling. The air is a heady mix of musk and desire.

The room is the size of a ballroom, with red velvet curtains hanging above the windows that sweep the gleaming floor and is scarcely lit by flickering candles. Plush velvet couches, the same color as the curtains, are scattered on either side of the room, occupied by people engaged in various forms of sexual interlude.

We pass a man sucking another man's cock lounging on one of the couches. I cringe hard at the loud slurping noises as heat travels from the bottom of my feet all the way to the tips of my ears. I quickly avert my eyes, but I'm hit with another sexual scene as someone dressed from head to toe in a latex suit eats out a woman sprawled on the table in front of the couch. Kaiden takes the champagne flute I'm holding and bends slightly before placing it alongside his on the table right next to them, unfazed.

Everyone is wearing some form of mask to conceal their identity. I can make out a few possessed humans, though, the *ethereal sight* alerting me of their tainted aura. Unconsciously, I reach for my onyx choker, and my skin itches with the need to free them from the possession. I shove the urge down because it would only ruin what we came here to do, and it would be pointless; I don't have any weapons on me anyway.

The atmosphere is heavy with sexual tension, moans, and sounds of pleasure breaking through the music. Servers wearing only lacy teddies or nothing at all but masks weave their way through the crowd, balancing trays filled with different colorful drinks. There's also a makeshift dance floor bustling with gyrating bodies dancing lasciviously to the beat. Hands and lips move freely as limbs tangle together in a symphony of carnal urgency, their expressions a mix of bliss and euphoria.

A fine sheen of perspiration covers my skin, and my pulse is racing. This party is crazy. It's like I'm trapped in a porno movie set, and like a bystander witnessing a car crash, I can't look away. I know it's the succubus and incubus pheromones causing all this, but coupled with the maddening attraction I feel every time I'm near Kaiden, I'm on the verge of combusting any second now.

Kaiden unexpectedly takes my hand in his and pulls me to the dance floor, slicing through the crowd of moving bodies. His touch burns through me all the way to the tips of my hair. The simple gesture seems so intimate and natural it makes me blush more fiercely than witnessing all the people blatantly fucking around us.

"What are you doing?" I ask, almost stumbling on my feet.

His lips twitch with the ghost of a smile. "We need to kill some time."

I swallow. Hard. "Can't we, like, stand in a corner and wait?"

"We need to blend in." And with that, he whirls me around in a swift, experienced move so quickly I lose my breath as he plasters his front to my back, one of his arms banded across my midriff and his other hand at the curve of my hip. I can feel every inch of his hard-as-steel body pressing into my back, and the temperature in the room suddenly gets a hundred degrees hotter as he starts to move his hips to the beat of the music.

Fuck me.

He's good. Really good.

It should be illegal for someone who looks like Kaiden to also be able to dance like this. Instinctively I lift my arms and snake them around the nape of his neck, starting to gyrate my hips and rub my ass against his hard length. I feel as though I've been thrust into a wicked dance of obsidian and light. And no one bothered to teach me the choreography. The problem is…I don't want it to finish, either. I could lose myself forever in this moment.

Everything seems to fade around us, and it's only me and Kaiden wrapped in our own little bubble. His touch sets me ablaze like a match thrown over a gasoline-soaked floor. I feel breathless, dizzy, high on his intoxicating smell, and so turned on I can barely see straight. Wetness pools at my core and leaks down the inside of my thighs, and I'm reminded of the fact that I'm not wearing any underwear.

"Mmm, angel. You feel so fucking good against me," Kaiden rasps in my ear, and his hot breath, along with the tendrils of hair framing his face, tickle the side of my neck.

Suddenly, Kaiden twirls me to face him, holding me against his chest while his fingers splay at the small of my back possessively and we sway to the music. My breath hitches in my throat when his hold tightens, pressing my body impossibly closer to his. His other hand comes up and cradles my jaw as his burning gaze sweeps my face.

"You're radiant, Iris I—" He clears his throat. The emotion blazing in his eyes like hot embers surprises me, so at odds with his usual quiet stoicism. Golden flecks swirl in the obsidian abyss. "I feel like I can't fucking breathe when I look at you. You shine brighter than the sun. I know I'm not worthy…but I want to bathe in your light." He pauses. Shakes his head. Then his eyebrows drop low. "No, not just want; I need to kiss you more than I need my next breath. I need your light to

burn me from the inside out, and if only ashes are all that's left of me, then it will all be worth it because at least I got a taste of Heaven." His voice is gravel wrapped in satin as his gaze zeros in on my lips.

"I—we—I don't want you. I—I can't. We can't," I croak, stumbling all over my words, trying to hold on to the little thread of sanity keeping me together. After all the time we spent together, I'm afraid that if he kisses me now…I'll never be able to come back from it. That without meaning to, I will hand him a tiny part of my soul that I'll never be able to retrieve. He's a demon and everything I should stay away from, but damn it, if I'm not two seconds away from throwing all caution to the wind. "I—"

I don't get to finish my sentence because, in the next second, Kaiden's lips slam over mine in a searing kiss.

Time stops.

And that tiny little thread?

It snaps. It catches fire. It unravels with the speed of light.

Every part of my body comes alive as he owns my mouth with sure, languid strokes that I can feel all the way in between my legs. The kiss starts innocent and soft but immediately transforms into the most intense, possessive kiss I have ever experienced. Tongues battling for control and teeth gnashing. Sinking my fingers into his hair, I pull him closer with a desperate moan as my nails bite into his scalp.

He swallows the sound, kissing me so thoroughly, as if he can't get enough of me, like he wants to brand me forever with the intensity of our shared connection and leave me ruined for every other kiss I'm going to have in the future because nothing can compare to this feeling. Nothing can even come close.

People are fucking all around us, but somehow the way we devour each other with undisguised hunger, our chests bouncing in sync, our hearts beating at the same delirious rhythm seems so much…more.

I'm losing myself in him. I'm drowning. He's pulling me down, down, down, in the unrelenting currents, and the thing is…I never want to come back for air.

Time seems to have lost all meaning, and I don't know which way is up when Kaiden slows down the kiss. His teeth sink into my lower lip with a little nip before he pulls away to trace the contour of my lips reverently with his thumb.

"If you ever want to kill me, Iris, all you have to do is deny me your lips or offer them to another man," he says gruffly, and I'm struck stupid by the fire in Kaiden's eyes. No one has ever looked at me like this before, with so much intensity. There's something more, too, as though the very fabric of his soul is reaching out to mine, and I get again the sensation that I somehow know him, that the connection we share runs deep, deeper than anything I have ever felt before.

I swallow through the lump in my throat. "This might seem crazy, but…have we, have we met before?"

He sucks in a shaky breath, and for some insane reason, I think he's going to say "Yes," when suddenly his eyes dart across the room, and the moment we shared dissipates like smoke in the wind.

"It's time." Kaiden takes a step back, and without giving me another look, he takes my hand in his, turns around, and pulls me toward the bar at the back of the room.

31

When we finally reach the bar, Kaiden tells me, "Wait here. I'll be right back." He then turns on his heel, and his big frame slices through the crowd. My eyes follow him as he stops near the door we entered earlier, where Maeve is waiting for him. She places a hand on his chest seductively, and they start talking. They stand so close to one another that they practically share the same breath. My nostrils flare, and my blood simmers as Maeve's hand sneaks beneath his suit jacket.

I turn around, afraid that if I keep watching them, I'll probably go over and rip her hair out and then punch Kaiden for letting her touch him after the moment we shared on the dance floor. Needing something to take me off the edge of the chaos I feel brewing inside of me, I stop the passing server and snatch a flamingo pink drink from the tray. My lips touch the rim of the glass when I remember Kaiden's words cautioning me not to drink anything. I put it down on top of the bar and curse under my breath because I really need a drink.

"Hey, gorgeous," someone says from behind me. As I turn around I come face to face with a well-built man wearing a jester mask and a royal blue suit. He bends, boxing me in against the bar before whispering in my ear, "You had my attention since the moment you walked in." His fingers wrap around my wrist tightly. "Let's go somewhere private."

A slow smile spreads across my face, and my fingers curl into fists. If I can't have a drink, maybe leveling this douche canoe will settle the rage bubbling inside my veins. Before I can throat punch the asshole, a big shadow appears, looming over us.

"If you want to keep that arm attached to your body, I strongly suggest you let go of her in the next second," Kaiden growls loudly.

The stranger lets go of my hand like I've burnt him, staggering backward. "Shit, man. We were just going to have some fun. That's what we're all here for, right? We're all sharing—"

"She's. Mine. And. I. Don't. Share," Kaiden snaps, his voice dripping with venom. He pulls me to his side before his arm circles my lower back possessively. "Now disappear before I pull out your lungs for daring to breathe so close to her."

The man's eyes bulge out of his head at Kaiden's words, and he leaves like his ass is on fire, weaving his way through the crowd.

"Let me go," I hiss while pushing Kaiden away, but he only tightens his hold on me.

He turns to me with a frown, his gaze sweeping over my partially covered face. "What the fuck has gotten into you?"

I catch a whiff of a cloying woman's perfume. White hot rage burns through me. "Let go of me. You smell like her," I spew.

A ghost of a smile touches Kaiden's lips. "Aw, is my angel jealous?"

"Being jealous would mean that I care," I bite back. "And I don't."

Amusement dances in his eyes. "Relax, baby. She was giving me an access card, that's all." He pulls on the lapel of his suit jacket, showing me the inside pocket where now sits a rectangular red card with golden edges. "Did you really think that I would let her touch me like that after I kissed you?"

I sniff, and my jaw flexes. "Well, you did look mighty cozy," I mutter.

Kaiden laughs before shaking his head incredulously, like he's sharing an inside joke with himself. "If you only knew, Iris. If you only knew."

His cryptic words leave me puzzled as he guides me toward the door behind the bar. He takes out the crimson card from his pocket and swipes it across the handle. The little red light in the middle of it turns green, and a soft click breaks through the music. Kaiden opens the door. A dimly lit, narrow stairway greets us. The door closes at our back, and I lift the skirt of my dress so I don't trip on my own legs as we start climbing the stairs. At the top, we reach a long corridor with black-painted walls. People are milling about the room, stopping to watch through the two-way mirrors littered across the walls.

Kaiden takes two drinks from a server's tray, passes me one, and loops an arm around my shoulder, whispering in my ear, "We're going to pretend like we belong and stop along the way to look at the scenarios. Then, when it's time, we're going to enter one of the rooms."

"'Kay," I say, and we continue down the corridor, stopping at the first two-way mirror. On the other side is some sort of a sex dungeon scenario with a woman hanging from a hook in the ceiling. She's blindfolded, two clamps hanging from her taut nipples, while a man uses a flog to spank her. Another man watches as a woman sucks him off. The wall behind them is full of whips, gags, clamps, and belts. My breath hitches in my throat. Kaiden seems to notice, and his gaze snaps to my parted lips, and then, he observes the way my chest falls rapidly.

"Does this turn you on, Iris?" he purrs in the shell of my ear. I bite my lower lip and give him an almost imperceptible nod, not able to speak at this moment, but he doesn't miss it. "Then I'll make sure to remember it."

We pass a few more scenarios, one with a foursome between

vampires on a massive round bed in a red room, another with a woman and two men in a basin infested with sharks. I think she's a siren. I don't even want to know how they pulled that one off. There's also a room with sex swings and another full of mirrors.

As we reach the only empty room at the back, Kaiden places our untouched drinks on a cocktail table and takes out the crimson card again, swiping it just like before over the door handle next to the two-way mirror. The light turns green. He holds it open for me to enter first. A plush, massive, round bed with satin red sheets sits in the middle of the room, and a couch is facing it, pushed back against the reflective surface of the two-way mirror on the wall.

Kaiden wraps his arms around me from behind before bending to whisper in my ear, "Do you trust me?"

I swallow, my stomach a ball of restless energy. "Do I have a choice?"

The door opens, and someone walks inside. The sound of shoes slapping against the floor reverberates in the dead silence of the room. "Ah, good, you're already here. Get her ready for me," a man with a commanding voice says.

Kaiden pushes my hair to one side and starts tracing kisses on the column of my neck while his hands palm my breasts over my dress. He starts rubbing my nipples in between his thumbs and forefingers.

My heart is beating so fast against my ribcage I'm surprised my ribs don't shatter to smithereens. Wetness pools and trickles down the inside of my thighs, and I let out a shaky breath.

"Relax, angel. I'm not going to let anything happen to you," Kaiden murmurs in the shell of my ear, only for me to hear.

"Turn around. I want to see," the same man says, and I guess it's him, Lucifer's chancellor. It has to be, right?

Kaiden does just that, whirling me around. Adramelech's gaze snaps to my face and then sails over my body slowly. He's beautiful, even with the serpentine mask covering half of his face, the vibrant green scales accentuating the deep umber hue of his skin and his unsettling eyes. They look exactly like a snake's eyes down to the pupils shaped like crescent moons. He's sitting on the couch, his legs spread wide with an erection tenting his pants.

"Kneel at her feet and eat her out," Adramelech demands.

Holy shit!

Is Kaiden really going to do this?

HERE?

My heart beats wildly in my throat, and I'm impossibly aroused at the idea that the people outside can watch us through the two-way mirror.

Shit, shit, shit.

I can't believe this is going to happen.

Kaiden circles me with sure steps, and his gaze never leaves mine as he kneels at my feet, drapes one of my legs over his shoulder, and parts one of the side slits in my dress. He lets out a sharp curse the moment his eyes find my naked center, then they slam into mine, all fire and brimstone. His hands move upwards on the curves of my hips beneath my dress. His fingers flex, biting into my skin and keeping me upright. I whimper and almost pass out when his tongue sneaks out and licks my slit from my back hole to my clit.

A sexy as fuck sound between a rumble and a low growl leaves Kaiden's chest as he starts feasting on my pussy like a starved man, his tongue wet and hot against my soaked slit. He starts sucking and biting on my engorged clit. Then, he flattens his tongue against it before licking me in maddening circles. He repeats the cycle again and again and again.

My fingers thread through his hair, and I push him closer to me, desperate for more as I pant and strangled moans of pleasure leave my mouth. My eyes slam shut, and my toes curl at the onslaught of pleasure. I'm flushed everywhere. Sweat dots my forehead and travels between my breasts as lightning seizes every nerve ending in my body.

I'm so close. So close.

Before I get the chance to come, Adramelech says, "That's enough. Come here."

Kaiden nips my clit and gives it one more suck before he stands, and I don't miss the inferno blazing in his eyes. His Adam's apple bobs hard in his throat, and his expression smolders as he licks his lips, not missing a drop of my arousal.

On shaky legs, I stride to Adramelech with Kaiden at my back and stop in front of him.

With a smirk, he says. "Open my zipper and straddle me." His gaze flits to Kaiden. "You're going to fuck her ass while I take her cunt."

Um, WHAT?!?

I didn't agree to this. Kaiden touching me is something else. As gorgeous as Adramelech is, I don't want him. I try to take a step back, but I slam into Kaiden's hard body and realize there's no way for me to escape. I really hope Kaiden has a plan because if not, I'm going to kill him.

Kaiden places a hand at my waist and squeezes me reassuringly. I suck in a choppy breath and place one of my trembling knees on one side of Adramelech's body on the couch and then the other, straddling him. The artery on the side of my throat is fluttering so violently it's about to burst as I start unzipping Adramelech's pants and feel his erection throbbing against my hand.

The sound of Kaiden opening his zipper slashes through the air like a loaded gun in the silence before he grabs my hips and lifts my dress at my back.

Adramelech's eyebrows furrow, and he sneers at me. "What are you waiting for? Take my dick out," he snaps as he circles my wrist in a punishing grip.

All of a sudden, Kaiden pushes me from behind, plastering me to Adramelech's chest, and with a swift move, he lodges the needle of the syringe in the side of his neck in a way that can't be seen from the outside since the couch is pushed against the wall right below the two-way mirror.

Surprise, followed by red-hot anger, flashes in Adramelech's eyes, but before he gets the chance to do anything, he passes out cold. Kaiden lifts me from Adramelech's body like I weigh nothing more than a feather, plants me on my feet, and pops off, appearing at the wall farthest from us, placing his hand on its surface. Fire spreads from his open palm, and in a matter of seconds, it engulfs the entirety of the wall.

The acrid smoke is so potent, I start coughing as screams filled with panic erupt alongside the fire alarm, which blares with a high-pitched sound. Sprinklers go off in the room but have zero effect because this is hellfire; it can't be put out using water.

"Give me a hand?" Kaiden asks as he appears next to the couch, and we both prop Adramelech on our sides with his arms around the napes of our necks like we're carrying a drunk, dragging his feet across the floor. He's heavy as fuck, and he's even taller than Kaiden, but with his weight distributed between us, it's not that hard to carry him.

The fire spreads toward us, but Kaiden simply flicks his hand, and the fire suddenly stops then sprints in the opposite direction like a live entity. My eyebrows shoot up, and I let a little gasp of surprise at his ability to control hellfire like that. Could it be possible that the Kabal mistook hellfire for *illum*? In my mind, that's the only reasonable explanation.

We get out of the room in the midst of a panic-induced frenzy. People are trampling each other in the narrow corridor to get to the exit. Kaiden tilts his head, pointing to a spot in the black wall, saying, "This way." He pushes with his shoulder on a concealed door that perfectly blends into the wall, and we go down the flight of stairs quickly to exit at the back of the mansion, facing the sprawling grounds and the garden with a hedge labyrinth at its center.

Kaiden's Escalade is waiting for us, and it's already running. We descend the last three steps and amble to the back of the car. Kaiden opens the trunk, and we push Adramelech's unconscious body inside. My chest bounces as I take huge gulps of fresh air, trying to get as much as I can into my lungs.

My dress is completely soaked and plastered to my body from sweat and water, but now that we're outside, a chilly breeze makes all the hair on my body stand on end. I watch as Kaiden secures Adramelech's wrists and ankles with chains that I'm sure must be spelled. He closes the trunk, and we get in the car quickly.

"You okay?" Kaiden asks as he throws the SUV into drive and peels away like a bat out of Hell, rounding the house and speeding through the same gravel driveway he drove through when we arrived.

"Yeah," I respond and watch the chaos we're leaving behind. The party attendees are spilling out of the mansion in a panic while the dark flames spread like wildfire under a huge cloud of smoke.

"What happens now?" I inquire after a few beats of silence.

"We'll get him to the basement in my building, and I'll torture him for information," Kaiden replies nonchalantly, his eyes on the road. The frost and detachment in his tone chills me to the bone.

"I want to be there when you question him."

"I don't think that's a good ide—"

"It's a good thing I didn't ask for your opinion then. As long as you're questioning him about me, I have every right to be there. And I didn't just risk my ass for nothing," I snap.

"Fine," Kaiden clips out, jaw taut with tension. He rakes a hand through his wet hair to push it back. Fuck me. He looks like one of those models that they purposefully douse with water before a photo shoot. He discarded his suit jacket on the backseat alongside our masks a little while ago, so his white dress shirt displays his perfectly etched chest and abs. As if he wasn't attractive enough, his tattoos stand out through the see-through fabric. And let's not even talk about the fact that his sleeves are rolled up to his elbows. The way the veins in his inked forearms snake along the corded muscles is making my mouth water.

I bet I look like a drowned cat next to him.

Ugh.

Trying to keep the dread crawling beneath my skin from sending me directly into the claws of a panic attack, I clear my throat. "So, is Maeve one of your exes?"

"Having an ex would imply that I do relationships. I don't do relationships, hand-holding, or kissing. Never have."

"Oh," I say and swallow. He did those things with me, though. Well, he only grabbed my hand so he could pull me to the dance floor, but it still counts as hand-holding in my mind. Not so sure it counts in his though. Probably not. "So she's like a fuck buddy or what?" I press, knowing that it will drive me crazy if I don't get a clear answer from him.

"I don't do those either."

I want to ask him what we are, how he defines this…thing between us—if there even is something to define—but I don't, not knowing if I truly want an answer to that, so I ask instead, "So, what does that mean, that you don't do kissing? You've never kissed someone before?"

Kaiden licks his lips, and the intensity in his eyes as his gaze locks with mine makes my heart skip a beat. "Until you, I have never kissed anyone, so no. You were my first and only kiss."

Whoa!

My eyebrows shoot up almost to my hairline. That is definitely not the answer I was expecting to get in return. "But why?" I ask stupidly while fumbling with my fingers in my lap. He has got to be lying, right? Does he really want me to believe that in all of his life, he's never kissed anyone?

He opens his mouth, then closes it as if he changed his mind at the last second. "I never felt the need to kiss anyone else. It always felt too intimate," he says after a few beats of silence, hiking a shoulder.

His response renders me speechless, so I turn around to look out the window as we cruise through the empty streets of Ashville.

"I need your light to burn me from the inside out, and if only ashes are all that's left of me, then it will all be worth it because at least I got a taste of Heaven."

Why can't I get his words out of my head? Why are they seared into my brain? My chest rises and falls with a choppy inhale as my heart thunders in my ears.

He kissed me.

He kissed *me*.

He kissed me.

He held me in steadfast arms on a magical night as fireflies danced all around us. He chased my nightmares away as the beat of his heart lulled me to a peaceful sleep. With a single kiss, he set my soul on fire and blew my world to ashes, turning it upside down. And as hard as it is to admit, all of my fears became true because it felt…transcendental.

Now, I don't know where I stand. What my role in this world is anymore. I think…Fuck, I think I'm starting to have feelings for him. We belong in different worlds. Our paths should have never crossed, but now they seem impossibly intertwined.

No, no, no, no, no, no.

You can't be with him, Iris!

You can't have feelings for a demon!

This can't be happening. It will ruin my life. It's just lust between us. Yeah, nothing more than lust. I'm reading too much into things. Maybe if I finally give into the temptation, I'll get it out of my system…get *him* out of my system. Then, I can move on with my life and forget all about Kaiden. My stomach takes a nosedive at that thought, but I don't look too much into it. I *can't* look too much into it.

So I focus instead on everything else that happened tonight. I never thought I would be into those sort of things…but if I'm being truthful to myself, I more than enjoyed it; I loved it. I wish Adramelech had let me come, at least, because the proximity to Kaiden in the car's cab is almost too much to handle. Thinking about everything that has happened tonight is making me all hot and bothered, and my nipples harden against the wet fabric of my dress.

Suddenly, Kaiden swerves right into a dark alley and slams the brakes, stopping the car in between two buildings. "What are you doing?" I ask as my eyebrows pull together in confusion. I whip my head toward Kaiden. With a gulp, my eyes drop to the death grip his tattooed hands have on the steering wheel. He turns off the headlights.

He's shrouded in shadows, the rays of moonlight filtering through the windshield, making his eyes gleam. Without a word, he's on me like a flash. He cages me in against the seat as he pulls the lever and flattens the chair while pushing it back to the max. Using his knee, he parts my thighs, then settles between them. A breathy moan escapes my lips when he starts rolling his erection over my center. He swallows the sound as his lips come crashing down on mine in a scorching kiss that steals the breath in my lungs and ignites a fire in every cell of my body.

With a forceful tug, he rips the thin spaghetti straps of my dress, eliciting a yelp out of me, and pushes down the corset, exposing my breasts. He takes them in each hand, using his thumbs to circle my nipples.

Kaiden pulls away and swallows audibly as his gaze travels the length of my body like a caress. "You're perfect. So goddamn beautiful." He dips and sucks one of my nipples into his mouth, teasing and licking before lavishing the other one with the same attention.

My hands come up to hold onto the headrest for dear life as my nails dig into the buttery leather. "Ahhh…so good," I pant. Back arching, I move my hips furiously, seeking more friction with my center over the bulge in his pants.

The windows fog over, and the air in the cab is thick with lust, mixing with Kaiden's decadent scent. He fists the skirt of my dress and bunches it at my hips, shoving his palms under my ass cheeks as he slides down my body and kneels in front of the seat, burying his nose in my pussy and inhaling deeply.

"You might smell like heaven," his voice comes out gruff, thickened by his desire. He spreads me open with his tongue, then spears it inside me. "But you know what you taste like, angel? Like sin. Like fucking mine," he breathes against my wet heat before he starts licking me like a man possessed. My hips buck and his fingers flex in response. They bite into my flesh as he keeps me against his mouth, not giving me any reprieve from his wicked tongue.

The low growl of his voice rolls over me, and pleasure sieges me as I ride his face, mewls and desperate sounds I have never made before slicing through the air in the cabin. Kaiden slides down a hand, and he pushes two thick fingers inside me as he sucks on my clit.

"Oh, God!" I moan through heavy pants as pain blends with pleasure, the fingers stretching me deliciously. My legs start shaking violently as my toes curl.

"There's no God, Iris, just me. I'm your God now. Whose knuckles are deep into your sweet pussy?"

"Y-yours, Kaiden. You are."

"That's right, love. Now be a good girl and come for me." He scissors his fingers against my G spot and bites my clit. Hard. Then licks the pain away.

"Fuuuuck," I cry out as pleasure like I never felt before detonates inside my body. It spreads through me like a lightning storm, frying my nerve endings and obliterating every coherent thought. Kaiden doesn't stop the onslaught with his fingers against my G spot. The orgasm goes on and on and on. My eyes slam shut as fireworks go off behind my eyelids, and I realize I'm experiencing my first multiple orgasm. Tears leak from the corners of my eyes and run down my cheeks from its intensity. It's almost too much.

I'm floating somewhere on a cloud with limbs turned to jelly, unable to open my eyes. I feel Kaiden cleaning me up with his tongue. He murmurs something I can't make out because tiredness pulls me under, and I succumb to it.

32

"Who put the bounty on Iris Harper?" Kaiden clips out through gritted teeth.

"I told you I don't know!" Adramelech's screams bounce off the wall as Kaiden sets him on fire for what must be the hundredth time today. The smell of charred meat wafts through the air, making bile surge in my throat. He's hanging from a metal hook in the ceiling, spelled chains around his wrists. His feet barely touch the cement floor.

We're in the basement of the building Kaiden lives in, or better said, the building he owns because I just found out earlier that he owns the whole freakin' neighborhood, and I still don't know how to process that information. He really wasn't kidding when he said the Conclave is getting into legitimate business.

The space is impressive; it looks like a giant windowless warehouse with top-notch security. He even has a biometric scanner at the door. Empty cages litter the wall on my far left, and I guess this is where justice is served, where all the dark creatures that break the number one rule of not killing humans are punished.

The sound of a phone ringing slices through the air, and Kaiden steps back from Adramelech, taking his phone out of his pants and glancing at the screen. He looks over his shoulder, and his crimson gaze finds mine, his scleras slowly going back to white. "I have to take this. I'll be right back," he tells me before striding to the door with steps that echo loudly in the cavernous space.

"I don't know why, but I don't quite believe you," I say to Adramelech as I stand from the chair I've been sitting on since we arrived a few hours ago. After I fell asleep in Kaiden's car, he brought Adramelech's unconscious body here, and then he drove us to my apartment. I woke in my bed, confused as to how I got there. After getting ready, Kaiden drove us to his building.

The thought that Kaiden must have carried me to bed is doing strange things to my heart. I can't get last night out of my head...the kiss, our talk, and then what happened in his car. A maelstrom of emotions war inside my chest, and my pulse scatters as the image of Kaiden kneeling between my thighs and feasting on me flashes through my mind.

Dammit, Iris, concentrate!

I blink, forcefully bringing my mind into the present. "You see, the Order taught us that Lucifer's right-hand demon is a well of information. That he knows everything going on. Why would you be his chancellor otherwise?" I challenge, striding to the massive table on my right, where torture instruments are laid out in an obsessive-compulsive order. Judging by how clean and organized Kaiden's penthouse is along with this place, I'm sure he's one of those clean freaks. Honestly, I'm surprised he didn't blow a gasket living in my apartment. Don't get me wrong; I like things clean and organized, but not at this level.

Picking up a serrated knife that has a weird symbol on the handle, I run my finger down its sharp blade. It looks spelled. Since I don't know what it does, I put it back in its place and take out a dagger from its holster at my belt. I make my way toward Adramelech slowly, with the gait of a predator cornering its next meal, as I flip it in the air a few times. "But do you know what you're most famous for? Your voracious appetite for eating the souls of innocent children and then feeding their little bodies to your snakes."

He smirks. "They do taste better than anything. Untainted souls are a delicacy."

"Sick fuck," I snap, and with a flick of my wrist, I send the dagger flying. It impales Adramelech's left eyeball with a wet *thwack*.

"You cunt!" He lets out a blood curdling wail, struggling in his restraints as tar-like blood starts pouring on the side of his face.

I smile like a cat. "Aw, did that hurt? I guess you've never experienced what a blessed dagger can do before. Well, let's get you two acquainted, shall we?"

His nostrils flare, and his serpentine eye glimmers with undisguised rage. "Do your worst," he hisses, and I step back to avoid the spittle flying from his mouth. He's only wearing the pants from last night, the skin of his exposed torso, a mangled mess of burns, still sizzling in the aftermath of Kaiden's power.

He didn't use any of the torture instruments on Adramelech, and I suspect it's because of my presence. He's probably afraid of my reaction, of how I'm going to perceive him after witnessing him inflict torture. Little does Kaiden know, I've dabbled in the art myself. Whenever I stumble across a demon higher in rank on my shifts, I make sure to question it about my mother's death before sending it back to Hell.

Since the umbra attack, there have been very few demons on the streets, so when Kaiden mentioned we were going to get Adramelech, I knew I had to be here, not only because I have a bounty on my head and want to know why, but because he might know something about the demon that killed my mother.

Folding my arms in front of my chest, I say, "Eliana Harper, my mother, was a hellseeker. She was killed eight years ago by a demon at the bottom of a canyon. Do you know anything about it, who that demon is?"

He arches a mocking eyebrow. "Aw, let me guess, Mommy Dearest's death messed up your sad little life," he taunts with a snicker.

A muscle thrums in my taut jaw as I wrap my fingers around the dagger's hilt and twist, eliciting another screech. "I asked you a question." With that, I take out the dagger and start carving out his eye to the sound of his wails. I don't enjoy this; in fact, my stomach lurches in my throat every time he screams. It's only practice that made me somewhat immune. The first time I tortured a demon, I spilled the contents of my stomach on the ground three times before I was able to continue.

Adramelech's serpentine eye smacks the floor and rolls, and I step back to see his face better. "Do you think there's a spell or magic powerful enough to grow back your eye? I don't think so," I muse, tone detached, cold as ice. "So, did you change your mind? Are you going to start talking now?"

The sound of Kaiden opening and closing the door reverberates in the vast space, but I don't turn around. The wards Malik put on the basement are so strong that he cannot disappear and appear at whim inside, so he needs to use the door like a normal person.

"Fucking hellseeker bitch," Adramelech spews.

"'Kay then, well, I guess you don't need the other eye either." I lift my dagger-holding hand and swing it toward Adramelech's remaining eye.

Just before the tip of the blade makes contact, he bellows, "STOP!"

I do.

His chest is bouncing with labored breaths. "There's a ledger Lucifer likes to keep with every single hellseeker death caused by a demon since the initiation of the Order. Your mother's name is not there. I would know; I'm the one writing in it."

What. The. Fuck.

I almost stagger back at hearing his words. No, that can't be right. I saw the file. The Order classified my mother's death as caused by an unknown demon. "You're lying," I seethe. It's the only explanation because if he's not, it means that the Order lied about my mother's death, and why would they do that? It makes no sense.

"I don't think he is. Lucifer does keep a ledger," Kaiden says from my right, startling me. If he is surprised to come back into the room and find me torturing Adramelech, he doesn't show it.

"Where can I find this ledger?" I inquire as I turn my head toward Kaiden.

He shoves his hands in his pockets. "In Hell, at Lucifer's palace."

"Can we get it?"

"It's too dangerous. It's the best guarded place in Hell. You can only enter with Lucifer's permission, and he's in hiding, remember?"

Fuck.

Looking back at Adramelech, I ask, "Who put a bounty on my head?"

His nostrils flare. "I already told you. I. Don't. Know."

I tilt my head. "Fine, then what do you know about the umbra?"

"The umbra?" he echoes, and his throat rolls with an audible swallow.

That alone tells me he must know something. "Yeah, don't play dumb. A few weeks ago, I was attacked by umbra demons in the national park. They came through a fucking portal and almost killed me."

Something akin to fear flashes in Adramelech's eye. But he still doesn't say anything.

"'Kay then," I say dryly and plunge the dagger into his gut, twisting before taking it out. I wait for the screams to stop. "Don't worry; your remaining eye is next. So…the umbra?"

He mutters a sharp curse, followed by a death stare my way. Sweat runs down in rivulets on his face and torso, tar-like blood gushing from the wound as violent tremors wrack his body. He hisses a serrated breath. "When the Celestial Treaty was signed, the seraphim put a secret clause in it. It obligated Lucifer to hide the umbra in the farthest corner of Hell and erase all traces of their existence because of a prophecy."

Folding my arms in front of my chest, I ask, "What prophecy?"

"I don't know what the prophecy says. I only know it exists."

"What about the portal? Do you know who opened it?"

"No," he answers quickly. Too quickly.

I cock an eyebrow and swing the dagger toward Adramelech's remaining eye again.

"FUCK! STOP!" he bellows.

I drop my hand and wait.

"I know a portal opened near Shadow Lake almost two months ago. It created quite the buzz in Hell since portals are forbidden. At first, I thought it might be a demon from the resistance, but I couldn't find any evidence. I didn't know umbra came through it, though, until right now…" He swallows. "I think they tore open the veil to create the portal."

My eyes widen. "They can do that?"

"Yes. They used to tear through the veil between Hell and Earth to collect souls, and that was before Lucifer banished them to the furthest corner of Hell."

I pinch the bridge of my nose, trying to calm the headache blooming between my eyes. Gritting my teeth, I turn on my heel and start pacing the length of the basement, my mind spinning. A warm hand placed on my shoulder stops me.

"You okay?" Kaiden asks. Canting his head to the side, his obsidian gaze captures mine and makes my heart flutter. He drops his hand at the side of his body, and I shiver slightly, already missing his warmth.

"Yeah…Do you think he's telling the truth?"

"I'm not sure, though you did scare the shit out of him when you were about to take out his second eye." A small smile tugs at his full, sinful lips.

"Yeah, well, you were taking too long, so I decided to intervene."

"You're good at it, torture. If you ever need a job…"

I huff. "I know you held back on Adramelech because I was here." Hiking a shoulder, I say, "I don't enjoy inflicting pain, but you get used to it when you do it enough times. It's something I had to do in order to at least try and find the demon who killed my mother."

"Didn't you say she died in a car accident when you were fifteen?"

"When the Order took me in, I learned that we fell into the canyon, and at the bottom, a demon was waiting for us. I don't know how I survived, obviously, since I can't remember anything about my past. But I saw the file. It said that the cause of death was inflicted wounds by an unknown demon." I fold my lower lip between my teeth, gnawing on it. "Do you think the Order lied about my mother's death?" I ask after a few beats of silence.

"I don't know, but you put too much faith into the Order. It's not like they're saints."

I scoff. "Yeah, well, they took me in after my mother's death and gave me a purpose. They didn't have to since I'm a half-blood, so excuse me for not choosing to believe a demon to the detriment of the people who gave me a new life."

Kaiden sucks on his teeth. "I understand this is a hard pill to swallow, but you have to at least take into consideration that the Order might have lied."

"I know, I just…I'm sorry. I didn't mean to snap at you, but it's the first lead I got about my mother's death, and it wasn't what I expected to hear." I heave out a deep sigh. "We need to find out what that prophecy says."

"Yeah, I know," he murmurs grimly, deep in thought, then scrubs a hand over his stubbled cheeks.

Taking out my phone from the back pocket of my jeans, I glance at the screen. "Shit, it's already nine. I have to go home and get ready for my shift. I can't miss another one."

"Okay. We can pick this up tomorrow and see if you can get anything else out of Adramelech regarding the prophecy. I'll call Malik from the car and let him know we finished for today, so he can come heal him. I don't know if he'll be able to do anything about the eye, though," he says before placing his hand at the small of my back.

"What happens when you finish getting all the information you need out of Adramelech? Are you going to kill him?" I ask Kaiden as we get out in the hallway.

"No, it's too risky. Even if Lucifer is in hiding, we can't risk him finding out. He might retaliate. Malik is going to erase his memories to make sure he doesn't remember being tortured."

My eyes almost bulge out of my head. I figured Malik was extremely powerful for a dark magic wielder, but not *that* powerful. "Can he do that?" I ask.

"The brain is always tricky to mess with, but I believe he can do it," he says, jabbing the elevator button.

33

I stare at my phone screen as a giddy feeling of anticipation sends shivers down my spine. Since that moment in his car, he hasn't touched me. Well, there's also the fact that we've barely spent time together in this past week.

"Did you manage to get any more information out of Adramelech?" Sam inquires, bringing me back to reality while adding the final touches to my makeup, sweeping blush with a fluffy brush on the apples of my cheeks. We're both sitting on top of my bed, getting ready for a night out. We haven't seen each other since she came back because she was swamped with work. Wedding season is crazy busy for a florist, and her taking a break for the purification rituals with her grandmother in the middle of it left her with a mountain of things to do.

"Unfortunately, no. Kaiden decided to lock him in one of the cells and leave him there for a few days." He couldn't ignore his Conclave responsibilities anymore, so he has been showing up only to accompany me on my shifts. Someone came by and installed the latest security system with all the bells and whistles, and he left a wolf shifter who works as security for him to guard my apartment and drive me around the rest of the time, which I found overkill. However, I couldn't actually argue with his decision because he threatened to go to Grayson again, so I clamped my mouth shut and went with it.

He also went apeshit on my ass when I told him I was going out with my best friend tonight and I didn't want him to come, but he calmed down when I said we were going to Sin. He simply stated that Carter, the wolf shifter, will drive us there. It felt suspicious as hell that he would back down so easily, but I counted it as a win because I really need a night out with my bestie to decompress.

"Do you think he was telling the truth about your mom?" she asks, snapping me out of my thoughts.

I swallow hard. "I don't know, Sam. But it's killing me. I've gone over his words a thousand times in my head. I need to take another look at that file. When I first saw it, I was fresh out of the hospital, and I was only fifteen. I didn't even know what I was looking at…" Bringing my fingers to my temples, I massage them in an attempt to dull the headache that's been pounding in the back of my eyes since I woke up today. "And we really need to find out what that prophecy says," I tell her.

"Only an oracle can help us with that, but as far as I know, they're pretty much extinct. I'll talk to Grammie, see if maybe she knows a way to find one," Sam says after a few beats of silence.

After finishing my makeup, Sam stands and saunters to the upholstered chair in the corner of my room. She brings the garment bag she arrived earlier with to my bed and unzips it. "Here, this one's for you," she says, passing me a beautiful but very short dress.

"I'm not wearing that."

She arches a perfectly etched eyebrow in my direction and purses her lips in annoyance. "And what are you planning on wearing, Your Bitchy Highness? Sweats? Your hellseeker gear?"

Popping a shoulder, I say, "Jeans and a top."

Sam takes a breath in like she's gathering all the patience in the universe and looks me dead in the eye. "Iris, we're going to an exclusivist club; you can't wear jeans. Now put this dress on and stop acting like a toddler."

"Fine," I mutter, rolling my eyes as I take the dress. "But the first round is on you."

A sly smirk lifts the corner of her lips. "Deal."

"I don't know, Sam. I kinda look like a hooker," I grumble ten minutes later, doing another once-over in the mirror while rotating. The reflection staring back at me looks like a grown-up, way-too-sexy version of Iris, with midnight hair styled in voluminous waves, eyes popping out like two pale sapphires, emphasized by the perfectly blended purple smokey eyes Sam did on me. I have to give it to her; she did an amazing job dolling me up. I don't know why I'm surprised, though. She always does.

The dress she made me wear is deep-plum, with a Chantilly lace corset on top that has a serious push-up. It makes my boobs seem even bigger, and the skirt hugs my body, emphasizing every curve, stopping in the middle of my thighs. It's the shortest thing I have ever worn.

"Expensive hooker, you mean. That Chantilly lace cost more than my entire outfit. You're lucky I don't have the boobs for it. Otherwise, I would be wearing it," she retorts while sipping from a glass of freshly poured white wine on my bed and waiting patiently for me to finish my freak-out session.

"Yeah…I'm gonna change," I say as firmly as I can, knowing damn well I'm in for a fight. The decision has already been made in her mind.

"No, you're not. I don't think you understand how hot you look, you dumbass! I wish I had your body. You should show it up more. Don't get me started again on those stripper tits. Every single guy in the club will be drooling when they see you. I am already, and I'm straight! I would totally go gay for you, and you know it." Standing up, a playful smirk painting her face, she smacks my ass and licks her lips suggestively.

I laugh at her exuberance, not feeling awkward anymore. It's hard to admit, but she's right; I look hot. She winks at me, and I have to take a moment to admire how sexy and beautiful my best friend looks tonight. She always looks incredible, always dressed to the nines, but now she's wearing a red-hot backless slinky number with a high neckline that wraps around her neck.

The hemline reaches her knees, and it would look modest compared to mine if it wasn't for the open back and a slit that cuts a few inches below the apex of her thighs. The color brings out her mossy green eyes. Her bright copper hair is straight and pulled into a high, sleek ponytail, her makeup flawless, as always.

"All right," I relent. "But I will be wearing my over-the-knee high-heel boots with it. I'm not comfortable showing this much skin, I need something to at least cover my legs. And hold my dagger," I mumble, referring to the only dressy boots I own and the most impractical ones because I spent almost a fortune on them, but I never wear anything aside from my combat boots anyway. I bought them on a whim, of course, with Sam being the devil's advocate telling me I should get them.

"Oh, the ones you bought with me last year. You definitely should; you're going to look like a sex kitten," she says enthusiastically as she claps loudly before taking a hearty sip of wine. "We're going to have so much fun tonight, and I'm finally gonna get some dick! I swear to God, I haven't gone on a dry spell this long in forever."

THE LINE OF people outside Sin seems even longer than the one from almost two months ago, if that's even possible. The flock of very well-dressed men and women forming the impressive queue throw us dirty looks as Sam drags me by the hand impatiently, bypassing everyone.

I almost do a double take at the tall, muscly man guarding the entrance. He's checking people's phone screens for their reservations. A bored tilt of his head toward the door of the sleek three-story building is the only signal he gives them before lifting the red velvet entry rope to let them in.

A brunette woman, wearing an even shorter dress than I am, screams loudly, "Hey! You can't do that," at us as we pass her. I shrug in response. Sam doesn't even acknowledge her existence, a sexy smirk tugging at her lips when we reach the top of the line.

As soon as the bouncer spots Sam, his whole demeanor changes, a big smile taking over his face. "Kitten!" he exclaims loudly.

"Hey, baby!" Sam says, practically purring, while throwing herself in his arms and French kissing him so deeply it looks like she's on a quest for his tonsils, not caring about all the people in line who are staring at the free show they're putting out. Her designer, black strappy high-heeled sandals don't even touch the ground anymore.

My cheeks heat at her brazenness. I pretend the entrance door of the club is the most interesting thing I have ever seen as they continue their improper hello.

The same woman who showed anger before grumbles loudly, "Unbelievable!" at our backs, but I don't pay her any attention since my best friend and the tree-trunk of a man she is climbing like a monkey seem to ignore her as well.

After what seems like forever, Sam finally unsticks her body from the bouncer's. Her feet touch the ground. She licks her lips with the expression of the cat that ate the canary as she whispers to him, "Meet me at the bar later. I got a new move to show you in the bathroom." She winks and throws him a suggestive smile while drawing circles on his massive chest, which has written "Security" in bold white letters over the black T-shirt.

Sometimes, I wish my enhanced hearing would work only when hunting demons; right now, it makes me feel dirty, like an unwilling voyeur to their intimate conversation. I want to scrub my brain of the image of what they are going to do in the bathroom later.

Sam suddenly seems to remember she isn't alone as she shuffles back at my side, gesturing from me to the bodyguard. "Iris meet Alex. Alex, this is my best friend, Iris."

I shake Alex's big hand, and he pulls me in a bear-like hug, surprising me. He then puts his massive hands on my shoulders, taking a step back. "It's nice to finally meet you, Iris! I've heard so many things about you," he says with a warm smile that makes his eyes crinkle.

The tattoo on his right wrist draws my attention. It's the Sigil of Baphomet, marking him as a member of the Obsidian Conclave. His features and massive body are a clear indication of Alex being a wolf shifter.

What the fuck?

Why didn't Sam tell me about this?

"Likewise." I smile back at him, trying not to blush because I know all about their sexcapades in minute detail. I also try to stay calm and pretend I don't suspect he's a wolf shifter until I have the chance to question Sam about it.

"Have fun, ladies," Alex tells both of us and then winks at my best friend while lifting the velvet rope for us to pass. "I'll find you later."

"You better," Sam shoots back as she throws him a look over her left shoulder, biting her lip while tugging my arm through the club entrance. She drops my hand as soon as we go over the threshold and almost runs through the dark-lit hallway.

I huff in annoyance. "Sam! What the hell? Wait, we need to talk!" She's acting like she didn't hear a word I said as two hunky bodyguards open a massive double door at the end of the hallway. I can't help but notice they also have the Sigil of Baphomet tattooed on their wrists, just like Alex. Where the hell did Sam bring me?

The first thing that hits me as we enter Sin is the heady smell of black cherries mixed with that of musk and fresh sweat permeating and thickening the air. The onyx stone embedded in the choker around my neck pulses faintly, making me aware of a demonic presence. I'm on high alert as I follow behind Sam, trying to catch up to her. Damn, she's fast when she wants to be.

"Do I wanna know?" by Arctic Monkeys blasts through the massive speakers. The powerful bass makes the dark floor vibrate. I can feel the vibrations in every cell of my body as a strange feeling of arousal overtakes my senses.

The club's interior exudes sophistication, the elegant ambiance created by the dark wood paneling and plush emerald couches in perfect synergy with the modern, almost futuristic oval-shaped bar placed right in the middle of the dance floor. Strips of LED lights are strategically placed under the bar and on its sides, making it the main point of attraction.

Because the floors aren't separated by ceilings it creates the illusion of being inside a massive theater. Stairs and rounded booths are on each side of the grand, black-tiled dance floor. The stairs lead to the private balconies on the second and third floors, where the VIP section must be.

Gilded cages hang from the incredibly tall ceiling and hold writhing bodies of women and men, wearing nothing more than lacy lingerie and boxers. Their faces are covered by black and red carnival masks that look extremely similar to the ones me and Kaiden wore at the succubus party. They are dancing provocatively, two or three in each cage, their bodies undulating to the hypnotic beat around each other. Some are even kissing and imitating the act of fucking. If I squint my eyes against the pulsing lights that shine from the ceiling through the cages, I can see a guy with a perfectly sculpted body, his skin the color of warm toffee and silver-streaked dreadlocks reaching the middle of his back, fingering one of the other dancers.

Judging by the way her body moves in pure ecstasy with the beat of the song, she doesn't mind being on display like that. I can't be sure that's what I see, though. The dimmed, mysterious light surrounding the club and the moving flashes of brightness offer only a few dizzying glimpses into their lewd show, freezing them in the act only for a second and giving way to darkness in the next.

I finally manage to reach Sam and tug on her hand furiously as she weaves her way through the throngs of people moving lasciviously to the beat in the middle of the dance floor.

"Sam, what the fuck? What is this place?" Anger drips from my tone as I shout to cover the music so she can hear me.

"Just a club, calm down. Let's get some drinks," she fires back at the same volume and turns her back to me again, trying to resume her route to the bar and pretend nothing is wrong.

I don't let her. I pull on her hand again, this time with more force.

"I'm not going anywhere until you answer me truthfully! Is Alex a freakin' wolf shifter?"

Sam spins on her heel. Annoyance pinches the planes of her face. "Yes, he is." She arches an eyebrow at me and folds her arms in front of her chest, waiting for my reaction.

I explode.

"And you didn't think you should tell me about it? You know I can't fraternize with dark creatures; I can get kicked out from the Order! Also, there are demons in this club. What did you think, that I wouldn't figure it out?"

The dance floor is so crowded, we are being pushed from all directions by the sweaty, gyrating bodies, lost in their own worlds, oblivious to our conversation.

"If I told you, you would have judged me." She purses her lips and shakes her head in disappointment. "You're doing it right now!"

"You slept with a wolf shifter, Sam!" I exasperate.

Her eyes narrow, and her nostrils flare, vexation lacing every word that comes out of her mouth. "Oh, be for fucking real, Little Miss Shacking Up With a Demon! Can you be a bigger hypocrite? Didn't you attend a succubus party with Kaiden fucking Black just a few days ago?"

A muscle thrums in my jaw. "You know I had no choice. Kaiden threatened to go to Grayson and tell him everything. I can't risk being kicked out of the Order. You know that," I scoff and match her posture, crossing my arms in front of my chest. "And I went to the party because I needed answers about the bounty on me. We were wearing masks; no one could recognize us there."

"Pfft, yeah, sure, keep telling yourself lies. What, did you trip and fall on his tongue? You've enjoyed every second of Kaiden moving in with you and going to that party with him; you just don't want to admit it."

Her expression turns even more sour. "Stop being such a goody two shoes and start living a little! You're living like a fucking nun, Iris. Life is slipping through your fingers, and you can't even recognize that. And so what if Alex is a wolf shifter? He is one of the nicest guys I have ever met, and he fucks like a beast, so I don't care! Neither should you. No one chooses how they are born or made into this world. Besides, it's not like I am planning on marrying him. It's just a fling; I'm having fun. I'm happy, and you should be happy for me too. I fucking support your every decision and cheer you for it. What kind of friend are you if you don't do the same?"

Her words are a double-edged sword meant to draw blood. And they do. They spear right through my heart and settle at the bottom of my stomach like battery acid because she's speaking the truth. Hindsight is a bitch, all right.

All the fury leaves my body bit by bit with the tongue-lashing I'm receiving from my best friend. "Shit, I'm sorry, Sam. I just…" I don't know what else to say, I feel like I'm being trapped between a rock and a hard place. I can't be here; if anyone finds out, I will be thrown out of the Order. But Sam is right; I'm a hypocrite with a capital H. Even if my wounded pride screams at me that she isn't.

"You just, what? I love you, but you can be so fucking obtuse sometimes. Stop following every archaic rule from the Order like it's your religion! Maybe you should start thinking for yourself for once," she snaps and looks to the side like she can't bear the sight of me in front of her eyes anymore. "I wanted to have a fun night with you, that's all. You haven't gone out with me in ages; I miss you…"

She shrugs and points at the door. "Go if you want; I don't care anymore. I'll be at the bar if you decide to stay." With that, she turns around, slicing through the crowd, and leaves me in the middle of the dance floor. I don't stop her this time.

34

The empty space left by Sam on the dance floor is quickly filled by enthusiastic dancers, crowding me with their sweaty bodies. *Ugh.*

I'm still pinned in place by my indecision, looking like a freak because I'm not moving; I'm just standing here, gnawing on my bottom lip while I try to make up my mind, surrounded by people that move in a trance-like state.

As I take my first step toward the exit, the decision seems immediately wrong. So I turn on my heel and shove my way through the crowd of moving bodies. Even if it's hard to admit, Sam is right. I'm a hypocrite, and judging Alex just by the fact that he's a dark creature is unfair.

When I finally reach Sam at the oval-shaped bar in the middle of the massive dance floor, she has her hand in the air, signaling to the female bartender who is mixing a cocktail vigorously. "One shot of tequila, please!"

The bartender serving this side of the bar is a twenty-something, really attractive woman, her skin the color of warm amber. She's got the most beautiful hair I have ever seen, bouncy, ash-brown curls reaching her shoulders. She reminds me of someone; I just can't conjure a face at the top of my head. She also has the Sigil of Baphomet tattooed on her bicep, peeking from the short sleeve of her black T-shirt. If I have to guess, she's also a wolf shifter. I have an inkling all the club employees are members of the Obsidian Conclave.

"Make that two," I say as loudly as I can so she can hear me over the music and plop down on the empty bar stool next to Sam's.

The bartender nods at me. Her honey-colored gaze stops at the onyx choker around my neck. Her eyebrows furrow slightly at the sight, but she doesn't say anything about it.

Sam throws her arms around me from her chair with a big smile. "I knew you wouldn't leave me stranded." One of the things that I love the most about my best friend is that her fury has a short fuse. She is always quick to forgive me when I fuck up.

Sighing, I hug her back, the heady smell of wisteria and jasmine that always clings to her skin surrounding me like a cloud. "I was a bitch. Can you forgive me, please?"

She passes me a lime wedge and places one of the shots of tequila that was already sitting on the bar in my hand. "Already did. Now, let's have some fun. Bottoms up!" she says as she clinks her glass to mine.

After I lick the salt on the back of my hand, I throw my head back and bring the glass to my lips. I try not to gag at the smell of potent alcohol hitting my nose, reminding me about the last time I got drunk. I down the shot in one go and suck on the lime wedge quickly in a failed attempt to get rid of the queasiness in my stomach. A shudder goes through me as the spirit burns the back of my throat and settles in my stomach, warming up my insides.

A meaty, sweaty hand on my left shoulder grabs my attention. A guy is standing way too close to the bar stool I occupy, looming over me.

"Hey, beautiful. Let's dance!" he screams in my ear with such force, droplets of spit fly from his mouth and hit the left side of my face. His hot breath reeks of pungent alcohol and onions.

Eww.

He's swaying from one foot to another, trying to keep his balance, clearly shit-faced.

I close my eyes for a brief second and tilt my head toward the ceiling, praying for patience. "No, thank you! I'd rather sit for now," I say back with a brittle smile and turn my head again toward Sam, ignoring him.

He moves his hand to my elbow and unsuccessfully tries to hoist me up from the bar stool, making it scrape abrasively against the floor. "C'mon, don't be a tease!"

My head snaps back at him. "Remove your hand, or I'll do it for you," I demand as calmly as I can, not wanting to cause a scene, but with every passing second, my blood pressure keeps rising.

"If you don't want attention, don't dress like a slut!" he snaps at me. More of his disgusting spittle lands on my cheek as he pulls forcefully on my elbow again.

"Uh-oh! Welcome to your funeral, buddy!" Sam chuckles out beside me.

Grabbing his sweaty fingers with my right hand and putting more force than necessary into my hold, I throw his hand off me, not before feeling the distinct crunch of his bones breaking.

He wails in pain, cradling his injured hand against his chest. "You, bitch! You broke my fingers," he spews before taking a few stumbling steps back. He knocks into two girls who are sipping on cocktails and spills their drinks all over their clothes.

"Asshole!" one of them mutters as she gives him the stink eye. She tugs her friend's hand, both disappearing through the moving bodies.

She got that right.

"Maybe that will teach you that no means no," I retort.

"Fuck you!" He takes a step forward and lifts his uninjured hand like he's about to bitch slap me. Before I can stand up and teach him a lesson, a big, muscly body appears behind the creep and grabs him by the scruff of his neck, making his feet dangle above the floor.

"Is there a problem here?" Alex asks over the loud music.

"This bitch broke my fingers," the creep answers with indignation. His attempt at wiggling out of Alex's grasp makes him look like a fish out of the water.

"I didn't ask you, fuckface. You clearly deserved it."

"Hey there, sexy!" Sam beams at Alex, receiving a smile from him in return.

I shrug. "I would hardly call the meat suit with a receding hairline and protruding beer belly a problem." Sam snickers at my remark. "Besides, I had it covered."

"Oh, I know you did. The boss sent me to deal with the asshole, though," Alex says calmly. "I'll go take the trash out, and then I'll have my break in about half an hour. I'll wait for you in our spot," he says, the last part for Sam only as he winks at her. Then he moves toward the exit, still carrying the creep by the scruff of his neck like he doesn't weigh more than a feather. Damn, wolf shifter strength is no joke.

"Yas! Momma is finally gonna get some," Sam chirps enthusiastically as a Cheshire cat grin takes over her face. She turns to order two more shots.

"I don't know, Sam…my last hangover is still making me question the decision of drinking alcohol."

"Nu-uh, you're not raining on my parade. So cut the shit, Debbie Downer! We're having fun tonight." She pushes the small glass filled to the brim with tequila and the lime wedge toward me. "I already have the miracle hangover juice in my purse for you. So, we can drink as much as we want."

"Fine," I relent and down the shot, this time in two gulps, the burn of alcohol traveling from the back of my throat all the way down to my toes.

Sam is messing on her phone, wholly absorbed by what she's typing. She's probably letting Alex know how excited she is about their incoming sexy rendezvous. And I'm swaying to the music, turned around on my barstool, observing the way people move on the dance floor.

Their undulating bodies seem to be driven by the haze of desire that blankets the club, like puppets on strings. I'm sure it has something to do with the mysterious dancers in the gilded cages above us. My onyx choker still pulses against my throat, but I can't identify any immediate danger or any possessed humans. So, my best guess is that incubi and succubae demons are dancing in those cages, their pheromones thick in the air. The dancers are probably members of the Obsidian Conclave as well. If that's the case, then it is a pretty ingenious way to feed the demons and attract humans to the club by heightening their sexual experiences and desires.

Still gazing over my surroundings, a weird-looking woman catches the corner of my eye. She is just standing there in the middle of the moving bodies, dressed in a pink vintage gown with a corset and a puffy skirt, clearly out of place. She looks like she belongs in a nineteenth-century-period movie, not in a club.

I blink against the pulsating red lights, hoping she will disappear like a figment of my imagination, but she unfortunately doesn't. Her form ripples like water when someone passes right through her body, making a beeline for the hallway where the bathrooms are located.

Shit.

Is that a ghost?

Oh God, not again.

The song that's playing changes to a more upbeat one, and Sam jumps abruptly from the bar stool. She drags me after her with an excited "Let's dance! I love this song!" to the dance floor. I look over my shoulder toward the woman, but she's gone. Huh, maybe she really was just a figment of my imagination.

Sam expertly elbows everyone in her vicinity, forcing them to make space for us, and starts swaying her hips in provocative circles while dropping low to the floor and coming up again. I'm not as good at dancing as she is, but I love it anyway, so I shake free of my inhibitions, letting the music guide my movements.

As Sam grinds her body against mine with the beat of the next song, a shiver works its way down my spine with the sensation of being watched. My eyes travel to the balconies above us until they meet obsidian eyes streaked with gold and crimson, watching me with the hunger of a predator stalking its next meal.

Time seems to stop as our gazes collide, freezing me in place. Everything goes quiet around me. The blaring music, the murmur of faded conversations, and the slurred half-shouted words of the drunken girls dancing in our vicinity. The only sound left is my heartbeat, a low drumbeat in my ears that seems to skip in irregular rhythms with every second I can't look away. I gulp hard at the image of Kaiden sitting on a plush emerald couch in one of the private balconies on the second floor, like a dark king on his throne, keeping an eye on his undeserving subjects, a lit cigarette between his fingers. He is so handsome it almost hurts to look at him.

Gone is the Kaiden that held me to his chest while I slept, the one that cooked for me and laughed so freely around me. This Kaiden seems relaxed, sprawled with an almost bored expression painting his face, but confidence and malice radiate from him in waves. Like a pungent cologne, the undercurrent of his power seeps into every nook and cranny of the immense space, ready to strike and snap your bones if you as much as dare to look in the direction of the cruel, dark king.

I'm so ensnared by the way he looks at me like he can peel every layer of my skin from my bones only with his eyes that I don't even notice until the very last moment the scantily clad woman with a razor-sharp bob and legs a mile long planting herself in his lap. Maeve bends to whisper something in his ear, one of her hands stroking over the dark fabric of his jeans, where his crotch is.

Everything comes rushing back as the caustic burn of jealousy spreads through my body like wildfire, taking me by surprise with the sheer force of it. It makes my breathing ragged as I clench my fists hard, the crescent indentations left behind in the palms of my hands bloody. Me and Kaiden, we didn't promise each other anything. I know that. So why do I feel like someone stabbed me right through the heart with a fiery dagger?

Nope, I'm not jealous over a demon.

Nuh-uh, not even a tiny bit.

"What happened?" Sam asks me, her forehead crinkling, concern evident in her tone as she turns around, trying to see what I was looking at just a second ago.

"Nothing," I respond, way too flustered for it to be nothing. Like the presence of Kaiden could ever be…nothing. Fuck. My heart bleeds all over the dance floor as needles stab at the back of my eyes.

Her head snaps back at me. "Iris, what the hell? You look like you've seen a ghost."

"Kaiden's here," I admit to the source of my distress.

"WHAT? Where?"

"VIP section, second floor balcony. Please be subtle." I beg her with my eyes.

She turns around again, and I guess she finds him in the crowd because she exclaims loudly, "Holy shit, he's way hotter in reality!" She keeps gawking at him.

So much for being subtle.

"Don't stare at him, weirdo!" I hiss at her, then pinch the bridge of my nose hard. Curling my fingers around her bicep, I drag Sam toward the bar.

"I don't know if I can look away…fuck, that woman is rubbing him like she wants the Genie to come out and grant her three wishes." Her mouth turns down in disgust. "Is that the woman you told me about? What's her name…Maeve?"

"Yeah," I mutter and continue pulling her with me to the bar. I can still feel Kaiden's burning gaze on me, but I refuse to look at him again. The two shots of tequila I downed earlier suddenly don't seem like enough. I need more alcohol in my system to erase the image of Maeve making herself at home in his lap and rubbing his cock. *Shit.* Just picturing it in my head makes my blood boil again.

"Four shots of Patrón, please!" I say to the bartender as I rest my forearms on the bar, waiting for our drinks.

"Woohoo! Now we're talking, baby!" Sam exclaims enthusiastically. "I can't have more than four shots total, though. I still have to meet up with Alex, and I don't like drunk, sloppy sex," Sam tells me as she downs her third shot of the night.

I do the same and suck on the lime wedge. This time, the burn of alcohol doesn't hold the same bite. After we both drink our fourth shots, Sam turns to me. "I need to pee. Come with?"

"Nah, I'll wait for you here. I don't want to break the seal."

"Are you sure? Listen, if Kaiden being here makes you uncomfortable, we can go," Sam murmurs as a concerned look takes over her stunning face.

I scoff. "Yeah, Mom. I'm sure."

She throws me a side-long glance. "No, really, Iris. You looked like you were about to cry when you saw him with that Maeve bitch. Maybe we should go."

And give him the satisfaction of knowing how hurt I really am?

Yeah, there's no way.

Rolling my eyes, I put on a mask of indifference. "I'm okay, Sam. I couldn't care less what Kaiden does. He can go fuck himself, or Maeve, for that matter. I don't give a shit."

The way she arches her eyebrow tells me she doesn't believe an iota of what I just said and sees right through my bravado but chooses not to say anything about it. "'Kay, I'll be right back. Drink some water. Your eyes are starting to glaze over."

After getting my confirmation that I will indeed drink some water, Sam weaves her way through the dancing bodies graciously. A few men standing at the far end of the bar follow her with their eyes until she's out of sight.

Alone, I turn to the bartender, order two more shots of tequila, and down them back to back. The spirit rolls over my tongue and in the back of my throat like water. I don't even need to bite into the lime wedge to take the edge off.

Taking my phone out of my cross-body bag, I shoot a text to Noah.

> **Me: I changed my mind. You can take me on a date if you still want to.**

The reply comes instantly.

> **Noah: How does dinner tomorrow at Ciprianni's sound?**

> **Me: Perfect.**

> **Noah: I'll pick you up at 8. Can't wait. Xx**

> **Me: See you tomorrow.**

While I'm swaying to the music near the bar, waiting for Sam and arguing with the annoying voice in my head that keeps telling me to turn around and look at Kaiden one more time, a guy with russet hair and hazel eyes approaches me sheepishly, holding a glass of bourbon on ice. He is a smidge taller than me, dressed in dark blue jeans and a white tee. He looks nice, soft, and conventionally attractive, but he doesn't make my heart stop or flutter in any way.

Like a certain Elite demon does, the annoying voice makes its presence known again.

Ugh, shut the fuck up!

His carefully styled hair flops over his forehead as he bends slightly and comes closer to my ear so I can hear him over the music. Thankfully, he doesn't come too close. This time, I will punch anyone even remotely sleazy who dares approach me.

"Hey, my friend over there and I saw you guys on the dance floor and wondered if you would like to join us for a drink or maybe dance." He points at his friend leaning on the bar across from us, nursing his drink.

I'm about to refuse him when the image of Maeve dropping into Kaiden's lap flashes through my mind again. The acidic burn of jealousy shreds my heart to ribbons for the umpteenth time tonight.

Why the fuck does it bother me so much?

"I would love to dance."

"Shit, really?" Two red spots cover his cheeks. "I mean, I didn't expect you to actually say yes. I came here at my friend's dare—"

"Um, Iris, Alex is waiting for me. He finally took his break. Are you good here?" Sam cuts him off and pulls me closer to her. I didn't even notice she came back from the bathroom.

"Yeah, sure, we're just going to dance," my words come out a bit slurred at the end, the alcohol buzzing through my veins, making me giggle. I'm not drunk yet; I'm tiptoeing the line between tipsy and drunk. Another shot will push me right over the blissful edge, though.

She throws me a confused look because she knows very well how much I hate it when guys hit on me, and I always reject their advances. "Are you sure? I can tell Alex to meet me after his shift."

"One hundred." I nod vigorously and circle my arms around her neck. "Have I told you lately how much I love you?" I plant a big, sloppy kiss on her right cheek, leaving behind the imprint of my lipstick.

Her eyebrows pull together in a frown at my gesture. "Fuck, you're already drunk. You did more shots after I left, didn't you? Now I don't want to leave you alone."

Rolling my eyes at her, I puff out an annoyed breath. "Um, hello, have you met me? I can drop-kick a demon; I think I'm going to be safe by myself. Besides, I'm just tipsy. I'm not drunk, I promise."

"Fine, but no more drinks." She points a finger at me. "I'm serious."

"'Kay, Mom," I snicker.

"When the fuck did I become the responsible parent?" Sam mumbles mostly to herself, still not moving from my side.

"Oh my God! GO already! Otherwise, you're going to complain all night that your vagina will shrivel up and die if you don't get any dick." I slap her ass and push her in the direction of the hallway where the bathrooms are located.

"Fine, I won't be long," she says to me and then looks over her shoulder to the russet guy waiting patiently for us to finish our conversation as he puts his empty glass on the bar. "Don't let her drink more alcohol! And if you by any chance do anything to hurt her, I'll cut off your dick and give it to my cat as a treat." Sam doesn't wait for him to answer and makes her way through the crowd of moving bodies.

"Damn, your friend is kinda scary," Russet Guy says as he approaches me again, taking Sam's place.

I laugh loudly and pull him with me on the dance floor. "You have no idea."

We wiggle our way through the crowd and finally manage to find a small empty space where we can dance without being pushed from all directions. He puts his hands on my hips and comes closer, his hot breath tickling my ear. "I'm Brad, by the way. What's your name, princess?"

Ugh, I'm already getting annoyed with him, but I need something to erase the memory of Kaiden from my brain. It's like he managed somehow to crawl under my skin because I can still feel his gaze singeing me, my body responding as if he's standing right next to me, touching me.

But that's impossible, right? Why would he still be watching me? Surely, he doesn't care that much, not if he let Maeve touch him like that while I was watching. He's busy anyway, getting a hand job over his jeans.

"I miss those perfect lips, angel. Can't wait to taste them again."

What a fucking liar. And I actually believed him.

Stupid, naïve Iris.

That's what I get for trusting a demon.

"I'm Melanie," I tell him, not wanting to give him my real name.

The song blasting through the speakers changes to a slower, more provocative tune, and my movements do, too. I close my eyes, letting the alcohol erase my inhibitions while the impulse to give Kaiden a taste of his own medicine overtakes me completely.

With the beat of the seductive song, I let my body be driven by the fog of desire and lust that blankets the club. I don't want to think; I want to be another one of the puppets on strings in the middle of the dance floor. I turn my back to Brad, raising my arms until I reach his hair, just like I did with Kaiden only a few days ago. I weave my fingers through it and start swaying my hips to the music. He melds his body against mine, and I can feel how happy he is about our dance.

He bends slightly, since we are about the same height, and kisses the side of my neck. His lips touching my skin don't get any response from my body, but still, I need more. I want him to kiss me, to erase Kaiden's memory from my lips. I turn around and close the space between us until we share the same breath.

"God, you're so—" Just as Brad is about to dip and kiss me, a tall, hard, tattooed body comes in between us, making me yelp in surprise, and lifts Brad by the throat so his feet dangle a few inches above the dancefloor.

35

"I wouldn't finish that if I were you," Kaiden's deep voice booms over the music, a sadistic smirk tugging at his mouth, the bottomless pits of his obsidian-colored eyes swirling with gold and red streaks. Anger radiates from him in waves as he drops Brad unceremoniously to the floor.

He falls like a sack of potatoes, knocking over a guy with spiky blue hair dancing near us. This seems to have broken the trance-like state of the people occupying the dance floor, who now give us a wide berth and throw concerned looks our way.

"What the hell, Kaiden?" I screech incredulously.

He doesn't pay me any attention as a muscle ticks around his jaw, still looking at Brad with murder in his eyes.

"What the fuck is your problem, man?" Brad shouts over the music as he finally straightens and puffs out his chest. His voice is scratchy, surely from his crushed windpipes. He looks up at Kaiden and immediately cowers, realizing he's at a clear disadvantage.

Kaiden has more than a head over him in height and a lot more muscle mass. I can't help but notice at this moment how hot Kaiden looks in his straight black jeans and a black shirt that's rolled at the sleeves, accentuating the cords of muscles on his inked forearms. His hair is pulled back into a ponytail at the base of his neck with a leather tie, a few shorter strands framing his face. He's wearing the same worn motorcycle boots as the day we met.

Kaiden looks down his nose at Brad the way a lion looks at a cockroach. "Leave. Before I pull out your spine with my bare hands."

"Shit, man. I, I u-um, I'm s-sorry. Is s-she, s-she y-your g-girl?" Brad babbles, stumbling all over his words. "We w-were j-just d-dancing. I d-didn't—I didn't know s-she was your g-girl."

Folding my arms over my chest, I huff in annoyance, "I'm not his girl."

At that, Kaiden's head turns to me with a raised eyebrow, his nostrils flaring. "Is that so, angel?"

"Oh, he speaks. What a fucking miracle!" I snap, my blood boiling over with rage.

One of the hunky bodyguards that opened the massive door for Sam and me earlier appears out of nowhere next to us, addressing Kaiden. "Do you want me to escort him out, boss?"

My eyes almost bulge out of my head as my lips part in shock. "What the hell? Boss?" I mutter mostly to myself. Of course, he's the owner of Sin. I'm surprised I didn't make the connection sooner.

Kaiden nods at the bodyguard, and Brad blanches, all the color draining from his face. He puts his hands up in surrender. "There's no need. I'll see myself out." He leaves without another word or look thrown my way, the bodyguard hot on his heels.

As the situation deescalates, the people around us resume their dancing and drunken conversations, still giving us a wide berth, though.

I throw my hands in the air in a fit of rage. "Fuck this shit!"

Before I can take even a step toward the bar, a strong forearm bands around my waist, keeping me in place. "Where do you think you're going?" Kaiden's breath is hot against the side of my face, his tone dripping with ire. A few of the strands that frame his face move with his exhale and caress my skin.

Trying to still my manic heartbeat, I take a deep breath in. In the next moment, Kaiden's decadent, spicy scent engulfs me completely, turning my legs to mush. All I want to do is lean back and feel his hard, hot body against mine. But the image of Maeve rubbing her hand all over him ignites my resolve that I have to get away from him. Immediately.

Grabbing his forearm, I try to remove it from my body, but it's like trying to escape a steel band; it won't budge no matter how hard I push at it. So, I do the only thing that I can think of and turn around to face him.

"None of your fucking business. Let me go!" I demand with urgency. Too late, I realize my mistake. Our bodies are flush, touching in all the ways that matter, and my brain seems to be fried by the electric shocks that zip from the back of my neck all the way down to my toes. My nipples harden against his chest, and I'm breathing hard, his intoxicating scent drugging my senses.

Kaiden's gaze darkens as he bends, his lips a hair's breadth away from mine. "Are you sure that's what you want, angel?" he almost whispers against my lips. His deep voice rolls over me like a caress.

"You're delusional if you think I want you to keep touching me."

A devious smirk tugs at his lips. "Ah, but you see, Iris. Only a few days ago, you pretended not to want me; then, you kissed me like your life depended on it. Didn't you come all over my mouth and fingers, too? So yeah, I'm calling bullshit," he says as the arm that is now circling my back comes down and grabs my ass, pushing me even closer to his muscular chest.

It's infuriating how right he is. My stupid body has a mind of its own, and it wants only one thing. Him.

With the added height from the high-heeled boots I'm wearing, I can feel his erection against my abdomen, his length spanning from the apex of my thighs all the way to my belly button. A moan escapes my mouth without my permission when I feel him twitching against me. Scorching heat courses through my veins and stops at my core, making my clit throb with need.

"Let me go," I repeat halfheartedly as I push at his chest. If I'm going to be completely honest with myself, with every second that he keeps touching me, I don't want to escape. Not truly. I sure as hell have the force to free myself...I just don't put too much effort into it.

"You don't know what you do to me, how unhinged you made me tonight." His free hand touches my inner thigh, right where the hem of my dress ends, his thumb drawing imaginary circles on the skin right at the seam of my panties, under my dress. My heart sputters as my underwear soaks completely with my desire. "Coming here to my club and looking like a fucking goddess. Giving every limped dick man an erection, making me want to gouge their eyes out for daring to look your way. I should punish you for letting that undeserving fuck touch what's mine and make me watch," his voice deepens as his fingers dig into my skin painfully. The added pressure makes me whimper.

"You were going to let him kiss you, and These. Lips. Are. Mine," he growls before biting my lower lip hard. Then, he sucks it into his mouth to chase away the sting. His minty breath with a hint of tobacco rolls over my face as he rests his forehead against mine. "You're all mine, angel. Fucking mine! I claimed you with my fingers and with my tongue, and soon enough, I'll claim you with my cock. I'm going to fuck you so hard, Iris, I'll ruin you for anyone else."

It takes a few seconds for my sex-induced brain to catch up with his words.

Realization finally dawns, and fury comes blazing in full force. I push hard at his chest, this time really meaning it, breaking our connection. This only adds fuel to my fire because it proves his point that if I wanted, I wouldn't have let him touch me.

"You think I should be punished? Me?" I laugh, but it comes out bitter, the hollow sound swallowed by the loud music around us. "Are you fucking kidding me? What about Maeve giving you a handjob over your jeans not long ago, huh?" I spew angrily, taking a step back. "'I miss those perfect lips, angel. Can't wait to taste them again,'" I mock, doing a poor imitation of his voice. "I'm so fucking stupid," I mumble angrily to myself.

He gets in my face again, our gazes locked in a silent war. "It's not like that. I was fucking watching you when she dropped in my lap. I didn't even notice her until I saw the hurt in your eyes. I shook her off, but you already turned around."

"Yeah, sure, and I was born yesterday. And why is she here then if you didn't bring her with you?" I seethe.

"She works for me. She's one of the succubus dancers."

"Oh, how convenient for you then." I huff a derisive laugh. "Eat shit, Kaiden!" With that, I turn around and stomp to the bar, elbowing my way through the dancing bodies. I receive a few annoyed looks when I push with unintentional force through the crowd.

I flag the attractive bartender and wait for her to finish serving the couple in line before me. "A shot of Patrón, please." I offer a weak smile. The happy buzz that I had going on evaporated completely with Kaiden's appearance, and I desperately need some more alcohol in my system.

She smiles back and starts pouring my drink.

"She's having water, Em. Give the shot to someone else," Kaiden's voice comes from behind me.

The bartender raises a curious eyebrow and looks at Kaiden. "Sure thing, boss."

"No, I'm not. Give me my drink, please," I say through gritted teeth, refusing to acknowledge his presence. Even if his eyes burn two holes in the back of my head and the heat of his body at my back seeps into my bones, his stupid, decadent, spicy scent making me weak in the knees.

The bartender's eyes jump from me to Kaiden. She shrugs, deciding she doesn't want to take part in whatever is going on between us. She pushes a glass and a water bottle my way before moving to serve another patron. I grind my teeth in frustration, itching with the need to punch Kaiden. My fingers circle the water bottle in a death grip, and I spin on my heel, facing him.

"Oh, you want me to drink some water? Fine, I'll drink some water." I open the bottle and throw the water at his face with a jerky motion. I snort with laughter at the sight of Kaiden dripping on the shiny black floor.

He isn't amused, though. At all. His eyes narrow dangerously into slits, and his nostrils flare as he levels me with a glare that can cut through skin and bone.

Before I can register what's happening, I'm upside down, thrown over his shoulder, once again with my eyeballs in direct contact with his delicious-looking ass. My hair covers my face and my purse slides down, almost falling to the floor, but I manage to catch it at the last second.

I can't believe he's doing this again. And in the middle of a fucking club where everyone can see my underwear. I wiggle and push at him. But it's like trying to break through a concrete wall. His arm is snaked under my legs, keeping me in place with no chance of escaping.

"What in the actual fuck, Kaiden?!? Put me down! Now!" I screech.

He doesn't answer as he effortlessly slices through the dancing bodies with me bent over his shoulder. People are staring and pointing at me while laughing at my expense. Heat burns the back of my neck, and my face is probably as red as an overripe tomato.

"Everyone can see my underwear, you brute! Put me down!" I snap.

"Stop wiggling if you don't want everyone to see your ass," he bites back as one of his hands tugs the skirt of my dress down, so I won't be indecent. He passes the people on the dance floor and goes toward the dark hallway, where the bathrooms are located. A few beeping sounds catch my attention as we stop at the far end of the hallway. It sounds like an electronic keypad, followed by the distinct beep and the sound of a door opening.

We enter another dark-lit corridor with multiple doors on each side. The moment the door we entered through closes behind us, the blaring music disappears completely, leaving me with the phantom feeling of the last song ringing in my ears. One of the doors to my right is slightly ajar, and I try to peek as best as I can from my position through the gap.

Moans and whimpers accompanied by the distinct sound of bodies slapping together reach my ears before a portion of a bed and the side of a naked woman riding a man becomes visible, her head thrown back in abandon. He's kissing her neck, but something looks off about the way he latches on to her. That's when I realize blood is dripping from his mouth onto her shoulder.

Shit.

This is a vampire feeding from an innocent woman.

"What the fuck, Kaiden? Is that a vampire? Put me down!" I shout and start banging my fists furiously on his ass. "We need to help that woman," I say with urgency.

"Did she look like she needed any help?" he asks with detachment in his tone as he takes long strides, opening yet another door to yet another dimly lit hallway. How big is this place anyway? And where is he taking me?

If I think about it, the loud moans and whimpers were a clear indication that she was enjoying herself quite a lot. But it still goes against everything I know and my instinct to protect an innocent human being.

"That's how vampires from the Conclave are able to feed safely without harming innocent humans. That woman volunteered to be fed from. A lot of women and men come here and give away their blood in exchange for a good fuck and the rush of vampire venom."

"How the hell is this even legal? And where are you taking me?"

"Because no one is harmed. Every involved party gets what it wants." He ignores my second question.

Without saying anything else, Kaiden opens another door to a room entirely encased in darkness. He flicks his finger over a switch to his right, and light floods the space, blinding me momentarily. He saunters to an L-shaped, brown leather couch and slides me down his body slowly, inch by agonizing inch, while keeping an arm at my lower back.

A few strands of hair are stuck to his cheeks, his face still damp. The front of his black shirt is completely soaked, accentuating every ridge and delicious muscle. I shiver when I feel the damp fabric against my skin. His eyes blaze with fury, and I'm breathing the electricity that seems to zap in the air between us.

Kaiden's tattooed hand collars my throat, squeezing. I gasp for air as his finger rubs on my pulse point gently. Heat pools at my core, and my heart rattles against my ribcage. My nipples turn to diamond-hard tips, rubbing on the fabric of my dress, making me crazy with lust. The way he holds his hand on my throat is not painful at all; it's more possessive than anything.

How sick am I for enjoying this so much?

He lowers his hand, and his nostrils flare as his breath ghosts the side of my neck. He reaches the spot where Brad kissed me and presses his lips there, alternating between sucking and licking. I drop my purse to the floor, not caring at all about the phone inside. His teeth scrape gently at my skin before he bites me hard, making me yelp at the unexpected pain that sends a pulse of need directly to my clit.

Kaiden swallows the sound with his lips, licking at my mouth and sucking on my tongue. I push his shirt up and rake my nails on his back. The marks I leave on his skin elicit a hum of approval from Kaiden that vibrates all the way to the center of my pussy. Grabbing the hair at the nape of his neck, I pull on it and press him harder against me at the same time.

He brings his hand to the apex of my thighs and cups me over the fabric of my soaked underwear. Pushing my panties down slightly, he sneaks one finger inside and presses the pad on my clit in wet circles. A moan escapes my lips, and tiny electric shocks take over my entire body.

"Dirty little angel, look how wet you are for me," his thick, raspy voice almost brings me to my knees as he slides his finger down to my entrance. He pushes it inside me, pumping it once, twice. Then he stops. Eyes on me, he lifts the finger to his mouth and licks it clean.

"No. Don't stop! What are you doing?" I ask with desperation. I feel like I'm going to combust if he doesn't touch me again.

"How was it that you put it? I must be delusional if I think you want me to keep touching you. So, what is it, Iris? Make up your mind already. Yes or no?" His lips turn upward with an infuriating smirk while he raises a questioning eyebrow at me.

"No!…Yes! Please, Kaiden—"

"Pick a safeword, Iris."

"W-what?"

"Did I fucking stutter? Pick a safeword."

I swallow through the lump in my throat. "I don't know…cherries," I say, thinking about the decadent black cherries wrapped in chocolate I receive every year on my birthday from my secret admirer. "But, why do I need a safeword?"

"Because you pushed me too far, and I'm finally going to deliver on my promise. Now remember your safeword. I'm only going to stop if you use it," he says, and all of a sudden, he turns me around and throws me over the couch armrest, with my ass in the air and my face smooshed against the cushion.

"What the hell?" I buck my hips, but Kaiden keeps me there, holding both of my wrists at my back in a powerful grip and immobilizing me with his legs.

I hear him opening his belt buckle, and I gulp as tremors wrack my body in anticipation. He pushes my dress up, bunching it around my hips. The belt whistles through the air before it comes crashing down on my right ass cheek with a loud *crack!*. The bite of pain surprises the hell out of me and makes my engorged clit pulse angrily.

"What the fuck, Kaiden? Let me go!" I scream.

"Use the safeword, Iris."

Crack!

"I fucking hate you!" I hiss but still don't use the safeword; instead, I kick his shin with my heel.

Crack! Crack! Crack!

Kaiden laughs. "If you hate me so much, baby, then why is your pussy drenched?" The leather belt flies down again and again and again until my ass feels like a bruised peach, and my panties become useless. Still, Kaiden is not using his full force; the pain is shocking but bearable, and each time the belt smarts my skin, it sends a lightning bolt of pleasure to my clit, bringing me higher and higher. My blood pounds a heavy rhythm in my ears as I seek friction on the couch armrest, desperate to reach the peak.

Suddenly, he pushes my drenched panties aside and slaps my clit so hard I see stars; then, he shoves three fingers inside me and pumps them mercilessly. In less than a second, I reach the high I so desperately craved and tumble down with his name on my tongue. The orgasm seizes every nerve ending in my body. It shreds them to ribbons before putting them back together. My eyes roll in the back of my head as my walls spasm violently around his fingers.

Kaiden milks my orgasm, pumping his fingers until I can't take it anymore. Then he kneels in between my legs and cleans me up with his tongue, his low rumbles mixing with my cries of pleasure as he fucks me with it. When he rims my back hole, I tense up and buck my hips, the act feeling illicit and dirty, but Kaiden grabs my hips and holds me in place as he continues to feast. I can't move, my body too spent, my muscles jellified, and soon I get used to the sensation.

He probes the pleated hole with his thumb and slowly slides it in as he sucks on my clit. I whimper at the foreign sensation while the bite of pain mixes with pleasure to fry my nerve endings. He just keeps it there, letting me get used to the fullness before he starts moving it in and out as his tongue switches between lapping at my clit and fucking my pussy. The second orgasm takes me by surprise. It ripples through me with the force of a landslide. My toes curl, and a sound I never made before pitches in my throat and tumbles out, echoing off the walls.

Kaiden stands, and I hear his disappearing footsteps, water running, and a drawer opening. I'm too spent and don't care enough to open my eyes, though. After a minute or two, he comes back and starts cleaning me between my legs with a warm washcloth. Then his hand caresses the stinging skin of my ass cheeks. I wince slightly, but it actually feels really nice. Opening my eyes, I look at him over my shoulder and see that he's using a cream. Carefully and gently, he spreads it around. When he finishes, he kisses each of my ass cheeks, puts my panties back in place, and tugs my dress back over my ass.

He snakes an arm around my middle and turns me around as he lifts me with an arm behind my knees and the other around my back.

He then plops down on the couch with me in his lap, careful to keep my ass out of direct contact with anything.

"You okay?" Kaiden asks, his knuckles grazing the side of my face. His eyes have that intensity in them again, like he's able to peer inside my soul just by looking at me.

I nod as heat scorches my cheeks. I feel shy all of a sudden, despite him just eating my pussy and my ass like a seven-course meal at a Michelin-star restaurant. Kaiden closes the space between us, framing my face with his big hands, and kisses me slowly and reverently, his tongue licking at the seam before parting my lips and pushing inside.

I snake my arms around his neck and slide off the leather tie from his hair to thread my fingers through the silky strands. Our tongues tangle in a fiery dance, and not before long, we are devouring each other's mouths. His cock is as hard as stone, and it twitches between us. In the heat of the moment, I move my legs and straddle him, our lips still fused together. Emboldened by the moment we're sharing, I slide my right hand in between us and press it where our bodies are joined over the massive bulge in Kaiden's jeans. A guttural moan rumbles in his chest at my touch.

"Can I touch you?" I say breathlessly before opening my eyes to look straight into Kaiden's.

His Adam's apple bobs hard in his throat. "Fuck, you're killing me." His eyes search mine. "You don't have to—"

"I want to, please!"

Kaiden's teeth sink into his lower lip. He nods without saying anything else. With trembling fingers, I unzip his jeans, freeing his impressive throbbing length. My breath hitches in my throat at seeing how big he is. His skin looks velvety smooth, and the crown is pierced with a barbell. I'm dying to touch him, so I glide my thumb over it slowly and let my instincts guide me since I've never done this before, hoping he's enjoying my touch.

Kaiden lets out a hiss. His eyes snap shut, wrinkles forming at the corners with the pressure. "Fuuuck," he swears under his breath when I circle his shaft and pump once, twice, making him twitch against my palm. A bead of precum drips on my fingers. I quickly gain more confidence as I start moving my shaky hand up and down in a slow, steady rhythm.

Liquid fire drenches my panties again at seeing Kaiden lost in the pleasure I'm giving him with every stroke of my hand, his eyes at half-mast, and his breath coming hard through his parted lips.

Feeling even braver than before, I slide down on my knees in between his spread legs. "I want to taste you," I breathe against his engorged head and dart my tongue out to lick at the barbell and the bead of pearlescent liquid clumsily, the metal cold against my tongue.

Kaiden inhales a sharp breath as a shudder passes through his body. I want to continue, but I don't know what to do next. My inexperience makes my cheeks flame with shame.

"I don't know how to…I've never done this before." I look up at Kaiden. "Will you show me what you like?"

His eyes are two hot coals. They blaze with fire while his gaze rakes over me. "Fuck, angel, you're going to be the death of me," he groans, standing up, and I shuffle a bit backward. He brings a hand to the back of my head to weave his fingers through my hair before fisting it. "Put your hand around the base and start pumping it. Use your tongue and lick the head like you would a popsicle and then suck."

I circle his throbbing cock around my fingers, fisting the base, and with my other hand, I hold onto his thigh. Darting out my tongue, I circle the crown, then wrap my lips around it and start sucking. It feels weird at first, especially with the piercing that I keep knocking my teeth into, but with every harsh inhale and raspy moan Kaiden is letting out, I forget about my inhibitions. He's hot and smooth as silk against my tongue.

"Just like that, angel. Now sheath your teeth with your lips and take me as far as you can in your throat."

Shit.

His dick is monstrous. How am I going to fit all of him into my mouth? I push away my fear and insecurities and take him in as far as I can. It isn't much, though. He's too big. He thrusts his hips, and I choke, panicking.

"Breathe, angel," Kaiden says as he lifts his other hand to my throat and massages it gently. "Swallow. It will help open up your throat."

I do, and it actually helps.

"I'm going to fuck your mouth. If it's too much for you, use your hand and tap my thigh. Do you understand?"

I nod around his length.

"Good girl," his voice is crushed velvet, the praise pulling at my heartstrings. His keen eyes don't miss the way I press my thighs together in an attempt to alleviate the throbbing need in my pussy, and he says, "Is my dirty angel turned on by sucking my cock? Rub your pussy on my leg, Iris. Let me see how much you want me."

I close the small space between us and start grinding on his leg with fervor as he starts fucking my mouth while keeping me pinned in place with his fingers digging into my scalp and the other hand circling my throat. The pressure is making me see stars, but I love it. It intensifies everything a hundredfold. Tears are leaking from the corners of my eyes, and spit trickles down my chin as his thrusts become more and more punishing.

"You're taking my cock so well, angel," his words are coated in gravel as he looks down at me through heavy-lidded eyes. Sounds of pleasure rattle from his chest, and I'm taken by surprise with how much I'm enjoying this. I'm on my knees in front of him, but it feels like I hold all the power. Fireworks go off behind my eyelids. I break at the seams, moaning around his length while my pussy spasms violently.

"Fuck, angel," Kaiden rasps in a low, sexy tone. "I'm going to come. If you don't want me to come inside your mouth, tap my thigh, and I'll pull out."

I open my eyes, hold his gaze, and relax my throat even more instead of tapping out.

He lets out a moan of approval before coming with an animalistic groan. Hot spurts of salty cum explode on my tongue and go down my throat as I swallow every last bit. The taste is not as bad as I imagined it would be.

Lifting me from the floor, he drags the pad of his thumb over my lower lip, an emotion shining in his eyes that I can't decipher. It's almost too much. A hummingbird takes flight inside my ribcage. I close my eyes, not being able to bear the intensity of his gaze anymore. He presses his soft lips to mine and kisses me languidly, taking his time while exploring my mouth. My insides turn to mush.

Loud pounding interrupts us. I flinch at the unexpected sound.

"Kaiden!" a rough, manly voice travels through the door. "It's urgent. Open up, man!"

Kaiden groans with annoyance and takes a step back, tucking his semi-soft dick into his boxers and zipping his fly. "What the fuck do you want, Logan?"

"Adramelech escaped."

36

"Motherfucker!" Kaiden booms with urgency as he strides to the door, opens it, and reveals a man larger than life.

"Hey there, sorry for interrupting," Logan says sheepishly as he runs his hand over the back of his neck. This guy is taller than Kaiden and built like a tank, his muscles bulging the fabric of his forest green tee. I realize why the bartender looked so familiar. She and Logan are carbon copies of each other, complete with the rich amber skin, ash-brown curls, sharp cheekbones, and whiskey-colored eyes.

Heat spreads in my cheeks as I wave awkwardly at him, not knowing what to say. He surely heard me and Kaiden with his wolf shifter hearing.

"Stay here, Iris. I'll be back to take you home. I won't be long," Kaiden instructs.

I scoff. "I have to get back to Samantha. I'm not leaving without her."

"Text her and tell her you're going home."

I snicker because who the fuck does he think he is to order me around? "Yeah, not happening," I mutter and amble to where they're standing on either side of the door.

Kaiden suddenly steps out and closes the door in my face, locking it.

"Open the door, Kaiden!" I scream as I start banging my fists on the wooden surface.

"Stay here. I'll take you home when I'm back," he repeats.

The sound of disappearing footsteps travels through the door, and I'm just standing here looking at it with my mouth agape. He *actually* locked me in his office. I bring my hand to the handle and press on it several times. It won't budge. Anger starts simmering in my veins.

That infuriating demon bastard!

Turning around, I take in my surroundings; I couldn't exactly concentrate on them before. The office is luxurious, and as with everything that Kaiden owns, it screams money, decorated in a combination of black and gray with warm, harmonious accents. The large executive chair behind the ebony desk is made of the same plush, dark brown leather as the couch and the two chairs in front of it.

Behind the desk, a huge piece of art hangs on the black-painted wall. It's a charcoal drawing, the same angel bowing on one knee that Kaiden has tattooed on his back. It's beautiful and heart-wrenching. I can't exactly explain the feeling it elicits, but the image tugs at my heartstrings in a weird way.

Striding to where I dropped my purse on the hardwood floor earlier, I slide it over my head and take my phone out to see if Sam called me.

Sam: Saw you with Kaiden.

I hope you're getting some because your exchange

was hot as fuck.

For a second there, I thought you were going to fuck in the middle of the dance floor.

Alex is taking a longer break to spend some more time with me.

Text me when you're done.

I'm surprised to see that just around forty minutes have passed since my best friend left me at the bar to meet with Alex. I'm suddenly parched, my throat feeling dry and scratchy. I need to drink some water, but I can't see any in the dry bar in the corner of his office, only a decanter of whiskey with two crystal highball glasses.

Surely, Kaiden didn't mean I have to wait in his office and die of thirst until he comes back. Who knows when he will be back, anyway. And why am I suddenly listening to something he said I should do? *Fuck that*. I pop into the bathroom real quick, take care of my business, and do my best to make my face presentable again. Getting out, I amble to the door and kick the handle hard with my foot. It shatters with a loud, satisfying sound.

I manage to trace my steps back until I reach the spot where that vampire was feeding earlier, but the room is now empty, and there isn't anyone else in my vicinity. As I come face to face with what I assume is the entrance that leads back into the club because of the muted music, I press my hand on the handle and notice it's locked only from the other side coming in. I expel the air in my lungs, relieved. It closes with a loud beeping sound behind me. As soon as I step out, the sudden deafening low bass assaults my eardrums and vibrates in the center of my chest as I find myself back in the bathroom hallway.

There's a long line in front of the women's bathroom, some of the girls barely keeping their balance, their words slurred and incomprehensible.

The last girl in line is sobbing uncontrollably into her consoling friend's shoulder. A snippet of their drunken conversation reaches my ears as I bypass the long line, "…he's a fucking idiot, Cara. He's also a Scorpio. Why did you call him? That's it. Give me your phone!"

Pushing through the dancing crowd, I shoulder my way to the bar, resting my forearms on the marble slab while I wait for my turn to order.

The bartender's eyebrows shoot up all the way to her hairline when she notices me, a wry grin tugging at her pouty lips. "You're back. You survived Kaiden's wrath."

I blush furiously and nod. "Yeah…can I have a water, please?"

A laugh bubbles out of her. "Are you planning on throwing it in someone else's face?"

"Nah, just thirsty." I smile back and tuck my hair behind my ear.

"C'mon, I'll get you something stronger on the house. You're my hero; the least I can do. You don't even know how many times I dreamed of throwing something at Kaiden's face. Plus, your tab is taken care of for the night; you can order the most expensive thing on the menu. You know, just to fuck with him." She winks at me.

"Maybe later, when my friend is back. I'll just have water for now."

"'Kay. Let me know," she says as she pushes a water bottle and a glass toward me and moves to the other patrons waiting to be served.

Taking out my phone, I fire a quick text to Sam to let her know I'm waiting at the bar, ready to go home. Tiredness starts to seep into my bones, and my stomach grumbles with hunger. I could kill for some greasy pizza or some French fries.

A flash of pink catches my attention from the dance floor. The woman wearing the weird looking clothes from earlier is twirling her ample skirts, her form rippling like water when people touch her.

No, no, no, no, no.

Please, no.

When I asked Kaiden about Tony's friend, he told me that the situation was taken care of. Since I haven't seen Tony in a long time, I assumed he moved on to the light, and I hoped I wouldn't ever have to see another ghost, but apparently, I'm not that lucky.

Shit.

Blowing out a weighted sigh, eyes still on the ghost, I pour the water into the glass and take a sip but choke on it when the woman pops out of thin air right in front of me.

"You can see me, can't you?" she asks, tilting her head at an unnatural angle.

"Fuck," I manage to get through the violent coughs. Jesus, I feel like I'm going to spit out a lung.

"Are you okay?" A girl standing next to me turns around and pats my back, concern pulling at her eyebrows.

I look over my shoulder, managing a weak smile as I nod and thank her. Placing the glass on top of the bar, I try to ignore the ghost.

"I know you can see me!" she shrieks like a banshee.

I can tell she's about to go ballistic on my ass, and based on the clothes she's wearing, she has been here for a long time. I don't know what she's capable of. "Fucking ghosts," I mumble under my breath and try to appear as normal as one can be, talking to myself in a club while looking for the salt shaker reserved for the tequila shots. Luckily, no one around me pays me any attention.

Bent over the bar, I finally find the shaker, pour some salt into the palm of my hand, and throw it at the ghost. Like a bad-functioning old TV, her form flickers and disappears with a bright light, but not before making the bottle of alcohol at a nearby table explode. The guys dancing around it are so shit-faced they don't even notice.

How is this my life right now? I honestly have no words. I feel like I'm going batshit crazy.

I don't get a chance to recover before a strange feeling seizes my stomach as the hair at the nape of my neck stands up at attention. Strong fingers grab my arm from behind. The sickly smell of overpowering cologne burns my nose and settles in the back of my throat. I spin on my heel quickly, but I'm not prepared to be face-to-face with Erik. I didn't expect to find another hellseeker here.

Shit!

He's dressed casually in jeans and a denim button-down over a white tee, so he's not working tonight. From an outside perspective, he's conventionally attractive, as all hellseekers are, his platinum-blond hair sleeked back, styled to perfection. He's about two inches taller than me with my high-heeled boots on, and he has a clean-cut, square jaw, the upper lip plumper than the bottom. He would look almost angelic if it weren't for the iciness in his gunmetal gaze. His arctic eyes give him the air of a psychopath. His beauty draws you in like a deadly, alluring flower, only to realize too late that you've been poisoned.

"My, my, what do we have here?" Erik says acidly, standing far too close to my face, his fingers digging painfully into my skin. He throws a menacing smirk in my direction. "Too bad natural selection didn't run its course to cleanse the bloodline and all."

What is he talking about? Is he referring to the car accident or something else? My heart dips as realization dawns. Could he be talking about that night near Shadow Lake when I was sent directly into an ambush with two draconic ravengers? Or the umbra attack?

I thought Grayson wasn't going to tell anyone since it's such a sensitive matter, and it's being investigated by the Kabal. But Erik is his family. *Wait.* I have no reason to make this big of a leap, but I can't help but wonder if he's the one who sent me in a trap that night. He could have easily gained access to Grayson's phone. From what I know, Erik doesn't live with him anymore, but I know he visits often. What if

Grayson went home after leaving the compound, and Erik was there?

He pulls on my arm and crashes the front of my body to his. Queasiness fists my stomach as his erection digs into my belly, his alcohol-infused breath washing over me, mixing with the powdery, sickly smell of his cologne.

Gritting my teeth, I push at him forcefully to break our connection. "What the fuck do you want, Erik?" I seethe.

He looks me up and down and licks at his lower lip. His eyes stop a second too long on my cleavage. It makes me shudder with revulsion, like I need to take ten showers for the dirty feeling of his leering gaze to disappear. He's also engaged to Britney, so him being here, acting like this, looking at me like a piece of meat, is even more disgusting in my eyes.

"Kiss me," he demands, closing the space between us and gripping my wrist with more force than necessary.

I'm taken aback by his words. "I would rather let a ghoul claw my heart out and eat it in front of me than kiss you," I fire back and shake my wrist free, taking advantage of the hellseeker speed as I bend and pull out the dagger I have sheathed in my left boot. I point its sharp tip at Erik's crotch. "Why don't you act like your hairline and take a few steps back," I bite back with a smirk.

"You think you're too good for me? You?" he practically spits the words at me as a menacing glint shines in his arctic eyes. "Quite the spectacle you put on tonight. You know…my dear grandfather asked me to follow you because he suspected you were a lying little bitch. Wait 'till he finds out his special little Iris is spending all of her time with an Elite demon. I'm going to blow his mind." He takes out his phone. "Oh lookie, what do we have here?" A slow, deranged smile spreads over his face while his finger slides on the screen to show me a multitude of photos.

My stomach takes a nosedive at the photos depicting Kaiden and me roaming the streets of Ashville together on my shifts, me getting on his bike on the narrow alley near the compound, and him kissing me in the middle of the succubus party.

What the hell, he followed us there? How did he manage to get inside and with his phone at that?

The last photos are of Kaiden throwing me over his shoulder earlier tonight. Bile surges in my throat, and my last meal is threatening to make an appearance.

"The whole world will know what a demon-loving whore you are," he cackles and turns on his heel, but not before bending over me and whispering in my ear. "When I finish with you, everyone in the Order will thank me for it." He walks away.

Panic sloshes in my veins like ice as my stomach fists into a ball.

Fuckfuckfuckfuckfuckfuck.

I put the dagger back in my boot and grab the glass of water I left on the bar, downing it in one gulp. Maybe I left the water in the glass too long, because it leaves a dusty aftertaste heavy on my tongue. I shake the weird feeling off and desperately try to think what to do next. The headache from earlier today comes back with a vengeance at the thought that I'm going to be thrown out of the Order. He's Grayson's family, probably in line to become the head of the Order since his parents died in a hellseeker mission a few years back. He can do no wrong, whereas me, the half-blood freak…Who will believe me if I say he's lying? Besides, he has proof, and Grayson told him to follow me.

Suddenly, claustrophobia grips me with sharp claws. The walls are closing in on me while the pulsing lights coming from the ceiling swarm in my vision, making me dizzy and feverish. I feel like my skin is pulled too tight over my bones, and I need to escape from my own body.

I need fresh air.

A bead of sweat rolls down my spine and another teeters on my eyelashes before falling into my eye as I take a few staggering steps toward the club's exit. Time seems to slow down, the people undulating on the dance floor in slow motion and throwing me weird glances as I sluggishly try to put one foot in front of the other.

The music becomes muffled, and the vibrations of the bass seem to pound in my head like a hammer. Something is wrong with me. I think about taking my phone out and calling Sam, but I feel bone weary. The prospect of taking my phone out of my purse overwhelms me. I can barely keep my body straight.

I trip on my own feet as the crowd of sweaty bodies pushes at me from all directions. In an attempt to balance myself, I grab a random guy's forearm so I won't face plant right in the middle of the dance floor. He throws me an annoyed look, but concern pulls at his eyebrows the longer he looks at me. The contour of his body is fuzzy at the edges. Trying to clear my vision, I blink a few times.

Does he have an identical twin or am I seeing double?

My knees buckle, sending me forward again.

Shit.

The guy catches me, breaking my fall, and asks me something as he circles his hand around my middle. He takes most of my weight on his side to keep me upright. But the words fly right over my head as his mouth moves soundlessly.

What is happening to me?

"Where, you, where, taking…me?" I ask sluggishly. The words come out of my mouth slurred and in the wrong order, not at all how I intended to say them.

He might have answered with "Outside," but I can't be sure.

The red pulsing lights and the bodies dancing in the cages above give me vertigo. In an attempt to still the heavy thumping in my head, I bring my fingers to my temple. It doesn't work, so I close my eyes for a second.

Somehow, when I open them, I'm outside in a back alley. The light from a broken lamppost flickers and heightens my drowsiness. I've completely lost the notion of time. I don't know how I got here. The smell of spoiled food crawls up my nose, making me realize I'm resting on a wall across two massive dumpsters, muffled music coming from the door at my right. I welcome the coolness of the concrete wall at my back. Its rough texture digs into the palms of my hands as I press them into the wall, trying to stay upright.

The guy I used to balance myself earlier is standing in front of me. A glint of worry shines in his emerald eyes as he says something. But again, his mouth moves soundlessly. I squint my eyes and try my best to concentrate on his words while he waves his hand in front of my face in an effort to get my attention. It takes a few tries before I manage to make sense of what he's saying.

"Do you have a phone?" he asks. "Maybe there's someone that can come get you."

I nod slowly in a weird, jerky motion but can't find the energy to open my mouth and voice the words.

"Shit, you're really wasted. Wait right here; I think I should get someone to help you."

I lift my hand sluggishly to somehow let him know that I don't want to be left alone in this creepy alley, when the door to my right opens. Platinum-blond hair shines in the flickering light.

"Baby, I've been looking everywhere for you," Erik says as he comes to my side and squeezes one of my hands in his, a look of worry pulling his mouth tight. Only I know he's faking it. The emotion looks wrong on his face, too exaggerated. His dead eyes give him away.

"Do you know her?" the guy asks Erik. My eyes slam shut since I'm not able to keep them open anymore, and I rest the back of my head on the concrete wall, trying to stay in the present.

"Yeah, she's my girlfriend. I went to the bathroom, and she disappeared. I guess she had a little too much to drink."

"Is this your boyfriend?" the guy asks me.

I open my eyes and blink, but I can't muster the energy to say no or at least move my head. Erik crushes my fingers with his, pulling a gasp out of my lips as my head swims. I'm seeing double again.

"Of course I am. Why would I lie? We've been together for five years. You're such a lightweight, baby. We had too many shots of tequila." Erik gives the guy a sincere smile, that he punctuates with a pat on his shoulder. "I got it from here. Thanks for taking care of her, man! Not many would do that. You should go. Enjoy the rest of your night."

The green-eyed man throws me a concerned look but seems to believe Erik because he shrugs and says, "I hope you'll feel better," toward me.

"N-no, no, don't go. P-please!" I finally manage to mumble on a broken whisper, but he's already gone, the door closing at his back.

"Still don't wanna kiss me?" Erik's alcohol-infused breath rolls over my face. Bile rises in my throat as he pushes his body into mine, crowding me into the wall.

"Let—let...me go!" I demand, trying to shove him away. But my voice is weak, and my limbs feel disjointed.

His laughter is followed by a deranged smirk that tugs at his lips and his cold, dead eyes. "Or what? What are you going to do?"

I suck in a choppy breath as realization kicks in. "You—you drugged me."

"Me? I could never," Erik says smugly as he pulls a fistful of my hair, his fingers digging painfully into my scalp. He flips open a switchblade and drags its sharp tip over the skin on my chest slowly. Blood drips down from the cut. "Everyone will know after tonight what a demon whore you are," he sneers into my face.

Those words again. Awareness slithers down my spine. Where did I hear them? I sluggishly sift through my foggy memories but come up empty.

"Little did my grandfather know when he asked me to keep an eye on you that I was already lurking in the shadows, waiting. I knew a half-blood cunt like you would eventually betray the Order, and I was right. I always am. You sold us out to fuck an Elite demon. I'm going to mark you, just like I did with the other demon whores, for all the world to see who you really are," he spews, his face too close to mine.

I don't understand. What other whores? What is he talking about? Demon-loving whore...demon whore. His word choice is so specific, and I've heard it before. I know I have. But where? My knees buckle as realization dawns. The women found dead with the same word carved into their skin.

Oh, God.

It was him.

He raped and killed those women.

He crushes his lips to mine, shoving his tongue in my mouth forcefully. I feel like I'm being thrown right into the past, into that high-school hallway, when I let him assault me. But I'm not going to play victim anymore. I somehow find the strength inside to bite his tongue. The taste of copper invades my mouth as he pulls back with a sneer, dropping the hand he had embedded in my scalp, taking a step back.

I give him a bloody smile. Then I spit in his face, laughing, but the sound comes out warped.

"You worthless, half-blood cunt!" He wipes at his face furiously and fists his fingers. His knuckles collide with my cheek. My head flies to the side, and white-hot pain explodes in my nerve endings before I black out.

When I come back to reality, I'm lying on the ground with Erik, crushing me under his weight. The asphalt chills me to the bone and digs into the back of my legs and arms painfully. I can only open my right eye halfway as red dots swarm my vision. The side of my face where he punched me feels swollen, and my temple throbs in pain.

A gust of wind ruffles my hair. It also travels between my thighs as though...I'm naked.

Nonononononononono.

Thrashing under the weight of his body is futile. I can't move him even by one inch. But I don't care. I keep on trying.

"Stay still! I need to cleanse that demon from your body," he snaps and backhands me. The sharp sting makes me groan. Then he resumes what he was doing earlier, unbuckling his belt. I look to the side to find something on the ground to help me escape.

Anything.

Please.

Anything.

But there's nothing I can use, only the scrap of fabric from my ruined underwear discarded near the dumpsters in tatters. Tears blur my vision and leak from the corner of my eyes at my helplessness. I feel so weak, so betrayed by my own body.

An iron fist grips my already shallow lungs at the sound of a zipper opening. My mind is a jumbled mess, desperation coating every sluggish thought. A sliver of hope unfurls in my chest as I remember the dagger in my boot.

As he pushes my dress over my hips and settles in between my legs, I somehow manage to pull the dagger out with trembling fingers and impale it in his thigh. He lets out a bellowing scream, throwing a string of curses my way. The blood coursing from the wound soaks my dress.

Adrenaline gives me a few more inches of clarity, along with the strength to push him off. I crawl as far as I can from his body. The moment of victory is short-lived as he manages to grab my ankle and pull me back. My knees and palms scrape against the cold asphalt with a bone-searing burn.

"You think you can escape? You stupid, half-blood cunt!" he spews furiously as he stands up, limping, and then takes out the dagger with a hiss. He sends his foot flying into my ribcage over and over again until I choke on my own blood.

I probably black out again because when I open my eyes, he has my wrists pinned above my head, and I'm crushed under the weight of his body. Every breath I take feels like I'm inhaling fire. As he settles between my thighs and the rush of adrenaline leaves my body completely, it finally dawns on me…there is nothing else I can do. An earth-shattering sob escapes my throat as I feel him at my entrance.

He's going to take something from me I can never get back.

Something breaks inside me in this moment. The turmoil turning my insides to ashes is slightly interrupted by the angelic voice ringing in my ears.

"Let go, Iris. Let the darkness inside you take over. Don't let him hurt you."

Suddenly, I'm thrown in the backseat of my mind, a mere passenger as power I have never felt before takes over every cell of my body. My eyes fill with a darkness so thick it seems to spill from the hollows of my orbits into the atmosphere as wisps of shadows start to emanate from my skin.

Erik shrieks in pain as I float from the ground in an upright position. I grab him by the throat and take him with me in a punishing grip, crushing his windpipe and grinding his bones. His eyes bulge as he sputters blood, coughing it in my face. Black vines spread all over his body at an alarming rate as if he's being rotted from the inside out.

The light in his eyes dims completely before I feel his vile soul leave his body. But I don't let go. No. I keep my grip strong and firm until there's almost nothing left of him but a pile of bones, cartilage, and loose-hanging scraps of leathery skin.

The power leaves as fast as it enters my veins. Like an elastic pulled too tight, snapping under the pressure, I'm thrown from the passenger seat back into my own mind and body. Still, the darkness doesn't vanish completely; it echoes in the chambers of my heart and in the recesses of my soul.

Dormant.

Waiting.

Erik's rotten corpse falls with a thud to the ground as I crumble on my knees on the cold asphalt. My teeth grind painfully at the impact. Then, my body starts shaking uncontrollably as my vision seems to go back to normal.

Someone screams my name, alarmed, but I'm not able to move. The cold ground digs into my cheek as my head falls to the pavement. Firey copper hair and mossy green eyes swimming with tears are the last things I see before I close my eyes and give into the void.

If you enjoyed this book, please consider leaving a review on ↓ **Amazon** *and* **Goodreads** ↓

If you haven't already read "Fated Hearts", the Echoes of Darkness Prequel — Ava and Logan's story — you can find it here:

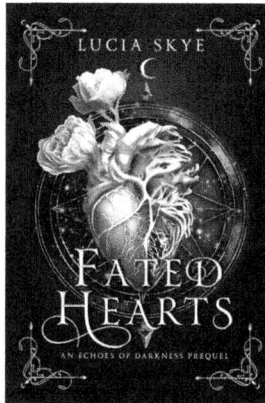

Ava

Waking up in the hospital with a harrowing diagnosis is a hard pill to swallow.

But it also opens my eyes to the truth.

Law school was never my dream. It was my mother's.

I've been living like a bird locked in a cage, and the bars are closing in on me, crushing me under

their weight.

I'm done letting others dictate my life.

The thing is…trying to cram a lifetime of experiences in a few months can lead you on a t reacherous path.

I let myself live. But at what cost?

Looking back, it was all worth it because it led me to him.

Logan

Reality is overrated.

Especially when my fated mate's wolf appears in my dreams, and shouldering my Alpha responsibilities becomes harder by the day.

And you know what they say about fate…

It's not only fickle. It also loves irony.

My life takes an unexpected turn when my eyes land on her.

A human.

She pollutes my mind. My dreams. My whole being.

I know I should stay away from Ava. My pack would never accept a human.

The question is, will I be able to resist temptation?

THANK YOU!

I cannot express enough gratitude for every single reader who took a chance on my book.

Everything I write is for you.

To my husband, for supporting my crazy dream, which literally started with me dreaming about Iris running through the forest. Also, for making sure I eat while getting lost in my own world.

To my editor. Ayden, you're a rockstar!!! This book wouldn't be the same without you pushing me to be a better writer.

And to my lovely ARC readers, your love and support means the world! A special mention of some special girlies: Kirstin, Arianna R., Becci, Nicole, Arianna L-C., Karina, JenJo, Sylvana, Ariel, Amanda (Hopmomma), Lindsey, and Hannah.

Also, to that person who left me a one-star review saying I should never write again, don't worry, I'm not thanking you. But I am working on the next book just out of spite. Ah, yes, I am that petty.

About the author

Lucia Skye

Lover of beautifully written words, strong heroines, anti-heroes, steamy romance, and swoon-worthy, broody MMCs, Lucia spends most of her free time, you guessed it…reading. Or better said, devouring books until the early hours of the morning because the main characters *finally* kissed after an agonizing slow burn, and she needs to know what happens next.

When she's not glued to her laptop, writing, drawing character art for her stories while listening to true crime podcasts, or daydreaming about falling through a magical portal in a mystical realm, you can find Lucia on the couch with her two fur babies, watching House of Dragon.

http://linktr.ee/LuciaSkye.Author

Find her on socials

Printed in Dunstable, United Kingdom

66820623R00221